Prudence

Prudence 1919

Prudence

BY DON L. TAYLOR

Published in the United States of America
by Prairieville Papers Publishing Company
Don L. Taylor, Waukesha, WI 53187

Written by the author of *The Prairieville Storekeeper*.

Copyright © 1993 by Don L. Taylor, Waukesha, Wisconsin, U.S.A.

Frontispiece photo by T.J. Florian.
Prudence is modeled by Mary Sue Harter.
Chapter heading art by Jeffery Schmid.
Book design by Joy Buslaff.

A limited edition of this book has been printed by
Thomas Press, Waukesha, WI 53186.

ISBN: 0-9639286-2-7

To Theodora Youmans
and her successors,
the free-spirited voting women
of America.

Acknowledgements

Historical information was obtained from a multitude of locations. The major sources include Genevieve G. McBride's article about Theodora Winton Youmans in the Summer 1988 issue of the *Wisconsin Magazine of History*; the autobiographical *Life Story of Dr. David Roberts* published in 1949; the official history of *The Thirty-Second Division in the World War*; *Wisconsin Women in Badger History* from the State Historical Society of Wisconsin; the summer 1986 issue of *Waco Heritage & History* featuring 'War Comes to Waco;' Volume V of *The History of Wisconsin* by Paul W. Glad; the memoirs of Philip LaFollette entitled *Adventure in Politics*; the *Journal of the Assembly and Senate* of Wisconsin; Eleanor Flexner's book *Century of Struggle: The Woman's Rights Movement*; Lawrence L. Graves' 1954 UW doctoral dissertation *The Wisconsin Woman Suffrage Movement, 1846-1920*; the secretary's minutes of the *Waukesha Women's Club*; G. H. Koenig's *Once Upon a Prairie, Haunted Wisconsin* by Beth Scott and Michael Norman; and of course Waukesha's newspaper, the *Freeman*.

Foreword

It was a joy to create the strong-willed character of Prudence, a 'liberated woman' ahead of her time, and to mingle her with Theodora Youmans, Dr. David Roberts, Leo Herbst and other real people.

My research into the era of the World War and Women Suffrage reaffirmed the truth that human nature doesn't change much through the swiftly moving decades of time. This is a story of long ago—Theodora died in 1932, the year I was born—but the intertwined themes are as current as today's TV news. The loves, the politics, the hopes and the fears are alive in all of us today.

The background scenes and events of this story are as accurate as I could describe them from the distant past. John Hille's sturdy house on River Road, where Prudence lived and loved, is currently occupied by Dorothy Ransome; the Vernon Marsh is imperturbable as always; the *Chicago & North Western* railway depot which witnessed the departure of Jon Hartmann and Leo Herbst when they went to war in 1917 is the home of *Saz's & Pep's Depot Restaurant* today. Literary license allowed some alteration of names and facts to enhance historical distance, but it won't take much effort for Waukesha citizens to recognize reality.

My thanks goes to countless friends and researchers who assisted with this labor of love. If my readers enjoy the story, discover some unknown history of our beloved homeland, and perhaps learn something new about human nature, then the work has been worthwhile.

Waukesha, Wisconsin
September, 1993
D.L.T.

Chapter 1

    A small weathered farm wagon with faded yellow wheels, drawn by a chestnut-tinted horse, rolled easily along the partially graveled country road alongside the greening grasses of the Vernal Marsh. A noisy red-winged blackbird circled the wagon, occasionally dipping in its flight to dart at the solitary masculine figure of the driver perched on the front board. The sky was cloudless and the sun was radiant in the late-morning sky, but the throat of the man's washed-out blue jumper-coat was securely buttoned against the brisk northwest wind. The ear-flaps of his dark cap were fully extended, and a yellow woolen muffler, knitted by his wife, was wound about his neck with the long tails flapping in the breeze.

    A black and gray mongrel dog of medium size, perhaps a shepherd crossed with countless other breeds, trotted briskly alongside the wagon. Occasionally the faithful companion, affectionately called 'Old Jake,' dashed out into the adjoining fields and marshlands chasing the faint scent of a long-departed animal.

    The horse stepped along the familiar road without requiring guidance, and the hunkered-down man was oblivious to his surroundings. He was thinking. His perplexity could be easily read in the stern lines of his features.

    He was a middle-aged farmer, no different in appearance than a score of other men in the middling good farmland south of Prairieville. Not lean, not fat; solid but not muscle-bound. His hands were calloused; his neck above the collar was toughened; his ruddy face showed its lifelong exposure to the elements.

    It was that craggy face which betrayed his present thoughts—a face lined with concern and wrinkled with confusion.

    'What's botherin' her?' he asked himself. 'Prudence has been a different woman these past few months. She used t' go about her chores quietly, without disturbin' nobody. For twenty-five years she's been cheerful and easy t' live with. But lately she's been kinda' moody. Kinda' restless. Kinda' pent-up, like there's something inside her about to burst out.'

The war in Europe had bothered her, he knew, especially as it appeared the United States might be drawn into it. Prudence was against war. 'She picked up a pacifist streak in that danged women's club in Prairieville,' he thought with rancor. 'That's what happens,' he mused, 'when you associate with people like Theodora Youmans.'

Or was it the fear of having their son dragged off to war? Jonathan, born in 1897, would turn twenty this spring. He was the right age to be a soldier. Just the other night as they were finishing supper Jon said, "I hope we go to war."

Prudence appeared stunned. "Jon! How could you say such a thing!"

Such a reproof was out of character for her. Prudence never let a shadow cloud her face, Zachary believed; Prudence never let a cross word slip from her lips.

"Why do you want to go to war?" she persisted.

Jon measured his words. "Because we should teach the Kaiser a lesson," he said quietly. "Those Germans have no business fighting their neighbors. If they get away with that, there's no telling how far they will go."

"You're right, Son," Zachary said with a quiet glance at his wife.

"Besides, if we go to war I might get a chance to see the world. I don't know any other way I'd get to Europe."

"There ain't nothin' wrong with Prairieville," his father said sharply.

"I know," Jon replied politely. "I want to spend my life in Prairieville. You know that. But it'd be fun to travel a bit first. I think I'd be a better man for it when I came back."

"*If* you came back," Prudence said pointedly.

Was that the source of the change in Prudence? A mother's natural urge to protect her offspring? Was that why she was beginning to speak out against the war?

Zachary listened to the steady clipclop of the horse's hooves on the hardpan road as he pondered the changing attitude of his wife.

She was a beautiful woman, he thought, with such a sunny disposition. He admired her the first evening he saw her, a gentle September evening he would always remember. He had heard from his parents that a new family was moving out from town. They had bought a quarter-section of land a couple of miles east. His father, along with other neighbors, had helped build their house, and it was time for the house-warming.

What he had not heard was that the new family contained an eighteen-year-old girl, the same age as himself. The instant he saw her through the raucous crowd in her new living room, he had been totally overcome by her presence. She was perhaps five-foot-five, with a statuesque body boasting seductive feminine curves that captured him instantly.

She was wearing a plain white blouse which transformed her into a bright angel in that dully lit room. Her large oval face expanded gracefully into a generous smile as she caught him staring at her—a smile which was highlighted by an even row of strong, white teeth. Their glances met. He saw a pair of very large cornflower-blue eyes and he could not look away.

Instantly, unaccountably, she felt a strange effervescence permeate her body like a myriad champagne bubbles rising through her blood.

A man and a woman suddenly became alive to each other.

The trappings of coquetry, romance, courtship, and matrimony have been made very complicated by society, but in truth the attraction of a man and a woman for each other is a very simple thing. Driven by the only absolutely essential requirement of life—the ongoing perpetuation of the species—two human beings are drawn toward each other with an elegant, irresistible magnetism.

Zachary was not a flirt, but before a single word was said between them, he reflexively arched his eyebrows at her—and in response, she winked her left eye.

He had known other girls, mostly from his school days. None of them had been worth his acquaintance, he had thought. And the girls on the nearby farms represented a stunted, droughty crop, he felt.

Now, however, this heavenly being exploded into his life, smiling at him, winking at him, making him feel like a man—a real man—for the first time.

He felt himself drawn to her—pulled into her—with irresistible energy.

They were introduced by their parents, and he could hardly stand the pleasure and the pain when she pronounced his name. "Hello, Zac," she said. That was all, but that was enough. He was forever lost.

It didn't matter that she was friendly with everyone in the room that evening. It didn't matter that she bestowed the blessing of her smile on each person who approached her.

In his heart, he had already begun to think of her as his own.

Even though she already had a suitor, a local farmboy who somehow had known her beforehand.

His name was Ephraim, and he was twenty-three years old, and he was there at the house-warming, and she spent most of the evening with him.

Zachary knew from the beginning that he would take Ephraim's place and marry Prudence. He never worried about it, even though it took her a year and a half more before she made her selection between the two young farmers.

He knew, because of the secret message carried in that wink—a message that told him she was his, even if she didn't realize it yet.

Looking back even now, from a distance of nearly twenty-seven years, his heart picked up its pace at the memory.

She was the most beautiful bride who ever spoke her vows in the entire county, everyone said. Her beauty was undiminished through the perpetual hard work on the farm, the birth of her daughter Sarah in 1895 and Jonathan two years later, and the unceasing duties of a devoted wife and mother. Her unfailing cheerfulness became a legend.

But now her good humor seemed to have changed into a moodiness which left Zachary mystified and confused. She was waiting for something, he felt, and while she waited there was a powerful pressure—some unknown force—building up within her.

'Maybe it's just normal for a woman going through the change of life,' he thought, dismissing the subject from his mind as he approached Reedsville, the tiny settlement with only a half-dozen houses.

His attention now was drawn to the sacks of corn in his wagon. The kernels would be ground coarsely by the mill, and he would return to his farm in a couple of hours with feed for the cattle.

"We're here, Kaiser," he sang out to his horse, and the knowledgeable animal automatically turned the wagon into Mortimer Reed's driveway. Zachary's sharp eyes searched the house for the well-known miller, but his friend was not in sight. Continuing around the circle to the mill, he gazed out across the watery expanse of the millpond, alert to the signals that winter was past and spring was rushing forward.

The ice was melted from the pond. The early March rains had performed their ageless ritual of cleansing the winter-weary earth. Measureless ambitions and energies were now free to be transformed from cold winter dreams to active realities. Rivulets of fresh water joined together to create lively streams which splashed headlong into the pond, losing their identity as they gathered, pent-up, to build enormous pressure against the dam.

'Jus' like Prudence,' he reflected anew. 'Everythin' still looks peaceful an' calm on the surface, but down below there is a restless energy strugglin' fer release.'

A steady torrent of white-frothed water gushed noisily along the stone-lined channel of the millrace, disappearing through the foundation walls into the depths of the two-storied wooden mill. Zachary thought for a moment of the solid practical use of that water as it powered its way through the turbines in this latter-day frontier settlement of south-eastern Wisconsin.

'Whatever there is inside Prudence,' thought Zachary, 'I hope it gets channeled to some good use. I hope it don't jus' break the dam.'

His reverie was broken by the cacophonous cawing of two black crows above the trees overhead. He looked up with a frown. Farmers reached for their shotguns when they saw those large raven-like birds, for they were capable of uprooting and eating incredibly long stretches of freshly sprouted crops.

Besides, despite his Christian disbelief in superstitions, he felt the dread of an evil omen whenever a crow appeared close at hand. Fortunately, the birds are wary creatures and usually keep their distance from humans.

After the crows had disappeared out over the pond, Zachary tethered Kaiser near the door and began carrying his corn sacks into the mill. His dog ran and jumped around him. "Careful, Jake," he cautioned.

Before he finished his task, he unbuttoned his jumper and loosened his golden scarf. He was not surprised to find the building unoccupied, nor was he perturbed. He knew how to operate the machinery as well as Mortimer; he had ground his own grain many times before. He carefully checked the stones, the gears, and the belts to make certain all was in order. Then he released the safety strap and slowly pulled the long handle into the operating position.

A low grumble accompanied the start of the machinery, soon overpowered by the sound Zachary loved—the sound of raw power being translated into usable energy. The upper millstone began to rotate, gradually picking up speed until it was a blur of motion. Satisfied, Zachary lifted a corn sack and dumped its golden contents into the supply hopper.

He was fascinated by the millstones in action. He possessed a poet's soul that anthropomorphized much of the farmer's life around him. He saw parallels to human life in almost all the natural cycles of nature. His crops in particular stirred his imagination as they were planted, tended, harvested, and consumed. Looking at the corn before him, he reflected that it was not of much use until it was grown to maturity, shucked, and ground.

'Jus' like humans,' he thought. 'We ain't much use 'til we're ground by the stones of life.

'All of us are bein' continually ground,' he mused, "til the day we die. Right now, I think the Almighty is workin' on Prudence, more than me. Maybe He's through with me fer awhile. But I wonder what He has in mind fer her?'

Such were his thoughts as he watched the whirling wheel perform its

5

work.

Less than a half-hour later, a second wagon pulled up near the door of the mill, joining Zachary's rig. The lean, middle-aged driver, wearing a sad, leathery face beneath a crumpled gray farmer's hat, hitched the dark horse to a ready post and lowered the tailgate to reach for a sack of grain.

He hoisted the sack onto his shoulders, knocking off his hat and exposing a shock of unruly black hair heavily streaked with gray. Leaving the hat on the wagon bed where it fell, the man walked the few steps to the door of the mill, opened it with one hand, and stepped inside.

The two horses remained as sentinels in the bright green clearing, surrounded by tall newly budded oaks and elms. Streaks of gentle sunshine streamed through the treetops, bathing the scene in a soft emerald glow. Two or three early robins strutted about on the short grass in their elegant, endless search for tiny edible creatures. The two horses occasionally acknowledged each other with a glance and a low nicker, while Old Jake forayed the shoreline of the millpond.

The growl of man-made machinery suddenly stopped, emphasizing the serenity of the surroundings. Only natural sounds remained—the rushing of the water, the chattering of a ground squirrel, the chirping of the ever-present sparrows.

Suddenly the door burst open and the newcomer strode out in a state of obvious agitation. His square face was grimly set, perspiring freely, and his black hair was scrambled and matted in disarray. He did not run, but his gait was hurried and purposeful as he covered the hundred yards or so to the miller's house.

"Mort! Mortimer! Where are you, Mort?" he called, his stentorian voice resonating through the two-storied frame residence.

He entered with evident familiarity, encountering the miller not far inside.

"Ephraim! Hallo!" Mortimer Reed advanced with a welcoming hand.

Ephraim ignored the hand. "Mort!" he exclaimed again. "There's been a terrible accident in the mill. Zac Hartmann has got 'imself killed down there. Musta' got 'is clothes caught in the gears. I shut the machinery down, but I couldn't get 'im free. There's a yaller scarf all tangled up in the cogs. I'll need some help gettin' 'im out."

"It can't be! Zac is as careful as they come."

"It's true, all right," said Ephraim. "I was jus' goin' in t' grind some corn, and I found 'im still goin' round and round and gettin' bloodier with each hit."

"Is he dead for certain?"

Ephraim gave a short nervous laugh. "Ain't no way there's any life left in that body," he said.

The two men walked briskly back down the flagstone path to the mill. Inside, Zachary's mangled body lay twisted amidst the gears of the mill just as Ephraim had described. Jake was nervously whimpering as he prodded his lifeless master with his nose.

It required the combined strength of both men to turn the gears backward enough to extricate the corpse. Together they carried it outside and laid it carefully in the bed of Hartmann's wagon. Kaiser turned his head and watched the proceedings in puzzled silence.

"I reckon we better get 'im home," said the miller.

"I reckon," agreed Ephraim.

Mortimer Reed paused. How's Prudence gonna' take it?" he asked skeptically. "She's such a gentle soul."

"Prudence'll be okay," said Ephraim. "She's gentle, all right, but she can be tough when she has to be."

"Mebbe we should take him straight to the undertaker," reflected Mortimer.

"Naw, I think Prudence would want 'im home first. Give the poor widder a chance to see 'im before we take 'im away. It'll ease the shock."

"Well, you know her better'n I do," responded Reed. "You've knowed her for some twenty-five years, if I can count 'em right."

"Yeah, I knowed her that long—even longer—but not as well as I wanted to," commented Ephraim wryly.

"Well, let's get goin'," suggested Mortimer. "I'll drive Zac's rig, if you want, and you can take your own. Mebbe you could run me back afterward."

It was a somber procession that rolled along the lonely road. The marshlands alongside contributed to the dismal emotions of the solitary horses and their men. It testified to a virginal promise, like an Eden, yet by its evident permanence and unchangeability it represented a promise still unfulfilled.

Its very name, the Vernal Marsh, suggests the brightness of a youthful springtime. Yet a perpetual youth remains forever undeveloped, forever blighted. Of course, there are changes in the marsh. The waters of the Pishtaka River flow in from the north, and flow out again to the south. The seasons come and go with faithful rhythm; the winter snows and the summer foliage alternate with unending determination. The inhabitants—lively minnows, sleepy turtles, slippery reptiles, little furry animals, animated birds—move about and are renewed according to their own cycles.

But despite these variations, the great body of the marsh has remained the same since the last glaciers moved ponderously across this patch of geography. Prehistoric savages entered a frigid newly made swamp as the glaciers receded northward some twelve thousand years ago. A succession of aborigines took their turns wandering through the bogs, leaving their artistic effigy mounds ten miles upstream at the site of today's Prairieville. Potawatomi Indians were the most recent tenants before modern civilization arrived. They traversed the marsh but did not linger, establishing their tent-grounds at more solid locations.

White settlers have occupied the area a hundred and fifty years— only a blink of time in perspective, but long enough to change all the surrounding territory. They have cultivated farms and established villages and cities. But, except for the straight-lined roads around its borders, the topography of the Vernal Marsh remains unchanged since its emergence from the glaciers. It has hardly been touched by mankind.

Quite to the contrary, the marsh has shaped the lives of the men and women surrounding it. It has made them patient, long-suffering, and imperturbable. It has conditioned them to an aggressive strength and honed them to a cutting sharpness seldom found so concentrated among such few residents. And in some cases, the aggressiveness has smashed through the imperturbability like a fox snatching a pheasant.

The roadside scenery became farmland as the two horses plodded along mournfully. Eventually a farmstead appeared in the distance, with a good-sized red barn dominating the skyline. A fat silo crouched alongside. Close to the road—River Road—was a square white stone house with a commanding presence.

Prudence knew something was wrong when she saw the two wagons pull into the driveway with Old Jake lagging behind listlessly. She met the men at the door, and they briefly explained the circumstances before she rushed to her husband's wagon and peered bravely into its interior.

She stood there unmoving, her strong but delicate fingers curled over the top of the wagon's sideboard. Her eyes remained steadily fixed upon the bloody golden muffler twisted about the battered body of her dead husband.

"Zachary," she whispered softly. "Oh, Zachary!"

The two men came up gently behind her. Ephraim stepped close alongside and put his arm around her shoulders, giving her a firm squeeze. She turned and embraced him with the unconscious ease of long association.

"He was such a good man!" she exclaimed. "A God-fearing man. So upright, so conscientious. And so kind."

"Yes, he was a good man," echoed Ephraim.

Reed was uncomfortable in the presence of death and its aftermath. He busily tended to Ephraim's horse, and then returned to stand nearby, creating a long embarrassed silence.

Ephraim finally spoke: "Now that you've seen 'im, Prudence, I s'pose we should hustle 'im over t' Gaspar's fer embalmin'." He moved toward the front of the wagon.

Prudence replaced her hands firmly on the sideboard. "No," she said softly. "He belongs here. Carry him inside."

Ephraim considered her request unreasonable, the whim of a freshly made widow. Based upon his years of acquaintance with her, he knew she was a rational and submissive woman, and he did not hesitate to overrule her. "No, Prudence. I reckon we'll just take 'im right on over now. It's the state law, ya' know, that he must be embalmed. The sooner done, the better, even though the weather is still cool. . . ." He put one foot on the front step of the wagon and reached up for a handhold.

Prudence turned abruptly and said "No!" again with such commanding force that Ephraim froze in the very posture of mounting the wagon. His eyes searched her face and saw a determination there which he had never seen before.

"No!" she repeated. "He's my husband and I want him to remain here."

"Prudence," said Ephraim with an air of patient wisdom, "he's gotta be embalmed."

"Then bring Mr. Gaspar here," she said firmly. "I will not permit you to carry Zac away."

Ephraim hesitated and finally yielded with the skeptical air of one who caters to an ill-tempered child. "Whatever ya' say, Prudence. Mebbe Art will come out."

The body was no longer warm when Ephraim and the miller lifted it respectfully and carried it inside to the sofa which Prudence had covered quickly with a clean white bedsheet.

They lingered to comfort her, but she took command. "Ephraim, please go down to the cornfield by the river and fetch Jon and Sarah. Don't tell them why. I want to give them the news myself in my own way.

"And Mortimer, would you mind settling Kaiser in the barn? I don't want to leave Zac."

The two men left silently to obey her requests, somewhat surprised at her sense of authority.

She turned back to her husband's body. With devoted resolution, she remained there throughout the day, talking with her children, questioning the undertaker, and generally taking charge. She courageously refrained from tears while others watched.

The dark coffin, swiftly procured by Ephraim, dominated the historic house. It rested in the center of the living room, supported by a chair at each end. Prudence spent the night there alongside the open wooden box which contained the last remains of the man who had been her beloved husband. A single white candle illuminated the scene, imparting an eerie sense of unworldliness. At first she sat silently, refusing to vent her emotions. But as she remembered the cheerful highlights of their life together, riddled with the inevitable regrets, she rose to her feet and draped herself over the grim wooden edge and leaned down to kiss his hardened lips. She began weeping quietly, mindful of her children sleeping in the rooms above.

After a while, she composed herself and addressed him. 'Where are you now, Zac! You've got to be in Heaven! You were always an honest, generous, considerate man, and you loved the Lord more than anybody else I know. You kept the Commandments, mostly, at least all the big ones. You were in church beside me almost every Sunday. You kept yourself sober and you never laid a hand on me in anger. I know you're in Heaven, if there is a Heaven, and I know there is a Heaven, because it says so in the Scriptures, and I believe what it says even if I'm not quite so sure as you always were.

'You're in Heaven now, I know,' she mused. 'But where is Heaven? I don't have any idea where it is. Up in the sky, maybe? Jesus was seen ascending up into the sky. So was Elijah.

'Or is Heaven simply a spiritual world which can be all around us? Are you here with me now, Zac, in a form I cannot see or touch?'

She imagined herself in the church service alongside Zac, sitting in the folding chairs of the Town Hall in the very room where they had been married. She could never enter that building without remembering her marriage, because her husband would never let her forget. Sometimes with his words, but usually just with his eyes, he would constantly remind her of their wedding day and its joyful meaning.

Zachary never outgrew his sense of awe and reverence at being her partner. He considered her God's gift given directly to him, a gift he possessed the first evening he saw her, a gift he never doubted, but a gift he never took for granted.

She was overwhelmed by his reverence for her, and from the very beginning he won her attention, her respect, and her admiration. Zachary exuded an inborn sense of authority which she could not contest, and it seemed both natural and inevitable that she should yield to his suit and disappoint Ephraim.

It was a choice she would have avoided if possible, for she truly loved both men, but once she made up her mind, she didn't look back. The fullness of Zac's devotion elicited from her a complete submission and a striving to satisfy him.

Not that the marriage was perfect. No two people can live together permanently in complete harmony. But Prudence and Zachary handled their disagreements gracefully, and usually were honest and forthright with each other.

Usually. But not always.

'What do you think of me now, Zac? Now that you know everything about me. Are you surprised? I'm not as perfect as you thought I was. I had my little rebellions which I hid from you. And my anger. Anger at never going to Decoration Day celebrations like I did when I was a little girl.

'But if you know about those wicked feelings, you must also know that I suppressed them because I wanted to please you. I wanted to stay on that pedestal where you put me.

'And of course now you know about that Great Sin of my life. Was it wrong? It must have been wrong, because I was afraid to tell you. It wouldn't have withstood your examination, would it? Your standards of morality are so high. I'm sorry, Zac. I'm sorry if you're hurt by what I did. But you can see, can't you, that I didn't do it for any selfish reason? I did it mostly for you. You know that, just as you know everything now.

'Do you hate me, Zac, now that you know? Don't hate me, Zac, please! I couldn't bear that! And I did it, really and honestly, for you, just as much as for me!'

During the night she alternated between musing tearfully and sleeping fitfully on the sofa. Whenever she was awake, she wondered uneasily how she stood in the esteem of her dead husband.

The guttering candle finally exhausted itself, but Prudence didn't renew it, for the first early glow of dawn was lightening the eastern sky.

Ephraim moved immediately to assist Prudence with arrangements for the funeral. "I got a plot in the Reedsville graveyard, across the road from the mill," he told her the day after Zachary's death.

"I was thinking we might bury him right here on the farm," Prudence replied.

"I don't think the law would allow you t' do that," speculated Ephraim. "And even if 'tis legal, I'd advise you agin' doin' it. Zac was a good man, but he's dead now. If ya' bury 'im here, you'll soon start thinkin' of 'im as a tombstone—an' you ought t' be rememberin' 'im as a livin' man."

This time she yielded to his advice. "You're right, Ephraim, I want to remember him as he really was—alive and vigorous."

He was pleased at her agreement. "Thank you, Prudence," he said modestly.

Her hand touched his arm and lingered there. "Thank you, Eeph," she said softly. "You've been so good to me, as always. Go ahead and make the plans for his funeral."

"Is there any particular hymn you'd like?" he asked.

She thought for a moment. "Yes—I think Zac would like us to sing *Work for the Night is Coming*," she suggested. "It was a favorite of his."

"Consider it done," he said. "And I'll get back t' you on what you need t' know."

"Thank you again," she said. "I appreciate it."

On the day of the funeral, Ephraim arrived early at the Hartmann farm to supervise the handling of the coffin by the pallbearers as they placed it in the horse-drawn hearse. He joined the inner family circle without invitation, and was readily accepted. With a sense of quiet elation, he rode alongside Prudence behind the hearse on the road to the Town Hall; this was the way he had always believed it should be.

During the funeral service, Ephraim sat with Prudence in the front row alongside Jon and Sarah. He even dared to place a comforting arm around her shoulder. His euphoria was such that he heard very few of the pastor's words, and was barely aware that they sang *Work for the Night is Coming* as he had specified. Afterward, quite naturally, he escorted her to the cemetery.

How sweet it was to have Prudence at his side at last! How bitter it had been, a quarter-century earlier, when she had chosen Zachary instead of himself! 'I have loved her longer than Zac,' he thought. 'And I loved her more deeply, too, despite the fact they were married a long time.'

He still kept the mementoes of their romance. They were stored in the tin box he bought at Perkins Hardware Store. For a dollar and a quarter, the box came complete with lock and key, ensuring his privacy in the early years when he lived with his parents.

He had met Prudence at a harness race near the Fountain Spring House, before her family moved to the farm. The ticket stub from that event was in his tin box, along with a tarnished copper penny he received in change after buying a bottle of strawberry soda pop for her.

It was love at first sight for Ephraim, just as it would be a year later for Zachary. She seemed receptive, though perhaps not as serious about being in love as he was. He reminded himself she was only seventeen— he was already twenty-two—and there was plenty of time for romance to blossom, even in an age when girls tended to marry young.

Ephraim's fault, perhaps, was that he was too patient. Unlike Zachary, he was inclined to let matters take their own course. It was not his nature to be aggressive, even when he was consumed with a passion for Prudence.

Therefore, he saw her only twice during the ensuing year before she moved with her parents to the farm near him. Each time she was with a large group of friends which prevented intimacy, but his ardor steadily increased nonetheless. She wrote him three letters during the year, and they too were eventually stored, the delicate stationery weakened by frequent re-readings, in the tin box.

He was elated when she moved to the farm, and he saw her several times while the new house was being built. She knew no one else in the area, so it was easy for him to monopolize her company.

But then came the house-warming—and Zachary. Although Ephraim stayed at her side during the entire evening, he was sensitive enough to recognize the spark of lightning which passed between her and the newcomer. In the following months, he pursued her diligently with every thoughtful and romantic device he could muster, and his courtship remained competitive for a long time. The fountain pen she gave him that Christmas was used as he composed ragged sonnets for her, but it too was eventually committed to the tin box when he lost her to Zachary.

After knowing Prudence and loving her, there was no possibility of accepting any other woman as a substitute. As the years passed, Ephraim came to be regarded as the most eligible bachelor in the farming community south of Prairieville. More than a few anxious girls tried to catch his attention, but his heart was designed for one woman only and it could not be changed. In the quarter-century since her marriage, he had not thought seriously about anyone else. His memories and his hopes were centered exclusively on her. 'She is the only woman I could ever love,' he reflected.

He did not become a nuisance, but he managed to see her often enough—usually at church—to keep up with the latest news in her life.

Ephraim's parents died unexpectedly soon after Prudence's wedding. He sold the family farm and bought one right across River Road from the Hartmanns. He wanted to be as close as possible to the place where Prudence lived with her husband.

Now she was at his side once again. He felt a strong sense of being restored to his rightful position. 'I'm back where I belong,' he declared to himself. Already, before his rival was covered with six feet of Reedsville loam, his courtship had resumed.

Chapter 2

In what he considered a neighborly courtesy, Ephraim voluntarily assisted Jon and Sarah with the farm chores both morning and evening beginning with the death of Zachary. He stepped forward with the authority of age and experience; he recognized the great cost of his timidity during his earlier courtship of Prudence and he was determined not to repeat the mistake.

Jonathan, however, quickly resented Ephraim's intrusion. "He acts like he's the new owner," he complained to his mother. "I appreciated his help during the first couple of days after Dad's death, but now it looks like he is trying to take us over. This farm belongs to our family, not to him!"

Prudence ignored Jonathan's complaints at first. She was totally occupied with her grief and didn't care to think about the farm or anything else except the death of her husband. Before long, however, she came to agree that Ephraim was pushing ahead too quickly. Reflecting on the behavior he displayed at the funeral, she felt uneasily that he was attempting to rule her own life along with the farm.

The daily chores were rather simple, consisting primarily of providing feed and water for the animals and chickens, milking the half- dozen Holstein cows which comprised the dairy herd, and hauling manure from the barn.

These chores were remorseless in their repetitious demands, but they required only a few hours each day. With the passage of winter, however, field work occupied all the remaining daylight hours. The ground must be prepared for sowing the hay, oats, and corn which comprised the basic crops of the dairy farmer in southern Wisconsin during the early nineteen-hundreds. March and April were the months for planting oats. The ground must be plowed and the soil disked and dragged to prepare the seedbed. Zachary died when this work had just begun, but with him or without him, the planting must be continued if people and animals were to have food.

It would be difficult for Prudence and her two children to handle both the chores and the field work. They did not deceive themselves. Alone after the funeral, they quickly recognized the difficulties facing them.

Despite the daunting prospect, however, there was no flinching from their task. It was evident that if they accepted help from Ephraim, they would have to accept his supervision as well, so they rejected any thought of his assistance. They were determined to run the farm by themselves, and they believed they were capable of success.

"I want to be independent at last!" Prudence declared.

To their dismay, Ephraim continued to arrive each morning at six o'clock to help Jon and Sarah. As soon as he stepped into the barn, he began giving orders.

He would say, "Jon, you can bring in the silage and fork it into the mangers. We'll get started with the milking. Sarah, mix the solution to wash the udders; I'll fetch the milking pails."

Prudence knew he was there; she watched from the kitchen window as he entered the barn. It was increasingly evident to her that he was trying to step into her husband's shoes in every respect. She was not necessarily opposed to the hopes she knew he harbored, but she felt he was being too aggressive. It was far too soon for her to consider the thought of another man, even a man she knew so well.

About a week after the funeral, she decided to send him away. She waited for him to arrive as usual in the light of a new dawn. Then, wrapping a shawl around her head and shoulders, she emerged from the warmth of her kitchen and walked the short distance to the barn. Ephraim readily accepted her invitation to share breakfast with the family. She resolved to tell him that they would not need any further help from him.

The subject seemed awkward over scrambled eggs and biscuits, though, and Prudence allowed other subjects to be discussed first.

"Where's Old Jake?" asked Ephraim. "I ain't seen 'im around this week a'tall."

"We don't know, Eeph," replied Jon. "He disappeared right after the funeral."

"We've heard he was seen once or twice over at the cemetery," Sarah volunteered. "Near my father's grave, of course. We went over a couple of days ago, but we couldn't find him."

"I hope he comes home soon," added Prudence. "He was such a good companion for Zac. They were always together. It's a double loss to have him gone too."

"Maybe we should get another dog," suggested Jon.

"Never," said Prudence quietly. "It would be an insult to Zac's memory to replace Old Jake."

After a long hesitation, Ephraim said abruptly, "Prudence, I bin thinkin' what you should do 'bout the farm . . . ."

"What did you have in mind?" she inquired attentively.

"Well, it's a big responsibility, and Jonathan is still very young an' inexperienced. I wouldn't mind takin' charge. I got enough time t' supervise yer animals and acres along with m' own. It might be the right thing t' do, at least for a year or two while you decide upon its disposition one way or t'other." He was watching her face, and he saw it cloud over with the hint of a frown. "That is, if you want me to," he quickly added.

"Jonathan may not have very much experience," she acknowledged, "but I can teach him what he needs to know. You have enough work to do at your own place and I would feel guilty if you worked over here, too."

"Oh, I got m' own work under good control," Ephraim said coolly, "and when I'm helpin' you, I don't consider it no work at all. It's a pleasure."

"That may well be, Eeph," she replied, "but all the same, we'd rather make it on our own."

"It's more work than you kin handle by yerself, Prudence," he cautioned.

"Maybe so," she conceded, her asperity beginning to reveal itself through the tone in her voice and the expression of her face. "But we've talked it over quite seriously, and we're going to give it a good try, anyway. Stop pushing us!"

"As you wish, Prudence," he replied in a surly tone. "I thought only that ya' might be grateful fer some help, with Zachary gone. We bin friends fer many years, an' friends are fer helpin'."

"I am grateful," she said, regaining her civility, "and I do appreciate the friendship we've enjoyed. You've been a help to me in so many ways, more than I dare mention. You have endeared yourself to me and my family once again. It's just—well, it's just that we want to be independent." Her smile was friendly, but firm.

He understood. "All right. I'll give ya' the chance t' run yer own farm. But yer not cuttin' me off from Sarah, are ya'?" His voice sounded stern, almost defiant, and he glanced toward the girl.

"No, Eeph, you know I would never do that," she replied with sympathy.

"That's good," he said with open relief. "I ain't too proud to admit I need help. I can't do everythin' by myself."

"I like doing your housework for you," Sarah interjected. "It's almost like having a home of my own."

"Yer a patient, hard-workin' woman jus' like yer mother," Ephraim remarked. "Ya' even look like she did when she was yer age. Ya' got yer mother's eyes, includin' the mischief. If ya' wore yer hair in a bun like her, you'd be twins. Yer the most beautiful young woman anywhere around. And judgin' by yer mother's history, the work won't hurt ya' none. Besides, you'll get yer own home soon enough, and this way you'll be ready fer it."

"Yes, I want my own home someday," she said wistfully.

"You shall have it, too," Eeph confirmed, "but don't be in a hurry. Wait fer the right man. Yer gonna be married a long time."

"Yes, Uncle Eeph." She had been taught to call him 'Uncle' as soon as she could talk. Ephraim was virtually a part of the family. "But it could've been Jimmy. It really could have."

"Don't be foolish, Sarah," Ephraim admonished. "Jimmy was a lazy, good-for-nothin' loafer. I told ya' so at the time. Ya' marry him and ya' got a lifetime o' trouble. Ain't that right, Prudence."

It was more of a statement than a question. A year ago she would have remained quiet, but now Prudence chose to answer. "You know Jimmy a lot better than I do," she said, "but it looks like he might have settled down now that he's married to Martha. They seem to be doing all right on that tenant farm."

"You jus' wait," he warned. "Wait an' see. They ain't goin' nowhere. He's lazy."

Jimmy had courted Sarah for nearly two years. She had been receptive at first, and at one time he thought he had won his suit. But when he finally pressed her for a decision, she followed Ephraim's advice. Amidst many hot tears she turned Jimmy away, and he married Martha three months later.

Ephraim ended the conversation by pushing back from the wooden table, scraping the linoleum floor with the chair legs. "The sun ain't standin' still," he admonished. "If yer gonna help clean my house this mornin', let's get movin'."

Moments later, as Ephraim and Sarah walked along River Road to his farmhouse, he told the girl, "You and Jon and yer mom can't possibly run that farm all by yer lonesomes. Yer gonna need some help."

"We're going to try," she shrugged.

"Tell ya' what," he continued. "I'll find a farmhand fer ya'. Somebody reliable, not jus' anybody."

"I don't think Mother will take him on," ventured Sarah.

"Well now, girl, you leave that part t' me," he replied. "I think she might take 'im, once she sees how much work there is to do. Give 'er two weeks—'til April Fools', and I bet she'll be willin'."

"We'll see," said the girl.

They stopped at the edge of the road—River Road, known as 'Lovers' Lane' by the local folk—before entering his driveway. He turned and looked into her face. He saw the features of Prudence when he was courting her: the same glowing rosy-apple cheeks, the gentle blue eyes, the walnut-brown hair, the eagerness of attitude. Her high school education had given her good grammar and a poised self-confidence, he thought with a twinge of envious admiration. Like her mother, she moved easily in the society circles of town where she had several friends.

"I'm doin' this as much fer you as I am fer her," he observed softly. "You are both very close to m' heart, and I can't jus' stand by and watch ya' work yerselves to death."

"I understand. You know how much we love you, Uncle Eeph. We count you as one of the biggest blessings in our life." She touched his arm with her hand, and turned her face downward with shyness as she continued, "I pray for you every day."

"Thank ya', Sarah," he returned. "I love you too, more than ya' can understand, and I need yer prayers. I know yer close to God. You are the most religious person I know—just like Zachary was."

"Mother always says I should be kind to you because you must be so lonely all by yourself, with no family."

"I'm not really lonely, Sarah," he replied as they began walking up the graveled driveway to his house.

They continued walking in silence until they reached the porch. He paused with one foot on the front step. Turning to her, he said earnestly, "Promise me one thing, Sarah."

"Of course, Uncle Eeph."

"Promise me you'll try to persuade yer mother t' take on a hired hand if I kin find a good man," he said.

As she thought about his request, her eyes turned up into the sky and her forehead puckered toward a spot centered between her eyebrows, creating vertical and horizontal wrinkles. The pucker meant she was thinking. It was a mannerism familiar to him; it was identical to the expression he remembered from the face of Prudence during his failed courtship as she wrestled with her fateful decision. That image had burned itself so deeply into his consciousness that it pained him suddenly now—even though more than a quarter-century had passed—as it appeared on the face of her daughter.

Her eyes danced down to his face. "I promise," she said.

They smiled at each other with complementary smiles—smiles that exhibited the complete trust and concern which permeated their hearts.

"I hope you understand that Mom loves you and respects you," she said simply. "I think perhaps she needs a little time to think through her new position in life, with my father gone."

"Of course," he agreed.

"Your natural instinct was to step in and give us your comfort and your guidance. That's really very noble of you, and I love you all the more for it. But don't rush it. Mom has to be alone for a while just to get over the shock."

"Yer right, Sarah. I know yer right. "I'll try t' be patient."

They went inside. As usual, the debris from breakfast was scattered around the kitchen. The black iron skillet, with remnants of fried eggs and bacon imbedded in its congealed grease, had been abandoned on the counter near the sink. A dimestore fork with bent tines and a mismatched knife were resting haphazardly on the solitary chipped blue willow plate atop the little kitchen table where he took his meals; the handle of a spoon was projecting above the rim of the enameled coffee cup which had once been white.

Ephraim quickly built a fire in the wood stove while Sarah filled the big iron teakettle from the drinking bucket. Like most of the rural homes in Wisconsin in 1917, the farmhouse boasted neither electricity nor indoor plumbing.

While she waited for the water to boil, Sarah busied herself clearing the table and scraping leftover food into a garbage can to be fed to the pigs. Ephraim pulled up a wooden chair and sat down backwards straddling its high back, watching the girl.

After working a few minutes without conversation, she said softly, "You said you are not lonely, even though you have no family. Why not? How do you keep from being lonely?"

He thought carefully, squinting against the light from the window over the sink where she was scrubbing the black skillet. "Why should I be lonely?" he responded. "I got everythin' I need—a roof over m' head, warm clothes fer m' back, an' plenty of food fer m' belly."

"Sure, your body is comfortable," she acknowledged, "but there's more to life than just being warm and dry and well-fed."

"Them's the big ones," he smiled. "What more would I want?"

"People! I should think you would want people! I should think you'd be lonely without other people in your life. I should think you'd want a family."

"I got *your* family," he reminded her, "just down the road. I love every one of you." He nodded his head tenderly, compressing his lips gently together. "Yer like a daughter t' me. So I don't feel lonely."

"But there's nobody in this house to talk to."

"That's true," he agreed.

"I'm not home alone very often," she said, "but when I am, I feel lonely. Especially after dark. The house makes all kinds of funny little noises. It's almost like the house itself is trying to frighten me."

He laughed. "A house is jus' a house. It don't have no will of its own. It can't think, or feel, or want to frighten ya'."

She turned to face him, and said very solemnly, "You're probably right, if you're talking about just any ordinary house. But our house is different. It's almost seventy years old. It was built by hand, by John Hilley—you know, the father of Bruno Hilley, who lives up the road with his sister."

"Oh yes, I know Bruno. I was thinkin' he might be a man who could help you on the farm."

A small shudder swept through Sarah's shoulders. "He seems like such a strange person," she said. "I don't feel comfortable around him. I don't know what it is—maybe it's his eyes, they seem to stare right through you as though his mind is somewhere else . . . ."

"Yeah, he's a bit unusual," Ephraim agreed. "Mebbe he's spent too much time in the swamp, livin' right on it as he does. I swear, that marsh kin infect ya' after a while. It's like a big living presence that kinda' overwhelms ya' and absorbs ya'. It kin do queer things to ya', I know what ya' mean."

"Maybe it runs in the family," Sarah said. "The old man—John—must have been more than a little odd. He had a French wife, and built the house to please her. He dug the basement by himself with nothing more than a shovel, my father told me. He hauled every stone for its heavy thick walls. He sawed the big beams for the roof, and nailed them in position. His angel permeates the place, my mother says. And sometimes when I'm alone in the house, I can feel him there."

"His ghost, you mean?"

"No," she said stoutly. "Not his ghost. That's superstitious. I don't believe in ghosts. It's his *angel*."

Ephraim laughed again. "An angel wouldn't try to frighten ya'."

"It doesn't make much sense, does it," she agreed with a smile. "But I"m just telling you my feelings, and feelings don't always make sense."

She returned her attention to the dishpan, but remained thoughtful. "You're never frightened, even though you're alone here almost all the time?"

"No, I ain't afraid o' nothin' here in the house."

"But don't you want *people* around?" she persisted. Don't you want someone to talk to?"

"Not jus' anyone," he said. "Most o' the people in this world are just rabble, and I couldn't stand t' be around 'em." His face became serious. "But I'd pay almost any price t' get the right person t' live wit' me."

"You mean as a wife."

"Yes, as a wife."

"Well then, why haven't you gotten married?" She knew him well enough to ask the question, but not well enough to perceive the obvious answer. "I think you'd make a wonderful husband and father."

He had never let her uncover his innermost passion, and he screened the truth from her even now. "I told ya'. I won't settle for jus' an ordinary person. I'm very particular. I want the right woman. An' I ain't caught the right one yet."

"If you caught the right one tomorrow, would you keep her? Would you marry her?"

"Of course!" he said quickly, almost too vehemently.

She opened a cabinet and put away the dishes she had just washed and dried. The brief clatter prevented her from speaking, but then she said, "How do you know the right person even exists? If you haven't found her in all the years you've been looking, maybe there isn't any such person." The thought of her own mother being the 'right person' was so impossible that it had never occurred to her, even though she knew there had once been a tentative romance between the two. She assumed, as he intended, that his ardor for Prudence had withered away years ago.

"Oh yes there is." He knew he was saying too much, but he couldn't stop.

"How do you know? Have you ever met her?"

"Yes. I met her a long time ago."

"Then why didn't you marry her?"

"She wasn't ready for *me*, I guess."

"Will she ever be? Do you really expect her to come to you, after so many years?"

"I hope so. That's what keeps me alive," he confessed even as he berated himself inwardly for revealing too much.

"Who is she? Does she live around here? Do I know her?"

Sarah could not remember any evidence of a romantic relationship during the years she had been keeping house for him. There were no sentimental mementoes, no desiccated flowers, no fragile love-letters. There was a locked tin box on top of the chest of drawers in his upstairs bedroom. It was always shiny and looked well-used; she assumed it contained money and valuable papers. The only picture of a woman in the house was a pencil sketch of her mother which she had seen many times propped up in its wooden frame alongside the box. It had been drawn by an itinerant artist, Ephraim told her, who had set up temporary shop in the Fountain Spring House in Prairieville. No, there was no evidence of the mysterious woman to whom he referred.

Ephraim was secretly grateful for her naivete; grateful that she had no inkling of his lifelong obsession with her mother. He was pleased at this innocent confirmation that both he and Prudence had successfully concealed his secret. By a tacit understanding, they had not openly discussed their long-standing romance for many years. They both preferred that it be forgotten by others, although they were aware of it daily themselves for a very tangible reason. He realized he must curtail his tongue at once.

"You ask too many questions," he said, rising abruptly from his chair.

"I'm sorry," she said as she carefully arranged the dishtowel on its rack. "But I'm asking these questions because I miss my father." Her face softened. "He died so suddenly. I wasn't ready for it. I feel stranded. And I'm so lonely." He was vaguely surprised to see tears spring from her eyes and roll quickly down her cheeks.

She took a step to leave the kitchen, but he slipped an arm around her shoulders and stopped her. "Don't cry," he said automatically. "It was mighty sudden, I know. Yer bound to miss 'im."

She turned in his arms and pressed her head against his shoulder. He could feel the violence of her sobs. He tried to lift her face so he could reason with her and comfort her, but she pushed his hands away and buried her head more deeply against him.

The intensity of her grief astonished him. Of course he had seen her cry at the funeral, along with her brother. But somehow he had been unaffected by their sorrow then; it had seemed rather tenuous. Perhaps they had been in shock, or they were simply wearing brave masks. Or perhaps he had been so aware of his new opportunity to win Prudence that he hadn't noticed the depth of their feelings.

But now he was suddenly brought up against the stark fact of Sarah's wracking agony, and he was stunned.

Ephraim looked into his own heart, and he could find very little distress over the death of his friend. He had not been horrified nor anguished, not even by the hideousness of the injuries. This realization did not amaze him, for he was acutely aware of the sharp sense of relief created by the elimination of Zachary from the drama of his life.

Nevertheless, to his surprise, for the first time he felt a pang of guilt over the fatal circumstances.

He quickly brushed aside his discomfort and turned his thoughts back to the girl who was clinging to him in desperation.

"Everything will be all right," he told her reassuringly.

"I just feel so alone and uneasy," she said, her eyes overflowing. "I'm so afraid of the war coming, and my father gone, and all."

He savored the feeling of her vibrant body pressed against him. Sarah always hugged him enthusiastically. Some people offer rigid hugs, resisting any invasion of their territorial space. Their hands hold their partner at a distance, avoiding any physical contact below the shoulders as though they fear an infection.

Not Sarah. When she hugged, her hands were employed to draw her partner closer to her in an embrace which virtually clamped their entire bodies together. It was the same uninhibited clutch Prudence had given Ephraim during their early days.

He forced himself to speak, but he spoke slowly. "Well now, Sarah, we can't do much about the war, can we? If it comes, it comes. And yer father is gone from this world an' we cannot bring 'im back, can we? But I'm here. Nothin' is goin' to hurt ya' while I'm around, and I ain't goin' nowhere. You can depend on me."

Sarah calmed herself as she often did, by turning her thoughts toward Heaven. "Forgive me," she said brokenly, "God is still in command of everything that happens to us, and all will be well. But I find it so hard to trust Him and let go . . . ."

"I know what ya' mean," Ephraim whispered. "Sometimes I can't jus' be patient and wait fer His will t' be done. There comes a time when the temptation t' take matters in m' own hands is simply overwhelmin'."

They lingered in each other's arms, each one for his own reasons reluctant to relinquish the embrace.

During the ensuing days, Ephraim resisted his intense desire to assist Prudence and her children on the farm. Following Sarah's advice, he even refrained from visiting them, although such abstinence required every bit of self-discipline he could muster.

Through Sarah, he maintained contact with the Hartmann family. She continued her regular twice-a-week visits to wash his dishes and keep his house in a modest semblance of order, and he was able to question her about the thoughts and actions of her mother. Ephraim seemed unusually eager to hear even the smallest detail, and she was quite willing to keep him fully informed.

Sarah found an equally receptive audience in her mother for information going the opposite direction. Prudence inquired daily about Ephraim's health, and listened with rapt attention to every comment made by Sarah about their neighbor.

Sarah used the opportunity to plead Ephraim's cause. She had not shared her family's resentment at his intrusion into their life and work. She admired him and was quite willing to accept his help.

"Mother, we certainly do need it," she argued. "Anybody can see that we aren't keeping up with the work."

"Well, yes, I'll have to agree it's more than we can handle. But I'm not ready to turn the farm over to Eeph."

"Don't be too hard on Uncle Eeph," said Sarah. "He only wants to help us."

"You're probably right, Sarah, but I feel uncomfortable with him."

"Maybe it's just a feeling that you're being disloyal toward Dad," Sarah suggested.

"That's possible," mused Prudence.

"If you don't want Eeph himself, maybe he could find us a hired hand," suggested Sarah.

Prudence considered that idea for a moment, and agreed. "If he can find us a good farmhand, I'd be willing to take a look."

Of course, Ephraim did indeed have a farmhand in mind to help Prudence. If she wouldn't accept his own efforts, Ephraim reasoned, the best substitute was his cousin. Robert was a bit of a drifter, a man who had collected a patient wife and two little children during his meandering journey through life. Unable to feed the three mouths which were his responsibility, he parked them with his mother near Janesville while he bounced from job to job. He earned what little he could with his limited skills and ambitions and sent most of his pay home to his mother.

Robert was willing, even eager, to answer the call. With that assurance, Ephraim could not force himself to wait until April first, the date he had informally designated when he first mentioned his plan to Sarah. His seasoned eye had observed that the fieldwork on the Hartmann farm was lagging, and he decided to act.

Sarah herself opened the conversation while she was washing an accumulation of dirty dishes in Ephraim's Spartan kitchen. "I think Mother might be ready to take on a hired hand, if you have a good one in mind," she said.

"That's good," replied Ephraim. "I was kinda' noticin' that the spring plantin' looks a bit slow."

"We haven't even begun putting the oats in yet," she lamented. There aren't enough hours in the day. We work from sun-up until after dark, but we can't get done. Now it looks like it'll rain tomorrow and put us even farther behind."

Ephraim placed a big hand gently upon Sarah's shoulder. "I suspected as much," he murmured. I bin farmin' all m' life, and I know how much work there is t' do. I tole ya' right off ya' couldn't do it by yerselves." His words were spoken kindly, without malice.

"That is certainly true," Sarah said.

"Mebbe yer right," Ephraim said. "Mebbe yer mother might be willin' now t' take on a hired hand."

Sarah quietly nodded her head in assent.

Accordingly, he accompanied Sarah to the Hartmann home when she had completed her work.

Prudence had missed him and felt somewhat guilty because she had so harshly rejected his recent offers of assistance. "I'm glad to see you again," she told him. "I was beginning to think I had lost you as well as Zachary."

It was the attitude he had hoped to find in her. "I was only respectin' yer wishes," he said modestly.

"Yes, I know," she sighed. "We do want to be the masters of our own farm, Eeph, but we don't intend to lose your friendship in the process."

"I should hope not," he commented.

"I want to be independent, Eeph, but I don't mind admitting that you were right about the work. There's an awful lot of it to do, and it's hard to keep up without Zachary being here."

"Yup. I knowed it. But you were right, too, in takin' control of yer own place. I let my worries fer you get outta' hand."

She smiled ruefully. "That's all right."

Ephraim gazed at Prudence with affection and concern. I bin figgerin' how t' help ya' git yer job done," he said tentatively. "Mebbe you'd like t' have m' cousin Robert come an' give ya' a hand. You never met Robert, but you heard me talk about 'im. He's a good worker."

Remembering her promise, Sarah endorsed the suggestion. "I think it's a good idea, Mother," she said. "We just can't get all the work done by ourselves. We've got to get some outside help."

Jonathan added his endorsement. "It looks to me like we'll be in the European war before very long," he said, "and I'll be off in the Army instead of working here on the farm. If Robert is too old to be a soldier, we ought to take him on. We'll need him, and maybe another one, besides."

Prudence put a restraining hand on her son's shoulder. "Even if the war comes," she said, "you don't have to be part of it. I couldn't think of you going off to fight!"

Jonathan covered his mother's hand with his own, but it didn't necessarily mean he would obey her. "We'll see," is all he said.

After an awkward pause, Ephraim addressed Jon's previous thoughts. "Robert's too old fer the war," he confirmed, "but he's young enough t' be a good worker. An' he won't meddle none in yer business, either. He'll jus' do what ya' tell 'im. You'll be the boss."

Prudence smiled. "You win, Eeph," she said warmly. "We'll be glad to accept his help."

"He kin stay at my house," Ephraim volunteered. "I'll be glad t' put 'im up. That way he won't be a bother t' ya', not at all, an' not much expense, either. He'd be satisfied with a half-dollar a day."

"I remember he's got a family to support," commented Prudence, "and I don't want to be cheap. We'd pay him five dollars a week."

"Naw, naw," protested Ephraim. "Not when I'm givin' 'im 'is room an' board. That's too much. Fifty cents a day is plenty. He'll work Saturdays and Sundays, too, so that's three dollars and fifty cents a week. Really, that's plenty. Don't give 'im a penny more."

Prudence laughed. "All right," she conceded cheerfully. "You win again. I yield to your judgment."

"Thank you, Prudence," he replied with a feeling of intense satisfaction. "Robert'll be here to work startin' Monday mornin.'"

When he left a few minutes later, Prudence gave him a hug. "You always come through, Eeph," she said. "You always help me when I need you."

Her warm embrace was all the thanks he needed. He winked confidentially at Sarah. Suffused with a feeling of deep contentment, he turned from the door and whistled tunelessly to himself all the way back to his home.

When he was gone, Sarah commented, "Mom, it's so good to know that you are happy again. I haven't heard you laugh since the day Dad died."

"There hasn't been much to be cheerful about," observed her mother.

"I like Uncle Eeph," confessed Sarah, "and I think he's good for you. He makes you laugh."

Chapter 3

Robert arrived at the Hartmann farm soon after breakfast on Monday morning, just as Ephraim had promised. He was riding a Harley-Davidson motorcycle; a duffel bag stuffed with his belongings rested in the sidecar.

Prudence examined him with a critical eye, and she was pleased. His face and hands were brown and toughened by the sun like Ephraim's, but he displayed a relaxed, easy-going nature. His ready smile revealed a broken tooth as well as a sunny disposition; he lacked the brooding intensity of his cousin. He was only about thirty-five, Prudence guessed, but when he removed his battered hat to speak with her, a bald head was disclosed which gave him a much older appearance. His protruding, angular cheekbones reduced his receding chin to near invisibility beneath his wide, thin lips. His eyes, set too closely together on either side of his narrow nose, were slightly crossed. She was glad he was not handsome.

It was evident he would not take command. His first words were, "If ya' see fit t' hire me, Ma'am, I'll do what ya' tell me t' do and I'll try t' do it t' yer satisfaction."

Jon and Sarah nodded their approval, and the terms of employment were quite acceptable to Robert. "Let me park m' junk over at Eeph's place," he told her, "n' I'll be right back t' start work."

Robert settled in as though he had worked the Hartmann farm all his life. He was well acquainted with farmwork, and quickly learned the new routine.

His help made it possible for Prudence to seek companionship with the women she had met in the Prairieville Women's Club.

None of them were her close friends—she hadn't taken the time to cultivate friendship—and some of them made it plain they didn't relish socializing with a farm wife, but she remembered several who were friendly.

When she thought of reaching out, the first person who came to her mind was Theodora Youmans, the newspaperwoman who had made a name for herself through clubwoman activity.

Theodora was nine years older than Prudence. She was a mature woman of the world who had established a career in journalism at the *Prairieville Freeman* even before marrying the publisher, Henry M. Youmans, in 1889. She heartily embraced the concept of women's clubs, joining three of them in Prairieville—the Beacon Lights, the Prairieville Women's Club, and the Ideal Club—in their early days. In 1898 she became president of the Wisconsin Federation of Women's Clubs.

Now Youmans was deeply immersed in politics, committed to winning the right to vote for women. She was president of the Wisconsin Women's Suffrage Association, a position she had held since the suffragists had reorganized following the defeat of their statewide referendum in 1912.

In her childhood Prudence had lived in Prairieville where she enjoyed close friendships with other girls of her neighborhood. Although she lived on a farm all her adult life, she never became accustomed to the solitude of the country. She was happily married to Zachary, she insisted to herself, but she hungered for the society of other women. The Prairieville Women's Club was formed at the turn of the century, and every few years afterward she wangled an invitation to attend one of their meetings. She treasured each occasion, but she didn't go very often because she knew Zachary didn't approve.

She had attended such a meeting early in January, a few months before his death. Theodora Youmans herself presented the program before her sister clubwomen; it was the first time Prudence had met her in person. The subject of her talk was "Woman's Hour" and it commanded the earnest attention of the thirty-seven members and guests. Although Theodora herself admitted that not everyone would quite agree with her, it was obvious from the applause and the comments that her views were well received. Afterward, Prudence went to Theodora like a moth to a lantern, and the two women took a quick liking to each other despite their disparate backgrounds. They recognized a mutual understanding at once, and Prudence quickly endorsed Theodora's efforts on behalf of suffrage.

"I deeply admire your work toward getting votes for women," Prudence told Theodora. "I don't know much about the world, but I follow your newspaper column every week. I thought it was magnificent the way you persuaded the state women's federation to endorse the referendum favoring suffrage a few years ago."

"Thank you," replied Theodora. "I almost didn't try, when the entire policy committee voted against me. But I just knew the delegates felt differently, and fortunately they supported the endorsement."

"All my time has been required on the farm," Prudence apologized, "and I wasn't able to help in the campaign. Of course, I never told my husband Zachary how I felt, because I knew he was against the idea of women voting. Nonetheless, it made me mad when we lost the referendum. I never could understand how we got beaten so badly at the polls."

"We were beaten by the farmers, the brewers, and the Germans!" declared Theodora. "They were all afraid we would outlaw drinking as soon as we could vote. I suppose they're right—most of us are as strong for temperance as we are for suffrage. Frances Willard, the woman who built the Women's Christian Temperance Union, combined the two issues with great effectiveness. Here in Wisconsin, certainly, the two causes—along with pacifism—have been inextricably intertwined for decades.

"You see, the farmers grow the grain, the brewers make the beer, and the Germans drink it," Theodora explained. "Together they make up quite a force at the polls."

"Well, I'm a farmer, and a German," protested Prudence, "but I'm against liquor—and in favor of women's rights."

"Yes. I understand, and I'm glad to hear your position," said Theodora with a smile. "But you can't vote. Your husband can—and did—and I heard you say he was against us. That's why we lost." Theodora smiled disarmingly as Prudence made a wry face. "Don't feel bad. The vote was nearly two-to-one against us. Your husband's vote didn't make any difference. And I understand perfectly. Henry and I don't agree fully on this issue, either, even though I am the president of the suffrage association."

That discussion during their very first meeting sealed a bond of sisterhood between Prudence and Theodora. In a more general sense, simply being in the society of other vital women touched a deeply buried sentiment within Prudence. She felt a vivid sense of awakening, a sense of challenge which exposed the insignificance of her life thus far.

Nevertheless, she didn't attend the next meeting in February, nor the following one in March. One reason was her lack of time. There was always an abundance of farm work to do, and she harbored such a strong obligation to her duties as a farmwife that she felt guilty spending a few hours attending a 'literary' club.

Additionally, it was inconvenient to travel to the meetings. Zachary insisted upon driving her if she went; he wouldn't let her go to Prairieville alone with the horse and buggy. He didn't complain about waiting to drive her home again, and he found errands to occupy the hour or two that she spent with the clubwomen. Nevertheless, the realization that he was wasting his time, coupled with the fear that she might be wasting her own time as well, added to her guilt and kept her from going to the meetings.

But the most important argument against attending the Women's Club was her knowledge that Zachary frowned upon her participation in townswomen's activities just as he opposed giving women the right to vote. He was an old-fashioned man and believed women belonged at home. They discussed the subject rarely, and never in any depth, but she knew his opinion without asking.

At first, she too had her doubts about becoming a clubwoman. Her parents were emigrants from Germany, arriving in Wisconsin as newlyweds, and she had been raised in the restrictive conservatism of the Old Country. It was quite unheard-of for a woman to venture far beyond the domestic sphere. The farm chores and the duties of motherhood, which fully occupied the hectic hours of every day, were infinitely more important. It was her moral duty to stay at home.

Then the years passed and she realized the children no longer required her constant attention. The farm work seemed repetitive and unfulfilling. She became lonely and bored, and the Women's Club offered relief from both symptoms.

The injection of a noble cause—suffrage—completed the transformation of her values. Suddenly it seemed her moral duty to enter a greater scene. She could scarcely stifle her new feelings. Although she maintained the appearance of a devoted farm wife, beneath the surface she was seething with the repressed desire to take a firm stand alongside Theodora Youmans and her friends.

Zachary was aware of the tumult within her, she knew, even without open confession. She didn't want to offend him, or rebel against his wishes, so she covered her feelings as best she could and continued spinning out the humdrum existence of her daily life.

Suddenly Zachary died, and her divided heart found its peace in widowhood. She was liberated to pursue her ambition. She could support the suffrage cause openly to whatever extent she chose, without being accountable to a husband.

Prudence assumed she had been quickly forgotten by Theodora after their brief January conversation, so she was surprised when Theodora appeared at Zachary's funeral. Her acceptance of the city woman's expressions of sympathy at the time was limited severely by her own grief, the small but pressing crowd of mourners, and the defensive presence of Ephraim.

She was surprised again when a card with a heart-felt note from

Theodora followed the funeral, reminding Prudence of their friendship and inviting her to the next meeting of the Women's Club on April 4th.

The invitation was received as eagerly as a drowning victim receives a life preserver, and nothing could keep Prudence from attending the meeting.

When the day arrived, she allowed Jon to harness Kaiser and roll out the buggy, but she insisted upon taking the reins herself to ride alone into Prairieville for the first time.

Driving along the country road to the Women's Club meeting, Prudence's heart was bursting with a sense of liberation and pride. She was free! Free to go to town, free to associate with her friends, free to pursue whatever cause she chose. The more she thought about Zachary's repression, the more exuberant she became over her deliverance.

Impulsively she pulled the wedding ring from her finger, glanced at it briefly with a sudden look of distaste, and threw it as far as she could into the hayfield alongside the road.

At once she regretted her action and felt pangs of guilt, but she did not consider going back to look for the golden ring which Zachary had once slipped on her finger with great tenderness. Instead she wondered at the intensity of her own repudiation of a quarter-century of a marital union which she now looked back upon as bondage.

Arriving in town, she remembered that none of the women of the club would come by horse and buggy. Virtually all of them owned automobiles. There were still some horses in Prairieville, but they belonged to old-fashioned tradesmen or people without enough money to afford a car. In the country, the situation was reversed—there were very few automobiles. Suddenly she was ashamed of being a farmer, and she pulled the wide brim of her hat down over her face as she drove across town to Thiel's livery—one of the few remaining—on Madison Street.

"I'll be back in a couple of hours, Kaiser," she told the horse, giving him an affectionate pat on his nose. Then she walked bravely to the Elk's Clubhouse at the corner of Clinton Street and Wisconsin Avenue.

The wide wooden steps beckoned her to the heavy front door. In a sense, she felt she would never return. She was leaving behind her old existence. She could not guess the future, but she would never permit herself to fall back into the enervating drudgery of being the submissive wife of a farmer.

She resolved firmly to cut her hair short as soon as she got home, as a symbol of her new life. Never again would she wear it in a tight little bun at the back of her head.

Then she lifted her skirts defiantly to climb the stairs and enter the building.

There were more than a dozen women in the meeting room as she walked in, but Theodora noticed her at once and stepped forward to greet her.

"I'm so glad you came," she said. "I know there's lots of work to do on the farm right now, but it will do you good to talk with other people."

"You're right," Prudence agreed.

Theodora treated Prudence like an old and very close friend, introducing her warmly to the club's president, Miss Martha Walton, and many of her sister clubwomen.

Prudence was impressed anew by the quiet, competent determination of Wisconsin's leading suffragist. Theodora Youmans was a short, well-built woman with a robust figure and a sprightly step. Her attractive face was handsome rather than beautiful. The widely flared nostrils of her solidly set nose gave the impression of impish pugnacity rather than meanness or anger. The spicy twinkle in her eyes added to the pleasing nature of her overall appearance.

Routine business was conducted, and officers were elected for the following club year to begin in the fall. Then Bertha Palmer, the newly elected president, made an eloquent plea on behalf of the National Red Cross Society. In the name of 'Preparedness', workers were needed for many different tasks.

"We'll be in the war in a matter of days," Theodora declared. "There is no doubt about it."

"Impossible!" answered Hattie Randle, wife of Prairieville's most successful furniture dealer and a dedicated believer in the peace movement. "After all we've done—Julia Grace Wales, Ella Neville—all of us—surely we're not going to allow ourselves to be drawn into that European quagmire!"

"I'm afraid we are," replied Theodora. "President Wilson's war message on Monday has received overwhelming support in Washington. The Senate will probably ratify the declaration of war today."

"How can that be?" asked Prudence. "Everybody I know is against it."

"The people aren't for it," confirmed Miss Grace Lusk, an English teacher in Prairieville High School. "After a class discussion one day last week, I asked my students for a show of hands on whether we should enter the European War. There wasn't a single student in favor of the notion. Children tend to reflect the views of their parents, so I would conclude that the mood of the citizens, at least in this town, is against President Wilson's demands."

"Absolutely!" declared Mary Lockney, wife of the knowledgeable lawyer who had represented the district in the state senate. "Senator LaFollette has fought the President at every step, and my husband Henry says he's not going to cave in now. He'll vote against the war resolution, beyond any doubt."

"Oh, I'd be sure of that," added Miss Catherine Tichenor, whose father was one of a long line of highly respected Prairieville attorneys. "Meta Berger—the Congressman's wife—says almost every member of the Wisconsin Congressional delegation is opposed to the President's demands."

"Yes, that's true," admitted Theodora. "We all know how strong the anti-war sentiment is here in Wisconsin. And for two good reasons: our penchant for Progressive-Socialist causes, and the fact that many of us come from a German background."

"The German-American Alliance says Germans and Austrians make up a third of the population in Wisconsin," Florence Estberg, wife of Prairieville's most popular jeweler, added.

"But the rest of the country is not like us," explained Theodora.

"I'm not so sure about that," objected Mrs. Lockney. "Just look at the nationwide attention given to Reverend Brockman's letter to the President."

"That was indeed amazing," conceded Theodora. "But the very fact that Paul T. Brockman, pastor of the Trinity Lutheran Church in Prairieville Wisconsin, achieves such notice is evidence that there's nobody else of greater stature taking the same position. In effect, the Germans in Wisconsin are the President's only outspoken opposition!"

"What did the letter say?" inquired Prudence.

"Reverend Brockman accused President Wilson of taking an active stance against Germany all the time that he was claiming to be neutral," explained Theodora.

"The pastor is right, too!" declared Mrs. Estberg. "He points out that when England came over here looking for money, Wilson's government kept very quiet while the war loans were being made. But when Germany tried to raise money in America, the President declared that it was a violation of neutrality and forbade any banker to respond to the requests. That's certainly not neutrality."

"And the same thing is true about the blockades, too," added Mrs. Lockney. "When England established a blockade around Germany and laid mines in the shipping lanes, President Wilson ordered our ships to stay away. But when Germany established a blockade around England and sent their submarines out to enforce it, President Wilson announced that we would ignore the threat. Then we blamed the Germans when our ships got sunk!"

"And just think of it!" exclaimed Mrs. Estberg. "It was food we wanted to ship to Germany—and Wilson wouldn't let us. But we were shipping war munitions to England, with his blessings!"

"And then the people got so outraged when the *Lusitania* was sunk!"

rejoined Mrs. Lockney.

"But you see—that's the proof that the rest of the country doesn't see this matter the way we do," said Theodora quietly. "Our political views are different."

"That's absolutely right," said Mrs. Helen Goff, wife of the leading restaurateur. "Other than Victor Berger, I can't think of another Socialist Congressman in the whole country—not a single one."

"That's true, I guess," said Mrs. Estberg. "We're used to Milwaukee having a Socialist mayor like Daniel Hoan. "But we are unique; no other great city in America elects a Socialist."

Grace Lusk shook her head. "I don't think traditional political views are really so important," she said. "It's not important what party you belong to. The desire for peace cuts across party lines. There are many people of all political persuasions who realize that violence is never the answer to our problems. Even Governor Philipp, a conservative Republican, has opposed the shipment of arms and ammunition to Britain."

"Yes," Mrs. Goff agreed, "but I think he was influenced by the feelings of the voters who elected him."

"Exactly," agreed Theodora. "We've got to remember that the voters' sentiments here in Wisconsin are as different from the national view as they are strong. We shouldn't let ourselves be blinded by these local opinions. You'll remember that the idea of an embargo on arms didn't get very far in Congress. The rest of the country is ready for war, even if Wisconsin isn't."

"Maybe the men are ready for war, but the women shouldn't be," observed Mary Lockney. "Women have always been peacemakers, as well they should be. Especially the women who know what's going on, which means us women who are in favor of having the vote. Women's suffrage and peacemaking go hand in hand, and we should never forget it."

"No, that's not necessarily true," protested Mary Newman Roberts, wife of the prominent veterinarian-businessman Dr. David Roberts. She and Theodora were close friends and partners in the suffrage effort. "It might be necessary to support the Wilson war effort to win political support for suffrage. Besides, not everybody around here is against the war," she asserted. "Look at the big turnouts for the Preparedness Parades all over Wisconsin. David says he can feel the mood of the people changing over to war. Isn't every one of us supporting Preparedness? I didn't hear any objections to Bertha's plea for the Red Cross."

As Mrs. Roberts finished her remarks, the knowledgeable women of the club turned automatically toward Miss Lusk. She felt their glances and was obliged to comment. "Of course we're for Preparedness," she said in a level tone. "But that doesn't necessarily mean we're in favor of going to war. I think a lot of us, myself included, support Preparedness so we can maintain neutrality. I think that is the position of Governor Philipp, too. He says a well-trained militia is important to insure neutrality."

"It is idle to assert we are preparing only for defense," Theodora said. "All countries say that, but just look at what's happening in Europe today."

"Then you are in favor of a declaration of war?" asked Miss Lusk. "Even though many suffragist leaders are against it? Olympia Brown herself even went to Washington last month to take part in the peace march." Brown, in her eighties, was one of the founders of the suffrage movement in Wisconsin and was regarded with veneration.

Theodora hesitated. For decades she had embraced peace, prohibition, and votes for women as though each depended upon the other for moral and intellectual support. But now she had been forced to change her view. She chose to support President Wilson and his war policies, following the advice of the suffragists' national leader, Carrie Chapman Catt. It was an open effort to buy political support for the cause of suffrage. Catt—and Youmans—were willing to sacrifice almost anything to achieve the right to vote—even though other suffrage leaders refused to compromise their pacifist principles.

"I am still a pacifist," Theodora declared slowly. "But I have come to believe that the Allies must win the war in order to obtain peace. That is the direction my pacifism leads today."

Prudence listened to the clubwomen with awed interest. Her own life was extremely sheltered, she thought. Work on the farm was so demanding that she seldom even read the weekly newspaper, except for the column of Theodora. She was poorly prepared to discuss political matters, despite her strong feelings against the war. She felt crippled by her lack of knowledge, and she longed to be like these women who seemed so well-informed and articulate.

The club's program for the day was given by Susan Guild, Dean of Women at Prairieville's Carroll College. It was an interpretative lecture featuring Wagner's *Ring of the Nibelung*—introduced as 'the world's greatest masterpiece.' Dean Guild had attended a performance of the opera in Berlin, and she described in great detail the magnificent stage settings, the 'sweetly told story,' and the inspiring music.

Selections from the opera were played on a Victrola. Prudence had never before heard music mechanically reproduced, and she was awed by the sound of human voices coming from the grooves of a phonograph record. 'What a day of wonders this is!' she thought to herself.

Miss Margaret Douglass then sang two short Wagnerian solos, ending the program with eloquent dignity.

Like political subjects, operas were new to Prudence. The clubwomen's apparent knowledge and appreciation of great music reinforced her feelings of ignorance and inferiority while simultaneously stirring her admiration.

Refreshments were served, and for a while the women sat or stood in small clusters to share a half-dozen different conversations. Prudence moved from one group to another listening unobtrusively and saying nothing.

All too soon, she felt, the group began to dissolve as women drifted away to head homeward. The afternoon had been so refreshing for her that she didn't hurry to leave. She lingered until the very end, until Theodora meandered toward the door with Mame Roberts and Grace Lusk. The newspaperwoman, who had been quite aware of the shadowing presence of the farm widow, turned with a hearty smile. "Don't hurry away, Prudence," she said. "We've been so full of business here that I'm afraid I haven't been a very good hostess. I have an hour free, now. Why don't the four of us stop at my house and talk politics?"

"Oh, I'd love to!" Prudence exclaimed, eager to prolong the afternoon's joy, and the four of them left the Elk's Clubhouse together. Theodora was energetic and quick-stepping, and soon they were entering the Youmans doorway on Carroll Street.

"I can't stay long," said Grace as the women settled into parlor chairs. "I'm going into Milwaukee for a dinner meeting."

"You may leave whenever you must," said Theodora graciously. "I just thought we might have a few minutes to get better acquainted with Prudence, as she wants to join us in our suffrage efforts."

"It was nice to have you at our meeting," Mame told the farm woman. "And I want to extend my sympathies, too; I understand you lost your husband quite suddenly a few weeks ago."

"Yes, that's right," said Prudence. Her eyes moistened. "It was a sudden shock. I miss him a great deal." Then she brightened. "The one good thing about it is that I feel more comfortable about being here with you. Zac didn't like me to attend women's meetings."

"Yes, you have told me that before," said Theodora. "A lot of men feel the same way, so don't feel bad about it."

"The days of male supremacy are coming to an end," declared Grace. "It's about time. Women have been oppressed far too long. As I pointed out in my book review, men have used the institution of marriage as a means of keeping women enslaved."

"Those are pretty strong feelings," observed Prudence, and then she remembered the vehemence of her own action in throwing her wedding ring into the field just hours earlier.

"Yes they are, but they are justified," insisted Grace with tightened lips. "Thank God we have groups like this Women's Club to rally us against our chains. Thank God for leaders like Theodora!"

"The Women's Club is good for all of us," declared Mame. "We learn things and develop our personalities. I'd think husbands would find us more interesting and appealing."

"Men are afraid of losing control," said Grace. "Men want to be the boss. They want women to be interesting, yes, but they also want them to be submissive and obedient."

"If that's what Henry wanted when he married me," laughed Theodora, "he sure must have been mightily surprised." The others laughed, too, at the thought of Theodora being dominated by anyone.

"Well, there is a good point there, anyway," said Mame. "I don't think I'm Mrs. Milquetoast by any means, but when the chips are down, I expect David to take the lead. Somebody's got to be the head of the family, and I think it should be the man."

"So do the men," said Grace quickly. "That's why it's so difficult to make any steps toward equality. That's why we women still don't have the vote."

The discussion continued for a half hour, when Grace expressed her regrets and left the house. Mame followed soon after, leaving Prudence alone with Theodora.

"Thanks for your hospitality," said Prudence, "at the club as well as at your home. I truly enjoyed myself. I haven't laughed very much since Zac's funeral."

"I'm glad you were here," responded Theodora.

"One thing puzzled me though," said Prudence. "Why did everybody look at Grace when Mame finished speaking? Is there some link between those two?"

"Yes, there surely is," answered Theodora. "Rumors are flying that Grace and Dr. Roberts are in love with each other. Someone saw them together in a Chicago hotel a couple of months ago."

"No! Really? Does Mrs. Roberts know about it?"

"Mame? Apparently not. She shows great respect for Grace's talents as a teacher, and even invited her to give a book reading at the Ideal Club—you heard Grace refer to it a few moments ago. The subject was most ironic—the book was *Love and Marriage* by the Swedish feminist Ellen Key. The author favors 'free love.' She says sexual activity is normal for men and women and shouldn't be restricted by the constraints of marriage. What really counts, she writes, is whether two people hold a deep mutual affection for each other."

"You mean Grace actually said things like that in front of Mame?"

"I wasn't there, but I'm told that she said all that and a lot more. And somebody told me that most of the time she looked straight at Mame."

"That just doesn't sound possible," Prudence commented. "Surely the rumors of a love affair between Grace and Dr. Roberts cannot be true! How could such a story get started, anyway!"

"For the last year or so, Grace has been helping the doctor with his new book," Theodora replied, "and they have spent a lot of time alone together."

"Well, I hope there's no truth to the matter," said Prudence. "Mame is such a nice woman."

"Yes, everybody loves Mame Roberts. It's so painful to think that anybody in the world could hurt her."

Even as they spoke, Grace was boarding the electric interurban train, headed for Milwaukee and a secret tryst with Dr. David Roberts for dinner.

Prudence changed the subject. She reached forward and rested her hand on Theodora's. "I admire you," she said. "I want to be like you. Most of us women have lives that are utterly unimaginative. It seems so wonderful for women to step out beyond their own little commonplace pathways. I want to learn about all the exciting things in the world. If I spend one more year in that swamp without getting out and doing something important for the world, I just know I shall turn into a mud turtle!"

"Well, there are some very positive things about being out in public," affirmed Theodora. "But there are some risks as well. Don't abandon the safety of your home life and jump into the swim unless you have considered all the angles."

"I've had plenty of time to consider all the angles," replied Prudence. "I'm ready to take the risks, whatever they might be. If I don't seize the opportunity now, it'll be too late to be a part of the great cause of suffrage. I want to work with you in getting votes for women. I no longer have a husband who needs me, and I want to do something important with my life. Will you let me join your efforts?"

"Of course. Half of my time is spent in trying to persuade women to become active in our cause. We're always looking for volunteers—especially women like you who are not afraid to work. We'll be glad to get your help—there is certainly plenty to do!"

"I have wasted my life," Prudence confessed. "Who really cares whether my flock of hens lays thirty eggs every day? What difference does it make if my heifers are washed and curried? Next year—even next week—nobody will remember. Not even me!"

"Don't be so hard on yourself," replied Theodora. "Even the little things we do every day, the routine things, have their own importance. Why, look at your family! You have raised two wonderful children. That is perhaps the most important thing any woman can do." She lowered her voice. "Let me make my own confession. There are times when I wish desperately I had children of my own."

"Really?" Prudence heard her own voice as though from a distance. She acknowledged what Theodora had said, but she didn't believe it.

"Yes, it is true," confided Theodora. "When I am gone, who will remember me?"

"But you've got so many friends," Prudence said, baffled.

"Well, let's say I've got a lot of acquaintances—a lot of women who are working in the same cause. But I have no real friends, nobody who will care about me in the years to come. You've got your children."

"But you have children, too!" protested Prudence.

"No, I don't," Theodora said abruptly. "My husband does. Henry has children from his first wife, but I have none."

"Oh, I didn't realize . . . ."

"That's all right. We've been friends only a few months. How could you know? You see, Henry's wife died a long time ago. I was working as a journalist in the office of the *Freeman*. After a few years, Henry and I were married."

"That must be difficult," said Prudence. "I can't imagine myself marrying again, now that Zachary is gone."

"Oh, you will," said Theodora. "Life gets pretty lonely without a spouse. That's what happened with Henry. He really needed a companion."

"Well, perhaps," Prudence replied in a disbelieving tone.

A footstep was heard on the porch, the front door opened, and the jaunty publisher of the *Freeman* strutted into the room. The two women rose. "You've not met my husband, Henry," Theodora said, motioning toward him with a flourish. "Henry, this is Prudence Hartmann, the woman I told you I was inviting to the Women's Club today. She's going to be helping me with my suffrage work."

Henry Youmans took her hand in his, but instead of shaking it gently as Prudence expected, he raised it toward him and leaned his face downward. His lips did not touch the back of her hand, but the gesture was so gallant and gentlemanly that she did not hear the words he spoke.

Later, walking down the sidewalk to Thiel's livery, her mind was whirling with excitement. The significance of the farm had been diminished in her eyes, and she was eager to move into a new and bigger arena. The importance of Theodora and the other clubwomen overwhelmed her, and a sense of exhilaration filled her whole body.

It seemed like a long ride home, for she was much later than expected and she feared her children might be concerned about her first solo drive into town.

Instead, it was Ephraim who was awaiting her in the farm driveway. "I'm so glad t' see ya'," he said, the relief evident in his face. "Sarah said you was goin' t' be back more than an hour ago." He took the halter of the horse while she stepped from the buggy.

"I'm sorry, I didn't mean to worry anybody," said Prudence. "I went over to Theodora's house after the meeting, and I'm afraid I stayed later than I intended."

"That's okay," Eeph said, but the frown on his face contradicted his words.

"You don't look like it's okay," she said with an impudent flash of her eyes.

"Well, I ain't real happy wit' you goin' in t' town by yerself," he growled.

"You're just like Zachary!" she exclaimed, laughing. "Thank goodness I'm not married to you."

Her lighthearted reference to the forbidden subject emboldened him. "Tell ya' what," he said brightly, "You marry me and I'll let ya' go in t' town by yerself."

"I'll think about it," she said with a teasing glance, turning toward the house.

"I'll take care of Kaiser," said Eeph. "Jon n' Sarah's in the barn, and Robert is still plantin' corn."

Prudence bustled about the kitchen preparing supper, still bursting with excitement. Later, when the pork slab was fried and the potatoes were mashed and her children were settled at the table, Prudence exuberantly related the events of the afternoon.

Sarah did not share her zeal. In her own gentle way, she said, "It sounds like the suffrage campaign could take a lot of your time. Do you really want to be away from the farm that much?"

"Oh yes, I'm sure I do!" Prudence replied enthusiastically. "I've worked on this farm for twenty-five years, and I'm ready for a break. It's time to give you two a chance on your own farm."

Sarah pondered for a moment, and then said very thoughtfully, "I'm not sure it's good for a woman to be out like that. I notice you are not wearing your wedding ring any more. . . ."

Prudence blushed. "I don't have a husband now," she said defensively.

"Dad's been dead less than a month," said Sarah crossly. "You ought to wear his ring as a tribute to his love and devotion. If you're out where people can see you, especially without your ring, it could lead to temptations."

Prudence laughed. "What kind of temptations?"

Her daughter hesitated. "Oh, I don't know," she replied. "All kinds of sins. I just think a woman should be at home."

Jon had listened in silence, but now he spoke in defense of his mother. "You're being unreasonable, Sis," he said. "Mom is a very smart and capable woman. I think we should encourage her to follow her instincts and get out into the world. It'll be good for her, and it'll be good for the world, too."

"I'm on my own now, Sarah," Prudence said ruefully, "and my children are grown. Lots of women are getting out of the home these days. I don't see why I shouldn't join them."

Sarah remained silent, so her mother continued, "Theodora Youmans is very knowledgeable and very capable. She knows what's going on, and she's part of it. That's the kind of woman I want to be, too. I want to do my little bit to change the world, to make things happen. I want to help her get votes for women."

Chapter 4

Theodora was right about the coming of war to America; she had a better sense of the country's mood than her club-sisters. Congress agreed with President Wilson's request and declared war against the Central Powers of Europe just two days later on April 6th, 1917. Only fifty congressmen and six senators voted against the measure.

Wisconsin's pro-German reputation was magnified by the fact that nine of her eleven congressmen followed Senator LaFollette's lead in vigorously opposing the declaration of war and voting against it.

The public outcry was immediate and extremely intense. "The odium of treasonable purpose and achievement," charged the New York Times, "will rest upon their names forever more." The New York Herald linked LaFollette's name with that of Benedict Arnold. Even though there were many citizens who opposed entering the war—LaFollette claimed the vote would be ten to one against it if a national referendum were held— public opinion castigated former dissenters after Congress acted. Badger State citizens in particular were viewed with suspicion, even hostility, by the rest of the country. Those who opposed the war were branded traitors.

Jonathan Hartmann was an early victim of such patriotic wrath. A few days after the declaration of war, he drove to Perkins Hardware Store in Prairieville. A group of boys were lounging at the edge of Gaspar Street outside the store when he completed his purchases, but he gave them scarcely a glance as he climbed onto the front board of the buggy and gathered the reins into his hands.

"Giddiyup, Kaiser," he called out to his horse.

One of the boys looked up. "Hey!" he shouted. "What'd you call your nag?"

"His name is 'Kaiser'" Jonathan replied cheerfully. "And he's not a nag!"

"Sounds like he's a German horse," a second boy declared. "You must be German, too!"

"No, but my grandparents were," explained Jonathan, not yet recognizing the boy's threatening tone.

"The dumb German can't afford an automobile," said another boy sarcastically, "but he's got a horse named *Kaiser!*"

"He's a traitor!" shouted the first boy. "Let's show him what we think of traitors!" He picked up a hard clod of dirt from the street.

"I'm no traitor!" Jonathan declared hotly. "I'm an American. Just like you!"

"Kill the Kaiser!" cried one of the boys.

"Look," Jonathan began, "it doesn't matter . . . ." his defense was cut short as the missile whizzed past his head and struck the wall behind him. He saw the other boys reaching down for various objects to throw. "Let's *go*, Kaiser!" he shouted, slapping the flanks of the horse with the reins. "Let's get out of here!"

A volley of assorted projectiles assaulted them as the buggy jerked forward behind the startled animal. Jonathan heard the staccato rattle of stones against the side of the buggy, and he saw several direct hits on Kaiser. He looked back just in time to receive a sharp blow above his eye. Stunned, he protected his face with an arm as the barrage continued.

The threats and curses of the boys assailed his ears long after Kaiser had galloped beyond the range of the stones, and his anger and outrage continued to swell as he made his way along the familiar roads to the farm.

"They threw rocks at me, Mom!" he told Prudence as he entered the house.

"Who?"

"Some boys in town. I didn't know them."

"Why would anyone throw rocks at you?" his mother asked.

"They called me a traitor because our horse is named 'Kaiser'" he explained.

"We named him that as kind of a joke," Prudence remembered.

"Of course," said Jonathan. "But they didn't know that. 'Kill the Kaiser,' they yelled, and then they threw things at us."

"That is absolutely horrifying!" exclaimed Prudence.

"Mom, why would anybody do that?" Jonathan asked. "There were lots of people against the war, but as soon as the decision was made, everybody put aside their own feelings and lined up with Uncle Sam. Don't they know that?"

"Apparently not," Prudence mused. "I think those of us with a

German heritage are likely to have a difficult time ahead."

"I'm glad we don't live in town, Mom," he reflected. "Those people don't seem to have much sense. Out here in the country, thank God, we don't have to put up with things like that."

"I think farm people are too sensible to give in to such hysteria," said Prudence. "Forget about what happened to you. We'll just have to remember not to use Kaiser's name in public until the craziness is gone."

The following Sunday, as Prudence and her two children were finishing their noon meal, the ugliness of war fever came closer to home. The sound of voices was heard, followed by the firm knocking of knuckles on the kitchen door.

Jon opened the door and looked into the agitated faces of a group of men. He recognized them as farmers from the area, although none of them were well known to him.

"Come on in," Jon invited with a tone of surprise.

"Have you eaten yet?" asked Prudence, rising quickly to greet the newcomers with typical farm country hospitality. "We're just finishing dinner, but we can set some more food out in a jiffy."

"No thank you, Missus Hartmann," said Albert Jones. "We got somethin' more important than food on our minds."

"Well, then, let's go into the living room where we can talk," she said. "Jon, bring some chairs along with you."

There were murmurs from the men as they followed Prudence out of the kitchen, but as soon as everyone was seated there was a stiff and very awkward silence.

"Well, what is it?" Prudence inquired.

The men all looked toward Jones, and he began speaking with some hesitancy.

"Well, Missus Hartmann, we came to talk to you about a neighbor of yours. We're a bit concerned about him."

Prudence looked puzzled. "Really? Who is it?"

"It's Bruno Hilley, Ma'am," said Joe Hunter.

"Why, what has happened to Bruno?"

"Well, nothin's happened t' him. At least, not yet."

"We still don't understand," said Jonathan impatiently. "Stop beating around the bush, and tell us what's on your minds."

After a short pause, Jones said, "We're wondrin' if he's a patriotic American."

"Yeah, we're thinkin' he's a slacker," said Marvin Neverman, using a term of criticism just coming into popular usage.

"More than a slacker," said Hunter. "Maybe even a traitor."

"Yeah, we heard he was against joinin' the war."

"He didn't want to help the British."

Prudence and her children were speechless with surprise. They looked blankly from face to face, seeing anger and hatred and contempt.

"Why on earth would you think such a thing about Bruno Hilley?" Prudence finally asked.

"Ya' see, he ain't got no family," said Jones. "Just his sister."

"An' we all know he don't do much in the way of farmin'," added Hunter, "although his place always looks beautiful."

"Yeah, where does he get his money? What does he live on?" Neverman chimed in.

"Well, it could be that his old man left him a bundle," said Jerry Nelson dubiously.

"But we don't know that," said Neverman. "We don't know nothin' about him a'tall. That's the problem."

"He ain't got no friends, neither," Jones continued. "Everybody says you're the only ones who know sumpthin' about him. Yer his nearest neighbor."

"Y'see, we was thinkin' that he oughter join Uncle Sam," explained Hunter. "He's a single man, an' he's got nothin' to keep him at home. He oughter be the first one t' enlist in the National Guard, t' kinda' set an example."

"Yeah, especially since his old man came from Germany and everybody thinks he might be a spy," said Jones.

"He's too old to be a soldier, isn't he?" asked Jon.

"Who knows how old he is," replied Jones. "An' who cares? Is there an age limit on enlistments?"

"That's not the point, anyway," said Hunter. "He's the most eligible guy we could think of. He could go to war, and nobody would miss him. So Marvin here and his brother Sylvester went to see him and tell him to sign up."

"An' he got so mad," said Jones, "that he threw them right out of the house!"

"He chased us out with a shotgun," said Neverman. "He was madder than anybody I ever seen in my whole life. He yelled at us, and cussed at us, and threatened to kill us. He even put a shell into the gun and pumped it. Believe me, we got outta there in a hurry!"

With the story finally told, the men stopped talking and they all looked at Prudence. She stared back at them, her thoughts churning, and finally asked softly, "Why are you telling us about this? What do you want?"

"Well, Missus Hartmann," said Jones, "as we said before, everybody says you're the only people who know this guy. We want t' know what you think about him. Do you think he could be a slacker?"

"Is he a spy?" demanded Hunter. "Is he a goddam German spy?"

Jonathan had listened to the story told by the men without commenting or showing much emotion, but now he could keep quiet no longer. Controlling his voice carefully, and speaking in quiet tones, he said, "Gentlemen, I find it hard to believe my ears. I don't know any of you very well, but you are too smart and too decent to be saying such things."

Prudence listened to her son with astonishment. How could her little boy sound so grown up?

"We've only been in this war a couple of weeks," Jonathan continued. "Maybe Bruno said he was against getting into the war, I don't know. I never heard him say anything like that, but there were a lot of us who felt that way. I'm not completely convinced myself we should have jumped into that European mess, although somebody has to teach the Germans to leave their neighbors in peace. But President Wilson and Congress have put us right into the middle of it, and it doesn't matter any more what we thought about it. We're all American citizens, and we're all patriotic, and we're all joining the war effort one hundred percent. And I'm sure Bruno Hilley feels the same way."

Jonathan paused and quietly surveyed the faces before him. The men said nothing, but nobody was smiling. Nobody was nodding in agreement.

Jon could feel the tension and animosity in the room, and it drove him to stronger words. "You men ought to be ashamed of yourselves," he scolded. "You don't really know Bruno Hilley, you said that yourselves. Just because he's a little different is no reason to think he's a traitor. Just because he's a bachelor, and lives with his sister, and keeps to himself mostly, is no reason to hate him.

"I don't know him very well, either," Jon acknowledged, "but I can tell you this much—he's patriotic. He's every bit as patriotic as I am myself, even if his father did come from Germany!"

Jones rose to his feet, his hat in his hand. "C'mon, men," he said. "There ain't no use stayin' here no longer."

Muttering among themselves, the men followed Jones from the living room and out of the house. Prudence and her children stood in the kitchen doorway and watched them leave. Jones turned back momentarily.

"Sorry t' bother ya', Missus Hartmann," he said politely. "We just wanted t' know what ya' thought about Bruno Hilley."

"Well, now you know," she replied curtly.

"We don't agree wit' ya' about him," Jones added. "We think he might be agin' us."

Afterward, Prudence said to her son, "I'm not sure you should have spoken so strongly to those men. They seem pretty angry, and they might think you're unpatriotic too."

"I suppose they might, Mom," replied Jon, "but I couldn't just sit still and let them talk about Bruno like that. It's not right."

A few mornings later, Ephraim walked into the barn where Jonathan and Sarah were finishing the morning chores. His face was writhing with rage. "Them bastards!" he shouted. "Somebody's smeared red paint on the front of yer house!"

They all ran to the front yard and stared at the three angry red letters which had been crudely scrawled on the white stones—'HUN'.

Prudence joined them there as they faced one another in agitated confusion. "I was afraid of this," she observed softly.

"What are we going to do?" asked Sarah, her voice quavering.

"I don't know," replied Prudence. "I guess we should just ignore it; I don't think there is anything we can do."

"Maybe we should tell the sheriff about it," Sarah suggested.

"No, we won't do that," Jon said firmly. "If there's anything to be done, we can do it ourselves. I've got a good mind to get my shotgun and give Albert Jones a warning he'll never forget. He's the one who did this, or maybe one of his buddies. There's no doubt about that!"

"Jon, Jon," his mother said with kindly reproof. "It won't help anything to threaten Mr. Jones. Leave your shotgun on the wall where it belongs. There's no sense in making matters worse."

"Things might get worse whether we make them or not," Sarah suggested.

"Oh, I don't think so," replied Prudence. "Men who write warnings secretly in the night don't have the courage to carry out their threats by the light of day."

"There's always another night," reminded Sarah.

Ephraim laughed despite the gravity of the situation. "Yer mom's right, Sarah," he reassured her. "Them dogs ain't gonna do nothin' more than whine at the moon. Jus' fergit what ya' saw here this mornin'."

Jon couldn't forget the matter so easily, however. As he worked at planting oats during the morning, he pondered the meaning of the epithet and wondered what significance it held for the future.

After the noon meal, instead of returning at once to the oat field, he walked down the road to the new Hilley farm. It was called "new" because Hilley had lived there only about thirty years; the original Hilley farm, established by Bruno's father, John, had been bought by the Hartmanns and of course now belonged to Prudence.

Jonathan found Bruno and his sister Elizabeth indoors as expected. The bachelor farmer deserved his reputation for being strange, Jon thought. The man was only in his forties, he knew, but he seemed ancient and ageless. He was short and squat, giving the impression of indestructibility. His bibbed overalls, ragged and unclean, emphasized the barrel-like build of his body. A square head with set jaw rested atop his bull neck. His black hair was unwashed and untrimmed, and from beneath that unruly mop his piercing, fathomless eyes squinted out at his visitor.

Elizabeth, by contrast, was a tiny woman who appeared submissive to her brother despite the toughness of her frame. In her youth she could have been pretty, thought Jon.

"Yah? What d'ya want?" Bruno's greeting was hardly a welcome.

"I hear you had some unpleasant visitors the other day," Jon said.

Bruno blinked his eyes but remained impassive.

"Some guys who wanted you to enlist in the army," Jon continued.

There was still no response. Jon felt his forehead begin to perspire.

"Well, I just wanted you to know we think they are nuts! Don't pay any attention to those guys."

"I didn't," grunted Bruno, his expression softening just a bit.

"That's good," said Jon.

"I got my gun and chased them away," Bruno volunteered, his eyes glinting.

"I heard about that," said Jon. "I'm glad you did it."

A short chuckle escaped from Bruno's lips. "The army is for young guys," he said, "like you."

"You're right," Jon replied.

He walked over to the window and peered out. "You have the best-kept farm in the county, Bruno. I don't know how you do it, but it always looks great."

"All it takes is hard work," Bruno commented. " 'Course, I get a little help from Ernie Fentz, the young kid from down the road a piece."

"Well, it's mostly you. Everybody knows you are a hard-worker," Jon said. Then, casually, like it was an afterthought, he added, "Say, if I did go into the army, would you be willing to help us on the farm?"

"Of course," Bruno answered. "Of course. I got time." He leaned forward a bit. "When you goin'?"

"Oh, I don't know. I'm still thinking about it."

"War's no fun," observed Bruno, shaking his massive head.

"That's true," agreed Jon. "But they'll probably make me go anyway, and I'd be better off by volunteering."

"Yah," nodded Bruno.

Jon moved toward the door. "Well, I just wanted you to know you've still got some friends around here," he said.

"Thanks. We both thank you," the German replied.

"Yes, thank you very much," Elizabeth spoke for the first time.

Jonathan returned to the oat field for the afternoon's work, his mind filled with thoughts of the future. He was solemn throughout the rest of the day.

That evening, he left the supper table with a restless, agitated mind. Without conscious purpose, he strolled out behind the barn and leaned against the corn crib, hands in pockets. The sun was nestling down to the western horizon, and the warmth of the day was dissipating.

He looked up into the cloudless sky where Venus, the Evening Star, was just becoming visible below the faint outline of the half-moon. "Where's Mars?" he asked aloud. "This is no time for Venus. It's time for war, not love."

When the last brassy tip of the sun had disappeared, he roused himself slowly and began wandering down the lane toward the river He could hear the faint honking of a small flock of wild geese in the distance; they were late migrating north for the season.

At the river's edge he turned and headed downstream, aimlessly following his childhood route to the vast mysterious marsh which charmed him. Now he could hear the distant call of peepers which gradually grew louder in his ears as he rounded each little winding bend of the waterway.

As he passed beneath the River Road bridge, a light, vaporous mist began to form almost invisibly in the air. He left firm ground behind and began advancing into the swamplands along an unseen but familiar track. The pungent aroma of the marsh, blended from a dozen different smells, was perfume to his nose. Soon he was alone in the natural world, isolated from all signs of human civilization. The moon was brightening in the fading afterglow of sunset, but the quiet darkness of night was settling around him, blotting out all but the closest landmarks.

He felt quite comfortable in this eerie setting. It was home to him as much as the thick stone walls John Hilley had pulled together years ago. Here he had spent joyful, exuberant days as a child free from work; here he had spent thoughtful, meditative evenings as he grew into adulthood. His sister Sarah grew lonely in the absence of people, but Jon drew consolation from the solitude. The soupy bogs, the sharp grasses, the prickly low shrubs—all combined to enhance his sense of communion with the Maker of the universe and everything within.

He crept unerringly to a dry grassy hideaway on a patch of higher ground in the midst of the marsh, screened on nearly all sides by tall reeds and low shrubs. He sank gratefully to the earth and stretched out supine, staring up into the eternal sky.

His gaze drifted downward to the familiar marshlands. He had learned many lessons from the hundreds of hours spent in those wet acres. He had been a little boy here, splashing along to chase frogs so his mother could fry their tender legs for his special treat. He had captured hundreds of snakes in his fruitless search for one of a poisonous species. When he was older, his father had given him a shotgun, and he had gradually learned the skills necessary to shoot ducks. Many an autumn evening he had bagged enough green-winged teals to provide supper for the family.

The marsh constituted his own special world, and he had explored it thoroughly. He knew every scrap of high ground and he knew every deep pool. He felt a sense of complete safety and comfort here.

Now, amidst these nurturing surroundings he wrestled with his feelings and his fears. He clearly recognized this moment as a turning point of his life, a time of testing which would define his character, but the right choice seemed obscured by a mental fog closing in on him just like the damp haze which was gradually obliterating the landscape before his eyes.

One part of him was chained to the family farm and these marshlands of his childhood. He could live and die right here content without ever wandering farther than Prairieville or Wonamuk. He loved his homeland with all his heart, and he felt a sense of belonging which would make him a stranger anywhere else on earth.

A network of fears reinforced his desire to stay on the farm—fear of the unknown, fear of battle, fear of pain and perhaps death. He always acted courageous and unconcerned whenever his mother expressed her worries, but in his heart he shared her feelings. If he answered President Wilson's call to arms, would he return home again safe?

Yet there was another part of him which fought for approval. It was partly a curiosity to explore the world. Like Prudence, he yearned for new challenges and excitement, but he was motivated even more powerfully by a sense of patriotism. The same love for his country which bound him so firmly also might compel him to leave that country to defend its interests.

Prudence waited with increasing concern for her son to return to the house. Sarah went to bed, leaving Prudence to her lonely vigil. She was reminded of the night she sat alone with Zachary's coffin. At midnight she could stand the suspense no longer. She slipped a blue denim jumper-coat over her shoulders and went to seek help.

Ephraim awoke with the first light rattle of pebbles against the window panes of his upstairs bedroom. He raised the sash and called out in a sleepy voice, "Who's there?"

Prudence replied with such urgent motherly concern that he was wide awake in an instant. He hurried downstairs and welcomed her inside, where she spilled out her story. "I think he must be out in the marsh," she concluded, "and I'm afraid he might be hurt, or lost."

"Not much chance of that, Prudence," Ephraim reassured her. "He knows his way around those bogs better'n anyone else, and he's careful enough t' keep from gettin' hurt. But I'll go look for 'im; I think I know where he'll be. This ain't the first time. Remember his fifteenth birthday?"

"Yes, I remember," she replied.

Ephraim went into the marsh by the light of the stars, for the moon had already set. The air was calm and cool, and most of the animals and insects had been silenced by the stillness of the night. The ground fog increased in density the farther he walked, but he knew his way through the marsh almost as well as Jon and he kept a steady pace. After half an hour, he approached Jon's refuge, and he was so certain of finding him there that he didn't bother to call his name.

Jon was sitting quietly on his little hummock, hidden from the world by the heavy fog, but still able to see the stars above. "C'mon home, kid," Ephraim said, and the youth rose stiffly to his feet.

They walked in silence for a long way before the older man said, "Decisions come pretty hard sometimes, don't they."

"Yes, that's right, Uncle Eeph," Jon replied in a low voice.

After a few more minutes of walking, Jon continued: "The trouble is, you don't get a second chance at most of the decisions in life. Time won't turn back, or even stand still. It's like being on a runaway horse, flying so fast it takes away your breath. You have precious little time to make any decisions about which way to go, and even when you decide, the horse might not follow your directions."

Ephraim laughed lightly. "You got it, kid. That's exactly what it's like. An' you'll find the speed pickin' up as ya' get older."

"I didn't feel this way when I was younger," Jon said. "It used to feel like I was kind of coasting through life, with Dad and Mom making all the decisions, and I didn't have to worry about anything."

"Yeah, well, them days is gone forever, boy. Yer on yer own now. Even if yer dad hadn'ta died, yer old enough that you'd be on yer own anyway."

"But how do you know what decision is right? How can you tell?"

"Well, if it's a matter of right an' wrong, ya' kin pretty much tell from the Bible, I guess."

"I know the Commandments," said Jon, "and I know my Catechism. But what if there is no right or wrong? What then?"

"There ain't no handbook, kid. Ya' gotta' kinda' feel yer way through the best ya' can."

Jonathan sighed. "Okay," he said, and they walked along through another spell of silence.

Then, "Have you ever made any tough decisions, Uncle Eeph?"

Ephraim laughed lightly again. "Well, kid, I can't say I've been troubled with a plague of life and death decisions. Livin' on the farm all by myself makes everything easier."

"Well, why did you decide to live on the farm? Why did you choose the farm you did, right next to ours? I know you didn't grow up there."

"Hmmm, why did I choose my farm? I never really thought much about it. When m' folks died at such an early age, I wanted a change of scenery, I guess. Their farm was too big fer me, anyway. My wants are very simple, an' I don't need a lot o' land. So I jumped at the chance t' buy the forty acres down the road. I always liked yer dad and mom anyway, and they had just gotten married and moved in with his folks. So it was natural t' move where I did, right close by. I ain't never been sorry, neither. Bein' near you kids has been like havin' a family o' my own."

"Why did you choose not to have a family yourself?" Jon persisted.

"It warn't really my choice, Jon. At least, it warn't a sudden one-time decision. It jus' kinda' developed that way over the years. I guess it's one of those things like you said where you don't have no control of yer own. Yer jus' carried along wit' the tide of events, so t' speak. If ya' could write yer own script, mebbe you'd do it different. In fact, I know I would."

They didn't speak again until they were approaching the Hartmann farmhouse. There, in the deepest darkness before the dawn, Ephraim reached out and stopped Jon, slipping his arm fully around his shoulder. The two men gazed briefly into each other's eyes. "Jonathan," he said, using the boy's full name for the first time in years, "I know what yer goin' through. I know what decision yer workin' on. An' I want t' encourage ya' t' make up yer own mind, and if ya' decide ya' gotta go off t' war, do what ya' know ya' hafta do. I love ya' with all m' heart, an' I always will. Yer mom an' I will support ya' in whatever ya' decide."

Then, spontaneously, the two men embraced each other with a rugged bear-hug. Their eyes were moist with emotion. Ephraim found himself wishing Jon were really his own son.

Prudence welcomed Jon home without complaint. It was nearly time to rise for the morning chores when he fell asleep in his own bed again, his mind at ease with the comfort of a decision properly made.

It was a decision which he announced at the breakfast table a few hours later. "I'm going to enlist in the National Guard," he said simply.

"No, Jon!" Prudence protested.

"It's the only way I can prove to everybody that we are true Americans," he said.

"Please don't decide with such haste!" his mother pleaded.

"I'm not being hasty, Mom," Jonathan replied. "I've thought about the war for a long time. You know that. And you know how strongly I feel that the Germans have to be taught a lesson. A lesson that only Uncle Sam can teach. I've been thinking for several months that if we got into the war, I'd want to enlist."

"But Jon, we'd miss you so much!" Sarah exclaimed.

"Well, I know I'll get awfully lonesome for all of you, too, Sis," he admitted. "But it's something I've just got to do."

"Your father's been dead only a month," Prudence pointed out. "Am I to lose you too, so soon?"

"You're not losing me, Mom," he insisted. "I won't be gone long. Once our troops get ready, it will go fast. We'll wrap this thing up and be back in a few months."

"I'd like to believe that," Prudence said. "But I don't think it's going to be as easy as you say. And I've got this terrible foreboding that you . . . that you won't live through it." Her voice was choked with emotion.

"Oh, that's nonsense, Mom. You're just over-reacting because Dad died so recently."

"I hope you're right," she said quietly. "I couldn't stand it if you were killed too."

"I'll be careful, Mom. Actually, I don't think there will be very many casualties among the American troops. With hundreds of thousands of guys going over there, the odds of dying are very, very small. I'll be okay."

"What will we do with the farm?" Prudence asked. "Robert's only been here a few days, and there's so much for him to learn."

"You're a good teacher, Mom," Jonathan replied. "You know a lot more about this farm than I do. And I know Bruno Hilley will be able to come and help with the work; I have already talked to him."

Prudence knew it would be useless to argue with her son. He was a man with great determination and independence, as he had demonstrated upon many occasions.

Jon and Sarah left the breakfast table to join Robert for the day's farmwork. As Prudence began washing the dishes, she thought back upon the many times she and Zachary had called their son 'stubborn'. He had done what he wanted to do, without much thought about what it meant to the family. It had been a challenge to raise him.

She remembered the events of his fifteenth birthday, having been reminded by Ephraim. Jonathan had received a second-hand bicycle—a gift for which he had pleaded vigorously. Bicycles were very popular in those years for both transportation and pleasure. The modern bicycles had both wheels the same size, and it was a mark of carefully cultivated prestige to ride one of them.

Jonathan was not interested in prestige—he simply wanted his freedom, and a bicycle would give him a great measure of independence.

He took advantage of his newly found freedom at once, by riding away from the farm immediately following the dinner at noon. He didn't have a preconceived destination; he simply pedaled along the country roads in a generally southwesterly direction, away from Prairieville.

How delicious was the freedom he enjoyed! He could go anywhere he wanted, now that he owned a pair of wheels—anywhere in the southern half of the county, at least.

He forgot about time; he forgot about his family. He rode until the deepening shades of dusk suddenly jolted him back to reality. He turned and headed back, but the sun went down when he was still miles away from the farm. An hour later he was spinning along in the darkness of a moonless night, and now he became increasingly worried about what would happen when he got home.

Eventually Prudence became worried enough to ask the menfolk to start looking for him. Zachary hitched up Kaiser and with Prudence at his side in the buggy, he began searching the country roads in the darkness.

Perhaps Ephraim knew Jonathan better than Zachary and Prudence, because he headed directly for the marsh. A half-hour's hike took him to Jon's secret hiding place. There he found the missing boy.

"I'm afraid to go home," Jon told him.

"Nonsense!" said Ephraim. "Yer parents are so worried about ya' that they wouldn't think of punishin' ya'. They'll just be glad to see ya' safe n' sound."

Now, with her hands soaking forgotten in the dishwater, Prudence remembered those events with great tenderness and joy. If only Jonathan were fifteen again, and could be kept safe at home on the farm!

Her reverie was interrupted by a sudden chill. It was not like a draft of air; it was more like stepping outside on a frigid winter day and feeling the remorseless cold permeate her whole body. She was alone in the house, but she felt another presence in the kitchen. She turned around, half expecting to find one of her children returned for some reason, yet knowing she would have heard the noise of the door. Of course, nobody was in sight.

With a shiver, she resumed her dishwashing, but the sensation of someone being with her did not disappear. It conveyed to her a heavy sense of dread and foreboding. Her heart began to pound. She glanced over her shoulder several times, seeing no one, and finally she called out "Who's there?" with no response.

Gradually her body warmed again, but when the dishes were done, Prudence could not remain in the house. She left immediately, and her steps automatically took her up the road toward Ephraim's house.

She found her friend resting on the double swing of his porch. "I knowed you'd come," he said. "I waited fer ya'. C'mere." He motioned for her to sit beside him, and when she did, he put his arm around her shoulders. Together they slowly rocked in the coolness of the April morning, gazing out over the bare brown fields.

They said nothing. She was unable to tell him of the unaccountable sensations she had felt in the kitchen, but he was aware of the emotions building within her and he knew her eyes were dampening even before he saw the tiny tears.

Suddenly she turned toward him and nestled her head against his chest. Her shoulders were shaking, and her breathing was deep and irregular.

"He decided t' join the army?" Ephraim asked quietly.

She nodded silently.

"I figgered as much."

The swing continued its slow steady motion, and Prudence broke into unrestrained sobbing. He drew her close to comfort her.

Finally she could speak. "I'm so afraid," she confided, "afraid that he will not come back alive." She began sobbing anew, so fiercely that she couldn't continue.

Again he simply held her as he would an injured child until she quieted. "After all, he is my firstborn son," she said, "and I am so afraid God will take him away from me as a punishment for my sin."

"God is gracious n' forgivin'. I don't think He would take yer only son away from ya'."

"He took King David's son."

"Yeah, I know. But not when the boy was twenty years old."

Prudence wasn't convinced, but she didn't argue the matter farther. She hunkered down alongside Ephraim and the two of them rocked slowly for a long time. Then Ephraim remarked, "Life is full o' surprises, ain't it."

"It certainly is," she agreed.

"We bin through a lot together, hain't we," he observed.

"Yes, we have."

"An' somehow I feel we ain't even started yet already."

"Maybe you're right."

Chapter 5

As Prudence sat in the porch swing with Ephraim, her mind went back sharply to the early days of her marriage with Zachary. They had been good days, probably the happiest days of her life.

The world was young in her eyes then—young, and pure, and filled with unbounded opportunities. The future was brimming with promised blessings that she felt rather than visualized. Of course, there would be work—there is always work on a farm—but work itself is a blessing, perhaps one of the greatest blessings of life.

The farm would yield its abundance, she knew. The low-lying fields, deep with rich black earth, would produce fifty bushels of corn to the acre. The oats would fill out full heads of golden grain. The thick alfalfa foliage would offer the finest grazing for their Holstein cows, which in turn would pour forth hundreds of gallons of fresh milk for sale.

Surrounding Zachary and her would be their healthy brood of children. It was assumed that they would have children. The subject hadn't even been discussed as a question before their wedding. Her visions of the future had always contained a couple of sons and a couple of daughters; maybe even more. The matter was not urgent to her; planting and raising their children would be as easy and natural as planting and raising their corn, oats, and alfalfa.

They had been married perhaps six months when Zachary's mother began making pointed comments about children. It was mid-winter, and the two women were busy shelling hickory nuts in the kitchen.

"There's a lot of work in farming," the senior Mrs. Hartmann was saying.

"Yes, there is," agreed Prudence.

"Zac is the only one we've got left to help us," observed Mrs.

Hartmann. "Zac is the baby of our family, you know, and all his older brothers and sisters have left."

"Yes, I know."

"We're not getting any younger, either. My husband, Peter, is nearly sixty years old. When you're sixty, you just can't work like you could when you were thirty."

"I suppose that's right."

"I've been trying to get Peter to slow down a little, especially since we know his heart is not strong. But there's so much to do that he won't listen to me."

"Yes, I've noticed."

"We've got to look ahead and plan for some help," Mrs. Hartmann said.

"Of course."

"To be blunt about it, Prudence, it's time for you to think about having children. Time is running out for us. A child isn't really a lot of help on the farm until he is nine or ten years old. Even if you had a baby now, Peter would be close to seventy by the time the child is able to work some."

Prudence was surprised; in her naivety she hadn't foreseen where the conversation was headed. Feeling embarrassed now, and a little offended, she did not reply.

Mrs. Hartmann plunged ahead. "I know there are young wives today who postpone having children because they want to prolong their honeymoon. They don't want to be burdened with babies, at least not right away."

Giving vent to her rising anger, Prudence hammered a hickory nut with unnecessary force, smashing it into jumbled fragments of nutmeat and shell. Her mother-in-law glanced up sharply, but she was so engrossed with her message that she continued her lecture without pausing for thought. "Such women are selfish—just plain selfish," she emphasized. With a vigorous shake of her head she added, "It's a sin!"

Prudence was stung by the comment from her mother-in-law. Looking back on that scene now from the distance of a quarter century, she felt the throbbing warmth of embarrassment and anger rising in her cheeks again. Her happy innocence ended that morning, she reflected ruefully, smashed like a hickory nut into irretrievable fragments. Her mother-in- law's condemnation raised the subject of fertility to the forefront of her mind, and for the first time she began to worry that she might be barren.

After all, they had been married for six months and she wasn't pregnant yet. Perhaps there would be no children for them. Perhaps she would never know the thrill of a tiny baby at her breast, nor the excitement of a young child frolicking on the lawn, nor the satisfaction of knowing that part of her, a son or daughter, would survive after she had passed from the earth. From that morning onward, she began to dwell upon the necessity to conceive and have a baby. No longer could she simply let nature take its course; no longer could she blissfully assume that babies would come automatically.

Zachary, ever sensitive to the feelings of his beloved Prudence, was aware of the change in her disposition, but she did not immediately reveal the reason for her unhappiness.

Throughout the rest of the winter, his mother pressed the subject whenever possible. Such opportunities were frequent because Zachary and Prudence were living in the same house with his parents. The senior Mrs. Hartmann would toss out a lightly veiled hint at almost every evening meal.

It might be the sympathy she would express for the weariness of her husband. "Peter, you look so tired tonight," she would say. Then, with a quick glance at Prudence, she would add, "You can't keep working this hard forever. Before too many years go by, we've just got to get some help for you and Zac."

Or she would mention the possibility of taking on a hired hand. "Effie told me her son is looking for work," she might say. "He's not very ambitious, but I suppose he would be better than nothing while we wait for a grandchild to come along."

One evening she mentioned the courtship customs of an earlier generation. "In my grandparents' day," she said, "we had a practice called 'bundling,' where a boy and girl would roll up together in a warm blanket on a cold winter evening. Houses weren't very much protection against the winter wind back in those days, and you couldn't just sit around without catching a chill. A woolen blanket was the answer. Besides, it allowed a boy and girl to snuggle down and get acquainted with each other rather closely.

"Young men being what they are," Mrs. Hartmann continued, "it wasn't unusual at all for the girl to end up with a baby.

"Lots of brides went to the altar very obviously in a family way," she remembered, "and it was perfectly acceptable."

"Really, Mother!" Zachary exclaimed indignantly.

"Every family needed children to work on the farm," she continued unabashed, "and a young man needed to be sure that his wife would be able—and willing—to have babies right away."

Prudence put the fork down on her plate with a clatter and rose hastily from her chair. The others looked up with surprise as she rushed from the room.

"What's gotten into her, I wonder!" exclaimed Mrs. Hartmann. "She is normally so cheerful and unruffled."

"It's no mystery, Mother," said Zachary, as he stood up to follow his wife. "You've been badgering the poor girl without mercy!"

He found her sobbing on the bed in their room. He sank down on the quilt alongside her, patting her shoulder to give comfort. "Now, now, Prudence, don't listen to my mother. She's so anxious for a grandchild that she doesn't realize what she's saying."

"Oh, she's a horrid woman," said Prudence between her sobs. "She knows perfectly well what she's saying. She doesn't care about my feelings at all!"

"She really does, Honey," said Zachary. It's just that she didn't stop to think how her words would hurt."

Prudence didn't reply; her shoulders were still shaking with anger and unhappiness.

"Of course," her husband continued, "it's true that we want to have children. I certainly do, and I know you do, too."

"You *know* I do!" she exclaimed.

He patted her shoulder, and left her alone to compose herself as he returned to the table.

His mother was not penitent. She said to her son, "In her heart, she is afraid a baby will be a bother, and that makes it difficult to conceive. If she *really* wanted a baby, she would relax and it would happen quite naturally."

Although Zachary loved Prudence with his whole heart, he couldn't avoid being swayed toward his mother's opinion as weeks and then months passed by without seeing any fruits of their union. Gradually, through the tender days of spring, when farm and marshlands alike were bursting with prolific promise, he began to harbor a resentment against the very woman he loved so deeply—a resentment she felt at once.

Now, swinging gently on the porch with Ephraim, Prudence traced the evolution of her feelings toward having children. As a bride she looked forward with pleasant anticipation to becoming a mother, but the continuous bombardment of suspicious and hostile comments from her mother-in-law gradually wore the luster from her hopes. Her eagerness was little by little battered into desperation. The subject became very sensitive, even painful, to her. She sensed that Zachary, who had originally been fully supportive of her, began to turn against her, and eventually the very foundations of her marriage were threatened.

She could still remember the first of their bitter arguments. It was triggered by something trivial, as many such arguments are. One of their heifers, Buttercup, had failed for the third time to have a calf. "She visited Homer the bull right on schedule," Zachary told his wife, "and I know everything went okay. It all seemed perfectly normal. Buttercup stood there in Homer's pen quite eager-like while we turned 'im loose. She pulled at 'er halter to look around at 'im, and I could swear she batted 'er eyes at 'im. He didn't need no proddin', of course. It didn't take very long. If anything, Homer was more spirited than ever. There's no reason why she shouldn'ta caught."

"What are you going to do?" Prudence asked.

"There nothin' much we can do," Zachary replied. "We done our best. We even had that young vet, Doc Roberts, out here t' examine 'er after the second failure."

Then Zachary had looked straight into his wife's eyes as he said with a brittle hardness, "I guess we'll have t' change 'er name to 'Prudence' and ship 'er off."

"Zac! What a cruel thing to say, to use my name like that," protested Prudence.

"Cruel?" he repeated with surprised innocence. "I don't mean t' be cruel. But it's reasonable fer me t' want children, ain't it? That's one of the reasons fer getting married, ain't it? I want a bunch a' kids a-workin' an' playin' right here on the farm."

"But Zac, don't you think I want the same thing?" she cried.

"Then what's wrong? Why can't ya' get pregnant?"

"I don't know, Zac, I don't know! I wish I could, I really do. But why does it have to be *my* fault? How do you know it's me!"

"Well, I ain't never seen a bull yet that failed," he replied. "Most of the heifers produce their calves, so the bull must be okay. But every once in a while there's a Buttercup. I don't know why any more than you do."

"But those are cows," Prudence reminded him. "We're talking about *us*."

"There's no difference," Zac said with assurance. "Cows or humans, it's all the same. I think my mother is right. There's somethin' holdin' ya' back. When ya' really want t' have a baby wit' all yer heart it'll happen."

His words were sharp and the hurt was deep. Prudence was too proud to cry, but her anguish was endless.

Ephraim, who had already moved to the farm next door, had succeeded in keeping a close friendship with Prudence even after she had chosen Zachary for her husband. He still loved her, she knew, but he was well aware of his secondary place in her life and he had accepted her marriage with good grace. He remained constantly alert and sensitive to her feelings, and she was grateful. The limited acreage of his own small farm often allowed him to help with Zachary's work as well. He did not explain, but she knew he was motivated by a compulsion to see her as often as possible.

It was no accident, then, that Ephraim quickly noticed the clouds which blocked the sunlight from her face and dampened the customary radiance of her smile. He soon found an opportunity to probe her feelings.

He was helping her pick green beans from the garden for their evening meal. Ephraim and Prudence were alone together, each of them working along a row of beans, plucking the succulent young vegetables from their short bushy vines.

"Somethin's bin troublin' ya' lately, Prudence," said Ephraim. I kin tell. Yer not yer usual self. What's the matter?"

"Oh, it's nothing," she replied, knowing that he would not be satisfied with her answer.

"Well, it *'tis* somethin," he said gently. "Tell me about it."

She dropped a handful of pods into her basket before repeating her denial with a slight shake of her head, "I'd rather not."

Ephraim straightened up for a moment, enjoying the warmth of the late afternoon sun on his shoulders. He knew she wanted him to press again. "Don't be bashful with me, Prudence," he said. "I know ya' have somethin' on yer mind. You'll feel better when ya' talk about it."

She stood up, clutching her basket, and looked into his eyes. She recognized the familiar expression of compassion and concern which he projected in times of distress. "Zac is mad at me," she blurted out, "because it seems I can't have any children." She bent over again quickly, searching for bean pods beneath the dark green leaves, hiding the tears which had sprung into her eyes.

"Surely it's too soon t' know whether you kin have children," Ephraim said softly.

"It's been more than a year now," she replied.

"I know when you were married," he reminded her. "Ya' gotta believe that's one day I will never forget!"

She ignored his implications. "A year is a long time," she observed.

"Even if ya' can't have children, how can he put the blame onta you? The weakness might be his, not yours."

"He is convinced the fault is mine," she replied.

"It's beyond knowin'," he insisted.

"He's convinced," she repeated.

Ephraim resumed his work, hurrying to catch up to her. "Even if it's yer fault, how kin he blame you? It's not somethin' ya' kin choose or not choose."

"He thinks if I wanted a baby bad enough, I could have one," she said, still looking downward.

"He's a fool, then!" exclaimed Ephraim. "He's a damn fool! I didn't realize he could be so stupid." He reached over and rested an arm across her shoulders. He wanted to take her fully into his arms to console her;

his whole body ached to comfort her.

She quickly turned away, divining his desire. "We mustn't. I've said too much. These things shouldn't be talked about outside the marriage."

He recognized her inner agony, and accepted her mild rebuff without offense. "If ya' can't talk about them inside the marriage," he said softly, "then ya' have t' talk to a friend. Ya' can't just bottle up yer feelin's."

She said nothing, and he continued. "I'm yer friend. I want t' be yer very best friend, 'cept for yer family. You kin talk t' me. It'll help ya' through it. An' I won't tell nobody. Ya' know that!"

"Yes, I know that," she agreed, looking fully into his eyes again. "You are my very best friend, and I'm glad you're here."

They finished the bean rows in silence, but in the following weeks neither of them could forget the conversation.

Now, rocking with Ephraim in the porch swing, she gazed up into his face. 'What a friend he has certainly been through all these years,' she thought. 'He has never wavered. He's always looked after me when I needed him. He comforted me during those early arguments with Zachary, and he is still comforting me today as my only son leaves to go to war. He has been willing to do anything for me. Perhaps I have expected him to do too much for me, too much for our own good. Yet he has never said *no* to me, never.'

She retreated again to her unhappy reverie. Even after twenty-four years, the memory of her humiliation burned within her. Under the constant barrage of complaints from his mother, Zachary had increased his own criticism of her childlessness, expressing his own growing bitterness. She became obsessed with the necessity for getting pregnant, and was constantly reminded of her failure. A thoughtless word or an unrelated incident would prompt the nagging ache in her heart, emphasizing once again her unfruitfulness.

Even Pastor Sternberg, the man who had performed their wedding ceremony in the Town Hall, added to her agony when he stopped at the farmhouse to visit her one morning.

Prudence welcomed him inside and poured a cup of coffee left over from breakfast.

The pastor, filled with good intentions, began by saying, "You've been married a goodly time now," and immediately Prudence knew what was on his mind.

"Yes, Pastor, it's been more than a year now," she confirmed.

"It's God's plan, you know, that we should bring children into the world and teach them to follow His Word," said Sternberg.

"Yes, Pastor, I'm quite aware of that," she agreed.

"I don't want to get involved in personal situations," the sanctimonious preacher said, "but you and Zachary should not wait too long before you begin your family. It is not wise to put off having children after you are married."

Prudence felt the blood rising to her cheeks, pushed by anger and embarrassment. "Pastor Sternberg," she said with choked voice, "don't you think we want children? Of course we want children. Don't you think we're trying to have children? Of course we're trying. I am on my knees constantly, begging the Lord to take mercy on me and give me a child!"

"Oh. I see. It is well, then, I suppose, if it is not your choice to remain childless. It must be God's will."

"It may be God's will, Pastor, but it is not our choice. You can be sure of that. We both want a child very much."

"You're sure? You're not holding off having children through selfishness, because you want time for yourselves?"

"Pastor, how can you be so cruel!" she cried. "I want a child more than any other thing on this earth. It's awful for you to accuse me of selfishness!"

He was not fazed by her words, nor by her obvious sincerity. "What have you done, my girl, to achieve your goal? Have you prayed in earnest? Have you rested properly beforehand, and remained undisturbed afterward? Have you. . . ."

"Pastor, I thought you said you wouldn't get personal."

"I'm only trying to help you," he replied evenly, "if indeed you are telling me the truth about your intentions. Have you been to see a doctor? I hear Dr. Joseph Braden in Prairieville gives very good advice in such cases."

"I think you've said enough," Prudence interrupted again, the brokenness of her voice betraying her outward composure. "Thank you for coming to visit me, but I think you should go now."

"I'm sorry if my thoughts have distressed you," said Pastor Sternberg as he rose from his chair. "I felt it was my duty to express them."

She told Zachary about the pastor's visit, including her own indignant reaction to the outside intrusion into her life. Her husband remained impassive, making little comment. He agreed, however, that she should see Dr. Braden.

On the appointed day, Zachary drove her in the buggy to Dr. Braden's office in the new Putney Block in Prairieville. She was apprehensive, but the doctor put her at ease immediately with his calm, sympathetic personality.

His examination was thorough, but unhelpful. "So far as I can tell, Mrs. Hartmann, you are in excellent physical condition," he told her. "There is nothing I can identify that might contribute to infertility."

He continued, in a professional but friendly manner, to suggest a number of ideas that might help her conceive, but none of the ideas was new to her. She had tried them all, without success. "I've even tried standing on my head afterwards," she told him ruefully.

During the ride home with her silent husband, she decided to make the best of a bad situation. She would remain cheerful and unconcerned, she told herself, even if she were never able to have a child.

Such a resolution, however, was difficult to follow, as each succeeding day brought new disappointment—and somewhere, between sunup and sundown, another disparaging comment from Zachary or his mother. Her emotional isolation continued to intensify. The only person who understood her, it seemed, was Ephraim, and she found herself increasingly dependent upon him for solace. He was unfailingly sympathetic and considerate of her feelings. She began to look forward with eagerness to the few minutes they found to share together each day—minutes in which she could expose her disappointment, her frustration, and her fear without bearing reproach. In her heart she knew it was wrong to rely so heavily upon him, but she couldn't help herself.

Another year dragged by—a tortured year which intensified the hostility between Prudence and her husband. The marriage endured only because of their commitment to the wedding vows. Prudence survived only because Ephraim supported her. Even so, the situation was untenable and everyone knew it could not continue forever.

It was the visit from Zachary's older brother that finally brought matters to a conclusion. Marcus Hartmann arrived home from San Francisco in late summer, bringing his wife and four children with him. He stayed only a week, but it was enough to trigger paroxysms of envy and despair in the childless couple.

There were three boys and a girl in the Marcus Hartmann family, and Grandma Hartmann doted upon them all. "What healthy, strapping boys they are. And how beautiful Angela is! See, Prudence, why I want you to hurry and have children?"

The emotional tension rose throughout the week. Prudence realized that Zachary's suffering was more intense—her agony had extended longer, so her endurance was greater. Zachary was so morose that he scarcely spoke to anyone while preparing for church Sunday morning. He dreaded the approach of the noon meal which was being prepared by his mother as a farewell banquet for Marcus and his family, who were leaving early Monday morning.

During the dinner, Zachary's mother once again maneuvered the conversation to the subject of having babies. This time, she told the story of how the English king Henry the Eighth divorced his wife Katharine because she couldn't give him a son.

"The Pope wouldn't give him the divorce he needed," Grandma Hartmann explained, "so King Henry threw the Catholic Church out of the country and created the Protestant Church of England.

"If kings have that right, then other people should have the same right. Kingdoms need a male heir, but so do farms." She looked sharply at Zachary, then Prudence, while everyone kept quiet from embarrassment.

When the dinner was finally over, Zachary drifted away from the house while the women were washing the dishes. He wanted to repair a fence at the far end of the south pasture, he told himself, but in reality he simply wanted to be alone, away from his brother's family.

The fence had been damaged by a large oak tree, rotten at the base, which had fallen on it during a recent storm. Zachary carried an ax, a hammer, and a pocketful of staple nails with him to make the repairs.

Arriving at the scene, Zachary found the tree had crushed several other smaller trees as it fell and was suspended several feet in mid- air, lying atop the fence.

The tree trunk was far too heavy for him to lift, so Zachary put his ax to good use in chopping it into more manageable lengths. As he worked, he meditated on the great disappointment being enacted in his life. How unfair it was that his brother Marcus could have three sons, and he apparently could have none. If a British king could leave his barren wife and take a different woman, why couldn't he? No, he loved Prudence too much for that. He could never leave her.

He was so preoccupied with his thoughts that he didn't realize his tree was working its way loose from the branches which held it. His left leg was extended below the heavy trunk, bracing his body as he worked. He was not aware of danger until suddenly the tree broke loose and dropped to the ground, twisting toward him as it went, pinning his leg beneath it. The sudden pain in his shinbone was so severe that he was certain it must be broken.

It was impossible for him to lift the heavy log off his leg, and the farmhouse was too far away for anyone to hear his cries for help. He picked up the ax with one hand and awkwardly chipped little pieces off the tree, but he quickly realized he could not possibly chop away enough wood to make any difference at all.

He would simply have to wait until someone missed him and came searching for him. That would take hours, he knew.

He gritted his teeth against the pain and fought off the lightheadedness which began to engulf him.

As the afternoon dragged by, the pain and shock of his injury, coupled with the dehydration of sun and wind, drove his mind into recurring waves of delirium. He drifted in and out of consciousness. He imagined a dozen different rescues but each one eventually proved itself false.

While the sun was setting, he heard the first voices from real people calling for him from a great distance. Even though he thought it must be another trick of his imagination, he tried to answer, but his voice was weak and he knew they could not hear him. He could tell they were searching for him, and he would have to wait only a little while longer.

It was fully dark when his father and Prudence came close enough to hear his feeble cries. Prudence dropped to her knees at his side.

"I'm here," she told him, kissing his brow again and again. "We'll have you home as quick as we can."

"If I had a son t' help me," he mumbled reproachfully, "this wouldn'- ta happened. I wish I was king."

Soon all the men had arrived and they were lifting the tree off his leg. His father and his brother raised him and carried him between them on the long walk back to the farmhouse.

Still delirious, he kept repeating over and over again, "I wish I was king. I wish I was king. I wish I was king so I could get a new wife. . . ."

Prudence walked alongside the whole way, tears streaming from her cheeks.

She realized her very marriage was at stake. After dressing Zachary's wounded leg, and finding to her relief that it was not broken, she stayed at his bedside through the rest of the night, staring out the open window across the dark swampland.

Although she had lived near the marsh for more than two years, she had not become well acquainted with it. She had been too busy, of course, in settling into a new marriage and keeping up with the endless work of a farm. She was well aware of the marsh, though, as a gigantic brooding presence, a constant reminder of eternal verities that do not change.

Now she was drawn to it by some inexplicable attraction. Instinctively she felt she would find solace in its boundless depths. She sank to her knees at the window sill and gave herself over to the sobs which shook her body and consumed her emotions.

Her prayers were fragments of thoughts which she couldn't complete, interspersed with expressions of raw emotions which pulsed through her mind.

Somewhere during the ensuing hours, as the evening dampness settled and a hazy crescent moon rose in the eastern sky, an inspiration for reckless, desperate action came to her and it would not be dismissed by her more rational mind.

Although she searched relentlessly for a different, more conventional solution to her troubles, she could think of nothing else. Again and again the same wild notion returned to her, each time with more force than before.

Soon she was devising detailed plans and even framing the words she would use. Ephraim was a vital part of the scheme. Without his confidential help her plan wouldn't work but she knew he could be depended upon absolutely. He would be shocked at the thought, but he would be thrilled at the possibility of being the father of her child.

By ordinary standards, she recognized, her plan would be considered immoral. Technically, she would be committing adultery, and she was aware that God's penalty for adultery under Old Testament law is death. But in a higher sense, she felt, she would be honoring her marriage by ignoring the Seventh Commandment. She believed it was her only hope to restore Zachary's love.

She went to Ephraim the next morning after Marcus and his enviable family had been taken to town to board the morning train. Ephraim had returned to the fallen tree and the broken fence, and he was busily finishing the job Zachary had begun.

It was a long walk across the open pasture. It seemed like the longest walk of her life. At first, Ephraim was a tiny speck on the distant fenceline, with the fascinating depth of the ageless marsh behind him. As she journeyed step by step, rehearsing her opening lines over and over, his form increased in size and detail until she recognized the blueness of the bibbed overalls framing his red plaid flannel shirt, and she could discern his motions as he chopped at the fallen tree so it could be removed from the fence. How sturdy and masculine he looked! She would carry that image of him—active, colorful, dependable—for the rest of her years.

He stopped his work as he saw her coming and stood watching her, the baffling, undefinable woman—another man's wife—who was the center of his own existence.

He wiped the sweat from his face with his blue bandanna. "Marcus an' his family get away all right?" he asked.

"Yes, they're gone, thank goodness," she replied.

He squinted at her in the bright sunlight, and he pulled the narrow brim of his straw hat lower over his eyes. "They sure broke up the peace o' the family," he commented, "with those perfect kids o' theirs."

"It's all Zac's mother could talk about," Prudence said, "and it made Zachary dreadfully upset."

"I could tell," he agreed.

"It's been building up for a long time, anyway. Marc's visit was just another straw on the load, and we're getting very close to the breaking point."

"I know."

They gazed into each other's eyes with a depth of understanding that belongs to old friends.

"This matter of having children is threatening my marriage," she said.

"It looks that way."

"Eeph, will you help me? Will you help me save my marriage?"

He looked bewildered. He reached up and took off his hat and ran his fingers through his hair. "Of course, Prudence," he said with confusion. "You know I'd do anything fer you. But how? What can I do?"

She knew the moment had arrived. There was no hesitation. "Eeph, I want you to try to give me a baby."

She saw the stunned disbelief in his expression, just as she had expected. She watched the sudden surge of excitement flash across his face, just as she had expected. And she heard him say in a hushed voice, "I would consider it a sacred responsibility," just as she had expected.

Against the backdrop of the eternal marsh, they agreed upon the particulars. It would be a one-time experience, not to be repeated; if the Lord wanted it to succeed, once would be enough. There would be no romantic emotions allowed, and there would be absolutely no commitment between them afterward. In fact, neither of them would ever speak of the matter again, not even to each other. The entire arrangement was to be impersonal, as though they were placing an order from a catalog.

A few mornings later, when Zachary and his parents were fully occupied with their tasks, Prudence took a quick, cool bath and dressed herself in fresh, clean clothes. She walked in a roundabout way toward Ephraim's house—a tiny speck of life against the verdant landscape, moving inexorably toward her destiny.

She had never been in Ephraim's house without Zachary, and she felt nervous and uneasy as she knocked lightly on the back door.

He appeared as well-groomed as she had ever seen him. He was wearing his Sunday trousers and white shirt without coat or tie, and somehow he looked simultaneously both formal and casual. His shoes were polished to a glistening shine. His hands had been scrubbed nearly raw, and his face was exceptionally clean-shaven. He was beaming as he welcomed her inside his home.

Ephraim studied her intently and inscribed her image into the permanent library of his memory. The nut-brown hair, brushed into a vibrant luster and fastened together at the back with an indigo ribbon. The azure eyes, enormous windows through which he saw the beauty and purity of her soul. The crisp white linen blouse, stretched taut across the breasts that he would soon see and feel for the first time. The thin dark belt which circumscribed the narrowness of her waist. Its circular gold buckle in the front, the ancient symbol of female fertility. The blue and white checkered skirt flowing endlessly from the fountains of desire.

"Would you like some coffee?" he asked, motioning her toward the kitchen.

"No, I don't think so," she replied. "I shouldn't spend very much time here."

"I understand," he said gently. "Come with me." He led her upstairs into his bedroom.

It was immaculate. Not a speck of dust appeared on floor, furniture, nor window sill. The bed was covered with a colorful hand made quilt, turned down to display a set of new white muslin sheets. The chest of drawers was adorned with a bright orange marigold in a small vase, alongside a shiny tin box. She recognized the pencil portrait of herself which had been sketched in Prairieville during her first date with Ephraim.

With tears quickly welling in her eyes, Prudence recognized anew the depth of his devotion.

"Thank you, Eeph," she said in a low, faltering voice.

"I'll disappear fer a while," he said.

When she was ready, she called softly and he entered a darkened room, shades drawn against the sunlight.

Prudence had concentrated intently upon the necessity for her unorthodox adventure, never anticipating what the experience would really be like. Therefore, she was truly astonished at the pleasure she enjoyed in Ephraim's arms. She had resolved beforehand not to make any comparisons, but it was impossible to squelch her memories of the grim, desperate encounters with Zachary in recent months. With Ephraim it was different. From the moment of his first touch she was overwhelmed with an irresistible sense of joy and ecstasy.

Although she had vowed to keep the transaction completely impersonal, it was impossible. How could she deny him her lips? How could she prevent the escalation of those kisses into a sublime passion? What could be more personal than the contact of his skin against hers for the full length of her body, or her legs unfolding to accommodate him? It would be inhumane to withhold even the slightest part of herself.

His inexperience was evident, but his desire to please her was so strong that she allowed him to learn her intimate secrets.

Throughout it all, she felt thoroughly comfortable. Somehow he dissipated her nervousness. He was powerful yet extremely gentle; he submerged her in strong but sensitive caresses which absorbed her deepest fears and tensions.

Utterly relaxed, she realized a feeling of blamelessness and justification which later she was unable to explain. The nagging perception rose to the surface of her consciousness that she might have made the wrong choice in husbands.

That night, Prudence enticed Zachary into her bed for the first time since his injury. She felt quietly confident that she would have a baby, and she wanted to believe it belonged to her husband.

That was all so long ago, she reflected now. Her daughter Sarah had been born twenty-two years ago, securing the stability of her marriage. Zachary quickly recovered the full measure of his love for the only woman in his life. Jonathan, Zachary's son, had followed quite naturally two years later, completing their family.

Ephraim had faithfully honored their secret, hiding what Prudence came to regard as the Great Sin of her life. Although she never spoke about it, the subject was never very far from her consciousness, and she had worried for years about what penalty might be exacted from her as a punishment. Now it was clear to her: she would lose her only son in the war.

She shuddered again and pressed closer into Ephraim's shoulder.

He understood her feelings. "There's nothin' we kin do about it, Prudence," he said quietly. "It's in the hands of the Lord."

Chapter 6

Prudence would have been perfectly content to let time stand still while she remained in the sheltering arms of Ephraim in his porch swing. But that knife-edge of our present existence, which marks the invisible boundary between the past and the future, moves steadily and inexorably forward for us all. There is no escape. Day followed unhappy day and Prudence could not stop or even slow the pace. Jonathan's resolution to enlist in the war had hardened and he only awaited the right moment.

The Women's Club gave Prudence an opportunity to divert her mind, and she eagerly drove into Prairieville for the club's final meeting of the season, a mid-day breakfast at Resthaven Hotel.

Resthaven was a gorgeous resort hotel built just before the turn of the century by Prairieville investors who hoped to profit from the hordes of summer visitors who flocked to the famous healing waters of the many local springs. Set upon a prominent hill on the east side of town, the hotel had been intended to rival the preeminent Fountain Spring House. Unfortunately, the popularity of Prairieville's springs was taking a mortal fall even as the walls of Resthaven were rising, and the new hotel was never able to stagger to its financial feet. Its splendid facilities, though, were open from time to time for the benefit of local citizens.

The brunch was capped with a frozen dessert, and a brief business meeting followed.

After a piano solo and a vocal duet, the group of nearly a hundred members and guests adjourned to the Sun Room for an amateur play.

Theodora Youmans sought Prudence out at adjournment. "How are you?" she inquired with genuine feeling. "I've been meaning to call you," she said, "I hope you will forgive me—I didn't mean to ignore you, but

I've been extremely busy trying to keep my suffrage team together."

"I know there are some differences of opinion," Prudence acknowledged, "but surely nobody would leave the 'team', as you call it."

"I wish you were right about that," said Theodora. "Some of my best working partners are on the verge of resigning."

"Because of the war?"

"Because of a lot of different things, but yes, the war is definitely highlighting our differences."

"Well, I want to help," said Prudence impulsively. "What can I do?"

"You can talk to all your neighbors about getting votes for women," Theodora said, as she had said to hundreds of women through the years. "We like to talk about freedom and equality in America," she added, "but all that talk is nonsense so long as half the citizens can't even vote!"

"Of course," said Prudence. "I've already been talking about it whenever I get a chance. But I don't see very many people. I want to do something more."

"Can you travel?" asked Theodora. "There are so many errands to be run, all over the state. Have you got time for short trips, maybe overnight sometimes?"

"Yes, I can travel," Prudence replied at once, ignoring the fact that she did not own an automobile and had never even ridden on a passenger train. "I've got the time available. I think that would be exciting!"

Theodora laughed with a hint of mischief in her tone. "It's pretty dangerous for you to volunteer like that around me," she said. "I've got to go up to Oshkosh in a few days to meet with Jessie Jack Hooper. She's pretty much in agreement with our views, but I want to be sure she understands the current situation. Would you like to go with me to meet her? Henry doesn't like me to travel alone."

"Just let me know when," Prudence replied. "I'd love to go."

Theodora's offer made her heart pound with anticipation, but her excitement was tempered by the knowledge that she had no experience as a traveler and had no means of getting more than a few miles from home.

Leaving the meeting at Resthaven, Prudence walked downtown to Spring City Auto, the Ford Motor Company agency on Main Street. She knew very little about machines, and she felt like a visitor from another planet as she examined a Runabout which was parked at the curb waiting for its new owner. She walked around it several times, admiring the polished fenders, the twelve-spoked wheels, and the smell of newness from the interior. The machine appeared very complicated to her.

Mr. Evans, the Ford dealer, was quick to join her. He began describing the joys and opportunities of owning a car, and her excitement mounted. But then he progressed to a description of the four-cylinder L-head engine with a displacement of a hundred and seventy six cubic inches, and her enthusiasm quickly cooled. Technical understanding of the automobile was far beyond her comprehension. Nevertheless, the car fascinated her and she knew it would be thrilling and satisfying to master it.

Hesitantly, she inquired about the price of the little Runabout. Mr. Evans told her it was 'only' three hundred and forty five dollars. That was barely half the amount required to buy a two-door sedan, but the figure seemed astronomical to her. She bade Mr. Evans goodby without revealing her name.

Soberly she walked over to Madison Street to retrieve Kaiser. He had no mechanical parts, she thought with grim satisfaction, and besides, he was enthusiastically glad to see her.

As she drove home in the buggy, however, she felt she could never be of much use to Theodora and the suffrage campaign without the ability to travel. Kaiser was fine for taking her into Prairieville, but she wouldn't want to journey very far behind a horse.

Most of the women she had met in the Women's Club had a motorcar, or at least their husbands did. She was the only one who traveled to the meetings in a buggy, she thought with chagrin. Zachary had always said there was no need for an automobile on the farm; it was a waste of good money. Horses were needed for the farmwork, and they could be used quite easily to drive into town with little extra expense. An automobile was not necessary for a farmer. But she was no longer a farmwife; she was more than that. She needed better transportation.

She did not have enough money to buy a car, she knew. The price, even for a little Runabout, was simply too much. Zachary had warned many times about the evil of borrowing money for anything other than a house or a farm. Their mortgage had been paid in full many years ago, and she would not consider going into debt for an automobile.

That evening, feeling guilty for having been away from the farm, Prudence joined Robert in the barn for the milking. Jonathan and Sarah were still in the field.

Robert had proved to be the right man for the farm. He was dependable and willing to work. His humility derived naturally from his plain appearance and lack of imagination. In addition, he was unselfish almost to a fault. "He's a generous man, wit' a heart of gold," Ephraim had asserted, quite correctly, and already he had won the respect and confidence of Prudence and her children.

When he listened to her afternoon adventures, and recognized her need for a vehicle, Robert responded in his typical big-hearted manner. "I got a set of wheels, Ma'am," he said shyly, "and yer welcome t' use 'em. I don't go nowhere no more."

She was puzzled at the meaning of his offer for a moment, knowing he did not own a car, but then she realized he was referring to his motorcycle. His Harley-Davidson motorcycle!

She laughed. She couldn't help laughing; the thought of herself riding a motorcycle was ludicrous beyond imagination.

He admired her too much to be offended at her reaction. Instead, he joined her laughter. "It ain't dangerous," he said. "Not wit' the sidecar on it. It steers easier than a car, and it turns a lot shorter, too."

"Oh, you are a dear, indeed!" Prudence exclaimed. "Can you really picture me riding your motorcycle? I'm a *woman*!"

Robert sobered at once. "Of course ya' can ride my motorcycle," he declared. "Ya' got the body of a woman, there's no denyin' that," he said; then he blushed furiously and went on quickly, "but you got the spirit of a man. I know ya' could do anything ya' want."

"Well," she said reflectively, "why not? Would you be willing to teach me how to ride?"

"Yes, Ma'am, I'd be quite willin' t' show you how."

The next morning, as soon as the chores were finished, Prudence heard the cheerful noise of Robert's motorcycle as he drove up to the door of her house. She stepped outside as he turned off the engine.

"Good mornin', Ma'am," he said, lifting his hat briefly. "C'mon, I'll show ya' the *Gray Ghost*—that's what everybody calls this beast, because it's so quick an' quiet." He stood alongside the front wheel, beckoning her to him. Ephraim hung back a little, jealously watching.

"Before ya' start, ya' jus' look over the machine to make sure it's ready t' go. Check the tires an' pump a bit of air in 'em if ya' need to." He squeezed the front tire in his vigorous grasp. "See, this is jus' about right. There's a bit o' give in it, but it ain't soft."

Prudence knew she could never pinch the tire with strength to match his, but she assumed she could tell from the appearance of the tire if it needed more air.

"Then ya' check t' see that ya' got enough oil and gas." Suddenly he felt a bit uncomfortable with his efforts to teach her something new. His voice faltered, and he stopped talking. He felt he was treading on forbidden ground, that his behavior was improper. Perhaps it was because for the first time he knew more than she did about the subject at hand—he, who was so ignorant and inferior. Perhaps it was because he was revealing some of the mysteries of a man's world to a woman. He was betraying his fellow men by initiating a woman into the masculine knowledge of machinery.

Or perhaps it was simply his nervousness at being in the presence of such an attractive woman. He was married, of course, and he loved his wife, but when he met Prudence he had been overwhelmed by her presence. She didn't compete with his wife; she was too exalted for such a comparison. He was simply awe-struck.

"Go on," prompted Ephraim, not at all happy with Robert's evident rapture.

Robert shook himself back to reality and uncapped the fuel tank to peer inside. "Ya' hafta tell how much gas n' oil ya' got jus' by lookin'," he said. "The tank on the left side is the main gas tank—holds about a gallon. There's an extra gas tank, a small one, on the right side. The oil tank is right behind it. Jus' take the caps off n' look in."

"Do you have to do this every time before you ride it?" she asked.

"Yep," he laughed. "It's best t' be sure o' what ya' got. An' a gallon o' gas don't take ya' very far, anyway. Mebbe forty miles."

"I see," she said.

"It may seem like an inconvenience at first," he said with half apology, "but you'll get used to it purty easy. An' that's about all there is to it, really, before ya' start 'er up."

He dared to look into her face, and he felt a resurgence of his admiration and awe.

"Well, then, let's start it," she said, "if you're willing."

"Oh, yes Ma'am," he replied, forcing his attention back to the motorcycle. He reached for his goggles and handed them to her. "Here. You need these t' pertect yer eyes. Sometimes there's little bugs, or just dirt in the air."

Prudence pulled the goggles down over the top of her head, sliding the lenses into place over her eyes. "They fit awfully tight," she said.

Robert was quick to reach for the elastic strap at the back of her head. His fumbling fingers adjusted the buckle. "How's that?" in asked, petting the back of her head to smooth her hair down again.

Ephraim bristled.

"It's just fine," she replied.

"Okay; get in," he told her, pointing at the sidecar, "an' I'll show ya' how t' drive it."

Prudence gathered her long skirts around her legs and climbed into the rather cramped compartment. Robert mounted the driver's seat and flashed a quick nervous smile across at her.

"You need goggles, too!" she protested.

"Naw, I'm used t' squintin'. Besides, we ain't goin' very far."

He smiled again, glancing covertly at her from the corner of his eye, and then began showing her the controls.

"Make sure it's in neutral," he said. "See, ya' jus' push this lever into this position." He showed her. "Then ya' retard the spark, like this. If the engine is cold, ya' gotta get the gas flowin', so ya' tickle the carb a little bit by pumpin' it a couple o' times." He showed her the little priming button on the engine.

"It all looks so complicated," she said.

"Aw, it'll be easy once ya' get used to it," he reassured her. "An' we're ready to start the engine now.

"It's got pedals on it like a bicycle," he explained. "In fact, ya' can ride it like a bicycle if ya' need to, but it'd be purty hard pedalin' fer a woman I s'pose."

"I think I'll let the engine do the work," she laugheded.

"Okay; well, ya jus' push down on a pedal as hard as ya' can. It usually starts right off."

He demonstrated, and the little machine was as good as he promised. The engine started up with an enormous husky roar. 'This is no ghost,' Prudence thought.

"Are ya' ready?" he asked. She nodded, and after a couple of short bursts of the throttle, he put the machine in gear and let out the clutch. They started forward smoothly but vigorously, heading down the driveway toward the road. Ephraim trotted alongside for a few yards, and then, feeling foolish, he stopped and stared after them.

"Once ya' get goin'," Robert explained, "it's real easy. Ya' just steer it like a bicycle, and control the speed with the throttle. The hardest part is shiftin' gears as ya' pick up speed. See? Ya' put in the clutch with yer left foot as ya' ease off the throttle, and ya' can shift the gears. Then ya' let out the clutch again as ya' feed it the gas." He tried to make it sound simple, wishing he could explain it more easily to her.

Suddenly he realized the end of the driveway was rapidly approaching and he had gained too much speed. He turned his full attention to controlling the motorcycle as he hit the brakes and wrestled with the handlebars. They turned sharply to the right on River Road, careening around the corner with such force that Prudence was sure the wheel supporting her sidecar was lifted a foot or more off the ground.

As they settled back to normal, Robert felt his face flame with acute abashment. "I'm sorry," he said in a very low voice, "I didn't mean t' scare ya'. I didn't think. . . ."

She laughed with delight. "You didn't scare me, Robert," she said. "It was thrilling! I haven't had such excitement since the time Kaiser got startled by the backfiring of a passing car. Let's do it again!"

"Oh no, no, no," Robert said. "I wouldn't. . . ."

When he recovered his composure, he said, "The brake pedal is here on the right side, and you push down with your foot to stop." He demonstrated. "An' don't let the speed build up like I just did. That was foolish of me."

They continued down River Road and turned toward Reedsville. It was a pleasant summer day with warm sunshine and fresh breeze.

There were broad grins across both their faces; Prudence was exhilarated by riding the motorcycle and Robert was exhilarated by riding with Prudence.

As they reached Reedsville, before turning north to continue their way around the perimeter of the swamp, Robert stopped the motorcycle.

"It's time t' trade places," he told Prudence. "Ya' ain't gonna learn it 'til ya' do it fer yerself."

"Do you really think I'm ready?" she asked.

"I showed ya' all ya' need t' know. Ya' wouldn't learn nothin' else if ya' rode wit' me fer a hunnerd miles."

She was already dismounting, a happy smile on her face. "If you think I'm ready, I'll give it a try."

She settled into the driver's seat, raising her skirts high above her ankles and tucking them beneath her. Robert was speechless as he stared at her bare legs. She noticed. "Maybe I should wear pants when I do this," she laughed.

Following his instructions, she let the clutch out very slowly and they began to move forward. It was thrilling to command the machine herself, to make it go whatever direction she chose. She gradually increased the speed, and even shifted gears without much trouble. They rode along quietly for a mile or two.

"There's nothin' t' jus' drivin' along," he told her. "I want you t' practice stoppin' and startin'. Jus slow 'er down and park fer a minute, an' then start up again. I want you t' do it over and over again so ya' get the hang of it."

Her first starts were quite jerky, and she killed the engine once or twice as she became accustomed to the feel of the required motions. Gradually she mastered the technique, and her starts and stops became smoother.

"Ya' learn fast," he said approvingly as they approached the Hartmann farm from the north.

"Let me go around again," she begged, and Robert agreed with a happy smile.

Ephraim, who had started forward to greet her, was left in the swirling dust of her tornado as she gave the machine full throttle and sprinted past him without a glance.

When Theodora telephoned a few days later to renew her invitation to accompany her to Oshkosh, Prudence was ready. With a sense of anticipation which made her spirits soar, she mounted the motorcycle which Robert had delivered to her door. Once again Ephraim stood by helplessly as she left; she scornfully refused his offer of accompaniment.

She waved her hand enthusiastically at the two men and headed off alone for Prairieville.

Her initial apprehension at riding solo was soon forgotten. The ride was brief, but her thoughts spanned vast distances and ideas. It was a dream coming true. At last, she was beginning to fulfill the ambitions which had fired her imagination.

Arriving at Theodora's house, she pulled into the driveway feeling very proud of herself. Henry and Theodora rushed out the door in astonishment, not believing their eyes.

"What's this?" Henry asked.

She feigned nonchalance, pretending that riding a motorcycle was an everyday occurrence for a woman. "I don't have a car," she shrugged.

Her friends laughed. "Well, I do declare!" exclaimed Theodora. "You are a happy surprise to me once again. Come on in; your hair will require a little arranging after your wild ride."

A few moments before a mirror prepared her for her next new experience—a train ride.

Henry was their chauffeur as he took the two women in his car to the *Soo Line* railroad station.

"Henry insists we should take the train," Theodora had explained. "It would be much more adventuresome in the car, just the two of us, but we'll save that for another day when the train is not so convenient."

The *Soo Line* train was not new to Prudence, although she had never ridden on it. She had heard the beguiling whistle of the trains as they paused at Vernal Station on the eastern border of the great marsh. Many times, especially in the quiet of the night, she had listened to the passage of the train and said to herself along with the poet, Edna St. Vincent Millay,

> *"There isn't a train I wouldn't take,*
> *No matter where it's going."*

Now she was actually climbing the steps into a railroad coach behind a gently chuffing steam engine, and she found herself marveling at this new miracle in her life.

Theodora accepted the train ride as commonplace, so Prudence kept her feelings to herself. 'There's no need for her to know how limited my background is,' she thought.

As the train rumbled northward from Prairieville it was soon passing through open farmland. Theodora was not prone to waste time, and she began to educate her neophyte friend with a discussion of the history and the rationale of the suffrage campaign.

If Prudence had been alone, she probably would have pressed her nose and fingertips against the windowglass and stared at the scenery. However, she restrained herself and forced her attention to the conversation of her eminent companion, sneaking only an occasional glance outside.

Prudence found the suffrage story, as related by Theodora, fascinating in its own right. She had admired the newspaperwoman for several years, and her admiration deepened considerably during the conversation.

Toward the end of the journey, Theodora began talking about the immediate disharmony among her associates. "Olympia Brown has already quit our Wisconsin Women Suffrage Association," she related. "It is a terrible blow, but she is gone and it is inevitable that others will follow. Ada James is almost sure to go, and perhaps Meta Berger as well."

"I know who Olympia Brown is," commented Prudence. "She's an older woman from Racine who was one of the first women to work for the right to vote."

"Yes, that's right. She's an ordained minister, and was actually an associate of Susan B. Anthony before coming to Wisconsin. She helped to organize the Wisconsin Woman Suffrage Association, and she was my immediate predecessor as president. She retired from that office when we merged with the Political Equality League. Olympia was instrumental in getting women the right to vote in Wisconsin school elections. That battle alone took years, and wasn't won until 1901."

"And now she's leaving the suffrage movement because of the war?" Prudence inquired. "She was in a peace march in Washington D.C. a couple of months ago; I remember Grace Lusk talking about it."

"Yes, she's one of the original purists in the movement. She firmly believes that all the women's issues should be lumped together—pacifism, prohibition, suffrage, everything. It's a moral issue with her, and there is no compromise. I respect her history, and of course she is entitled to her own opinions, but I think we'll never achieve suffrage if we follow the course of 'all or nothing'."

"She was president of the Wisconsin Woman Suffrage Association when we lost the referendum in 1912, wasn't she?"

"Yes, she was. And in my opinion, that battle should never have been fought. We weren't ready, and the voters weren't ready. We didn't just *lose* the referendum; we were *crushed*! The results knocked us out of the suffrage battle, and we're still out. Wisconsin is considered unwinnable by the national suffrage leaders, and they're probably right."

Theodora was carrying a small box containing pamphlets and other campaign materials. Prudence rummaged through the box, and was delighted to find a yellow ribbon, about six inches long, with the simple inscription 'VOTES FOR WOMEN' on it. Her passion for the cause had been magnified by the morning's discussion and she pinned the ribbon to the front of her dress to proudly proclaim her position. "I hope I get the chance to talk about suffrage with somebody who's not on our side," she commented.

"You'll get lots of chances like that," Theodora predicted.

Jessie Jack Hooper met them at the station. She was a quiet, dignified woman with a broad face and steady eyes. She suggested they talk during lunch, and she led them to the *Athearn Buffet* at the hotel on High Street.

During the meal, Prudence's yellow suffrage ribbon was noticed by many of the people who passed by their table. Prudence quickly recognized the extent of the division of opinion on the subject, for some of the faces scowled as they saw her message and others smiled. Nobody, it seemed, was neutral.

After lunch, Mrs. Hooper took them to the offices of the *Northwestern* for an appointment with the publisher. As they waited in an anteroom, a proud, portly man marched into the room from the sidewalk, puffing on a large cigar. He was well-dressed in a dark blue suit with a white carnation pinned jauntily in his lapel. He was about to pass by when he noticed the yellow ribbon. He paused momentarily, took one more step, and then returned to face Prudence. He frowned.

"Ma'am, I see you are in favor of women's suffrage," he said without introduction. "I have never met a knowledgeable suffragist, and I would like to ask you a few questions. Do you mind?"

Suddenly Prudence lost her rabid desire to debate suffrage with an unbeliever. She glanced at Theodora and Mrs. Hooper, expecting to be rescued from her plight. Instead, she saw the two women rise as a dignified gentleman in a light gray suit bustled toward them from the other direction. She realized the publisher had arrived to receive them.

Theodora turned briefly toward Prudence, as though to invite her along for the interview. Then, upon reflection, she said, "Prudence, please excuse us for a few moments." She nodded toward the man with the carnation. "Here's the chance you were looking for," she said in a low voice.

Theodora looked up at the stranger and smiled. "Mrs. Hartmann, here, will be glad to answer your questions." Then she turned and was gone down the hallway with the publisher before Prudence could object.

Prudence looked at the glowering masculine face before her and summoned every bit of courage and dignity she possessed. "I am Mrs. Zachary Hartmann," she said quietly. "What are your questions?"

The man's face softened a bit. "I apologize, Ma'am, for failing to introduce myself. I am Jacob Miller."

"I am pleased to meet you," said Prudence, boldly extending her hand. He reached down to grasp it with a light touch, bowing his head slightly toward her.

"Thank you, Ma'am," he responded.

"Now, let me ask again, what are your questions?"

"Well, Ma'am, you've answered one of them already, for you have indicated you are married. But let me go on. What does your husband think about your views in favor of votes for women?"

"My husband, sir, is dead, and therefore I cannot ask him," replied Prudence without hesitation.

Mr. Miller inhaled a deep breath of cigar smoke, and then softly blew it toward the ceiling in a couple of fragmented rings. "Ah-h-h," he said in a knowing manner. "That explains it. I didn't think any reasonable husband would permit you to flaunt such a point of view."

"I am not flaunting my point of view," said Prudence.

"Oh, but you are," he insisted. "The wearing of your ribbon is an ostentatious display of a viewpoint which you know is controversial if not downright offensive to many citizens."

"I'm sorry if my viewpoint offends you," said Prudence, "but why is it offensive to suggest that all citizens should have an equal right to vote? Our country is founded on the principles of equality for everyone."

"You are wrong, Ma'am. Our Founding Fathers spoke of all MEN being created equal. They did not mention WOMEN. Men like Thomas Jefferson would never have dreamed that someday women would be claiming equality with men. It is obvious to everyone that women are different than men in many, many ways."

"Different, yes, but still equal," insisted Prudence. "Different physically, but equal politically."

"But that physical difference results in a political difference," said Mr. Miller.

"Explain yourself," challenged Prudence.

"The wisdom of God has appointed women to be the wives and mothers," Mr. Miller began as though he were lecturing a child. "Women are to create the homes and have the babies and rear the children. They should be concerned with domestic matters. It is for men to go out into the world to earn the living and fight the battles. They are to be concerned with matters of business and politics."

"God made it so women have babies, and men don't," agreed Prudence, "but God gave brains to women just like He gave them to men. God gave brains to women, and He expects women to use them."

"Ah, yes," nodded Mr. Miller smugly. "Women are to use their brains, but to what purpose? God intended women to use their brains to improve their homes and their families, not to interfere with men in the outside world."

"How do you know that?" asked Prudence. "Why shouldn't women use their brains to improve the 'outside world', as you call it, as well as their own homes?"

Mr. Miller looked offended, as though she shouldn't have challenged him. "Well, they just shouldn't," insisted Mr. Miller. "Every decent person knows it instinctively. It goes against nature. Women should be nestmakers. Historically, they have stayed at home. That's where they belong. The Bible tells us that."

"I don't remember reading that in the Bible," said Prudence. "Can you remind me where it says that?"

Mr. Miller paused thoughtfully for a moment. Once again he sent a ragged circle of cigar smoke upward. "Yes, I'll tell you where. It's in the Book of Proverbs. The last chapter. The writer describes the role of a Virtuous Woman in working hard to take care of her family—getting up early in the morning, feeding everyone in her household, making clothes to keep her family warm in winter, and so on. Then he refers to her husband as a man who sits with the elders of the land at the gates of the city. I think that pretty well tells it all—the Bible says women should stay home and take care of their domestic duties, while their husbands handle the civic affairs."

Prudence had a fair knowledge of the Bible, and she was thoroughly versed in the well-known passage in which Solomon describes the Superwoman of the Scriptures.

"Mr. Miller, I am quite familiar with Chapter thirty-one of the Book of Proverbs. That Virtuous Woman has been the model of my life. In fact, I can quote the words that describe her. It is true that she takes care of her family. But in addition, it says that 'she is like the merchants' ships; she bringeth her food from afar.' It says that 'she considereth a field, and buyeth it: with the fruit of her hands she planteth a vineyard.' And again, it says 'she maketh fine linen, and selleth it; and delivereth girdles unto the merchant.' It sounds to me like that Virtuous Woman is very active in the outside world, in the world of business. She's active in everything from agriculture to manufacturing to real estate."

"I think you're taking those words out of context," said Mr. Miller. "I commend you for memorizing verses from Scripture. Unfortunately, I haven't done so, and I find myself at a disadvantage here. But it is evident that all the business our Virtuous Woman engaged in was for her home—to provide food and clothing for her family. I think it's acceptable for her to be in business like that. But that's where it should stop. Women should tend to their families, and not get mixed up in other kinds of business."

"Mr. Miller, it seems to me that every business in the whole world exists for the purpose of taking care of families and people, of filling human wants and needs. What other business could there possibly be?"

"Well, um, I think you're generalizing too much. I would say that a woman should merely take care of her own family, not the rest of the people outside."

"Not if you follow the Book of Proverbs," Prudence said. "That same Virtuous Woman 'stretcheth out her hand to the poor; yea, she reachest forth her hands to the needy.' That tells us that she should be involved in things outside her own family."

"Well, it's all right for her to give to the poor," admitted Mr. Miller. "That is certainly a Christian virtue. But it's pretty plain that everything you've talked about here involves her working hard to satisfy her family's needs and perhaps the needs of the poor. I still say she shouldn't take part in politics. It's her husband who sits with the elders of the land. The Virtuous Woman stays at home and keeps her mouth shut."

"Quite the contrary, Mr. Miller. It says specifically that our Virtuous Woman 'openeth her mouth with wisdom; and in her tongue is the law of kindness.' It sounds to me like she is involved in politics—it even talks about laws."

Mr. Miller tried to suck another lungful of smoke, but the cigar had gone out. He removed it from his mouth and examined the tip with disbelief. Then he jammed it back between his lips without lighting it and resumed his conversation. "I knew I should have studied my Bible more faithfully," he said. "You are picking words and phrases from here and there, and stringing them together to fit your case. Unfortunately, I am not able to do the same. But you know in your heart, just as I do, that the Bible instructs women to stay at home and let the men handle everything in the outside world."

Prudence smiled, not in triumph but in the satisfaction that she had not been overwhelmed in her first confrontation with a man concerning the suffrage issue. She was content to let him have the last word; they both knew he had not proved his case.

The conversation was clearly over, and she expected Mr. Miller to excuse himself and move on. Instead, he just stood there, glancing restlessly around the anteroom, showing no indication of leaving.

After an awkward silence, Prudence resumed the conversation. "Tell me, Mr. Miller, aside from the Bible, why a woman should not be allowed in the 'outside world,' as you call it. What is so awful about it?"

"It just isn't right for women and men to mix together away from their homes and their spouses. You'll see—there will be jealousies and arguments and all sorts of silliness. Men won't keep their minds on their business, not with women around. Professional standards will be compromised, and the work won't get done. And even worse things can happen—men and women will have love affairs, and homes will be broken, and children will be neglected."

"You don't have very much faith in people, do you?" said Prudence.

"You don't think husbands and wives can be faithful to each other when they are out of sight?"

"Not when they're thrown together hour after hour, day after day. Even a saint can be tempted."

"I'll agree that people are inherently sinful," Prudence conceded. "But I can't believe they will become more sinful if women are given the right to vote. Have you got any proof of what you say?"

"No, of course not. How can I? We won't know for sure unless it happens, unless women succeed in forcing a law through so they can vote. By then, it'll be too late."

She chose not to reply, and after waiting a few moments, Mr. Miller moved toward the doorway. "I can see you aren't going to change your mind," he said, "so I might as well be going." His step on the way out was not nearly so crisp as it had been on his way in.

"Goodby, Mr. Miller," she called after him cheerfully.

She was still smiling when Theodora and Mrs. Hooper reappeared at the end of their interview. "Thanks for tossing me right into the ring," she said. "I didn't get knocked out."

Chapter 7

Zachary had been a man of rigid opinion and stern control. Prudence, beneath her placid exterior, had been chafed repeatedly by his prohibitions. Her most frequent frustration was the denial of her desire to travel alone away from the farm—a desire which she quickly fulfilled after his death by going to the Prairieville Women's Club meeting.

Another vexation was his almost pathological disapproval of non-religious public gatherings. "The devil loves crowds," he would say cryptically whenever she suggested they watch a parade or join a friendly celebration.

Her father had a temperament quite the opposite; he seized every excuse for a day off and invented a few excuses of his own. As a child growing up in Prairieville, Prudence and her family had commemorated virtually every public occasion.

The best of these was the annual Decoration Day observance. Some of the fondest memories of her early years were the recollections of the parades, speeches, and treats which surrounded that glorious day. Her father, a veteran of the great 4th Wisconsin Infantry which saved the Union's position on the first day of the Gettysburg battle, had marched proudly in each parade. She remembered how pleased he was, always, when her mother told him again that his uniform fit him even better than when they were married at the end of the war. Prudence herself had taken pride in polishing his shoes to a shining luster whenever he marched.

Those joyous adventures ended abruptly when she married, for Zachary immediately projected his solemn, solitary disposition to his new wife. He rejected her proposals to take a day's respite from the farm between milkings and go to town for any of the holidays she had enjoyed so much. He wouldn't even allow her to see her father march in the Decoration Day parades. There was plenty of work to do on the farm, he said, and there was no time for frivolity nor idleness. Her entreaties and her tears were to no avail, and she gradually learned to suppress her feelings.

Now, with Zachary's restrictions only an unhappy memory, Prudence prepared to celebrate Decoration Day with great enthusiasm. It would be a welcome relief from the sorrow of her husband's sudden death and the foreboding surrounding the military enlistment of her son.

Robert was given permission to spend the holiday with his wife and family in Janesville, and he roared off on his motorcycle as soon as the morning chores were completed.

Prudence served an early lunch, and they prepared for their journey into town. Ephraim was in high spirits as he harnessed Kaiser and hitched the buggy. He was whistling a familiar church hymn, *Count Your Many Blessings*, and he gazed out across the farmland toward the river with a contented expression which seemed out of place on his face. A bluebird fluttered past on its way to a small birdhouse on a distant fencepost; he watched its movements with pleasure.

When the buggy was ready, he drove up alongside the farmhouse and helped Prudence into the front seat beside him. Sarah and Jon climbed into the back.

He was overjoyed at the invitation to join the family; it would be his first opportunity to escort Prudence on a public outing other than going to church. After the death of Zachary, he had expected to move quickly into what he perceived to be his rightful position as head of the family, although he recognized there must be a decent interval before he actually married his woman. Instead, Prudence had played him hot and cold, turning him on and off, creating uncertainties in his heart where, by all the lights of reason, he had expected solid acceptance.

But now, at last, he was holding the reins on a family expedition with Prudence at his side. He sat up straight and stiff as Kaiser trotted toward town. His face was joyfully alight although he said little. The early afternoon weather was fair, but he would not have noticed if a freak May snowstorm had suddenly enveloped them. Jon and Sarah were eagerly chattering in the back seat, but he did not hear them. He was aware of nothing except the woman at his side, his elusive prize, the comely woman wearing an elegant straw hat held in place with a diaphanous white shawl.

For the first time, he would be seen on the streets of Prairieville escorting Prudence as though she belonged to him. She would hold his arm as they walked, he knew, and she would glance at him occasionally with that look of warm comfort bestowed only upon partners of long standing. Their friends and acquaintances, scarce as they might be, would see them and understand the depth of the new relationship which was being confirmed. Even the strangers who chanced to pass by would recognize the presence of an uncommon devotion. He could feel a sacred consonance engulfing them and radiating around them like a celestial hymn.

Prudence herself felt the comfort of his presence. The thought of having Jonathan march away to war frightened her and made her feel insecure. Ephraim's closeness was a consolation. She was well aware of his devotion to her, and it softened her feelings of helplessness.

Why, then, had she resisted his overtures immediately following the funeral? It must have been nothing more than a reaction to the sudden change in her life, a natural inclination to proceed slowly, a desire to think things through. A union with Ephraim certainly seemed so natural, so inevitable. It would fulfill a sense of order in her life.

Ephraim could never dominate her the way Zachary had; there was nothing to fear. Perhaps it was true that they needed each other, she mused; perhaps they had, beneath it all, belonged to each other for many years.

He turned to look at her. "Prudy," he said, using an affectionate nickname for the first time, "Prudy, thanks fer invitin' me along today. It's a real pleasure fer me to be here wit' ya'."

She touched his arm gently for a moment. "It seems so right, doesn't it," she agreed.

Prairieville was crowded with automobiles, horses and buggies, and people on foot. Kaiser picked his way to Thiel's livery and stopped at his customary hitching post. Ephraim helped Prudence from the buggy, and the family began walking uptown. They could sense the martial atmosphere. This was no ordinary holiday; the citizens were in a serious mood befitting the existing state of war.

The downtown streets were lined with people of all ages, standing and sitting, waiting for the parade to begin. Ephraim and his 'family' found an open space on Main Street near the Five Points in the center of town, and staked out their own vantage point.

"I've heard that they've invited a group of men to march in Civil War uniforms, along with our modern-day soldiers," remarked Prudence. "They're calling it *The Boys of '17 and The Boys of '60*."

"Are there going to be some real Civil War veterans with them?" asked Jon.

"That's what they say," said Prudence. "I haven't been to a Decoration Day parade for many years, but I suppose there are still some veterans able to march. They'd be pretty old by now. My father marched every year, you remember, until he died. Let's see, he'd be seventy-seven if he were still alive. I don't suppose he'd be marching very fast."

"I wish I'd seen him march," said Jon.

"Yes, I wish you had, too," said Prudence wistfully. "But Zachary was right, there was always a lot of work to do on the farm. And it seemed like the weather was always perfect on Decoration Day—perfect for farming, that is."

"Who are *The Boys of '17?*" asked Sarah.

"I'm not sure," said Ephraim.

A spectator alongside turned to them. "Don't you know?" he asked. "It's all the guys who have signed up to fight. The biggest group is Prairieville's infantry company. It's been in the papers. Haven't you heard of it?"

"Yes, I know all about Prairieville's Company," said Jonathan quietly.

"I remember reading a story or two," said Prudence. "But it was only a brief mention. I really couldn't tell you much."

"It's a new company," said the man. "Dan Martin—he fought in the Spanish War—Danny has been named captain, and he's trying to raise a full company of men. He's got Harry Welch and Dick Austerman as his first and second lieutenants."

The conversation was interrupted as Dr. David Roberts, Prairieville's prominent veterinarian, approached them, looking for an open place along the edge of the street where he and his wife Mary could stand. Prudence pushed Jon and Sarah closer together to create an opening. "Mame!" she called out to her friend from the Women's Club. "Come and join us. There's room."

"Thanks, Prudence," said Mrs. Roberts as she and the doctor squeezed into the crowd alongside them. "David was out on an emergency call, and we're late getting here."

"Isn't this exciting!" exclaimed Prudence. Everybody seems so thrilled to be here today to cheer for our country. The war fever has really taken hold."

"Yes, what a change in temper," commented Mame. "Remember our discussion at the Club in April? The women were surprised when I said the public attitudes were hardening for war. At that time—just two months ago—the prevailing opinion of the people was still very much against getting into the war."

"And today," said Prudence, "there was an American flag at almost every home as we drove into town. That's a remarkable display of patriotism."

"Yes, and look at this crowd!" exclaimed Mame. "I've never seen so many people at a Decoration Day parade in my whole life."

"Everybody said we would never support the idea of taking sides because so many of us are from German backgrounds," remarked Prudence. "But attitudes changed almost overnight as soon as Congress declared war."

"I guess it proves we're all Americans first, regardless of where our ancestors came from," observed Mame.

"I wonder how many boys will volunteer to go fight, though," mused Sarah. "That will show us how deep their patriotism is. Maybe when it comes to risking their lives, they'll hold off."

"We'll find out pretty fast," said Mame. "Captain Martin is trying to raise an infantry company of a hundred and fifty men from Prairieville. He's got nearly a hundred so far, but the first burst of enthusiasm has ebbed and nobody's coming in to volunteer any more."

"Some of the boys are signing up elsewhere," observed Dr. Roberts. "Not everybody wants to sink into the mud of the trenches. My nephew, Frank, wants to fly—he's signing up to be a military pilot."

"Yes, and many of the guys from the well-to-do families are wangling their way into officers' schools if they want to support their country," observed Jon with obvious disapproval.

"I hope there's enough money to train all the boys and equip 'em and get 'em overseas to fight," remarked Dr. Roberts. "Sales of the Liberty Bonds are not going very well."

"At least, not in Wisconsin," Mame added. "I've read that the bonds are selling well in other parts of the country."

"I suppose they'll blame the German influence in Wisconsin for the poor sales here," Jon suggested.

"I'm sure they will," said Ephraim wryly. "Germans get blamed for everything."

"At least the Red Cross Tag Day was a success last Saturday," commented Mame. "The girls raised more than a thousand dollars for a very good cause."

"It was the best Tag Day the town has ever seen," said Dr. Roberts. "I know a couple of men who ended up with more than fifty tags pinned on their suits."

"Tag Day?" asked Sarah. "What is Tag Day?"

"Oh, it's just a way the Red Cross girls have of raising money. They ask for donations from people passing by on the street, and give out a little tag for each gift. People pin the tags on them to show that they have made a donation."

"Prudence," said Mame brightly, "you should have been over at the G.A.R. Hall this morning when the schoolchildren brought their bouquets of flowers."

"You mean for the soldiers' graves?" asked Sarah.

"Yes," replied Mame. "It was such a touching scene! With the warm weather so slow in coming this year, there weren't a lot of garden flowers available. Instead, the children picked wild flowers from the woods and fields. You've never seen such a variety of beautiful flowers in your life. And the little children were so sweet!"

Their attention was drawn to an attractive woman strolling by in front of the crowd. She paused for a brief instant, fixing the veterinarian in her gaze. "Hello, David," she said in a warm, friendly tone, as she gave him a big smile. She did not acknowledge Mame's presence and she moved on quickly without waiting for a reply and without looking back. It was only after she was gone that Prudence realized it had been Grace Lusk. A quick glance at Mame disclosed a face filled with annoyance and disgust, highlighted by hardened eyes and compressed lips.

"Look!" said Sarah. "Here they come!" She pointed up the street at the first phalanx of horses prancing into view.

The various bands of marchers swept past them in waves. There were Boy Scouts and there were members of civic and fraternal groups. A contingent from the Women's Relief Corp was included. Military music was supplied by the marching band of the Industrial School, the reformatory where juvenile delinquents from all over the state were learning trades and hopefully being rehabilitated.

The centerpiece of the parade, however, was the contrast presented by *The Boys of '17 and The Boys of '60*. The Civil War veterans had been numerous and full of vigor when Prudence as a little girl had witnessed their marching. She had never considered them young, because they were the age of her father, but she had always thought of them as being in the prime of adulthood, well capable of defending their beloved country.

Now their ranks were sparse and their uniforms, many of them ill-fitting, appeared worn and dingy. The men themselves looked ancient and decrepit, and she caught herself hoping that they would be able to finish the parade route, that none of them would collapse and dampen the spirits of the crowd.

Then the young recruits for the European War followed briskly with all their vigor and determination. As she watched rank upon rank of young men marching along with exuberant energy, Prudence found herself searching out the ones that were the most handsome. There weren't many who appealed to her. She thought to herself that she was very particular about men. She was attracted only to the very best; the most handsome, the strongest. Like Zachary, she thought ruefully—and Ephraim.

Instinctively she glanced over at Ephraim. She studied his face. Yes, it was handsome, and strong. But for the first time she saw wrinkles at his cheekbones and around his eyes. Wrinkles. 'Ephraim is getting older,' she thought. He would be fifty in June. 'No wonder his face is wrinkled. No wonder his jowls are beginning to sag. Yes, his face is still handsome, but it is showing the effects of his seasons in the sun and wind.' She pictured him as she had seen him so often, unchanging through the years, wide-brimmed hat shading his face, a red bandanna around his neck to protect him from dust and chaff. 'Unchanging?' she thought. 'No, not unchanging. It's just that I didn't notice the changes until now, all of a sudden.'

She thought again of her father, who had died fifteen years before. 'I never noticed the changes in him, either,' she thought, 'although surely he was looking old and wrinkled by the time he died so unexpectedly. He was sixty-two. Only twelve years older than Ephraim is now. The changes come so gradually, and one is not aware of them until there is a sudden dreadful announcement.'

She continued to gaze at Ephraim, looking past her two children. 'How many years has he got left?' she asked herself. 'Ten years? Twenty? Life is so short,' she reflected, 'and it has not been kind to Ephraim. He has always been waiting for something. For what? For me? But I've not been available for twenty-five years. How can one have a good life when one is always waiting for something that is not likely to happen?'

She looked again at the young men marching in front of her. She was close enough to see their faces. There were no wrinkles. No sags. Their faces were examples of vitality, of eager expectancy. Yes, there were several of them she considered handsome. She felt an urgent need to love and be loved. 'I could give myself quite readily to one of these men,' she fantasized. 'What fun it would be! I've been waiting for something, too,' she realized. 'My life has been held in suspense for years, just like Ephraim's. Maybe it's time to do things my own way. To let go. To live life to the fullest, while I'm still young. Before it's too late.'

Suddenly she felt a distance between herself and Ephraim. 'I don't feel old, like he looks,' she thought. 'I am only forty-five. I am young and full of life, like those boys marching out there in the street.' A sense of quiet terror clutched at her heart. 'Or am I? Am I looking older, too?' she wondered. She wished for a secret mirror, at once, just for a moment. 'No,' she thought, 'I wouldn't have the nerve to look into it.'

Even though she could not examine her features physically, she pursued her brutal introspection. 'Is the best part of my life already over? Did I waste it? Am I any better off than Ephraim? Did I enjoy myself the way I should have, all those years with Zachary? What purpose have I served with my life?' She thought back on those difficult early years—the farmwork, caring for two little children, the endless days of diapers and dishes and despair.

Her heart warmed with affection, romantic affection, for those young recruits, tinged with a touch of envy. 'They have their whole lives ahead of them, unlike me,' she thought. 'And yet, somehow I feel very close to them. I am part of them. I am still young, like them. I've still got a big part of my life before me.'

She looked closely at Jonathan, standing between her and Sarah. 'Is it possible that I have a son as old as those soldiers marching past?' she thought. Immediately her face flushed with embarrassment. 'Of course. Those boys are the age of my son,' she realized with mortification. 'How ridiculous I am to imagine a romance with one of them! What a fool I am being!

'I'm glad Jon can't read my thoughts. He would think I am crazy, to think such sinful thoughts. But his face is a picture of thoughtful concentration. I wonder, does he feel as close to those young men as I do?'

Jonathan, she knew, had not yet followed through on his avowed intention to enlist in the National Guard. The decision, made during his nocturnal meditation in the marsh, was absolutely firm. However, at that time it was too soon; there was nothing in the newspaper about where to sign up. Then the spring farmwork became so pressing that he delayed his action even though he had learned about Dan Martin's efforts to attract enough men to form Prairieville's own infantry company.

Now, watching the marchers before him, he was indeed feeling the call to join them. He determined that he would enlist before the day was over. He would seek out the men from Prairieville's Company and tell them he wanted to join them.

It didn't take much effort. As soon as the parade ended, some of the marchers from the *Boys of '17* came back to mix with the crowd, looking for men of military age.

Two of them spotted a thin young man not far from Jon. They approached him boldly. "Hey, kid, you look old enough to fight. How 'bout joinin' us?"

"Thank you, but no thanks," said the youth politely.

"Why not? Ya' 'fraid? Ya' ain't a coward, are ya'?"

"No," replied the youth, his lips white.

"It's time to rally 'round the colors, kid. Ain'cha patriotic?"

The youth said nothing, but he glanced nervously behind him and took a half step backward.

The two soldiers pressed forward. One of them, a short dark-skinned boy with an impudent moustache, demanded, "Wha'cher name, kid?"

"I don't have to tell you," he replied, his chin trembling.

"Don't lip off to me," the soldier warned. "You don't do that to Blackie if ya' want to stay healthy."

"I know what yer name is, anyway" said Blackie's partner, a tall blond soldier. "Yer a kraut-head. Ya' won't fight against the Germans because yer a German yerself. Yer a traitor!"

"No, I'm not," the youth replied. "I'm not a traitor."

"Well, if yer not, then come along with us and sign up. We're from the new Prairieville Infantry Company. Our books are open, over in the Clarke Block."

The youth hesitated, not knowing how to answer. "I c-c-can't," he stammered. "I just can't. Not right now."

"Yer gonna' be drafted anyway, ya' know," said the blond soldier. "Ya' might as well beat the draft, and sign up with us. That way, yer gonna be with friends when ya' go overseas."

"I can't," the youth repeated. "Not yet."

"He thinks he's too good for us," said the dark-skinned soldier, his upper lip twisting his moustache into a sneer. "He's from one of the 'better families' in town, ya' can tell from his talk. He don't wanna mix with us common guys."

"Yeah," his light-haired partner agreed. "Blackie's right. That's why we can't fill our ranks. Hell, we ain't even halfway there yet."

The two soldiers had been gradually encroaching upon the youth with tiny shuffling steps. Now they pushed forward openly. "Mebbe we should help persuade ya' a little," one of them said. The youth shrank back from them, again glancing behind as though measuring his chances for escape.

"Let me go," he said. "I want to go to the rally in the Colonial Theater."

"You'll have plenty of time to get to the rally," said Blackie, "after you sign up."

Jonathan had been watching the drama with great interest. "Leave him alone!" he suddenly ordered.

Blackie and his blond partner stopped and looked quickly at the newcomer who spoke with such confidence. "Who are you?" one of them asked.

"My name is Jon, but that doesn't matter," he replied. "What does matter is that I want to enlist. You can forget about this man. I'll go with you quite willingly."

The two soldiers were taken aback at the new volunteer. They immediately lost interest in the thin youth, who quickly turned and disappeared into the crowd.

"C'mon, kid," said Blackie, recovering himself. "Let's go an' getcha signed up."

Prudence quickly extended a restraining hand. "Wait, Jon," she said. There was urgency in her tone.

"Wait, nothin!" declared Blackie. "Let's go." He grabbed Jon by the arm.

Ephraim quickly intervened. "Let go of him!" Blackie looked up, eyeing the muscular frame and determined face of the toughened farmer, and slowly withdrew his hand.

"Jon let's talk about this before you do something rash," resumed Prudence.

"Mom, this is not something rash. You know I've been thinking about it for a long time, and I made up my mind a month or so ago."

"But once you sign the papers, you can't back out. Let's just talk about it a little bit first."

"What's there to talk about? There's a war, and Uncle Sam needs men, and I'm the right age. I'll be drafted anyway; June fifth is Registry Day and I'm required to declare myself."

"No, Jon, you just turned twenty. You're supposed to be twenty-one. Registry Day is only for men from twenty-one through thirty."

"But Mom, I'm only a year away. I think I'm old enough."

"Yeah, he's old enough. We'll take him at twenty," the blond soldier commented.

"You don't have to do it, Jon," begged Prudence. "Please. Don't. Wait until you're twenty-one."

"I don't want to wait, Mother," said Jon patiently. "By then the war will be over, and I don't want to miss it."

"Oh, I don't think it'll end so quickly. It's been going for four years already, and from the news I read the battle-lines aren't changing very much."

"But once Uncle Sam gets into the fight, we'll win it in a hurry. Sure, it's kind of a stalemate right now, but the addition of a whole bunch of new troops from America will make a big difference. This is a once-in-a-lifetime chance for me, and I don't want to miss it."

"There's not much chance that you'll miss it. But if it's going to go as easy as you say, there's no need for you to get involved. They won't need you."

"Mother! Don't talk like that. I don't want to shirk my duty. If I don't join up, I'll always feel like I was a coward. I won't be able to hold my head up straight."

"Well, if you insist on joining the army, why don't you see if you can become an officer? I think officers get treated a little better."

"Mom, I don't want any special treatment. I am just a common ordinary guy, and I want to be treated like any other guy. I want to do what is right for my country."

"But we need you on the farm, Jon," she said. "We've been counting on you. You're the only son we've got."

"We've talked about that, Mother. Bruno will take my place until I get back."

Sarah had been quiet throughout the discussion between mother and son, but she could restrain herself no longer. "Let him go, Mom," she advised. "I'll be proud to have a brother fighting for his country. I wish I could go, too. But they won't let girls fight, so Jon will have to be my fighter."

She paused, but nobody spoke, so she continued: "Jon, just make sure all those guys come back soon. As I watch them march by, I keep thinking that somewhere out there is my future husband. I don't know who he is. But make sure he comes home again while I'm young enough to get married!"

"That's the problem," protested Prudence. "Some of those boys won't be coming back. And I couldn't stand it if you got killed over there, Jon!"

"I won't get killed," he replied. "But if it's God's will that I do, I'd rather die doing my duty than to live as a coward the rest of my life."

"Don't say that!" cried Prudence, as Sarah said simultaneously, "Good for you, Jon!"

"I'm sorry, Mom," Jon said soothingly. "I didn't mean to upset you. But I am absolutely determined to enlist and serve my country. And while I'm doing that, I may get a chance to see some of the world beyond Prairieville."

"Eeph, talk to him," she implored with tears in her voice.

"Prudy, it won't do no good. He's made up his mind, and nuttin' is gonna change it. Besides, it's the right thing t' do. If ya' step back a ways and look at it, you'll agree."

Jonathan smiled at his mother. "Come with me, Mom. I think we've missed the rally at the Colonial Theater, but I have a pretty good idea of what Reverend Logan would have said there. Come with me while I sign up and pick up some information. Then we can go home together."

They followed Blackie across the Five Points to the Clarke Building, where the enlistment office was located. The young man behind the desk was friendly but very businesslike. His name was Leo Herbst, he said, as he stood up to welcome the newcomer.

"We'll be glad to have you in our infantry company," said Leo with a smile.

"Thank you," replied Jon.

"You look like you are in good health," observed Leo.

"Yes, I am."

"Take off your shirt," Leo requested.

He walked around Jon, inspecting his torso. Then he felt the sides of Jon's neck below the ears, stared into his eyes, and watched him do a few stretching exercises.

"Open your mouth so I can check your throat," he instructed.

"Ah-h-h," said Jon with his tongue out.

"You pass," said Leo, reaching for a paper. "Sign right here."

There was no time to reconsider. Prudence gulped audibly as her son leaned over the desk to write his signature boldly on the contract. The moment was quickly over.

"We practice marching and drilling every evening at seven," Leo said, "up in the park at the corner of South Street and Barstow. You don't have to be there for every practice, but you should come for the next few evenings because we're getting ready to show off our close-order drill on Registry Day next Tuesday."

"I'll come every night," said Jon.

"Except Sunday," Leo told him. "We don't practice on Sunday."

"All right," said Jon.

"And we expect our unit to be called up by the middle of June. We'll be going to Camp Douglas, they tell us, to get started. Then we go to Texas."

"The sooner the better," said Jon.

The buggy ride back to the farm was in somber contrast to the joyfulness they had all felt on their ride into town that morning. Ephraim had felt such a strong sense of communion with Prudence then, but her estrangement now was painfully evident. He could not guess at the complexity of her thoughts, so he ascribed her reticence solely to her fears for Jon. All of them kept their own stone-faced thoughts, and it seemed that even Kaiser plodded along without the usual spring in his step.

Ephraim helped Prudence from the buggy at the door to her farmhouse, and he put his arms around her in a protective hug. She responded with unusual coolness, it seemed to him. "I'll put Kaiser in the barn," he told her, "and go straight to the milkin'."

After the chores were finished, after the evening meal was eaten, after all had gone to bed, Prudence was still agitated. She finally fell into a fitful sleep in her lonely bed, but it wasn't long before an appalling vision spread into her mind. She was a spectator amid a violent and terrifying battle being fought in deep darkness around a military trench. The night sky was laced with green streaks like hellish Northern Lights. Enormous explosions shook the ground and the whine of unseen bullets drove her into the safety of the excavated fortress.

Flares and fireworks overhead illuminated the depths of her shelter and she realized that the soldiers before her were all little boys—five or six years old, perhaps of kindergarten age. They were dressed in proper military uniforms and they wore steel helmets. Their guns were tipped with fixed bayonets. The boys were solemn and business-like as they went about their tasks. They wore white bandages which flashed in the murky gloom of the earthwork as Prudence realized most of them were injured and bleeding. Their uniforms, their weapons, and even the dirt walls of the trench were smeared with blood.

Suddenly she stepped upon a live body lying in the mud and a dry scream welled noiselessly from her lungs. Several of the uniformed children were now discernable on the trench floor—injured? Dying?

She fell to her knees in the mire and even before she looked into the face of the nearest child she recognized her son Jonathan. Another scream of anguish rose from her lungs. It broke from her trembling lips and she wakened from her fitful sleep to find herself shaking in her own bed at home.

Her nightgown was damp and sweaty. She lay on her mattress a few moments, recovering her full senses, and then she rose and crept across the hallway to Jon's room, half expecting to find him as a child of kindergarten age.

She looked in upon his untroubled face, and listened to his quiet breathing. Impulsively, she leaned over the side of his bed and kissed him lightly on the forehead. He stirred, but did not wake.

Satisfied but still uneasy, she returned to her lonely room to face the remainder of the night.

Registry Day arrived less than a week later. Governor Philipp called it "Duty Day." It was a day set aside by a proclamation of the President of the United States. Every young man between the ages of twenty-one and thirty was required to register so he might be selected for military service.

Authorities in Washington feared there would be riots and violence in Wisconsin because of the strong anti-war sentiments of the Germanic population. President Wilson was prepared to send troops to the Badger State if necessary to maintain order.

In Prairieville and throughout the county, the registration was to take place, precinct by precinct, at the polling places.

"It's like voting, except that voting is voluntary," explained Prudence after reading the newspaper. "The registration is compulsory. Even immigrants who have not yet become citizens must register."

Jonathan harnessed Kaiser and drove into Prairieville after lunch for the day's events.

Even though it was not required for him, he went at once to the Town Hall and signed up because he wanted to wear the khaki arm band given to each registrant by a Red Cross volunteer. He would have felt guilty without one. He told them with pride that he was a member of Prairieville's Company, and they laughed with him about how funny it would be if the men from the draft board selected his name for conscription and had to go to France to find him.

There was a parade, of course. Following hard on the heels of Decoration Day, it was the second big parade in less than a week. The

Registry Day parade was more professional, however, featuring the cadets from St. John's Military Academy in the western part of the county.

Prairieville's Company had held four drill practices since Jon's enlistment, and he had faithfully appeared for each one. Leo was his friend from the very first day, and proudly taught him everything he needed to know. Although he was still an amateur soldier, Jon had caught on quite naturally to the various commands and steps. Therefore, still wearing his farming overalls and plaid shirt, he took his place alongside Leo with the other members of the Company in the drill demonstration which followed the parade.

Afterward, he watched the ball game at the White Rock ballpark between the cadets from St. John's and a hometown team sponsored by the Jiffy-Jell company.

Registry Day passed without violence in Wisconsin. Federal troops were not needed. In fact, the Badger State was the first in the nation to report its registration completed. State officials sent a telegram at four A.M. the next morning announcing a tabulation of 218,700 eligible young men. General E.H. Crowder, the United States Draft Director, replied as follows to Governor Philipp in Madison: "I have come to expect the impossible from Wisconsin!"

Prudence did not go to Prairieville with Jonathan for Registry Day. She did not find it a cause for celebration. Her heart was filled with dread for the future—the future after Jon would march off to war.

After the noon dinner dishes were washed and put away, she began cleaning the house in an attempt to get her mind off her fears. The ploy didn't work. As the hands of the hallway clock moved with agonizing slowness in their prescribed circuit, she became almost panicky in her vivid imaginations of scenes from the war.

By this time in early June 1917, the war had settled into vicious fighting in the fields of France. Despite the slow and clumsy communication of the era, everybody knew the horrors of trench warfare, and everybody had heard the stories of British propagandists—stories of brutal Huns who bayoneted babies and raped Belgian nuns and tortured prisoners of war.

As she worked, Prudence remembered her nightmare and couldn't put it out of her mind. She re-lived the details over and over again, becoming more agitated with each memory. Her house-cleaning efforts became ever more vigorous, until she was fairly leaping around the room with frantic but purposeless action.

Realizing her foolishness, she finally she gave up trying to dust the furniture. She sank exhausted into the living room sofa in a turmoil of despair.

Lying there limp, she felt a coolness engulfing her body. At first she thought it was the natural result of her sudden inactivity, following the physical frenzy of her housecleaning. But soon the chill was accompanied by the same sense of a physical presence which had disturbed her in the kitchen when Jonathan had announced his decision to enlist. Frightened, she lay without moving while she cautiously opened her eyes and looked around. She quickly confirmed that there was no one in the room with her, as she knew.

Nevertheless, the chill insistently rolled over her body in waves, almost like the nausea she had felt in the early days of each pregnancy, increasing in intensity with each recurrence.

Her attention was suddenly attracted by a shadow in the window. It was motionless and she did not know how long it had been there but she recoiled in fright. It was a man staring through the window into the room, his silhouette starkly visible against the brightness of the afternoon daylight. She could not discern his face, but his head and shoulders were clearly outlined. He was wearing an ordinary farm hat, but no other details of his features or his clothing were recognizable.

"Zachary!" she cried instinctively, for the hat reminded her of him.

There was no reply, no sign of motion from the dark faceless shadow.

She did not know whether the man saw her on the sofa, because his eyes were hidden in the darkness of his face, but she felt that they stared at each other for many long minutes. She was unable to move. She was unable even to think. Her heart had stopped beating, she knew, and she felt no reason to breathe. Her hands were clammy with a cold sweat.

The shadowy specter extended its hand toward her, palm upward, in a gesture of intimate urgency.

She leaned forward in response but when she attempted to rise from the sofa the man quickly turned, showing the familiar profile of Zachary, and disappeared.

Immediately the chill was gone from the room and her full energy returned. She jumped from the sofa and dashed to the window to look outside.

There was no place for anyone to hide on the open lawn, and certainly no human being could have escaped so quickly even by sprinting. Yet the yard outside the house was empty. No one was there.

Chapter 8

The romance between Grace Lusk and Dr. David Roberts, revealed to Prudence by Theodora after the April meeting of the Women's Club, was known only through the quiet gossip of women in the club until it burst into the open in mid-June.

Grace's passion for the doctor had soared to heights she could no longer control. Their relationship had started innocently enough, when she assisted him in the writing of his book, *Cattle Breeds and Origins*. But while they worked together during the ensuing months, she fell in love with him passionately and possessively. The two had been to Chicago together several times, including a recent trip during which she pressured him to declare his love for her openly and leave his wife. He refused.

During May, Grace telephoned the veterinarian frequently, and the two met secretly at the County Line station of the interurban train between Prairieville and Milwaukee. They quarreled whenever they talked. At mid-month, Grace became jealous because Dr. Roberts refused another tryst in Chicago and took his wife to the theater in Milwaukee instead. He decided it would be best not to see her again privately.

The National Holstein-Freisian Breeders Association of America was holding their annual convention in Worcester, Massachusetts early in June, and Dr. Roberts had been thinking about going to it for it would benefit him professionally. He could scarcely afford the time away from his veterinary practice, and he was involved in selling some of his cattle at a current Holstein sale. Still, it might be the best thing for everyone if he gave Grace's passion a little time to cool.

Before he made a decision about the trip, Grace phoned and insisted upon meeting him again. He resisted the proposal, but she pleaded with him so insistently that he finally yielded to her and they met on the first day of June in the parlor of a Milwaukee hotel. They had dinner together in a private dining room. After they ate, they moved to a seat near the window.

"I have something to say to you," she began.

"Yes? Well, what is it?" the doctor asked.

She returned to the old subject, the impossible request. "I want you to tell me that you love me more than anybody else. I want you to tell Mrs. Roberts that we are in love with one another and that she must give you up."

"I can't do that, Grace," the doctor said.

"You must!"

"I cannot."

"Doctor, it was enough at first for me to see you every few weeks. It was enough because I knew you were passionately in love with me. You told me so. You showed me, with every action available to a man. In effect, you stopped being Mame's husband a long time ago and became mine. I was willing to wait, because I knew you loved me and because I knew that you would straighten everything out at the right time."

"Grace, I have never misled you," Dr. Roberts said. "I told you from the beginning that my marriage is sacred to me and we must not interfere with it."

"But you told me you loved me," she protested.

"Yes, Grace, I told you that, and I meant it," he reassured her. "But I've always insisted that our relationship must be kept confidential. We must not hurt Mame, no matter what we feel."

"I don't want to hurt Mame," Grace agreed. "She is a wonderfully good woman and doesn't deserve to be hurt. But I can't wait for you any longer. I don't deserve to be hurt either, but you are hurting me with every day you keep our love secret."

"I've always said our love must remain confidential, and you have agreed with me," he insisted.

"Well, that won't work any longer," she said wearily. "We've gone too far. I am your wife in everything but name, and it's time to end the charade. You've got to tell Mame, and you've got to do it now."

"But how can I do that without hurting her?" he asked.

"I don't care how you do it, but you must do it."

"You're being unreasonable, Grace. I would never have asked you to help with my book if I had known it would lead to this. You've known from the beginning that I would never break up my marriage with Mame."

Clearly flustered, the reddened schoolteacher rose from her seat and took a step or two toward the back of the room. With nervous fingers, she unfastened her wrist watch and laid it carefully on a little table between them. Then, with a resolute hand, she reached into her black purse and pulled out a small pistol.

Pointing the gun unsteadily at her astonished lover, she declared, "I am going to give you just five minutes to make up your mind as to whether you will tell Mrs. Roberts what I want you to tell her."

Dr. Roberts stood up and faced her. He could not believe what was happening. Grace couldn't be serious about the gun, he thought. Surely she must be joking, and he was in no mood for jokes. He moved toward her to confiscate the weapon.

"Stop!" she ordered, reading his intentions. "Don't come another step or I will kill you right where you stand."

She was serious. Deadly serious, he could tell. He froze, staring at her, expecting any moment to feel the impact of a bullet entering his chest.

There was a long pause while both of the protagonists silently took measure of each other. Then Grace pointed to a Bible lying on the table alongside her watch. "Dr. Roberts," she said evenly, "place your left hand on the Bible and raise your right hand. I want you to swear that you will go home and tell Mrs. Roberts that I am in love with you and you are in love with me and she must give you up. If you don't promise to do this, I will kill you and then kill myself and end it all."

Dr. Roberts thought for a brief moment, but then he saw the steel-eyed determination in her face and he did not want to die. He followed her commands and swore the oath, saying to himself that the words were of no consequence because they were spoken under duress.

"When do you want me to tell Mrs. Roberts?" he asked.

"Tomorrow," she directed.

He quickly decided to attend the Holstein-Freisian convention. "Why, tomorrow or the next day we are going East," he told her, "and I can't tell her before we go. It would ruin the trip. Let me tell her when we return."

Grace protested the delay, but after the doctor begged repeatedly, she finally agreed. "When will you be back from the East?" she inquired.

"I am planning to return by the middle of June."

"Then you will tell her?"

"Yes," he replied, saying to himself that he would agree to anything just to get through the day safely.

"Remember, you have promised," she reminded him.

"Grace, is this the way you feel about this whole affair?" he asked, hoping to restore her senses.

"This is the way I feel about it," she replied without hesitation.

"I am sorry," he said.

Having forced him to say what she wanted to hear, she was ready to conclude the meeting. "Don't try to take the gun," she warned. When he assented quietly, she replaced the pistol in her purse, straightened her clothes, and abruptly left the hotel.

With a sigh of relief, Dr. Roberts resolved never to meet Grace again. He drove home alone, a severely chastened man.

The next morning, Grace phoned the Roberts' residence and asked to speak to the veterinarian, who was not home. Although she didn't say exactly why she had called, Grace's tone of voice was so intimate and emotional and demanding that Mrs. Roberts was considerably disturbed. She had heard hints and rumors linking Grace to her husband, but this was the first overt evidence of trouble.

Returning to his home at noon, Dr. Roberts chanced to pick up the mail from the box near his front door. A personal envelope addressed to Mrs. Roberts caught his attention at once, for he recognized the handwriting of Grace Lusk. He slipped the letter into the inner pocket of his suit coat before entering the house.

When Mame told her husband about the phone call from Grace, he was further surprised and very angry. The letter and the phone call provided clear evidence that Grace had lost her senses and would no longer keep their relationship confidential. He decided he had better get out of town as soon as possible. "Pack our things," he told Mame. "We're leaving tomorrow for Massachusetts."

Grace had told Dr. Roberts that she would go to California in mid-June after the school year ended. She had a friend in Santa Barbara, she said, with whom she intended to spend the summer. The doctor was quite certain it was a male friend—he had heard she had other lovers.

To be certain Grace was gone before he returned to Prairieville, Dr. Roberts lingered in the East with his wife after the end of the cattle convention, traveling through Massachusetts and New York. They spoke of Grace only once, in a Boston hotel room, when he asked Mame, "Are you happy on this trip? Are you enjoying yourself?"

"Yes, Dave, I am," Mame replied, "but I would be a whole lot happier if Grace Lusk had not telephoned our home before we left."

"Mame, don't let that worry you," her husband said. "I love you more than any woman on the face of this earth and I want you always to remember that!"

Back in Prairieville, Grace waited anxiously day after day while Dr. Roberts was away. She thought about him constantly, and walked past his house on Wisconsin Avenue every few hours to see whether he had returned.

Finally, late in the evening of June 20th, she noticed lights in the windows of his house. He was back! And he had promised to tell every-thing to his wife as soon as they returned from their trip.

She walked past his house several times in the dark, hoping to find him outside, mustering the courage to confront him, to learn if he had kept his promise. She could see him through the window of his house, dining with his wife, his mother-in-law, and his nephew.

Finally, with pounding heart she climbed his porch steps and rang his doorbell.

Dr. Roberts fairly leaped from his seat at the table to answer the door. He stepped outside onto the porch to confront Grace, closing the door behind him.

"I have come to find out if you have told everything to your wife," Grace said at once.

"No, Grace, I haven't told her. We've just returned this evening. But I will tell her tomorrow."

"You're lying to me," Grace said excitedly, her voice rising. "You have put me off week after week, and you think you can do that forever. I want you to tell her right now. Right now, you understand?"

"No, Grace, I can't do that. I don't want to spoil the evening. I'll do it tomorrow."

The door opened, and Mame peered out. "Whatever you two are talk-ing about, you should say in front of me," she challenged them. "Come on inside where we can talk."

"No, I don't think that would be a good idea," Dr. Roberts said. He took Grace by the arm. "Let me walk you home."

"Mame is right," said Grace. "I think we should have it out right now."

"That would never do," argued the veterinarian. He took a step across the porch, dragging a reluctant Grace with him. "Let's get going," he said to her. Over his shoulder, he said to his wife, "I'll be right back."

Grace wasn't ready to leave, but she allowed the doctor to propel her down the steps and along the sidewalk. He was furious with her, and told her so. She was disrupting the peace of his home.

"It's one thing for us to meet in Milwaukee or Chicago, where we won't be seen by anybody we know," he scolded. "It's quite another thing for you to telephone my wife or come over to see me at home. I insist that you not do that again."

"Only if you keep your promise to tell her the truth," Grace said.

They walked angrily through Cutler Park, Dr. Roberts escorting her almost to her door on West Park Avenue. "Don't try to contact my wife again," he warned her as he turned to leave.

When he returned to his home, he was not surprised to discover that Mame was raging with bitterness and jealousy. She had sent their nephew home, and her mother had retired upstairs to her room.

"What's the meaning behind all this?" she demanded as soon as he was inside the house. "What's going on between you and *that woman*?"

"Well, Mame, it's not what it looks like."

"Then why did she come to our house tonight? What was she here for? I heard what she said. What is it that you're supposed to tell me?"

Dr. Roberts decided it would be best to brazen it out. His body stiffened into a posture of offended innocence. "The truth is, Grace seems to have fallen in love with me," he said. "I don't know why. I've never encouraged her."

Mame slapped both hands over her mouth to stifle a hysterical scream. She sank into a chair at the dinner table. "Oh, I thought so!" she exclaimed. "Those things I've been hearing, those horrible things, are true!"

"What things have you been hearing?" her husband inquired in a deliberately calm voice.

"Oh-h-h-h-h!" Mame doubled over atop the table, pushing aside dishes still filled with the remains of a half-eaten meal. A crystal wine goblet toppled, spilling its contents onto the tablecloth.

The doctor stared at the red stain which spread rapidly, unchecked, across the pure white linen, but he did not move.

Mame was sobbing now, her shoulders shaking violently.

"What things?" her husband repeated insistently.

Mame tried to answer, but could only choke out a few words through the heaving convulsions of her body. "Those stories—those rumors!" she spluttered.

"What rumors?"

"You know—people have hinted—people have whispered—your trips to Chicago—you have taken—*that woman*—to Chicago—secretly—you two—behind my back—you know!"

"Mame, Mame," he said, moving to her side and stroking her shoulders. "Mame, it's been nothing but business. Nothing but business. We went to see about publishing my book."

"She—*that woman*—went with you?"

"Yes, she went with me. It was all open and above board. Not a single thing was said or done by either of us that would reflect against us. We stopped at the same hotel, but she had her room and I had mine." He was recounting the way it had been on their first trip. He blocked from his mind the later trips; he didn't want to think about them.

She shook her shoulders to rid herself of the touch of his hand. He obliged, backing away a few steps.

"Mame, please!"

Slowly she raised her head from the table. The front of her hair was smeared with meat sauce. Her blotched face was wet with tears. "How could you!" she exclaimed. "How *could* you! How could you allow *that woman* to get ideas about you!"

"I didn't know," he replied. "I didn't know it was happening. It just happened, that's all."

"How *could* you!" she repeated.

"Mame, I treat every woman with respect and dignity. You know that because you know me. Most women get pretty tired of being taken for granted, but I never take anyone for granted. I treat every woman like a queen."

"Oh-h-h," Mame groaned.

"But I am not guilty of making Grace Lusk love me. I did not want her to fall in love with me. When she did, I could not help it. She did it of her own free will. I have tried to talk her out of it. I am sorry for her. I truly am sorry for her."

"Oh-h-h-h," Mame groaned again.

"I have tried to discourage her foolish fantasy," he continued, "but she is the damnedest little fool who ever lived. She has been chasing me to death."

Dr. Roberts strode back and forth across the highly-charged room, glancing at his distraught wife from time to time, protesting his innocence and his inability to cool the romantic fires raging in the heart of the schoolteacher. Finally he paused before her, and fixed her in his gaze. "Mame," he said as earnestly as he could, "I want to remind you of what I told you in Boston, for it is completely true and honest. I love you more than I love any other woman on the face of this earth, and I want you to remember that always."

With a great effort, Mame was able to quiet herself enough to reply. "I want to believe that, Dave, you know I do, but this is so terrible . . . it is so terrible!"

"Yes, I know it is terrible," he agreed, "but just trust me and everything will be all right."

They continued talking for a long time, and Dr. Roberts believed he was beginning to win her confidence and get the matter under his control. But then she startled him with a new determination. "Dave," she said, "I am going to see *that woman* tomorrow and talk to her."

"I don't think that is a good idea," her husband cautioned.

"My mother thinks I should do it," she replied.

"No, Mame, your mother is wrong. You mustn't see Grace. It will serve no useful purpose. Don't do it!"

"Why not?"

"Because she is extremely distraught and she doesn't know what she is saying. She has suddenly declared her love for me and she is very upset because I told her I do not love her in return. I have told her that I love you. And she has become very angry. Very unreasonable. She might say anything, even things that are not true, because she is so angry."

"I don't know, Dave, I just don't know. I want to talk with her. Mother thinks I should. I will call her first thing in the morning. I want to hear whatever she has to say, even if it isn't true."

"No, don't do that," he told her again. "Mame, I forbid you to see her. I forbid you even to call her. She will make up stories. She will lie to you. Her imagination has gone wild, and you can't believe anything she says. I forbid you to go."

Mame was not convinced, and the marital argument continued for an hour or more. Finally, exhausted from repeating the same thoughts over and over, they ended the discussion without a reconciliation and Mame went upstairs to prepare for bed. She was still crying.

Dr. Roberts, deeply troubled and fearful, went into the basement of the house and cut the telephone wires.

The next morning, Mame walked next door and succeeded in making a fateful phone call. Grace Lusk said she had something important to say, and they made an appointment for ten o'clock in Grace's office in the Y.M.C.A. building on South Street.

By chance, however, Dr. Roberts intercepted his wife on the steps of the Y.M.C.A. as he returned from the Post Office. He took her by the arm and marched her back to his office on Grand Avenue.

"Stay away from Grace Lusk," he told her again. "She is so upset that there is no telling what she might do."

"She wants to see me," Mame insisted. "She has something to tell me and I might as well hear it straight from her lips."

"Don't do it," he warned. "Remember, I am your husband and I forbid you to see her."

The veterinarian kept his wife with him the rest of the morning, but after lunching at home they separated as he returned to work. Fearful of what might happen, the doctor asked his business manager to watch his house and shadow Mrs. Roberts if she went anywhere.

The doctor's fears were well grounded. After a while, Mame left the house also. She walked in the shade beneath the beautiful elm trees which lined Wisconsin Avenue, past the Baptist Church and through Cutler Park. She took the same route her husband had followed the night before when he escorted Grace back to her boarding house.

Grace was alone in that house on West Park Avenue when Mary Roberts entered. At last, the two rivals for the love of the dapper doctor confronted each other in a showdown. The conversation was brief and to the point. "What do you want to tell me?" Mame asked.

"I want to tell you something that Dr. Roberts should have told you many months ago. I am in love with your husband and he is in love with me. Surely you have known for a long time that you were no longer first in his heart—that he cared for someone else. It must have been obvious to you."

"No, it has not been obvious," replied Mrs. Roberts with as much composure as she could muster. "How long has this been going on?"

"More than a year," Grace replied, taking a perverse delight in seeing the shock and pain in the eyes of the woman who was an obstacle to her happiness.

"You are mistaken," Mame said bravely. "You may have fallen in love with my husband, but the feelings have not been mutual. He does not love you. He is a kind and considerate man, and you have mistaken his kindness for affection. I repeat, he does not love you. I demand that you quit chasing him. I demand that you leave him alone, that you stop all communication with him immediately!"

Grace laughed, a staccato, cynical laugh. "I am not mistaken. When he entertains me at dinners in fancy restaurants, when he tells me I am the only one he cares for, when he kisses me with hot, eager kisses the way he used to kiss you, when he takes me to Chicago and reverently undresses me and sleeps with me—when he does these things you think he does not love me? I am mistaken? Hah!"

"You're lying through your teeth," said Mrs. Roberts. "Your imagination is running wild. You're making up stories to satisfy your fantasies. You're just trying to break up our marriage. You liar! You home-wrecker!"

"Don't you call me names, you self-righteous snob!" cried Grace. "Everything I say is true and you know it but you won't admit it because you want to look proper. You want to hang onto your husband for appearances even though you know his love for you died a long time ago. You have bullied him into submission."

"You little slut!" exclaimed Mrs. Roberts, her dignity collapsing. "You filthy whore! David loves me and no one else. I'll get him over here and prove it. I'll prove you're lying. David will come here and you will hear him say that he loves me more than anyone else on the face of this earth, just as he told me last night." She stepped over to the telephone and picked up the receiver.

While her nemesis was placing the call, Grace went upstairs to her room and returned with the same .25 calibre pistol she had used to threaten Dr. Roberts.

The veterinarian was not in his office to receive the phone call from his wife. His business manager had reported back to him with the ominous news of Mame's visit to Grace, and the two men were racing toward the boarding house on West Park Avenue.

They arrived just as two sharp gunshots were heard from within, followed after a pause by yet another.

Rushing inside, the two men found Mary Roberts dying on the floor of the parlor, while Grace Lusk was standing at the top of the stairway, weak and wobbling from a self-inflicted wound in the chest.

Dr. R.E. Davies was called. He arrived within a few minutes, and after bending over the blood-stained body, quickly declared that Mrs. Roberts was dead.

As she heard the fateful words, Grace sank to the floor at the top of the stairs. His attention drawn by her agonized moan, Dr. Davies looked up at the prostrate woman and asked, "What happened?"

"I shot her because she called me such awful names," Grace told him. "But I didn't intend to kill her. Oh, I want to die, I want to die!" She pressed her index finger to her breast. "Doctor, where is my heart? I want to shoot myself in the heart. Where is it, precisely?"

Dr. Davies directed her finger to a safe location on her chest. She put the muzzle there, and promptly shot off the tip of her finger, the bullet missing her heart again.

The chief of police, Don McKay, arrived with the coroner, and Grace was taken to the municipal hospital.

In the top drawer of Grace's dresser, a letter was found addressed to Mame, but never sent. It began with a disclosure of the love affair between herself and the doctor. At its conclusion, Grace wrote:

> *In the eternal triangle our souls require for their solution the elimination of one character. The two who should remain are the two whose affection is mutual. . . . Will you sometime read Ellen Key on* LOVE AND MARRIAGE?

The book *Love and Marriage,* of course, was the book Grace had reviewed for the Ideal Club at the request of Mame Roberts. It preached the philosophy of 'New Thought' which some people believed was an excuse for lapses from the moral code.

News of the murder whipped through the little town like a prairie fire. Theodora Youmans, at the newspaper office, was among the first to hear it. She went immediately to Grace's hospital bedside. There she found a very remorseful woman.

"My life is over," Grace told Theodora. "I had found what I thought was the great love of my life, but I have been sadly deceived. Dr. Roberts was simply toying with me while he led a respectable family life. He never intended to make our relationship honorable."

"Oh, Grace, how could you do such a thing? Mame was such a kind and generous woman. . . ."

"Yes, I know. She was the innocent victim. Deceiving her—hurting her—that was the one dishonorable thing Dr. Roberts and I did. Our love itself seemed so perfect and pure—he even said it was. But it couldn't be, because Mame was there. And she didn't deserve her fate."

"Quite right, she did not."

"Well, it's all over now. And I've made such a mess of it."

"We can't un-do it, can we," commented Theodora.

"Maybe there's some good that can come of it," suggested Grace. "I've been thinking clearly today for the first time in months. Mame's awful death was a shock that woke me up from the horrible nightmare I was living. It's all so plain to me now, and maybe there is some other woman who will see my example and change her own life before it is too late. I am of no importance, but my story is. I've thought and thought and thought, and that is the only possible good that I can see."

"It certainly is a powerful lesson," agreed Theodora.

"It is easy to understand why women get into affairs with married men. Women are usually interested in men who are the same age, or perhaps even older. But once you get past twenty-five, most of the men are married."

"Yes, that's true."

"You associate with men in business, and when you are together you don't remember their families. You come to think of them as unattached."

"But you were close friends with Mame. The two of you worked together in club work, and in our suffrage campaign. You probably saw her as much as you saw Dr. Roberts. She was no stranger to you."

"Yes, yes, that's true. But I seldom saw them together. I know it sounds foolish, and it is, but I came to think of them as two separate people, not attached to each other."

"I guess so," murmured Theodora.

"Then when you fall in love, you suddenly remember that you haven't the right. But that's the last thing you want to think of, so you put it aside and don't think about it at all."

"It's possible, I suppose."

"Then the heartaches begin. We try to right a wrong by straightening out, not our end, but the other end. It's that little selfish something in human nature. We deplore it in others, and when we see people act selfishly we can always see quite clearly how they should have done differently. But if we were all decent, generous, unselfish souls, as everyone should be, we wouldn't be here trying at so little and failing at so much."

Theodora had prepared herself to console her friend and fellow clubwoman. She had expected to do most of the talking, and had wondered how she could avoid the subject of the recent murder. But Grace wanted to talk, and she wanted to talk about the subject that was in the forefront of both of their minds.

"I was raised properly in a good family," Grace went on. "I had strict parents and good brothers always watching over me. I've always considered myself a good woman. But the great love came over me, and it came wrong—all wrong. It isn't safe to let yourself become the least bit fond of a man who is married. The first step that takes you away from friendship and toward love—that's the one to avoid. When you go home nights thinking about a man and go to sleep with his face in your mind and wake up thinking of him in the morning—perhaps having dreamed of him during the night—it isn't safe to go on with the friendship."

"We didn't realize. . . ."

"Of course not. How could you know? I put on a mask. I tried not to show my true feelings. But I was hungry for love and I found that his interest in me was very comforting and it kept me from being lonely. Of course I should have turned my back on the whole situation, but I could not -I simply could not! I loved him too, too much, and I believed with all my heart that he loved me the same way."

"I feel so sorry for you," Theodora said softly.

"You see, there is only one way a man can prove that he loves you, and that is to ask you to marry him. But a married man can't ask you that. A married man won't divorce his wife and marry the other woman. He'll keep up his double life as long as he can and drag it out as long as possible."

"You're probably right."

"Men love intrigue—it keeps them young. Then when the game is up and the man must quit one or the other, it is you, the other woman, he leaves to weep your heart out. It is you who must get back where you started, and you can't do it if you have gone too far."

"It is indeed a sad, sad story."

"For me it is too late," Grace repeated. "But if my story is heard by some other woman who can wake up and change her life while there is still time, perhaps some good can come out of my terrible ordeal."

Theodora and many other friends made frequent trips to the hospital until Grace's attorneys, fearing the spread of colorful gossip, ordered an end to all visitations.

Gossip there was. Salacious gossip, in the beginning. But as the days went by, Theodora recognized a subtle change in the tenor of the talking. At first the comments had centered upon the personal case at hand, but soon she realized the public opinion of the town was hardening in a posture unfriendly toward women's rights in general and clubwomen in particular.

"Women shouldn't be discussing free love," one man told Theodora. "It just gives them ideas."

"Books like Ellen Key's shouldn't be allowed to circulate in this country," said another.

"Women's clubs shouldn't be reviewing subversive literature."

"The whole idea of literary clubs for women is wrong. Nothing good can come from a bunch of women getting together by themselves."

"Women belong at home. Look what happens when you let them get out of the kitchen."

Isolated on the farm, Prudence did not learn of the terrible event until she read it in the newspaper a week later. By that time, the private funeral was over and Mame's body had been delivered to its grave in Prairie Home Cemetery by the pallbearers including Henry M. Youmans.

Instinctively, Prudence wanted to be with Theodora, to close ranks with a fellow clubwoman. She drove Kaiser into Prairieville at once, and met with Theodora in her office.

The newspaperwoman related to Prudence the events of the tragedy, and began to explain the significance of what was happening. "The whole concept of women's clubs is coming under fire," she explained. "After all, our clubs are only about twenty years old. Many people were against the idea in the first place, but the criticism had pretty well disappeared. Now all the old objections and complaints are being shouted again from the rooftops. Now we have become laughingstocks on the streets of the city."

"Laughingstocks?"

"Yes, and worse. You see, we had set ourselves up as harmless 'literary clubs' to gain acceptance by the community. In truth, that was simply a cover for our more fundamental purpose of joining together in unity to pursue the goals of the whole women's movement. It was the only way we could meet. Of course, we have been literary clubs in part, as we have tried to educate ourselves by reading and reviewing books together. But now, even a simple thing like a book review is being looked upon as dangerous and undermining to the public morals. It's humiliating, and it strikes a body blow to our hopes for suffrage."

"Yes, I understand," said Prudence. "I remember only too well the accusations of that nasty man in Oshkosh last month—he predicted that when men and women mix together away from their homes and their spouses, there will be jealousies and arguments and love affairs. I don't think he mentioned murders—he didn't want to go to extremes—but I guess it has already happened."

"Well, it's certainly going to be hard to overcome arguments like his, in the light of this murder of one clubwoman by another. As if we didn't have troubles enough just by ourselves."

"Troubles?" asked Prudence.

"Yes, Zona Gale—our First Vice President—has resigned from the Wisconsin Women Suffrage Association because the organization is supporting Wilson and his war effort."

"You told me that might happen," observed Prudence.

"Yes, I saw it coming. And it probably will get worse. Meta Berger, wife of the Congressman, is taking her place as First Vice President, and I don't know how long Meta will stay with us. She too opposes the war."

"It looks like we've reached a low point in our campaign," said Prudence.

"Yes," Theodora agreed. "Things haven't looked this bad for us in Wisconsin since the referendum was defeated five years ago. And the irony of it all is that I truly believe our support of Wilson will pay off in helping to pass an amendment to the Federal Constitution which will bring us the final victory."

"I want to help," Prudence said.

"We need your help more than ever now," Theodora said. "Mame and Grace were two of our best supporters. Now they both are gone."

"The job may be harder now," said Prudence, "but it will make our victory all the sweeter!"

Chapter 9

"Look at them Northern Lights, Sarah!" Ephraim exclaimed. The sun had disappeared beneath the western horizon an hour or two earlier while she was cleaning his house. Now the work of the long July day was finished, and they were halfway through the short walk along River Road to her home. They had walked almost halfway before they became aware of the heavenly spectacle overhead.

They paused in the dark stillness of the moonless night and stared upward at the extraordinary display of Aurora Borealis.

"I've never seen them so beautiful," she breathed softly. Her arm slipped around his waist, and he responded in the same manner. They stood motionless for a long time as the broad avenues of light coursed across the heavens. The misty whites of the basic streams were tinged with pale mint and raspberry, continuously but almost imperceptibly pulsating and changing in hue.

"It's magnificent," commented Ephraim.

"God's creations are magnificent beyond comprehension," agreed Sarah.

After further meditation, Ephraim said, "The sky is filled wit' many moods tonight. It reminds me o' Prudence."

Indeed, Prudence was never very far from Ephraim's mind.

"How does it remind you of my mother?" prompted Sarah.

Ephraim struggled to put his feelings into words. "Oh, I dunno. Mebbe it's the peacefulness of it all. The silence. The mystery. The feelin' that somethin' important's happening but we can't know what it is, we can only guess at it. We can only see the quiet little expressions that flash across 'er face. Well, they don't flash suddenly, they just seem to. Actually, they develop so gradually that you ain't aware of 'em comin' n' goin'. One minute her face is sayin' nothin' at all, and then suddenly you recognize somethin' very clearly in 'er features, like surprise, or impatience, or joy, or . . . or love . . . and then ya' blink yer eyes and look again and it's gone. Only you'd swear that nothin' changed. She didn't smile, or frown, or wrinkle 'er nose. Not a muscle moved durin' the whole time, yet fer a brief moment there was somethin' in 'er face that gave you a look at somethin' that's usually hidden."

"I think I know what you mean," said Sarah.

"An' then the next time ya' look at 'er ya' see somethin' entirely different. But yet it's always the same face."

"Yeah, you're right," said Sarah.

"Well, it's like that day we went t' town fer the parade," Ephraim continued. "Remember?"

"Yes. I remember."

"On the way t' town, I kept lookin' at 'er face because it was so happy. It was soft, or somethin'. Every time I looked it was somethin' fresh, and beautiful, but different from a few minutes before. Like the Lights." He pointed up into the sky. "Sarah, I coulda' swore she loved me then. Like I'd never known before. She smiled at me. She made me feel like I was somebody. Somebody important. That's what a woman—the right woman—kin do fer ya'. Know what I mean?"

He saw a sudden startled insight flash across the girl's face, and he realized with astonishment he was telling her more than he had ever revealed before.

"Oh, I suppose I shouldn't be sayin' these things t' ya," his words stumbled on. "If the sun was shinin', an' ya' could see my face, I wouldn't dare to say 'em."

He paused, embarrassed and confused.

"Don't stop," she begged. "Go on. I want to hear what you're saying. I really do."

"I've said too much," he muttered.

They stood there at the edge of the road, two figures fused into one dark shadow, while the sky sheltered them with its cold, shimmering exhibition.

The girl's comprehension deepened and she turned her head to gaze at his uplifted face; in that instant she recognized something that had developed quietly in her consciousness without much of anything changing, like the Northern Lights; it had been there right in front of her for a long time without her seeing it. "You told me once," she said quietly, "that you met a woman a long time ago—the 'right woman,' you said."

"Well, I thought so then," he said, trying to downplay the subject.

"She wasn't ready for you then, you said, but you still hoped after all these years that someday . . . ."

"Yes," he said slowly. He realized she had stumbled onto the truth, at least a part of the truth, and he wasn't sure he wanted her to know.

". . .Someday she would come to you and be your wife."

"A guy gets crazy thoughts sometimes," he responded, "but then ya' get straightened out agin."

She stared at him, trying to read his face by the dim light of the heavens. "You're talking about ... you're talking about ... my mother!" she exclaimed.

He finally looked down at her. "Well, there was a time," he said simply. "There was a time I thought yer mother was the right woman."

"My mother. My mother! You've been in love with my mother for all these years?"

They were looking earnestly at each other, oblivious now to the phantasmagoria above them. "I guess I could fall in love wit' her agin," he said evasively.

"Oh, Uncle Eeph!" she cried, turning toward him and clutching him to herself in desperation. They hugged each other without speaking for a long, long time, her head firmly nestled against his shoulder.

When she finally spoke, her voice was so soft that he could scarcely hear her words. "Of course, I knew you had courted Mom back before she was married to Dad. I never really thought about it as I grew older. I guess I just assumed it was a fleeting emotion, a brief and rather innocent phase of your youth."

"That is what I wanted everybody t' think. I put my sentiments aside. I could hardly ha' been a close friend of the family if I was forever houndin' yer mother, with her bein' a married woman an' all. So I had t' cover up my feelings."

"Oh, Uncle Eeph!" she exclaimed again. "How touching! How beautiful! And yet, how sad!"

"No, Sarah, not sad. I been happy just bein' around her an' the family. I been able t' see her, an' talk with her, almost every single day. I am a lucky man. Indeed, I am a very lucky man."

"Did Mom know you how you felt all this time?" asked Sarah.

"I s'pose she did, but we never talked about it. I done my best to be around t' help her fer whatever she needed, without ever lettin' 'er be uncomfortable about it. I think she likes it, knowin' she can always count on me."

"Now that Dad is gone, have you told her you're in love with her?"

"Not in such direct words. It's too soon t' talk about it. But she knows it. She couldn't help but know it."

She squeezed him again. "Somehow," she murmured, "this makes me happy inside. Everything is going to turn out for the best, I just know it. And I am very, very happy about it."

116

"You don't mind, really? Ya' wouldn't mind if someday I could get yer mother t' marry me?"

"No, I wouldn't mind. It would seem perfectly right. After all, you have been so very close to our family. I've always considered you a most wonderful uncle; Mom has taught me to think of you in that light. And ever since Dad died, I have looked upon you as something even more— I've thought of you as my father, almost."

She leaned back and looked up into his face again. "It would be wonderful, simply wonderful, to have you as my new father!" Then once again she wrapped her arms around him. He responded by gently stroking the back of her head.

After a while, he said, "I was tellin' ya' earlier about how the Northern Lights reminded me of Prudence."

"Yes, I remember. Do go on."

"Well, it's in the quiet way they come and go and constantly change. Your mother was so happy on the way t' town fer that parade, but then somethin' changed. I could feel it comin' over her while we watched the boys marchin'."

"What could you feel?"

"I don't rightly know. But she kept lookin' at me sideways, and there was feelin's written on her face that I ain't never seen before. She wasn't content no more. I don't think she said a single word on the way home that day, an' she wouldn't look at me, either. She's been that way ever since. I've been meanin' t' ask ya' about it."

"I've noticed it too," Sarah agreed. Especially since Registry Day. I came downstairs that day in the middle of the afternoon after cleaning my room, and I found Mom extremely upset. She was nervous and trembling, and her face was so white I thought she had seen a ghost. But she insisted nothing was wrong, that she had just gotten too hot washing the dishes. That didn't sound right to me, but she wouldn't say anything else."

"I know she's worried about Jon goin' in t' the Guards and goin' off t' war," said Ephraim. "But is that the whole thing? Or is there somethin' else?"

"What else could there be?"

"Well, she ain't mad at me, is she? Did I do something wrong durin' that holiday?"

"I don't think so," replied Sarah. "I'm certainly not aware of anything like that."

"That's good," said Ephraim.

"I'll let you know if I find out anything," Sarah said. "And from now on, I'm going to think of you as my new father."

"Be careful about that, Sarah," he warned. "Yer mother has a mind of her own, an' if she thinks we're takin' anything for granted, she'll get as stubborn as an ornery old cow."

"I'll be careful," she said, and the two of them resumed their journey to her home, walking charily with heightened sensitivity to the worlds emerging around them.

Sarah kept his confidence, as he knew she would, but she began a quiet campaign to assist Ephraim's modern-day courtship of his old-time sweetheart.

A few days later, Prudence and Sarah attended the wedding of Theodora's stepson, Henry, who had returned from his military training in Chicago.

Prudence found Theodora still depressed by the murder of Mame Roberts, and full of self-doubts about her ability for the moment to pursue the suffragist campaign.

"I'm supposed to go to a meeting in Beaver Dam next week to discuss women suffrage, but I just don't feel up to it," Theodora confessed. "I haven't told the women up there yet, but I think I'll call them tomorrow and back out."

Prudence glanced quickly at her daughter. "Do you think I could spare the time to go?"

"Of course," Sarah replied without hesitation. "Jon is still home; they haven't called up Prairieville's company yet. Robert is there, and Bruno Hilley is helping out already. And I'm almost as good as a man when it comes to farm work."

"Almost as good?" repeated Prudence, smiling. "You work harder than they do, and you know it. You're worth twice as much as any of them."

"We'd better not tell them that," laughed Sarah.

"No, that's our little secret," Prudence agreed.

"Men are so funny, aren't they?" commented Theodora lightly. "It's not enough for them to know that they are bigger and stronger. They also want to think that they are smarter and more important, too."

"That's what this suffrage campaign is all about, isn't it?" said Prudence.

"Yes, I guess it is. We women want to prove that our opinions carry some weight, too."

"Equal weight," added Prudence. "Equal weight. A woman's vote should count just as much as a man's."

Theodora sighed. "But sometimes I wonder whether maybe we're being too pushy. For generations, we've been humble helpers for men. We've been content to stay at home and keep house and raise children and support our men. Maybe that's the way it should be. Maybe we shouldn't be in such a hurry to give up our humility."

"It says in the Bible that God created woman to be a "helpmeet" for man," offered Sarah, "and after the Fall, God told the woman that her husband would rule over her."

"Leave it to Sarah to remind us of God's word," Prudence remarked kindly. "She is our resident theologian."

Theodora wrinkled up her face. "Well, when you get to the New Testament," she said, "St. Paul says men and women are equal in the sight of God. So why shouldn't we be bold enough to ask for equality when it comes to voting?"

"There's no reason why we shouldn't," agreed Prudence. "There's nothing wrong with that."

"And yet . . . and yet . . . and yet just as we begin to win what we want, Grace Lusk comes along and reminds us of what the consequences of our boldness can be."

"There's no connection," Prudence said. "Murders have been going on in this world ever since Cain grew jealous of Able. It has nothing to do with the rights of women."

"I keep telling myself that," said Theodora. But somehow, my confidence is a bit shaken right now. That's why I don't think I could plead our case very well for my friend up in Beaver Dam."

"Well, I can," said Prudence. "And I want to go."

"All right," Theodora agreed with relief. She dug into her cavernous handbag and pulled out a scrap of paper. "Here's her name—Jordan. Mrs. Matilda Jordan. I'll write that down for you, along with her address. The meeting will be at her house on Park Avenue. There's a light luncheon, I believe, and a gathering of perhaps a dozen women. I think it will be a friendly group, but one is never sure with such a controversial subject. Anyway, it's next Thursday at noon."

"I'll be there," promised Prudence.

"Okay. I'll call her to let her know."

It was milking time when they returned home; the cattle had gathered themselves in the barn lot and were waiting patiently for the gate to be opened. Prudence was so excited about her assignment that she told Sarah to take care of Kaiser while she went to search for Robert.

She found him in the cow barn; he was just finishing pouring the daily ration of ground grain into the mangers for the cattle.

"Robert!" she called excitedly as she stepped up into one of the stalls to approach him.

"Yes, Ma'am," he said, looking up from his task. "Oh, Miz' Hartmann, you shouldn't be here in the barn with yer fancy clothes on. You'll get all smelly!"

"You're probably right, Robert," she said, "and thank you for being concerned about me. But I don't care if I do get all smelly. I'm so excited!

I've got a chance to go to Beaver Dam next Thursday for a meeting, if I can get there. Would you let me take your motorcycle? Please?"

He looked down into her eager eyes and he smiled. "Of course ya' can take the Harley," he said. "Are ya' goin' off t' one o' them suffrage meetin's?"

"That's right," she said. "It's my first chance to do it all my myself, without Theodora being along."

Robert suddenly turned serious. "Are ya' sure yer ready to go such a long way by yerself?"

"Sure I'm sure. What could go wrong?" she asked.

"Oh, almost anything could go wrong. Mind you, my motorcycle is in top-notch shape. I'm proud of my *Gray Ghost* an' I spend hours an' hours takin' care of it."

"I know you do, Robert."

"But still, ya' could get a flat tire—the front one's a bit thin, and I been thinkin' I oughta' shell out the cash fer a new tire one of these days. Or ya' could run out of gas, or ya' could have some kind of mechanical breakdown."

She laughed. "I'll be careful to put gas in it when it gets low," she assured him. "And I'll be glad to take my chances on a breakdown. I know how much time you spend fussing over that prize, and I'm sure it's very dependable."

He grinned. "Well, yer right. I love that li'l two-wheeled beast, and I take good care of it."

"As for the flat tires, I think I could learn to fix a flat. Would you be willing to teach me sometime?"

"Ya' know I would," he said, smiling again. "T'morrow's Sunday. We'll go t' church early as usual, an' we'll have dinner at noon, 'n how 'bout takin' a lesson on fixin' flats soon as the dishes are done?"

"It's a date, Robert," she laughed. "We'll go to church together, and you and Eeph come and have dinner with us. Then we'll have a school on fixing flats. You be the teacher, and I'll be the student."

It had become a habit for all five to squeeze into the buggy every Sunday morning and let Kaiser take them to the Reedsville town hall for church. They had no regular pastor during those years, so they relied on a minister from one of the churches in Prairieville to come out each week. The services were held early in the morning to allow the minister to return to his home church for the regular eleven o'clock service of his own.

Afterward, sometimes Prudence would invite Eeph and his cousin to join the Hartmann family for their noon dinner.

On this occasion, as always, the men were quick to accept.

"Thank you for yer hospitality, Ma'am," said Robert. "Eeph and me will be glad t' come. It's always a pleasure t' have dinner wit' yer family. It sure beats what we fix by ourselves, an' we don't have t' do dishes, neither."

Prudence found it hard to go to sleep that night, filled as she was with two fresh anticipations. In just four days she would be off, all by herself, on her first adventure as a suffragist. And she would be taking her first long motorcycle trip! It seemed to her that life had never been so full of promise.

It was cloudy the next afternoon, with occasional light sprinkles of rain—enough to be annoying, but not enough to help the crops. As soon as dinner was over, Robert walked back to Eeph's house and returned with his motorcycle. He took it to the floor of the barn loft to be out of the rain. Prudence and the others arrived, dishes washed and dried, and found him ready with his tools and materials.

"I'm here, Robert," she announced.

"Yes, Ma'am," he said with his usual politeness. He stood upright, ramrod straight, and stepped out from behind his machine.

"If the tire goes flat while yer ridin', ya' gotta' be sure ya' keep a tight control. Especially if it's the front tire, ya' can lose control of the motorcycle an' ya' could even crash. The secret is to have a really firm hold on the handlegrips. If ya' feel the ride gettin' kinda' squishy, ya' better tighten yer grip as hard as ya' can, an' slow down an' stop until you can check out the tires and make sure they're okay.

"The long and short of it is it's real important to check the tires carefully each time yer gonna' take a ride."

"Are you still sure you want to drive that machine, Mom?" asked Sarah. "It sounds pretty dangerous to me."

"Yes, I'm sure," replied her mother. "It's one of the most enjoyable things I've ever done in my life. And I'll be careful."

Robert let the air out of the front tire. He grabbed a wrench and showed Prudence how to remove the wheel from the motorcycle. With difficulty he separated the tire casing from the rim and pulled the inner tube from the casing.

"Once ya' have the inner tube in yer hands, it's an easy matter t' put the patch on it if ya' can spot the leak. Usually you can find it simply by pumping air into the tube, and listening fer where it leaks out. But if that don't do the trick, then ya' hafta' pump up the tube and hold it in a bucket o' water to see where the bubbles come from."

"It sounds pretty complicated to me," Sarah complained.

"No, I think I understand it," said Prudence. "I think I could handle it if I had to."

Robert showed Prudence how to glue the patch on the tube. "These new patches are easy as pie," he said. "Used t' be, ya' had to heat 'em up t' make 'em stick. Now ya' jus' put the glue on and let it dry fer a few moments."

He reassembled the tire, inflated it with a hand pump, and replaced it on the cycle. "That's all there is to it," he said. "I've showed ya' the whole job, but ya' won't really learn it unless ya' do it yerself. So I'll jus' stan' by and watch while ya' do it all over again."

Prudence laughed lightly. "Thanks, Robert, but I don't think I need the practice. I watched you quite carefully, and I think I know enough about it to muddle through if I ever have to."

"You're a great teacher," commented Jon, "but I hope my mother never has a flat tire out on the road."

"Well, I hope so too," said Robert. "But it's good t' know how t' fix it if ya' hafta. Are ya' sure ya' don't wanna run through it once right now, just to be sure ya' got it?"

"Thank you, Robert, I'm very grateful, but I've had enough mechanical lessons for one day."

It was raining a bit harder now. Prudence walked over to the big doorway of the loft and looked out at the house and the fields beyond. Ephraim came up alongside and she allowed him to put his arm around her waist.

"I know how proud ya' are," he said, "an' how much you want t' be independent. But I'd like t' go wit' ya' when ya' go t' Beaver Dam. Wit' that sidecar attached, there's room fer us both."

"No, Eeph," she replied. "I appreciate your gallantry, but I want to go by myself."

"Don't be foolish, Prudence," he admonished. "It's a long trip on a motorcycle, and the roads ain't good. The chance of having trouble along the way is pretty darn strong. An' I'd want t' be there t' help ya'."

"Thanks again," she said firmly, turning away from him, "but this is something I've got to do alone."

Sarah and Jon likewise failed in their attempts to argue against her solitary journey. She was determined to go by herself. "I'm expanding my horizons," she told them. "I'm testing my limits, to see what I can do."

Prudence devoted the rest of the afternoon to cutting and sewing a big yellow banner with the slogan, 'VOTES FOR WOMEN' displayed across it in bold black letters. She attached it to a wooden mop handle so she could wave it easily.

During the next few days, Prudence prepared for the meeting in Beaver Dam, writing a brief outline of her remarks and giving little talks to herself in her bedroom mirror. 'Don't get so nervous,' she told herself. 'After all, it's only a gathering of a few of Matilda Jordan's friends in her home. Just pretend it's a social visit.'

By Thursday morning she felt she was as ready as she would ever be.

She dressed in new blue denim pants and a plaid shirt borrowed from Zachary's closet. She was in high spirits, and hummed a march from John Philip Sousa as she bustled about after breakfast.

Robert rode his motorcycle to her door as he had promised, with Eeph trotting alongside.

"One last word, Prudence?" Eeph begged.

"No," she said, putting both hands over her ears. "Don't say it, for I won't listen to you."

Robert's tools and equipment were loaded into the sidecar, along with her small satchel containing a skirt and blouse for the meeting. She included a few suffragist pamphlets given to her by Theodora, and road maps for the three counties she would ride through. She mounted the homemade yellow banner on the back of the cycle so everybody could read the proud words, 'VOTES FOR WOMEN' as she rode past.

She slipped on her goggles and mounted the *Gray Ghost*, having allowed an extra hour's cushion for the journey. The sky was overcast with the clouds of the changing weather drifting from the west, but the approaching rain was developing slowly. She expected to be back home long before it arrived in Prairieville.

Jon and Sarah joined the two men in seeing her off and wishing her well. Eeph stood alongside for a few moments, grasping the handlebar. "Are ya' sure ya' won't let me come along an' help?" he pleaded.

"I'm sure," she replied.

"There's a lot violence in the air," Eeph said soberly. "Mebbe it's the war fever. You know they've been beatin' up Germans all over Wisconsin. Honest American citizens who happen to be from Germany."

"Now who's been telling you things like that?" Prudence asked with a patient smile.

"Bruno told me about a lot of it. He says he knows of a couple of cases where they actually murdered Germans in Wisconsin."

"Oh, I think maybe Bruno is imagining things."

"No, Mom," said Jon earnestly. "I've heard about it during our drill practice. Even the governor is worried about it, because of the unprovoked personal attacks."

"Well, I'll be very quiet about my German background," said Prudence, laughing gently. "I won't flaunt my Iron Cross or salute the Kaiser in public."

"Let me come wit' ya'," pleaded Eeph once more.

"No, Eeph," she replied firmly. "Today I'm on my own."

"Be careful, Prudy," he warned again. "There's violence in the air, I tell ya'. If they'll fight about the war, they'll fight about women votin', too, I bet."

"Eeph, I will be careful. I promise you. And now, let me go, or I'll be late to my very first rally."

She started forward, and Eeph ran alongside for a few yards. "Be careful, Prudy, be careful!" he shouted.

With a cheery smile and a wave of her hand, she spurted ahead. He dropped behind and stopped at the foot of the driveway as she turned north on River Road and increased her speed.

Once again she experienced the exhilarating sense of liberation as she dashed along, feeling the wind against her face. The Pishtaka River paralleled the road for a mile or so, and she smelled its cool damp air. Red-winged blackbirds circled high around her head; she knew they were chattering at her but she could scarcely hear them over the puttering of her motorcycle. She saw a pair of blue-winged teal flying low along the riverbank.

The road turned abruptly, and she crossed the river on a short steel bridge, spotting a turtle at the edge of the water. Then she began the short climb uphill to Reedsville Road, and the marshlands were left behind.

It was a perfect day for cycling, with no sun and little wind. She found her heart singing for joy, with the song occasionally erupting into lilting words thrust out before her as she hurried along the dusty backcountry roads.

There was very little traffic. Occasionally she met an oncoming horse and wagon or passed a farm tractor, but most of the time there was no other vehicle in sight in either direction.

She stopped occasionally at quiet intersections to check her maps. Her navigation was true, and she arrived in Oconomowoc within the hour's time she had anticipated. After filling the gas tank, she took the road toward Watertown. It was more heavily traveled, but then she found quiet dirt roads for the last part of her journey.

Within a few miles of her destination, the road became badly rutted with the washboard effect common in that age. The incessant bumps jarred her body and threatened her thin tires, even through she throttled back and traveled cautiously.

Her concern proved justified a few minutes later as she heard a loud pop and realized the front tire had gone flat.

"Oh, no!" she sighed as she steered the motorcycle off to the flat edge of the road and dismounted. "I guess I'm going to find out how well I learned my lessons."

Grimly she unpacked Robert's tools and set to work. She had already removed the wheel, and was attempting to free the tire casing when she was joined by two husky boys from a nearby farm.

"Here," said the older boy. "We'll help ya'." He knelt down and took the wheel from her hands.

The two boys worked without talking, and Prudence stood by and watched as they pried the tire from the rim and removed the inner tube.

"Here's yer problem," the boy said, flexing the empty tire casing. "There's a break, see?" He pushed against the tire from the inside, and she could see his finger through the break.

"Joe, run up to the barn and get that leather liner, ya' know what I mean?"

Joe nodded and set off at a trot while the older boy turned his attention to the inner tube. Having marked the tube's location against the tire, he now matched it with the break and quickly identified the leak. By the time Joe returned, a new patch was in place.

"This'll last fer a little while," Joe said, slipping the liner inside the tire before stuffing the tube back in place. "But ya' ain't got much tread left on this tire, an' ya' better get a new one as soon as ya' can."

When they were done, Prudence pulled Zachary's old wallet from her pocket and offered to pay the boys, but they solemnly refused. "No thanks, Ma'am," said the older one, "we was jus' glad t' help."

They wouldn't even give her their full names. "I'm Jim and this is m' brother Joe," is all she could elicit from them before they turned and walked away.

The road was rough for another mile or two, so Prudence rode very slowly to minimize the bumps. Having allowed extra time, she arrived at Matilda Jordan's lovely home on Park Avenue in Beaver Dam well before noon and found three women waiting for her. They were amazed to see her alight from a motorcycle, but Prudence quickly brushed aside their comments and asked to be shown to a room so she could change clothes.

"We had planned to meet right here in my home," Matilda said, "but so many women wanted to hear you that we decided to go down to a little restaurant called *The Wedge* on Front Street. It's only a couple of blocks away, and we can walk."

There were about twenty-five women seated at tables in a large open room at *The Wedge*. Prudence marched bravely to the front and raised her yellow banner where all could see it. She was treated with deference, which served to increase her apprehension. She had very little appetite for the beef broth and sandwiches set before her. She had thought it would be a small gathering of friends in a parlor, but now it was a large formal group in a public setting. This would be her first appearance as the main speaker anywhere, and she began to wonder whether she had volunteered too quickly. She was comforted by the thought that nobody at the meeting knew her, and she could leave town as soon as the meeting ended.

She was amused when Matilda Jordan introduced her as "one of the leaders of the Wisconsin Women Suffrage Association," but she was too frightened to smile at the exaggeration. She rose, trembling like a music student at her first recital, and began.

Her opening remarks detailed some of the history of the suffrage movement, as she had learned it from Theodora. She was nervous at first, and she found herself stuttering—something she had never done before in her life. Then one of the women sitting close to her podium smiled at her in a sympathetic manner, and Prudence decided to talk to her as though there were only the two of them in the room. Later she found another friendly face near the back of the crowd, and she alternated her attention between the two listeners.

When the history lesson was over, she launched into her three-point speech about why women should be able to vote. As she warmed to her audience, her fears dissipated and she began to speak with poise and authority.

"First, we should vote because women are intelligent," she said, "and can contribute good judgment to political discussion.

"Second, we should vote because women are compassionate, and can bring the quality of mercy to the level of government—maybe even saving us from warfare.

"Third, we should vote because it is right. Men and women are equal in the sight of God, and should be treated equally in the laws of man."

Toward the end of her talk, she saw three teen-aged boys drift into the back of the room. She never knew whether they wandered in accidentally or with arguments in mind, but it soon became obvious they did not like what they were hearing. They remained standing, lounging insolently against the wall, making disruptive comments to each other in tones that gradually became louder. They would not heed the reproving glances of the women who turned to scowl at them. Prudence ignored them as best she could, and continued speaking, but she was glad she was nearing the end of her remarks.

The hecklers grew bolder as the minutes passed, and soon they began shouting their taunts directly at the speaker. "Siddown, lady, and shuddup!" and "Go back to the goddam kitchen!" they cried, along with other profane insults.

Prudence tolerated the clamor as long as she could, but her patience eventually came to an end. She grasped her yellow banner and walked slowly toward the back of the room toward the boys. As she approached, they became quiet, waiting to see what she would do. Stopping ten feet away, she fixed them in her gaze and tried to look very stern. She shook her mop handle at them, making the banner flutter before their faces. For ten or fifteen seconds there was complete and utter silence in the room. When she spoke at last, her voice was heavy with scorn. "Grow up, boys," is all she said before turning on her heel and striding back to the front of the room.

The owner of *The Wedge* appeared, having been summoned by a waitress, and he escorted the boys from the room without further disturbance.

Prudence finished her talk, and the women lingered in conversation for nearly an hour. They were strengthened by the knowledge they were not alone in their efforts, and they enjoyed the comradeship of their sister from Prairieville.

The three rowdy boys were waiting for them on the sidewalk outside the restaurant, and she had to run the gauntlet of their scoffs and threats as she and Matilda began walking. By the time they reached the Jordan home, the boys had been left behind.

"You did a magnificent job," Matilda told her as she emerged from the bedroom dressed again in her traveling clothes. "I can see why you're one of the leaders."

Prudence smiled. There was no reason now to tell her friend that this was her very first public speech. "Where's the nearest filling station?" she asked. "I want to have a full tank of gas to start home with."

Matilda gave her the directions, and Prudence cranked her machine into life. "Goodby," she shouted. "Thanks for the chance to talk with your friends."

Later, as the tank was topped off and she opened Zachary's wallet to pay for the fuel, she saw a dark open touring car cruise slowly past. Her three tormentors were in it, and when they saw her they steered close to the curb and began yelling threats at her. She looked away from them. The attendant remarked, "What's wrong with them guys?" but she didn't answer.

When she mounted her machine again, she looked around carefully but there was no sign of the black touring car.

Heading out of town, she slowed to a crawl as she encountered the stretch of washboard road where her tire had gone flat. While she was creeping along, suddenly the car rattled past her at bone-jarring speed, covering her with a cloud of dust. A hundred yards ahead, almost at the entrance to a farmstead, the car turned sharply and stopped. The driver jockeyed it back and forth until it was sideways in the road, completely blocking her path. She had no choice but to brake to a stop, her heart beginning to pound. She sat transfixed in the saddle while she watched the menacing gang leap from the car and begin swaggering toward her. They were close enough that she could hear their snarling threats.

"You tole' us t' grow up. Huh! We're gonna show ya' we ain't just boys, like ya' called us."

"Yeah. Yer gonna find out yer dealin' wit' men. Real men."

"We'll teach you to come stirrin' up trouble where yer not wanted!"

She glanced behind her with the thought that maybe she could get the *Gray Ghost* turned around and escape.

"Don't even think about runnin' away. We'd catch ya' and run ya' down."

"Yeah. We're gonna fix ya' so you'll never leave home again!"

"You need a man pretty bad right now, don'cha. Too bad, lady, yer all alone. But don't worry none. There's three grown men here t' take care o' ya'. Real good."

The road was narrow, and lined on both sides with a fence and a thick row of scrub brush. She realized her machine wouldn't turn short enough and there wasn't time for any maneuvering. Helpless, she just sat there and watched as they marched closer.

Maybe Eeph had been right. There was violence in the air in Wisconsin during this summer of 1917. There had been rocks thrown at Jonathan and his horse in Prairieville; what would these young scoundrels do to her now? She had been foolish, perhaps, to travel alone and speak out for the rights of women.

She thought briefly about leaving the motorcycle behind and making a dash for safety. She looked around her again; the closest farmhouse behind her was at least a half mile away. Even though she was wearing pants, she could never out-run these hoodlums. And if she showed her fear by running, it would probably embolden them even more. When they caught her, as she knew they would, they would show her no mercy. She knew enough about dogs to know that her best chances lay in wearing a brave face and showing no fear.

In that moment, she felt a renewed understanding of how much she needed Eeph; how much she depended upon him. How she wished he were at her side!

She sat straight upon the seat of the *Gray Ghost* and faced them with resolution. Her very audacity made them stop for a moment.

"Ain'cha scared, lady?"

"Why ain'cha runnin'?"

"We mean business, an' ya' better look out!"

Her courageous posture couldn't hold them off very long. One of them picked up a stout tree limb from the roadside ditch.

"I'll knock ya' right off yer perch," he said grimly as he started marching toward her again, his two buddies at his side.

It seemed to Prudence that the birds stopped singing and the breeze stopped blowing and the whole world stood in silence as the three young bullies strode forward. She sat without flinching in the eerie noiselessness of the moment, partly because she must not let them intimidate her and partly because she was frozen with fear.

Suddenly a deafening roar shattered the stillness, and a puff of dust rose leisurely from a spot in the road only a few feet in front of the gang leader. He stopped in his tracks as everyone turned quickly to see the smoking muzzle of a shotgun braced on a fencepost and held in human hands. Prudence recognized the young farmer at once—it was Jim, the one who had fixed her flat tire that very morning. His brother Joe was in the shadows behind him. The two boys climbed nimbly over the fence, brushed aside the thick shrubbery, and emerged onto the road.

"Ma'am, we'll walk ya' past that auto*m*obile," said Jim, and he motioned her to start moving. The three trouble-makers stood aside and let her pass, falling in behind as they all moved slowly forward along the road. Prudence steered her machine around the stopped car, and paused briefly to thank her benefactors.

"That's all right, Ma'am. Now git goin'. We'll delay these punks long enough fer you t' git safely on yer way." Jim raised his shotgun and aimed at a rear tire.

"Don't!" shouted one of the boys. "That's my dad's car and he'll kill me!"

Jim didn't even hesitate. With a loud blast from his shotgun, the tire collapsed. "Ya' got a spare," he said. "You'll be able t' get back t' town. An' don't ya' ever come out this way agin!"

Prudence glanced behind her as she rode away and she saw Jim and Joe walking up the road to their farm. The three boys stood momentarily gazing at their stranded auto before they set to work changing the tire. Then she turned the corner and they all disappeared from her sight.

Chapter 10

Prudence chose not to tell Ephraim or her family about the frightening confrontation on her way home from Beaver Dam. They would scold her audacity, she knew. They would try to prevent her from traveling alone again, so she said nothing. She had no intention of quitting her suffrage efforts, and she wanted to travel and campaign without hindrance nor argument. She believed in the cause with all her heart. In addition, her activity helped assuage the dread of her coming separation from Jon.

The mobilization of Prairieville's Company had been delayed for weeks because the Army was not ready to receive the men at Camp Douglas. The orders were finally received, however, with very short notice.

The fateful day was pleasant and sunny, with gentle fluffy clouds of pure white floating in a sapphire sky. The cheeriness of the scene was set in direct contrast to the morbidity of the occasion.

The familiar route into Prairieville had never been more delightful. It seemed to Prudence the whole world was engaged in a deceptive conspiracy to lull them to complacency, to anesthetize them into a false confidence of safety and security.

The cliff swallows had never been more active along the riverbank, darting and sailing through the soft morning breeze around the buggy as though they understood their mission of diversionary entertainment. The peepers at water's edge vigorously expressed their joy, ignoring the time and the season. A trio of red admiral butterflies flitted gracefully around their heads for a time, afterward trailing in their wake for a half-mile or so. The fragrance of alfalfa, curing in the hayfields alongside the road, wafted into their nostrils with a gentle reminder of God's nourishing bounty.

The grasses had never been so green; the air had never been so fresh; the roadside daisies had never been so pure. The world was singing its song of joy, thought Prudence, trying desperately to mask the gruesome reality of war and death awaiting them around the next corner of time.

In any life, there are isolated moments of great potency and import that remain fixed in memory forever. For Prudence, standing in the sunshine along Grand Avenue on August 11, 1917 comprised one of those unforgettable moments. The sight of that rag-tag group of somewhat more than a hundred, mostly in street clothes, seared into her psyche like a branding iron on the flank of a young heifer. Prairieville's Company of boys—how could she call them men, when to her they were scarcely past kindergarten age—Prairieville's Company marched crisply south down the center of the hushed avenue to the cars of destiny, the waiting cars of the *Chicago & North Western Railway.*

"What an exciting time!" commented Ephraim, at her side. "What a great opportunity fer a young man."

Prudence, buried deep in her distressing thoughts, said nothing.

"A chance t' go abroad!" exulted Ephraim. "Some of those boys would never travel beyond the borders o' Prairieville County, if it weren't fer this. Ain't it strange, how good things can come outa' bad things. War is horrible, as everybody knows, but it gives these boys an outlook on the world that they would never get any other way."

"It will give them the satisfaction of doing something for their country," suggested Sarah.

"Yeah. Yer right," responded Ephraim. "But I was thinkin' o' somethin' more down t' earth. Those guys are gonna meet a lot o' different people. They're gonna get an education they could never get outa' books. They're gonna see a lot o' this country. I hear most o' the trainin' is done down south. Heck, they may even get t' see France!"

"I wish I could go with them," pouted Sarah. "It's not fair that boys get to do all the exciting things, and girls have to stay home."

Prudence laughed in spite of her gloomy feelings. "That doesn't sound like you, Sarah. Not long ago, I remember, you said it was not good for a woman to be out in the world."

"When did I say that?" asked Sarah.

"When I was talking about the campaign for women's rights. You said a woman should stay at home."

Sarah reflected quietly for a moment. "Well, yes, I guess I did say that, didn't I? It's true, there are a lot of risks for a woman outside the home. Look at what happened to Grace Lusk."

"Nothing is all good or all bad," commented her mother. "There are choices you must make everywhere you walk. If you're going to live in this world, you're going to have to take some risks. But that's what it means to be alive. You should experience everything the world has to offer and learn to make the right choices."

"I suppose you're right, conceded Sarah. "But everything seems so frightening."

"It ain't frightenin'," said Ephraim. "It's excitin'! Just think o' Jon, livin' wit' a bunch o' other guys, all his friends. They'll be goin' places t'gether, n' doin' things t'gether, mebbe even gettin' t' go across the ocean an' seein' what the world is like over there."

"That would be fun," said Sarah. "That's what I meant before—it isn't fair that boys get to do all those things, and girls can't!"

"Would you really want to be a soldier, Sarah?" asked her mother. "Would you really want to live in a muddy trench, and not be able to wash properly, and have to shoot other people?"

"Well, if the boys have to do it, so should the girls," she replied stoutly.

"Remember, the Huns would be shooting at you, too," said Prudence.

Sarah was silent for a moment as she pictured herself in the trenches of France, ducking her head from the bullets whizzing past. "Oh, I don't know what I want!" she suddenly exclaimed. There's a part of me that wants all that adventure, and there's a part of me that wants to stay home and hide in the house."

"I know what you mean," murmured her mother.

The crowd now surged around the end of the military column, following in a stampede to the train depot. The company fell out of ranks on the platform, as captain Martin allowed his men the natural consideration of leave-taking from family and friends. Prudence worked her way through the throng until she reached Jon. He looked so young. She pictured him again as a schoolboy, but when he hugged her she felt the arms of a man around her shoulders. There were tears in her eyes.

"Don't cry, Mom," he said gently. "I'm just off for a little romp. We'll wipe up those Huns in a flash and I'll be back working the farm before you know it."

She could not trust herself to speak, but she squeezed him as hard as she could.

Lieutenant Welch came past, announcing the imminent departure of the train. "All men get on board!" he commanded. "All men on board!"

Jon gave his final farewells, picked up his duffel bag, and turned away. Prudence watched him climb the steps into the coach directly behind his friend Leo. His head was up, his shoulders were squared, and he did not look back.

The local band known as the *Woodmen of the World* struck up a cheery tune as the coaches jerked forward to begin their journey.

Prudence joined the crowd in waving at the departing train, even though she could not see Jon within. After it was gone, her composure broke for a moment and she pressed her head on Ephraim's shoulder. "Oh, I just know he'll never come back!" she sobbed. "He'll never see Prairieville again!"

Ephraim comforted her as best he could. "Now, now, Prudy," he said soothingly. "Don't fret. He's in God's hands, and God is gracious in all things."

The three of them returned to the livery wordlessly.

The buggy seemed empty during the ride home. With Jon gone, there was space to spare. 'The family circle is broken, perhaps forever,' Prudence thought to herself.

Family? Yes, family. Increasingly, she was thinking of this group as a family. She was thinking of Ephraim as her husband, father to her children. It was a comfortable thought, a thought that gave her security in a treacherous world. She knew she could depend upon Ephraim. He had proved his devotion to her time and again through all the years of her remembrance.

She reached over and pressed his hand. He glanced down at their intertwined fingers, and a slow smile spread across his features. In response, she looked up into his face, and felt a welcome consolation. If only he weren't so old. . . .

In the following days, Jon wrote letters faithfully from Camp Douglas to keep the family informed of his new experiences. Although Wilson and the Federal government had been preaching 'Preparedness' for more than a year, the War Department was not ready for the great influx of citizen soldiers who responded to their country's call.

"*I finally have a uniform,*" Jon wrote after two weeks. "*It was so fresh and new, but by the end of the first day I looked like I was returning from the war instead of just going to it.*

"*There are fifteen thousand of us here at Camp Douglas. Certainly, that will prove to everybody that Wisconsin is just as patriotic as any other state in the Union. We are all tired of hearing that Wisconsin is filled with traitors who won't support the war effort.*

"*We are dreadfully short of everything in the way of supplies. Of course, I didn't expect the luxuries of home. But we don't even have enough basic items like tents and blankets. I share a mess kit with Leo. Luckily, we do have enough food to put in it!*

"*It is rumored that Governor Philipp has given up on getting supplies from Uncle Sam, and is going to use the state treasury to buy the things we need. . . .*"

John's rumor was right. Adjutant General Orlando Holway was sent to New York to spend nearly three quarters of a million dollars on military equipment, and he completed his mission with such dispatch that the Wisconsin troops had adequate supplies by Labor Day.

It was just in time, for in mid-September the Wisconsin guardsmen were ordered south for training at Camp MacArthur near Waco, Texas.

"By the time you get this letter," Jon wrote, "we will be half-way to Texas. There is no time for us to see each other before we leave.

"But don't feel bad about it. I am glad we have been transferred so quickly. We are all anxious to get our training over with and go fight the Huns. The sooner we get going, the sooner we'll be back."

Prudence remained sitting at the kitchen table for many long minutes and re-read Jon's letter over and over again. 'Why are there so many good-bys in this world?' she asked herself. 'I thought the worst was over when we said good-by at the train station in Prairieville, but somehow I feel even more desolate now that my son is gone from Wisconsin.'

She imagined him on a troop train, with every passing minute putting more and more distance between him and his home. 'How sad he must be,' she thought. 'He's never been away from home before. And he has to do it all by himself, with nobody from his family to give him comfort.'

She could not bear her agony alone, the agony of separation. Clutching the letter in her hand, she rose from the chair and removed her apron. With a deep sigh, she trudged out of the house.

It was mid-afternoon, at the time of the autumnal equinox. The days were shortening rapidly as the growing season came to a close. A sense of urgency spurred the efforts of the three men who were harvesting the season's crops. They were in the west field which was snuggled in a bend of the river. Robert was driving the team of horses—Kaiser and Bismarck—pulling the machine which cut the corn and left it tied into bundles with binder twine. Ephraim and Bruno had the job of loading the bundles of corn onto a wagon pulled by Ephraim's team, and transporting the fodder back to the barnyard.

The technology of farming was changing rapidly. Although corn—a crop native to North America—had been used to feed livestock for centuries, it had only been thirty-five years since a Wisconsin agricultural scientist, Franklin King, demonstrated that the whole corn plant—stalks, leaves, and ears—could be best preserved if it were chopped into bits and stored in round silos. The process depended upon packing the chopped corn so tightly that no air would penetrate. Without air, the corn would keep for many months without spoiling. The slight fermentation of the green fodder also aided its preservation. The milk production of dairy cows increased dramatically when they could be fed green corn throughout all four seasons.

Only a year before his death, Zachary had invested in a new 'silo-filler' to chop the corn and blow it through a big pipe up into the silo. The silo-filler was driven by another product of advanced technology—a tractor. Zachary's tractor hadn't found much use in the fields, but it was a perfect power source for the corn chopper, through a long belt-drive.

Prudence couldn't wait for Ephraim and Bruno to return to the barnyard with their wagonload of corn. She marched solemnly along the lane to the field, clutching Jon's latest letter in her hand, overwhelmed by her sense of loss.

The two men paused in their efforts as they watched her solitary feminine figure advancing toward them. Her red and white checkered dress was a sharp contrast to the greens and browns of the field. Ephraim felt a familiar tug at his heart as she approached. He knew she had an important message to convey, or she would not have interrupted them. 'How lucky I am to be the one she seeks!' he thought. 'How lucky I am that she is becoming my woman, at last.'

"He's gone, Eeph," she blurted out as she drew near.

"Who's gone?"

"Jon. Jon's gone."

"Yes, of course Jon is gone," he said. "He's been gone more than a month already."

"No, Eeph, I mean he's really gone. He's on his way to Texas. Here, read his letter for yourself."

He took the proffered paper and carefully perused it. He was not a good reader, and he formed each word with his lips as he went, but after a few minutes he had digested the contents of the page.

"Well, we knew he was goin'," he remarked.

"But so soon?" she complained. "And without seeing us?"

"We're at war," Ephraim said simply. "An' we're all patriotic."

Bruno bristled. "It's about time everybody realized we're all patriotic," he said grimly. "I'm gettin' tired of people accusin' me an' Elizabeth o' bein' traitors."

"Is that nonsense still goin' on?" asked Ephraim, remembering the visit from Albert Jones and his friends just after the Declaration of War.

"It sure is," affirmed the short, stocky German.

"What have they done to you lately?"

Bruno's eyes darted wildly all around the cornfield before he replied.

"First it was the Liberty Loan drive," he said. "I had several visits from men who wanted me t' give money t' the war. But Elizabeth an' me ain't got no money t' spare. Our farm ain't very big. It looks nice, sure, because we spend a lot of time fixin' it up. You can keep things lookin' pretty decent if ya' work at it, and it don't take much money. Elizabeth n' me talked it over in the beginnin', an' decided we weren't gonna give no money to the war. We ain't got much, an' we don't think we shoulda' gone t' war anyhow. So we ain't gave a single penny, an' we don't intend to."

"Whew!" breathed Ephraim. "I knew ya' ain't very strong on the war, an' that's okay, but I didn't know ya' had refused t' donate anything at all t' the Liberty Loan."

"Well, we ain't done it. An' we ain't gonna'. The more they threaten us, the more determined we get."

"Threats? What do they do to threaten you?" asked Prudence.

"Oh, nothin' t' hurt us none. A couple o' times they put up signs on our gate sayin' we don't give t' the Liberty Loan. Once they smeared yellow paint on our mailbox. Nothin' too serious."

"You've got to be careful," said Prudence. "Congress has passed the Espionage Act, you know, and they can arrest you if you say anything against the war."

"Yeah, we know that. We know about the Espionage Act, and we've heard about some of the arrests. We ain't dumb. We know ya' can't say nothin' nice about Germany or the Kaiser, even if it's supposed t' be a free country, an' we know ya' can't say nothin' against Uncle Sam's policies. So we just don't say nothin' at all. When they come to talk to us, we pretend like we can't understand English. We pretend like we're foreigners."

Prudence laughed. "I'm sure that makes them all the more nervous about you," she observed.

"Probably so," agreed Bruno. "But if we don't say nothin', what can they do? They can't prove what we're thinkin'.

"'Course, then they came back with some guy who could talk German. So we pretended we couldn't understand German, neither. They got really mad, but they finally left." He saw no humor in the incident, although both Ephraim and Prudence chuckled.

"What if someone hears you talking English when you're out somewhere?" asked Prudence.

"We don't go nowhere. We ain't never gone nowhere. 'Cept fer comin' over here, an' goin' t' the store, we stay at home."

Prudence laughed again. "Well, maybe you can get away with it. Have they stopped coming by your house?"

"They stopped fer a little while," Bruno said, "but they were back again last week."

"What did they want this time?"

"They wanted us to sign that pledge from the Loyalty League."

"Oh, yes. I remember," said Prudence. "Albert Jones stopped at our house, too. We signed it for him."

"Well, we didn't." said Bruno stubbornly.

"Why not? It won't cost you anything. And certainly you are loyal enough."

136

"Of course we're loyal. It if was just that, we'd sign, if they'd explain it t' us in German. But I read the whole pledge, and it goes on t' support the war. An' we don't believe in the war. We think we have a right t' our beliefs. We ain't gonna' give in."

"Well, I think maybe you're being a little foolish," observed Prudence. "If I were you, I'd sign their childish pledge and give them a little bit of money."

Bruno stared at her with an air of injured innocence. "But Miz Hartmann!" he exclaimed. "That ain't right! We don't really believe in the war, and it would be wrong for us t' lie about it, wouldn't it?"

His righteousness penetrated her heart. "I suppose so," she replied. "But be careful! The people who support the war are very powerful, and it can be dangerous to cross them."

"I'll be careful, Miz Hartmann," he promised. "An' if all else fails, I got my shotgun!"

Robert had been crossing the field back and forth while they talked, and he was nearly finished with his task of cutting and bundling the corn. Only a narrow strip of the tall, tasseled, green plants remained down the center of the field.

"We'd better get this corn into the silo," remarked Ephraim, glancing at the declining sun. "If we hurry, we can probably get this field cleaned up good before chore-time."

Ephraim and Prudence walked alongside the wagon while Bruno drove the team. Prudence lowered her voice so Bruno couldn't hear her. "I am worried about him," she observed. "He doesn't seem quite normal. I wonder if the threats are beginning to affect his mind."

"I was thinkin' the same thing," confessed Ephraim. "His whole body seems to twitch and jerk when he talks, and his eyes seem so cruel and . . . and so far away."

When they went to church the next Sunday, several of the parishioners told them about the treasonable speech of Senator Robert LaFollette on Friday.

Until now, those who attacked the Senator could find very little ammunition. He and his little band of "willful men", as President Wilson labeled them, had successfully blocked legislation which would have authorized the arming of merchant ships. Wilson armed them anyway, and the Germans promptly sank several of them. LaFollette then opposed the President's demand for a Declaration of War, although the House and Senate overwhelmingly joined the President in declaring war upon Germany. The Senator then opposed military conscription, and again Congress endorsed the President by a lop-sided majority.

The Senator spoke with the voice of moderation and reason, and was accordingly hated with unusual intensity. His opponents, however, could find no legal or moral foundation to lynch him because he submitted to the laws once they had been passed. Their strongest argument was that he failed to support the President, but even the most rabid war-hawks could not call that a crime. In America, all citizens have the Constitutional right to express disagreement with the President and his program. But the temper of the times was heated beyond the boiling point—during the war, dozens of Wisconsin citizens were arrested and fined under the Espionage Act simply for criticizing U.S. policies. Bruno was right to keep his mouth shut; LaFollette would have been well-advised to do the same.

Instead, he used his senatorial position to call for Congress to define our aims in fighting the war. Once again, his opponents whipped themselves into a fury, denouncing him as pro-German and anti-American.

With that background, LaFollette appeared before the convention of the farmers' Nonpartisan League in St. Paul on September 21, the day Prudence received her letter from Jon. The auditorium was packed, with thousands of people outside in the streets hoping to get in. The convention leaders previewed a copy of his speech which defended his demands for Congress to participate in a written declaration of America's war aims. They told him it was too controversial, and he put aside the manuscript. As he entered the hall, however, the ovation from the crowd demanded his response, and he delivered a rousing speech extemporaneously.

He talked about financing the war, and about his proposals to levy a high tax on war profits. He said he had not favored entering the war. The crowd cheered, and he added, "I don't mean to say that we hadn't suffered grievances; we had—at the hands of Germany—serious grievances . . . . They had interfered with the right of American citizens to travel upon the high seas—on ships loaded with munitions for Great Britain."

A heckler asked about the *Lusitania*, a ship sunk by the Germans in 1915 with the loss of more than a hundred American lives. LaFollette replied that the Lusitania had been carrying six million rounds of ammunition for the Allies, implying that it had become a fair target.

The reporter for the *Pioneer Press* of St. Paul sent out a report of the speech over the wires of the Associated Press—but he mis-quoted LaFollette as saying, "We had no grievances against Germany"—exactly the opposite of the true words. He reported that LaFollette justified the sinking of the *Lusitania*. He reported that LaFollette blamed the profiteering of bankers and munitions makers for America's entry into the War.

Newspaper headlines from coast to coast attacked LaFollette the next day, and the Senator from Wisconsin was branded a traitor. In the weeks following, Minnesota's governor Joseph Burnquist began proceedings to petition the U.S. Senate to expel LaFollette. The Board of Directors of the Madison Club revoked his membership, calling him a "disloyal citizen". A group of faculty and students at the University of Wisconsin in Madison burned LaFollette in effigy on the campus. *The Wisconsin State Journal* branded the Beta fraternity house as a "hotbed of sedition and German propaganda" because LaFollette's son Phil lived there. Four hundred members of the University faculty, along with the university President Charles Van Hise, signed a petition to the U.S. Senate accusing LaFollette of giving aid and comfort to the enemy.

It would be seven months before the truth would be revealed before a Senate committee and the Associated Press would publish a correction and an apology. In the meantime, Senator LaFollette and the State of Wisconsin were vilified across the country, and the warhawks became vicious and violent.

Jon wrote frequently from Camp MacArthur, telling many of the details of his military organization and training.

"As soon as we arrived," he wrote, we found ourselves in the new 32nd Division of the U.S. Army. Leo and I am no longer part of Wisconsin's 4th Infantry Regiment; we have been transferred to the 127th Infantry Regiment of the 32nd Division.

"Brigadier General William G. Haan has taken command of our division, because our previous commander, Major General James Parker, has already left for France. Of course, this has got to mean that we will be in France within a few months.

"Because of this, there is a sense of real urgency to our training. We are told again and again that there is no time to waste. Many of the men have been here a month or more, including our new friend Karl, and they are just finishing the first four-weeks course. Mom, you'll simply love Karl, I know you will. He is very handsome, and he is such a gentleman! He's almost five years older, so he's the natural leader of us 'three musketeers.' He is helping us catch up, as the group is already beginning the second four-weeks course. Leo and I missed almost all the first course. It takes four such courses to complete our infantry training. If you follow this to the logical conclusion, you can see that we are scheduled to complete our training by Christmas. We have a head start on most of the other divisions in the country, we think, so you don't have to be a genius to figure out that we could be sent overseas as early as January. We are continually told not to speculate about this, but of course that only increases our conjectures. . . ."

Such news did not provide much comfort to his mother. She went about her daily tasks mechanically, almost in a daze. She prepared the meals, she kept the house clean, she helped with the chores. She even made another long ride on Robert's motorcycle, equipped with a new

139

front tire, to preach women's suffrage at a small rally in Sun Prairie. But everything she did was overshadowed by a dread for Jon's future.

He had written that their training would be completed by Christmas, so she began to expect him home for the holidays. She felt, unreasonably, that if she could see him once again on the farm, even for a short leave, she could be sure he wasn't gone forever. It assumed the form of a test for her, like the fleece of wool used by Gideon to assure himself of the will of God: if Jon returned home for Christmas, he would live through the War and return to the farm safely afterward. While she nourished this secret test in her heart, she waited daily for the mail to arrive.

"We've got a whole system of trenches dug just outside the camp," Jon wrote in October. *"We use it to practice trench warfare in preparation for the battlefields in Europe. All of us were kind of 'green' at first, and in our mock battles we were 'killed' over and over again. . . ."* You can be sure his mother's heart blanched when reading those lines. *"Now we consider ourselves veterans of the trenches, and we are experienced enough to keep our heads down.*

"I like the rifle range best of all. I have learned how to aim, load, and fire my Springfield rifle. Karl and Leo and I are all pretty good and we consider ourselves marksmen already. Afterwards, we have to field-strip our weapons and clean them so they will continue to fire with great accuracy. This is a skill that will help me when I get back to the farm. I wonder if they will let me buy my rifle at the end of the war?"

In November, a new monster materialized in Jon's letters to frighten Prudence—poison gas. She hadn't even heard of this awful weapon, but now her son gave her the details. "Yesterday we were taught how potent a gas can be," he wrote. "A building was set aside for the demonstration, and it was equipped accordingly so it could be flooded with 'poison' gas. I don't know what they actually used for the gas, but I'm sure it wasn't the deadly mustard gas we have all heard about. It was bad enough, though.

"First we were made to dash through the building, from one end to the other, without any protection from the gas. It took three or four minutes, I'd say, to make it through the building—long enough that it was impossible for you to hold your breath. Believe me, your eyes were stinging even before you got the first whiff in your nostrils. But when you finally had to gasp for air, the damned stuff just about knocked you flat. A couple of the guys actually collapsed on the floor and had to be dragged out. Karl and Leo and I made it all the way, but by the time we escaped outside we were crying and choking and totally immobilized. . . ."

His mother was crying, too, as she read his words. After wiping her eyes and blowing her nose, she continued reading: *"After we had mostly recovered from that horrible experience, we were issued regulation gas*

140

masks and instructed how to use them. Then we had to go through the building again. This time it was like a stroll in the park. There was nothing worse than a slight discomfort.

"They certainly made believers out of all of us. I'm going to make sure my gas mask is within my reach whenever I'm in combat. I'd throw away almost everything else before I'd give up my mask."

The intensive training made soldiers out of the farmboys in a hurry. They took their work seriously, and maintained strict discipline through it all. "We follow orders every minute of the day," Jon wrote. "There is no relaxing after hours; even our games are prescribed for us. There is a schedule for eating, a schedule for using the laundry, a schedule for sleeping. Karl says we even shower by the numbers!

"Now we are approaching the end of our training. We think we are the best-trained, toughest group of soldiers in the world. No doubt we'll find ourselves tested on the battlefield, but we go with a great sense of self- confidence.

"And we're all hoping for a brief furlough at Christmas in a couple of weeks. We know there's a job to do, but rumor has it that we don't sail until January so maybe we can make it home before we go.

"Leo is particularly eager to get back, because he has just become engaged to his Prairieville sweetheart, Clara. He sent her a diamond ring through the mail this week."

Prudence read the last two paragraphs over and over, and pinned the page to the curtain in front of her kitchen sink so she could see it while she worked. The Lord was answering her prayers, she thought; the boys would come home for Christmas; the woolen fleece in her imagination was wet with dew.

The next week, though, brought a letter which dashed her hopes. *"Bad news, Mom,"* he wrote. *"We've been told there will be no furloughs given to anyone for the holidays. No exceptions. We're told not to guess, but I think that means we're on the sailing list for sure."*

As soon as Prudence read those lines, her determination re-doubled to see her son before he sailed. 'If he can't come here,' she said to herself, 'then I'll go there! I'll take Sarah with me for company, and I'll go to Texas. Perhaps that will fulfill the Test of Gideon.'

Ephraim tried vainly to talk her out of the long journey. "This may be the last chance I have to see him alive," she said dramatically. "If I didn't go, and he dies overseas, I would never forgive myself."

"Now, Prudy, the chances o' him gettin' killed in the war are almost nothin'. Don't worry so much about it. An' it's foolish to go all the way to Texas just t' see 'im for a day or two."

"I don't care how foolish it is," she replied. "I'm not going to change my mind."

He recognized the flint-like determination in her tone. "All right," he conceded. "But I'm goin' along t' make sure ya' get there all right."

"That's not necessary," she said. "I'm confident that Sarah and I can find our way there safely without help."

"Well, I'm comin' along anyway," he said doggedly. "It's the middle of December, and there ain't much work t' do on the farm. Bruno and Robert can take care o' it."

"As you will," she replied.

Less than a week later, on the Sunday afternoon before Christmas, the three were in a coach of the *Missouri Kansas Texas* railroad, the *Katy Line*, rumbling southward from Dallas nearing their destination on the Brazos River.

Ephraim glanced over his companions with a smile of complacency. The journey had gone well for him. He had known Prudence for a good quarter-century, and lived next door to her for years, but this was the longest continuous stretch of time they had spent in such close proximity to each other. They had proved to be extremely compatible. What a pleasure it was for him to travel with his daughter and her mother, especially since it now seemed probable he could soon wrap up the loose ends of his life and tie himself permanently to these two women with the bonds of matrimony.

Jon and Leo met them at the train station with a warm smile and close hugs for everyone. "Our training is pretty well over," Jon explained. "I'm on duty tomorrow morning, but then I'm off until Wednesday, the day after Christmas."

They shrugged off the horde of Negro porters who wanted to transport them and their luggage. It was only five blocks to the hotel, Jon told them, and Northerners were quite capable of walking that far in the cool December air.

He walked them to the best hotel in town, the Raleigh, where he had secured a suite of rooms for them on an upper floor. There was a comfortable sitting-room or lounge overlooking the prosperous-appearing cotton town, with a small bedroom on each side. Ephraim would occupy one of the sleeping rooms, of course, with Prudence and Sarah sharing the other.

They unpacked some of their clothes, and took a few moments for rest and refreshment. Then they moved downstairs into the colorful dining room named *The Purple Cow*.

Jon and Leo kept up a steady monologue during dinner, regaling them with anecdotes of their training.

At last Sarah found an opportunity to tell them about the bomb which had exploded while being examined in Milwaukee's Central Police Station just a month earlier. Nine police officers had been killed in the blast.

"The home-made bomb had been placed next to the Italian Evangelical Church, but it was found before it exploded," she explained. "It was intended for pastor August Giuliani, we are sure, because he has been so outspoken in support of the war."

"We know the war has stirred up a lot of hatred and violence," commented Jon. "There's no telling where it will all end up if we don't finish it off in good time."

Sarah was impressed by her brother's stories and his evident maturity. Prudence listened to him quietly with an expression of wonder on her face which Ephraim had never before seen.

At the end of the evening, Prudence inquired about Clara. "Did she like the ring you sent up to her, Lee?" she asked.

"Well, to be honest, she sent it back to me," confessed Leo.

"Oh, no! Why?"

"It was too big to fit her finger," Leo replied. "So I've got it back at the jewelery store here to get it made smaller."

As they rose to leave the table, Jon gave them instructions for the next day. "You can sleep late tomorrow morning," he told them. "You're probably exhausted after your trip, and I'm on duty as I said before. But I'll come and get you about three o'clock in the afternoon, for some of us from our company are celebrating Christmas Eve with a party. We've got a corner of the mess hall reserved just for us. Karl makes friends with everybody, and he wangled a special evening meal for us."

"That sounds like a good idea," Ephraim commented.

"Then on Christmas morning I'll show you the sights of Waco. I've never toured it myself, so I'll learn something too. It's the county seat and the biggest town for miles around. The Army's official Christmas Dinner is at noon, and then almost everybody is off duty the rest of the day."

"The time will go too quickly," observed Prudence. "Our train leaves for home early the next morning."

"That's just as well," said Jon. "We all go back to our regular duties then anyway, so I couldn't be with you."

It was late when Jon and Leo left the *Raleigh Hotel*. They returned to their Camp just before the curfew closed the gates for the night.

Prudence and Sarah retired circumspectly into their cramped bedroom, with Ephraim ensconced in his own room off the other side of the lounge.

Sarah soon fell into a sound sleep, but Prudence remained restless and awake, thinking of Jon and worrying about the future.

After a while, she rose quietly and wrapped a robe around her shoulders over her nightgown. She tiptoed quietly into the lounge, closing the bedroom door softly behind her.

Stepping to the window, she pushed the curtains open to gaze out upon the bright quarter slice of moon. She began meditating, offering prayers for Jon and his safety.

The night air in central Texas was mild despite the calendar, and she endeavored to open the window. The sash was stuck, and the panes rattled slightly as she forced it up a few inches.

A few moments later she heard a soft rustling behind her, and she turned her head in the dim light to discover Ephraim.

"I couldn't sleep either, Prudy," he said softly. He hesitantly closed the short distance between them, and put his arms around her from behind. She was not embarrassed.

They stood there for a long time, silently sharing their common emotions, before he whispered, "I love him like a son, too, Prudy. I consider him our child just as much as Sarah. I know he's Zac's, of course, but I love him like he was my own."

He leaned his head over her shoulder and gently turned her face around so he could kiss her cheek, then her lips. It was a tentative kiss, yet it seemed resolute and unchallengeable.

Their lips lingered until she turned in his arms, at a slight signal from him, and they clasped their bodies to each other in a desperate, hungering, spontaneous action. They kissed each other passionately for a brief time. He could feel the soft contours of her body pressed against his. With inspired realization, she was thinking wildly, "I've been yearning for this ever since the day of my Great Sin." She was amazed that she felt no sense of guilt.

The next afternoon, Jon escorted them to Camp MacArthur and pointed out some of the places he had written about—the trenches, the rifle range, the poison gas demonstration building. He told how he and his comrades had picked cotton from the fields before they first pitched their tents. The tour was fascinating to his family from the farmland, but Prudence let her thoughts drift to the previous night, to the magical moments with Ephraim. She was still slightly dazed from their spontaneous joining together. It was the first time they had kissed since the day Sarah had been conceived. She glanced at him covertly, and found his eyes pensively studying her. The camp was swarming with hundreds of young soldiers, but she seemed alone in the world with Ephraim.

'And yet,' Prudence thought, 'he is so old. So old, and so dull. I'm still young and I want a sense of excitement and adventure in my life!'

They concluded their tour at the big building which was their mess hall. Perhaps a dozen young soldiers were seated around tables in a spacious corner. Leo was near the center of the group. Sounds of loud conversation and boisterous laughter echoed through the cavernous hall.

The men suddenly became quiet and turned their attention to the newcomers. Jon introduced them in turn to his family.

Halfway around the circle, Jon introduced his friend Karl. Prudence had not noticed him in particular, but upon the mention of his familiar name she gave him her full attention. She was startled, for he resembled Zachary as she had first seen him in her family's new home twenty-seven years before.

Her heart fluttered. She was suddenly overwhelmed with the old sensation of champagne bubbles effervescing through her blood.

Their glances met—and locked. Karl was not a flirt, but before a single word was said between them, he reflexively arched his eyebrows at her—and in response, she winked her left eye. Her face became covered with a maidenly pink blush, and her heart began beating so fiercely that she could feel the pulse in her neck.

Ephraim observed the silent exchange with eyes that quickly recalled the same scene which had sprung into Prudence's recollection. The arched brows, the wink—he had seen it all before, and it had burned in his memory for years. His heart lurched with envy, and a physical spasm racked his body. He was not afraid of Karl, for he could not foresee the future, but he fervently wished that the expression of tender yearning which he now witnessed on her features had been directed at him.

He reassured himself with the reflection that her love for him was probably deeper and more enduring for the very fact that it was not so intense, but then he remembered the hard fact that the first recipient of her hungering emotional glance had been a man she married and loved until his death.

Sarah did not notice the exchange of glances between Karl and her mother, but she too had a sudden emotional jolt from the encounter. For the first time since Jimmy's courtship, she felt a strong attraction for a young man. 'I could grow to like him an awful lot,' she thought to herself.

Later, Prudence could not recall any of the extraneous details of that Christmas eve dinner. There was no recollection of the menu, nor the conversation, nor the other people who were present. It was as though she and Karl were alone together, communicating without words. She could feel his personal presence like an electrical charge permeating the room. That he felt the same toward her she had no doubt, for whenever she permitted her glance to rest briefly upon him, she found him simultaneously returning the favor.

She must have conversed with him during the dinner, innocent questions and answers—how could she not exchange a few words with her son's new and best friend? Yet later she could not remember a single sentence of what they had said.

They parted that night, the first time they had met each other, with nothing more than a casual 'good-night', but she felt he could read her whole life and soul in those two words.

The next morning dragged interminably for Prudence, even though Jon provided an excellent tour of Waco with a horse-drawn cab and a Negro guide. She barely saw the towers of Baylor University, nor the remarkable suspension bridge across the river, nor 'the tallest building west of the Mississippi'—home of the Alico Life Insurance Company. Her mind was set ahead in time, eagerly awaiting the noon dinner when she hoped to see Karl again.

At the end of the tour, she dashed into a ladies' shop and bought an expensive flowered dress. The purchase was uncharacteristic for her, especially since she scarcely glanced at the price.

She wore her new frock to the mess hall for the army's official Christmas Dinner. Karl was there, but to her intense disappointment he politely allowed Ephraim to maneuver him to a place at the table where she could not converse with him nor even observe his face. Instead, he was seated directly across from Sarah, and the two young people became comfortable friends long before dessert was served.

Prudence found herself next to Leo. He proved to be an accomplished conversationalist, but her mind and heart were centered on Karl. She hurried her family through dinner and as they stood to leave the table she moved to Karl's side and invited him to accompany the family through the remainder of the afternoon.

"Oh, I wish I could, Mrs. Hartmann," he said with a tone of regret that seemed almost tangible to her, "but I promised to go with my team to play ball against another company."

She replied with the same measure of deep regret, "I'm so sorry. It has been such a pleasure meeting Jon's best friend. I suppose we shan't see each other again, as we are leaving for Wisconsin tomorrow morning."

"Probably not," he replied with soft politeness. "But I enjoyed meeting you, too; Jon has said so many wonderful things about you."

She feared that was her last sight of him, for he would be sailing for France with her son. However, to her great joy he and Leo both appeared on the platform of the train station the next morning as they were preparing to board.

Karl said little, at least little that she remembered, but when it came time for farewells she clasped Jon tightly to her, gave Leo a light embrace, and then boldly hugged Karl with all her strength. Sarah followed her example, giving warm hugs to all three boys.

Those final moments on the station platform of the *Katy Line* were remembered by Prudence in vivid reality for the rest of her life. Her innermost emotions were wrenched open by her fear that she would never see her son again. At the same time, Karl's embrace, which was the first physical contact between them, palliated her wounds and provided a welcome comfort to her agonized soul.

Chapter 11

The long train ride home, through Dallas, St. Louis, and Chicago, was charged with high emotions among the familiar trio. Prudence was engrossed with her fantasies about Karl, and could think of little else. The physical presence of Karl's body pressed against hers in farewell was a memory she tossed about in her mind again and again, each time seeking to ensure herself of his mutual feelings.

'There's no doubt about it,' she told herself repeatedly. 'He felt the same attraction for me. I could see it in his eyes. Of course, he couldn't say anything openly, because he is Jon's friend and we were never alone. But I know he likes me, just as I like him.'

She would have been surprised to read her daughter's thoughts, which were centered on the same person. Sarah was considerably less sure of herself. 'Karl is such an attractive man,' she thought. 'He seemed to enjoy my company and my conversation. I wonder, does he like me? I wonder if we'll ever see each other again. I hope he comes back to Prairieville with Jon sometime.'

Karl was in the forefront of Ephraim's mind, too, as he observed the sadness on the face of the woman he loved. 'I can't believe what I saw! I can't believe Karl n' Prudence could be attracted to each other romantically. She's old enough t' be 'is mother! Surely it ain't true. I'm just imagining things.'

Nevertheless, he was so troubled by his thoughts that he was driven to confront Prudence directly. He decided to act at once, while they were on the train together with hours of leisure.

"There's somthin' I wanna' talk over wit' ya'," he began as he sat facing the two women in the opposite seats.

His words startled Prudence from her reverie. Her doleful eyes glanced up at him. "Yes?" she inquired.

Having opened the conversation, Ephraim wasn't sure how to proceed. After an uncomfortable pause, he said lamely, "Ya' been lookin' mighty gloomy."

She kept her eyes on his face as she answered slowly, "Of course I'm gloomy. I have just said good-by to my only son. I may never see him again."

"Well, I think yer bein' a bit meller-dramatic 'bout that, Prudence," he said. "We talked about it afore. There's millions o' young men goin' over t' fight the Huns. Sure, some of 'em ain't comin' back. But if they all stayed snug at home, there'd still be some of 'em wouldn't live to see the end o' the war. Nobody is absolutely positive they're gonna draw their next breath, or keep breathin' fer one year or fer ten."

"We're all in the hands of the Almighty," Sarah reminded them.

"But even so," continued Ephraim, "the odds is overwhelmin' that Jon will live through the war n' come back n' get married n' raise a bunch of kids n' cry at our funerals when we die n' then fergit us in the normal course of events."

"That's right, Mother," Sarah agreed. "So don't waste your time worrying about it. There's nothing you can do, anyhow, so just leave it to God."

"I guess that's all I can do," sighed Prudence, turning her face to stare through the window at the cottonwood trees lining the little creek they were passing.

The conversation faltered, and Sarah rose to her feet. "I'm going for another stroll," she announced, swaying with the motion of the train. It had become almost compulsive for her to walk the length of the train every hour or so, quietly observing her fellow passengers.

When she was gone, Ephraim resumed his earlier observation. "I know ya' pretty darn well, Prudy, and I think there's more on yer mind than havin' Jon head off t' war."

She didn't respond, but continued to stare gloomily through the window, her face turned away from him.

"C'mon, tell me what's botherin' ya'," he wheedled.

She shook her head stubbornly, refusing to look at him, but her face turned the color of early strawberries.

He waited a moment longer, his eyes yearning for her, his knees nearly touching hers. Their bodies were rocking and shaking in unison as though directed by a master choreographer as the train hurtled along the rails toward Chicago. 'I wish our spirits enjoyed that same kind of harmony,' Ephraim thought ruefully to himself.

Aloud he declared, "Yer thinkin' o' Karl, aincha." He examined her expressionless face. "I saw the way ya' struck it off with 'im."

Still she did not speak; she did not even return her gaze inside the coach to look at him.

"I don't wanna reproach ya', Prudy," he said, "but I wanna remind ya' o' one thing. Only one thing. The kid is only half yer age. Look at 'im like ya' would a son, that's all." Again he scrutinized her face, trying in vain to draw her eyes to him.

"I jus' wanna perteck ya'," he said with respectful deference. Then, with more firmness, he added, "Don't make a fool outa' yerself."

Not once did she look at him during the gentle lecture that emerged from his wounded soul, nor did she give any visible indication that she heard his words. He didn't need an answer. Her silence confirmed the worst of his suspicions.

It was scarce comfort that Karl would remain hundreds or thousands of miles away. Despite his deficiencies in education, Ephraim understood enough of human nature to know that Karl in his absence might be a more potent rival than if he were present in the flesh. As an imaginary being, more or less, Karl could be molded without protest into almost any shape Prudence might desire.

With a deep sigh and a shrug of hopelessness, Ephraim ended his attempt to engage Prudence into a discussion of her feelings toward the young man she had recently met.

As soon as Prudence returned home, she went to Daniel O'Brien's photography studio on Broadway and had her portrait taken. She didn't admit the reason, not even to herself.

In her concern for Jonathan, Prudence had neglected her suffrage activities during recent months. Now she resumed her political interests. She met with Theodora in the Youmans' parlor on the last Sunday afternoon of December.

"The campaign is coming to a head," declared the newspaperwoman. "We've had so many victories all around the country in 1917! North Dakota, Ohio, Indiana, Rhode Island, Nebraska, Michigan. Even in the Solid South, we won the right for 'primary voting' in Arkansas for the first time. And of course, winning the referendum in the state of New York was the capstone of the year.

"The pressure is mounting. Congress can't ignore the Anthony amendment forever. A vote in the House of Representatives is almost certain in January, and this time it won't be an overwhelming defeat like it was in 1915."

"We can win in the House?" asked Prudence.

"Yes, it is quite possible. But it's going to be very, very close. A swing of one or two votes could make the difference."

"What can be done to help?"

"Well, you can write a letter to President Wilson, asking him to come out in our support. Jessie Jack Hooper, who has been working in Washington with the National American Woman Suffrage Association, says he is on the verge of declaring his position in our favor."

"What about our Congressmen? The ones from Wisconsin? How are they going to vote?" inquired Prudence.

"The toughest ones are William Stafford from Milwaukee and Ed Voigt from Sheboygan. We think the rest of them will probably vote with us."

"That's certainly a big change from the last time the House voted," remarked Prudence, who had learned a great amount of suffrage history during the months she had known Theodora.

"You're right. The last time, just three years ago, nine out of the eleven Congressmen from Wisconsin voted against the amendment. One of those nine, of course, was Bill Stafford. He's been quite outspoken in his position, and I don't think there is any hope in turning him around. There's no question about the fact that he represents the beer interests."

"What about Congressman Voigt?"

"He seems to be pretty strong in his position against a Constitutional amendment," Theodora related, "although he doesn't preach against woman suffrage on principle. He says the states should decide, and he still points to the Wisconsin referendum in 1912 where we lost so decisively."

"Let's talk to him while he is home for the holidays," suggested Prudence. "Maybe we can give him something to ponder when he returns to Washington."

"I've been thinking the same thing," said Theodora. "I'll see if he will grant us an interview."

The Congressman was quite willing to receive the two women, and they made their pilgrimage to his home in Sheboygan soon after New Year's Day.

The journey required a change of trains in Milwaukee, but with an early start the two women arrived at their destination by mid-morning. The depot seemed nearly deserted, and they stepped outside to confront an empty street. A light snow had sifted down from the clouds blown in from the lake during the night, leaving a sugary dusting which freshened the dreary snow-banks. Few of the townspeople had swept their walks, and the shoes of the two determined suffragists scuffed the half-inch of white fluff as they bent their determined steps to their destination on their inspired mission.

The weather seemed extremely cold to Prudence, who had basked in the summer-like climate of central Texas just two weeks before. The crispness of the morning air, still drifting in lazily from the lake, made their noses tingle and quickly brushed a rose-like tint upon their cheeks.

The warm moisture from their exhalations left white condensation vapors which swirled around their faces and trailed briefly behind them as they hurried on their way.

Edward Voigt was a decisive-looking man with an intense expression. He personally met their knock upon his door and welcomed them inside. His mouth was smiling but not his eyes as he hung their coats in the hall closet and escorted them into the parlor.

"It is a pleasure to be visited by two such charming members of the fair sex," he said somewhat awkwardly.

"Thank you, Congressman," replied Theodora. "It is good to see you again. And I'd like you to meet my friend, Mrs. Prudence Hartmann."

He acknowledged her courteously and continued to stand as the two women seated themselves in the overstuffed chairs. "Let me get you some coffee," he said.

"That's not necessary," said Theodora, "don't trouble yourself."

"Oh, but I insist. It will take only a moment. You've come a long way, and January weather in Wisconsin is rather brisk."

"Well, that's true," conceded Theodora. "We walked from the depot—have you no cabs in Sheboygan?"

"I'm afraid this is not Milwaukee, Ma'am," he replied with another forced smile.

When they had their coffee cups in hand, the Congressman opened the subject directly. "Of course I know why you're here, ladies," he said. "You and I have talked about the issue of woman suffrage before, Mrs. Youmans. You know, of course, that the Anthony amendment will soon be brought before the House."

"How soon?" asked Prudence.

"I understand it might be as early as next Thursday, the tenth," replied the Congressman.

"It will be an historic moment," said Theodora. "My First Vice-President, Mrs. Jessie Jack Hooper, is in Washington and she thinks the amendment is going to pass."

"That is possible," said the Congressman, "but far from certain."

"It's been quite some time since I have heard your position on the matter, Mr. Voigt," said Theodora. "My recollection is that you were somewhat opposed to the amendment. But times are changing, and the momentum for favorable action is increasing steadily. It looks like women are going to win the right to vote; the only question is how soon it will happen."

"You may be right," he replied.

"It looks inevitable," Theodora continued, "and we'd certainly like to have your vote on the winning side."

"I think you know my position," he said somewhat stiffly. "I haven't changed it at all."

"Well, I don't know your position, sir," said Prudence gamely. "I'd like to hear it directly from your lips."

He nodded sagely. "Gladly, Mrs. Hartmann. Of course, I have nothing against women. I haven't fully made up my mind on whether women should be given the vote, but I take my job very seriously. I represent the voters of Wisconsin, and they have spoken very clearly in a referendum that they did not want woman suffrage."

"But that was six years ago, Mr. Voigt," observed Theodora. "A lot of things have changed in six years."

"You are quite right," he agreed smoothly. "Many things have changed. But we don't know whether our voters have changed their minds in favor of woman suffrage. I would like to find out, of course. If the voters ordain such a change, I will certainly agree with them. However, I believe very strongly that the decision should be made by each individual state, for opinions can be different in different states. If Colorado wants women to vote, that's fine with me; if Alabama says no, that's fine with me, too. I insist that we should have the right to make that decision in Wisconsin. The Federal government shouldn't be allowed to coerce us."

"But Wisconsin won't give women a fair chance!" objected Prudence.

The Congressman raised his eyebrows and pursed his lips. "Why not, may I ask?"

"Because of the brewery interests," Prudence explained.

"Oh, I see," he replied, nodding his head thoughtfully. "Well, Madam, let me remind you that breweries do not vote. Only people vote. . . ."

"Yeah, only men!" Prudence interrupted.

". . . . And regardless of what makes people vote the way they do, the elections in this state are completely fair and honest."

"Sometimes the voters can be swayed," Theodora said quietly. "When it comes to a question that is so very important to the breweries, they can spend an awful lot of money to influence public opinion."

"Even the people who run the breweries should have the right to promote their cause, just as you have the right to promote yours," said the Congressman pointedly. "And I have complete faith in my fellow voters to make the right decisions after hearing opinions from everybody."

Theodora tried a different angle. "It looks like President Wilson is going to support the amendment," she said. "If our President recommends passage, will you go along with him?"

"Mrs. Youmans, I am quite firm in my decision on this matter. I will oppose the amendment at the Federal level, because I think the decision should be made by the voters of each state. I don't want the Federal government to force it down our throats."

"But the Federal government can't force it down the throats of the states," said Theodora. "The amendment, if it is passed by Congress, must be ratified by the states before it becomes part of our Constitution."

"That would be fine, Madam, if every state were required to ratify it to make it official. But only thirty-six states are necessary. That means that up to twelve states could oppose the measure, and it would still become law. And I don't think that's right."

There seemed to be no point in further discussion, so the women rose to leave. "Thank you for hearing us," said Theodora.

"Thank you for coming," Congressman Voigt replied. He bestowed upon Theodora another of his now-familiar false smiles. "I respect your position as president of the Wisconsin Woman Suffrage Association, and my door is always open to you."

As they walked back to the depot, Theodora remarked, "I despise men like that, who hide their true opinions behind a mask of legalities. You know in your heart that he is opposed to women's rights in general, and woman suffrage in particular. But you are not able to argue the case directly, because he takes refuge in the defense of states-rights."

"There isn't much hope for him to vote for the amendment, it seems," Prudence observed.

"No, I don't think so. But you never know for sure; if he sees it's going to pass, and women are going to be voting, he won't want to get caught opposing them. It might cost him his office at the next election. No matter how slim our chances, it was worth the trip to Sheboygan because Jessie tells me the decision could be decided by a single vote."

"Are you going to Washington to watch the proceedings in person?" asked Prudence.

"No, I don't think so. I can't take the time."

Prudence sat in meditation for a few moments. Her trip to see Jonathan two weeks earlier had marked her first excursion outside Wisconsin, and she had learned how easy it was to travel.

"I've never been to Washington," she mused aloud. "This might a good time to go, in mid-winter, when there is very little work around the farm."

"Of course," encouraged Theodora. "Why don't you! Jessie can get you into the visitors' gallery so you can watch with the rest of the women."

"Well, the big drawback is money," said Prudence honestly. "If the hotels in Washington are as expensive as the *Raleigh Hotel* in Texas, I sure couldn't stay very long."

"I think Jessie can take care of that for you," said Theodora. "We're expecting quite a number of women from around the country, and we've found all sorts of places for them to stay. If you're really interested, I'll ask Jessie about it."

Prudence hesitated only for a moment. "There's still the cost of the railway ticket, but I'll never have another opportunity like this one. Yes, go ahead. I want to make the trip."

The dull winter sun had already disappeared when Prudence left Prairieville for home, and it was dark and cold on the empty road. Kaiser made his way with sure steps along the snow-covered track, however, giving her plenty of time to consider the exciting prospect of visiting the nation's capitol.

Awaiting her on the kitchen table was a letter from Camp MacArthur. Her name and address was scrawled in a boyish hand, and for a quick heart- stopping moment she thought of Karl. Then she felt a surge of shame as she realized her disappointment that the letter was from her own son.

"I pray that you and Sarah and Ephraim had a safe journey home. It was such a joy to be with you again, if only for a few hours. Thank you with all my heart for coming down to see me.

"Although we have not been told of any official date for our departure, it is pretty obvious we are about to leave. We have been told that of all the divisions in training around the country, we are the best one—therefore, we should be the next to go. We expect to be moved to the east coast any day now, and we have been ordered to get ourselves ready for immediate shipment."

The letter continued for several pages, describing the feverish excitement of the boys who were anxious to see France. Prudence scanned the lines quickly, expecting to learn news of Karl, but she was disappointed. She returned to the beginning and read the letter more carefully page by page, hoping to discover some small reference she had missed, but there was nothing.

After eating supper with Sarah and washing the dishes, Prudence sat at her writing table in the living room and wrote a brief letter in reply. She told of her visit with Congressman Voigt, and her intention to journey to Washington for the historic vote on the Anthony amendment.

On impulse, she addressed the letter jointly to Jonathan and to Karl, and slipped into the envelope a wallet-sized copy of her own portrait recently taken at O'Brien's.

Ephraim was opposed to her new journey when she first told him her intentions. "It's too dangerous, Prudy," he protested. "I won't let ya' do it."

"Eeph," she said sternly, "I'm going to go whether you approve of it or not, so there's no use in discussing the matter."

He quickly shifted his ground. "I'll go wit' ya', then," he said in a determined tone.

"No, Eeph, this is an occasion for the sisterhood of suffragists. You would be out of place there, and I would be embarrassed to have you along. If I'm capable enough to vote, then I'm capable enough to travel alone to Washington."

He remonstrated until he realized that his persistence was irritating her. His arguments were useless. She had made up her mind and that was that. "I am an independent woman, thank goodness," she told him, "and I will not be submissive to your protection!"

Her choice of words, hinting that she was lucky not to be married to him, gave great distress to Ephraim. Later, to make amends, he gave her the money to buy the railway tickets she needed. "I didn't mean t' make ya' angry wit' me," he apologized.

The vote on the Anthony amendment was definitely scheduled for Thursday, January 10th. Mrs. Hooper found a very inexpensive room for Prudence in a private home on Fifth Street in Washington, completing the arrangements. Just a few days later, Prudence found herself on the Tuesday morning train to Washington. She was pleased with her own bravery and audacity.

'What great adventures are opening before me,' she thought with amazement. 'A year ago, who would have imagined I'd be on this train today, heading off to the nation's capitol to take a small part in history? I've been talking with Congressmen; I've been to Texas; I've been involved in great events.'

She took a cab from the train station in Washington to her house on Fifth Street, which she discovered was within walking distance of the capitol. Her hostess, Mrs. Hudson, was a genial matron with two small children and no husband. She was not interested in politics, but she was friendly and very talkative. Her meager living was earned by taking in boarders.

Wednesday morning was devoted to sight-seeing. Mrs. Hudson insisted upon being her guide, leaving her children in the tender custody of their aunt.

Never was there a more complete tour of our nation's capitol in a single day. Mrs. Hudson knew where to go by the most direct route, and she knew what to do at each site. Prudence was overwhelmed by a succession of great historic places—the Lincoln Memorial, the Washington Monument, the White House, the Smithsonian, the Tidal Basin, the Jefferson Memorial, the Supreme Court Building—the memories of all these novel scenes became hopelessly jumbled in her mind. Mrs. Hudson whisked her from spot to spot, talking incessantly as they went. Prudence was relieved when they finally returned to the friendly house on Fifth Street for a hearty supper and an early bedtime.

The next morning, as she took her seat in the gallery of the House,

Prudence was met with a buzz of good news from a variety of women who were strangers, yet friends:

"President Wilson has come out openly for the Suffs!" declared one of the group, her face beaming.

Prudence quickly realized that the nickname 'Suffs' was short for 'suffragists.' She herself was a Suff.

"It's true," agreed another outspoken observer. "He declared his position to Congressman Raker yesterday."

"Congressman Raker is the chairman of the House Committee on woman suffrage."

"The President can't back down now. Even if we don't win today's vote, Wilson will have to support our campaign."

"Well, with the President's support, we'll certainly win today, won't we?"

"Of course. The President wouldn't have taken a stand if he wasn't sure of our victory."

"Don't be too sure! The vote is too close to count. We've got every last supporter on the floor that we can get, but there's an awful lot of Antis down there, too. We may still be one vote short."

"I saw Congressman Sims of Tennessee come in a moment ago with his arm in a sling."

"Yes, he's got a broken arm and a broken shoulder—but he wouldn't let the doctors set the bones because it might have kept him away."

"I hear Congressman Crosser of Ohio left his sickbed to make the vote for us."

"Yes, and so did the Republican House Leader, Congressman Mann from Illinois—he's been in the hospital for six months, but he's down there on the floor right now."

"I saw him come in—he couldn't even stand up by himself."

"And did you hear about Congressman Hicks of New York? He left his wife's deathbed. She knew she wouldn't live long enough to see him again, but she wanted him to come and vote—she was that devoted to the suffragist cause."

"Yes, I hear she died last night, while he was here in Washington."

"Now there's a real Suff for you!"

The proposed amendment to the Constitution was the essence of simplicity:

> *Section 1. The right of citizens of the United States to vote shall not be denied or abridged by the United States or by any State on account of sex.*

> *Section 2. Congress shall have the power to enforce this article by appropriate legislation.*

The roll call began amidst hectic last-minute appeals from members to each other. In contrast to the confusion below, the women were hushed as they kept a record of the votes as best they could. As the end of the roll approached, members began switching their votes, and the clerk was utterly unable to determine the outcome.

A second roll call was announced, and the disorderly scene began to repeat itself.

"How does it look?" Prudence asked Mrs. Hooper.

"I'm just as confused as the clerk," confessed her redoubtable friend, "but I think we're still a vote short of the two-thirds required."

The second attempt, like the first, was inconclusive, as the clerk was uncertain of the results, and a third roll call was ordered.

"Look what's happening!"

"It's a man coming in on a stretcher!"

"That's Congressman Barnhart, from Indiana—he's going to vote in our favor."

Once again the scene was enacted. By this time even Prudence knew which way most of the votes were going to be cast: Congressmen from the southern states were virtually united in their opposition, along with their colleagues from eastern industrial states like Pennsylvania and Ohio.

On the positive side were the Representatives from the west and the Midwestern states. The men from the state of New York, very much aware of the mandate expressed in their recent referendum, voted 40 to 4 in favor of the amendment.

Even on the third time around, a recapitulation of the vote was necessary before the outcome was certain. Suddenly the amendment's supporters on the floor began cheering and shouting to the gallery, and only then did Prudence and the rest of the women know that they had won.

The final tally proved that virtually every vote was needed, even the weak 'aye' from Congressman Barnhart on his stretcher. The Anthony amendment passed, 274 to 136. A switch of one vote from Aye to Nay would have defeated it.

Prudence was delighted to note that eight of the Congressmen from Wisconsin voted in favor of the amendment, with only Stafford and Voigt in opposition. The eleventh Congressman did not vote.

Spontaneously, in somber, measured cadence, the massed throng of inspired women gave expression to their pent-up emotions by singing 'Old Hundred'.

PRAISE GOD, FROM WHOM ALL BLESSINGS FLOW. . . .

Prudence was caught up in the grandeur of the moment. She felt exalted as never before, even though she knew the battle was not yet over. She joined in the singing, rising to join hands with the women on each side.

PRAISE HIM, ALL CREATURES HERE BELOW. . . .

They began swaying from side to side, as their solemn hymn resonated through the marble corridors of the capitol. They were celebrating the magical moment of a monumental victory long deferred. It had been an arduous journey from the makeshift meeting of Elizabeth Cady Stanton in Seneca Falls seventy years before. It was like arriving in heaven after a long and turbulent life.

In the *Prairieville Freeman* the next Thursday, Theodora wrote:

> *We have won. We are over the top. We have captured*
> *one of the three most important trenches on the way*
> *to complete enfranchisement.*

They had taken a big step forward, but victory was still far away. Before them lay the trenches of Senate concurrence of the amendment and ratification by the states.

Back at her Prairieville farm a few evenings later, Prudence patiently explained the political realities to Ephraim. "Passage by the U.S. Senate is virtually assured," she told him. It will probably take a few months, because the Senate by tradition is slower-moving than the House of Representatives. But it will come."

"Of course it will," agreed Ephraim vehemently. Anything Prudence wanted, he wanted too. And any dream she held, he was sure would come to pass.

"The real difficulty will be in securing the ratification by the states. Even by our most optimistic count, none of us can confidently name thirty-six states which will support the amendment."

"There's no trouble in Wisconsin, is there?" Ephraim asked. "Wit' you n' Missus Youmans n' everybody workin' so hard fer it, it's a sure thing, ain't it?"

"No, not really," she explained. "There is still a very strong sentiment against women's rights in this state. Don't be fooled by the fact that our Congressional delegation voted in favor of the amendment by a large majority. The state legislature will not be nearly so friendly."

"Who's in the state legislature, anyhow?" asked Ephraim.

"Oh, Eeph," she exclaimed, "surely you remember that Assemblyman John Buckley and State Senator Charles Mulberger represent us."

"Well, are they for us or agin' us?"

"I'm afraid they are against us," she said. "But we've got a lot of time to convince them. The amendment probably won't be passed and ready for ratification until late in the year or possibly early in 1919."

"There's an election this fall, ain't there?" asked Ephraim.

"Yes, there is."

"Is Buckley gonna be up fer re-election?"

"Yes, he will be."

"Then I'm gonna run against him. I gotta' be sure that our amendment gets ratified."

"Oh, Eeph," she laughed. "You're wonderful! You're always trying to do good things for me, and I love you for it. But somehow I can't quite picture you as a legislator in the State Assembly!"

Ephraim looked perplexed and possibly a trifle offended. "I'm gonna run, anyhow," he muttered.

Chapter 12

A blizzard of rumors heralding an imminent departure for France had been flying through Camp MacArthur since Thanksgiving, and shortly after Christmas the 32nd Division received official orders for transfer to the Port of Embarkation at Hoboken, New Jersey. The first troops left Waco on January 2nd. It was announced that Jon's infantry would be the first to move, but their orders were not forthcoming. Day followed routine day and Jon was still in Waco.

The formal training program of sixteen weeks had been completed in December, so the January days were filled with impromptu drilling, target shooting with the Springfield rifles, and any other makeshift work which the company officers could devise to help combat the inevitable monotony. They had hurried through their training, only to sit and wait.

Many of the infantry companies were commanded by a single officer, but the Prairieville Company was allowed to keep its three original leaders—Captain Dan Martin, First Lieutenant Harry 'Red' Welch, and Second Lieutenant Dick Austerman. The Company had arrived at Camp Douglas the previous August with a hundred and fourteen men.

Under orders from the United States War Department, the 32nd Division was reorganized at the time it reached Texas. Company size was increased to two hundred and fifty soldiers, requiring the consolidation of various units. The men from Prairieville remained together, as they had been promised, forming the basis of a new company in the 128th Infantry Regiment. They were joined by many other Wisconsin men, and even a few men from Michigan—including Karl.

The Prairieville boys were allowed considerable freedom during January. Jon and Lee and Karl often played schafkopf in the evening, huddled close to the little stove at the door of their tent. Red Welch often joined their game. On several occasions, Red protected them when a military policeman caught them deep into the hours of night-time curfew.

Red repeatedly encouraged them to go into town for an evening to break the monotony of camp life. Jon and his two friends were not given to carousing, and they had seen Waco only in the company of Jon's family at Christmas. They began suffering the boredom of camp fever by the end of January, however, and they finally accepted evening passes from Red.

"Hey, you guys goin' t' town?" asked a rowdy tent-mate who was known for his skirt-chasing.

"Yeah, I think we will," said Jon.

"The 'Reservation' on Second Street has been closed by federal order," their comrade reminded them, "so you can't get a woman legally in Waco. But girls are girls, and you'll be able to find what you're looking for." He winked.

"Thanks anyway," said Jon, "but we're not looking for girls."

"Okay," Lothario shrugged. "Some guys do, and some guys don't."

It was a short ride into Waco in the back of a military vehicle along with three other soldiers. When they climbed out they were downtown. The other three seemed to know where they were going, and they soon disappeared.

"Well, this is the big city," said Jon ruefully as he gazed around.

"Not too impressive, if you ask me," commented Karl.

The winter sun had already set, and the evening darkness was interrupted by the lights of the business district. The three country boys began their stroll, glancing into the windows of the closed shops and pausing to consider an occasional tavern or restaurant.

They had expected to be with a crowd of people, but the streets were quiet. Here and there they saw a cluster of unfamiliar soldiers. Most of the passersby were white men, with a sprinkling of Negroes.

"Well, let's pick someplace and eat supper," Jon suggested.

"I guess that's what we came for," agreed Karl, "but I haven't seen anything yet to catch my fancy."

"We could always stop in at *The Purple Cow*," Jon said. "The *Raleigh Hotel* is only a few blocks away, and the food was pretty good when I ate there at Christmas."

"We can start walking that way if you want," suggested Leo, "but let's keep our eyes open. Maybe we'll see something we like on the way."

As they walked, Karl thought of the holidays. "Y'know," he said, "we had a wonderful time at Christmas. I really enjoyed your family when they were here. Ephraim, Sarah, and your mother—all three of them seemed like such good people."

"Yes, I think they are wonderful, too," rejoined Jon. "But Ephraim isn't really part of the family, you know. He's a neighboring farmer who has been helping us ever since Dad died last spring."

"Yeah, I know. I know your dad is dead. Your mother is alone. My father is alone, too, since my mom died."

"Yes," Jon nodded. "Maybe we should get them together."

Karl laughed. "I don't think so. My father is nothin'. Nothin' but trouble. I wouldn't wish him on anybody. Especially not your mom. She was so nice."

"Yeah, my mother is a wonderful woman. Oh, we've had our bad moments, especially when I misbehaved, but I guess that's normal in any family. And I guess I'd have to admit that she was right to punish me once in a while. There were times when I was a little rascal."

"I can imagine," commented Leo.

"But I always knew she loved me," confirmed Jon. "Even when I was bad. And I have always loved her, too."

"I loved my mother, too," confessed Karl. "She and I were very special friends. We looked out for each other when Dad was mad at us."

Karl paused, and Jon glanced at him to encourage him to continue.

"Yes, my mother was a very good person," resumed Karl, "and that would just make my old man all the madder. He'd yell at her when he was mad, especially when he was drinking. She'd just sit there quiet-like, without shoutin' back, but you could see the fear and the terror in her eyes."

Karl's voice choked with a sudden emotion, but in the dim light his friends didn't know whether it was anger or sorrow.

"Sometimes that'd be enough for him, just to see how frightened she was. But sometimes he'd start hittin' her. Maybe every month or so. I think it depended upon how drunk he was. He'd walk over to her, right in the middle of yellin' at her, and just suddenly hit her, or sometimes he'd just pretend to hit her. Sometimes he'd hit her more than once. He'd just keep at it, even though she didn't fight back, until he got tired of it. If she fell on the floor then he'd kick her. She'd be all black and blue the next day, all over her arms and her legs and her face."

"That's awful!" exclaimed Leo.

"When I was just a kid, I couldn't do much to help her. He'd just push me aside. And I was scared of him, too. But as I got older, I began protecting her from him whenever I could. The last couple of years, things were a lot better. He didn't dare touch her when I was around."

"Why didn't she call someone for help, or leave him?" asked Jon.

"Who could she call? Where could she go?" Karl asked. "Her parents both died when she was young. We lived in a run-down house, 'way out in the country. Didn't even have a phone until the last couple of years. Without his paycheck from the factory, how would she feed me and my two sisters? She *had* to stay with him, and put up with it. There wasn't any choice."

"How long ago did she die?" Jon asked.

"Just a year ago. Right at the end of winter. She suffered from a horrible cough. Sometimes she would cough all night."

"What did the doctor say?"

"She wouldn't see a doctor. I tried to get her to go. She was afraid he would put her in a hospital somewhere—she had T.B., I think. She said she would rather die. And she did. I think she was ready to go. Both my sisters were married and gone, and I think she realized I was staying home only for her. She never asked me, but I think she knew it."

"That's a terrible story," said Jon. "You've never told me any of that before. I didn't know."

"Well, I don't like to remember it, much less go around talking about it."

"That's why you joined the army, then," Jon declared. "It was right after your mother died."

"Yeah, that's right. I quit my job in the factory and joined the National Guard. I didn't even tell my old man 'good-by'. I enlisted quietly, and kept everything a secret from him. I wanted to surprise him—he'd come home one night and I wouldn't be there and he wouldn't have any idea where I had gone."

"Does he know where you are now?"

"Oh, I suppose so, if he bothered to ask questions around town afterward. But I haven't heard from him. And I don't care. I hope I never hear from him again."

As Karl finished his story, the two boys were climbing the steps of the *Raleigh Hotel*. They went inside, and they found the throng of people they had expected downtown. *The Purple Cow* was crowded to capacity, and they were told it would be a few minutes before they could be seated.

"Did your family like the *Raleigh*?" asked Karl.

"Yes, they liked it a lot. The rooms were clean and the service was good. Of course, we don't have a lot to compare it to—I think it was the first hotel they ever stayed in."

"Your mother was so nice," Karl said again, tenderly. "She reminded me a lot of my own mom."

"Well, most moms are pretty decent people," agreed Jon.

"Has she had a hard life?" inquired Leo.

"Who? Mom? No, not really," said Jon. "She's worked hard, of course; we all work hard on the farm. But my dad treated her real good. He didn't drink. None of us in the family drink. I'd say she has had a really wonderful life. And now she's acting like a young heifer in the springtime. She has good friends in town, and she is working hard to win votes for women. I just got a letter from her a few days ago. She's going to Washington D.C. to watch Congress vote on the Anthony amendment."

"No. Really? That sounds like big-time stuff," commented Karl. "I had no idea your mother was such an important lady!"

Jon laughed. "She's not big-time. I love her, but she's not big-time. She just kind of grew into this campaign for woman suffrage, mostly because she happened to meet a woman in Prairieville who heads up the campaign in Wisconsin."

"Well, it sounds big-time to me if she is going to Washington. I can't ever imagine my own mother doing something like that."

"If you like impossible scenes, then listen to this," said Jon rather proudly. "When she goes around the state campaigning, she rides a Harley- Davidson motorcycle!"

Karl laughed. "I like the woman!" he exclaimed. "I like her. She is not only a very nice lady, but a very exciting one to boot. When does she go to Washington?"

"I don't remember. Here, let me look." Jon pulled Prudence's letter from his pocket, and laid it on top of the grand piano in the hotel lobby. He set aside the small O'Brien portrait of his mother, smoothed the wrinkled pages of the letter, and began perusing it.

Karl peered over his shoulder. "Hey!" he exclaimed. "She addressed it to you and to *me*! Why would she do that?"

"Oh, I hadn't noticed." He shrugged. "I don't really know why she did that. I . . . I guess she liked you."

Karl noticed the photograph. He picked it up carefully and studied it. "Your mother is a beautiful woman," he commented thoughtfully. "And she looks so young!"

The lady in charge of the restaurant appeared at the entrance of the dining room, and Karl asked her how much longer they would have to wait.

She looked exasperated. "I really don't know," she replied. It will be a while yet."

"Could you suggest a nearby restaurant which would be less crowded?" inquired Karl.

The woman wrinkled her face. "You can try the cafe where the university kids go," she offered, giving them directions.

Jon turned to his friends. "Let's go," he suggested, folding his letter and replacing it in his pocket. "I think I'd prefer a smaller place."

"That's fine with me," responded Karl, and the three boys left the hotel and resumed their stroll.

Only a block or two away, they found the small cafe. Its tables were occupied with young men and women, including several boys in uniform.

They waited to be seated, and they signed their names in the guest register as requested: Jon Hartmann and Leo Herbst and Karl Krupp.

The two boys who entered behind them didn't like their names. "A bunch of Germans, huh?" the taller one huffed. "Since when do they let krauthead traitors in the army?"

Jon faced them. He remembered the young boys who had thrown stones at his horse and wagon as he was leaving Perkins Hardware back in Prairieville, and his stomach tightened. "We are American citizens," he declared, and we're every bit as loyal to Uncle Sam as you are."

"Hah!" snorted the boy. "Of course you would say so. You wouldn't admit it if you were a spy or a traitor."

"Yeah," said his comrade. "We know how to deal with German traitors. We've got some at Baylor University, even on the faculty, and we led the fight to get them out."

"Well, we're not traitors and we're not getting out," Jon said bravely.

"Maybe we'll throw you out, right now." muttered the student. "We don't want to eat at the same table with Huns."

"Don't try anything," Jon warned. "We've got an awful lot of friends." He looked over his shoulder at a table occupied by four soldiers, as if they were part of the group.

The troublemaker followed his glance, and backed down. "Let's go somewhere else," he said to his companion. "I don't want to eat with the Huns."

Jon and his friends watched them go. "I can't believe this," said Jon, shaking his head sadly. "One of the reasons I joined the army was so that everyone would know that I am a patriotic citizen, even though I come from a German family."

"It certainly is incredible," agreed Leo.

After they were seated, Karl said confidentially, "I've been thinking about changing the spelling of my name, so it won't sound so German."

"Changing it to what?" asked Jon.

"Just changing the first letter from 'K' to 'C'," he explained. "Karl with a 'K' is so Teutonic. But Carl with a 'C' is pure American."

Jon smiled. "I suppose so. But it doesn't seem like much of a change to me, especially when your last name is 'Krupp.' That sounds awfully German to me. Are you going to change that, too?"

"I'd like to change it," Karl said. "But I think I would have to go into court and get it legally changed, because it's my last name. For my first name, I think I can just decide to do it by myself. I don't think I have to even tell anyone."

"I don't know," admitted Jon, "but it sounds reasonable. So from now on, you are Carl with a 'C'?"

"Yes. I'm going to do it, right now." He laughed. "For the rest of our lives, we can point back to this moment in a Texas cafe and say, 'that was where I changed my name!'"

"Okay," said Jon mischievously, stretching out his right arm with a table knife held lightly in his fingers, touching his comrade's shoulder with the flat of the blade. "I dub thee Carl with a 'C'. There. It's done. Rise, Sir Carl, and face your future."

During the meal Leo revealed that Clara had returned the engagement ring to him a second time. "She doesn't like the setting," he explained. "She says it sticks up too high. I guess I'll have to take it back to the jeweler again."

"She sure is hard to please," commented Carl. "Do you think she'll ever be satisfied?"

"I hope so," said Leo. "I don't really know."

When they returned to camp that night, there was high excitement.

"I think we'll be heading out soon," Red told them. "The exact date still hasn't been announced, but it's got to be within a few days. We were told to get everything in company headquarters ready to go on a minute's notice."

Despite their eagerness, they were destined to wait impatiently in Texas for several more weeks. They watched other members of the 32nd Division march out of camp headed for the troop train while they remained behind, anxiously waiting to get into action.

At last, near the end of February, their turn came to leave. They marched to the railway station with their belongings on their backs, and waved goodby to the city through the grimy windows of their coach.

Jon wrote home from the East Coast early in March.

"I'm sure that you heard about the sinking of the troopship, the Tuscania, by a German submarine," he began. *"Some of the boys from the 32nd Division were on board, including Ed Boemke from Prairieville, they say. Maybe there were others, too, but we don't know yet."*

Yes, of course Prudence had heard about the Tuscania. She had worried and prayed and given him up for lost even though she knew he was still safe on solid ground in America.

"It looks like we have simply replaced one waiting place for another," he continued. *"I thought we would never get out of Texas. We watched all the other units going, and it seemed like we were the last one. Now it is the same story here in New Jersey. We were actually on board our troopship, waiting to leave port, when one of the boys came down with some awful disease. It's a form of meningitis, they say. So they quarantined a dozen of us, including Lee and Carl and me, and jerked us back off the ship.*

"The rest of our company has already disappeared overseas, but we are stuck here.

"I don't know how much of this letter they will censor, but it's impossible to keep secret a troop movement of this size. Virtually the whole 32nd Division is gone, including all of our regiment. And here we sit, doing nothing, while the rest of the world goes rolling along."

Prudence read those lines with mixed feelings. Jon wasn't in the trenches yet. But was it any better to have him exposed to meningitis? He might very well die in an army camp on this side of the Atlantic!

"Meanwhile, Lee's sweetheart, Clara, returned his engagement ring to him for the third time. There's a chip in the diamond, she says, and she wants another gem which has no flaw.

"We think her girlfriends are jealous, and when they criticize her ring then she finds fault with it too!

"Anyway, he bought another stone and had it set in the ring and he sent it back to her again. He hopes this is the last time he sees the darned thing until he gets home and sees it on her finger!"

Jon wrote about the angry students in the cafe who had taunted them for their German names. *"As a result, Karl has changed the spelling of his name to Carl, with a 'C'.*

"And by the way, Carl was gratified that you remembered him," she read with a blush. *"When he saw that you had addressed your letter to him, as well as to me, he was surprised and very pleased. He says to tell you that you are a very beautiful lady, and you look very young, especially for someone who is so important in the women's political scene. He's right, of course. He is impressed with your suffrage activity as well as your good looks. Honestly, I think I could have passed you off as my older sister when you visited me. All the guys who met you thought you were very nice."*

Prudence felt embarrassed. At first, she wasn't exactly sure *why* she felt that way, but her face was quite warm when she finished reading Jon's letter. As she pondered the matter, however, she came to believe that Carl was sending her a coded message. He was confirming his warm feelings in response to her own, but he was careful enough to say everything in a way that would not be obvious to Jon or to others who might read his letter.

She quietly put it aside at the back of her little writing table in the living room. She didn't want anyone to think she was hiding a letter from Jon, but she secretly hoped Sarah would not see it there.

But of course, Sarah *did* see it there. She saw it, and she picked it up eagerly, and read it, and she too was surprised when her face grew warm.

Prudence and Sarah did not discuss Jon's letter. In the past, they read his letters and commented on them, exploring his thoughts and picturing him in whatever he was doing. Now it was different. When Sarah finished reading this letter, she replaced it almost guiltily upon the writing table. She and her mother averted their eyes from each other, and neither of them chose to speak. The silence quickly became unendurable, and she went to her room.

It was inevitable that Sarah should seek her solace from Ephraim. She sneaked the letter from Prudence's desk later in the afternoon and read it aloud to him in the loft of the barn while he was pitching hay down for the cattle. When she finished, he sank heavily onto a pile of hay alongside her. They sat there together, huddled in the deep aroma of the dried alfalfa, their parallel gazes lost in the gloomy obscurity of the cavernous loft.

"Somehow, that letter makes me feel very unhappy, Uncle Eeph," she ventured after a while.

"I ain't very happy about it, either," he admitted.

"I thought Mom acted a little bit funny down in Texas when she was with Carl," she said.

"Yes, it was pretty obvious," he agreed. "She was actin' like a spring chicken." He paused. "She's a good-lookin' bird, everybody would agree, but at her age she ain't no spring chicken."

Sarah watched the myriad of little specks of haydust dancing through the slender shaft of sunlight shining through a knothole. She thought idly of the millions of such motes gently swirling unseen through the empty spaces of the enormous hayloft. Only a tiny number of them were illuminated by the narrow sunbeam; the rest were invisible and ignored. She could smell them; she could virtually feel them in her nostrils as she breathed—but she could not see them, except for the few that chanced to drift through the spotlight.

'There are so many things in life that are hidden from sight,' she mused to herself. 'You know they are there, and you can feel their effect, but you can't see them.' She had lived with her mother all her life, and yet there was so much about her that she didn't know, and could not comprehend.

Aloud, she said, "Uncle Eeph, I want you to marry Mom."

"I want that, too," he breathed.

"It would be the right thing for both of you to do," Sarah said.

"Yes, it would," he agreed. 'You don't know how right you are,' he thought to himself.

"How can we get her to see that?" she asked.

"I dunno', Sarah, I dunno'."

They sat silently, neither of them ready to rise. Their sunbeam was abruptly cut off by a vagabond cloud, but after a few moments it was restored again.

"You kinda' liked Carl, didn' ya," observed Ephraim.

She hesitated only for a second. "Yes, I did. I enjoyed talking with him during our Christmas dinner."

"You'd like t' get t' know 'im better?"

"Yes, I would."

"He's on his way t' France now."

"Yes," she acknowledged. "But he'll be back. I know in my heart he'll be coming to Prairieville."

"Yep, I think yer right. I think we'll be seein' 'im agin."

She hesitated longer this time before speaking. "Uncle Eeph, you didn't like the idea of me seeing Jimmy. You're sure you don't mind me seeing Carl?"

"Carl is different," Ephraim said flatly. "Carl is okay. Carl is a man who's gonna make somethin' outta himself. You can tell that just by talkin' t' 'im."

"Thank you, Eeph. I depend so much upon your good judgment. And I like Carl already, an awful lot. And I hope Mom doesn't spoil everything."

He picked up an alfalfa stem and began chewing on it idly as he reflected.

"Well, Sarah, we've worked on things t'gether before. Let's work on this one. Let's get me married off t' yer mom, and let's get you n' Carl t' be friends—real good friends."

"I'd like that very much," she said.

He rose to his feet, and reached down to help her up. "We're partners, then," he declared.

"Yes, Uncle Eeph, we're partners, as always." They sealed their covenant with a long and expressive hug.

Prudence was not aware that Ephraim and Sarah had arrived at such an outspoken understanding, but she felt a certain measure of discomfort at the implications of Jon's remarks in his letter.

'How can I be so attracted to a man who is really just a boy? A boy who is young enough to be my son?' she mused to herself. 'Is Eeph right? Am I making a fool out of myself?'

She retrieved the letter from the desk where Sarah had replaced it, and read it again quite carefully. 'I don't see any hint of reproach in Jon's writing,' she thought. 'If I were acting improperly, surely Jon would have indicated some criticism, however slight. But there is nothing critical at all in what he says. Quite the contrary. He seems to be proud of the fact that I look young and beautiful.'

She carried the letter upstairs to her bedroom, and put it into the top drawer of her dresser. Then she paused to look into the mirror. She wiggled her nose and pulled lightly at her face below her eyes.

'My face may not be as fresh and tender as a baby's,' she thought, 'but it doesn't look like an old woman's, either. It's still strong and healthy. I could easily pass for thirty.'

She smiled at her reflection in the glass, revealing the straight lines of her white teeth. "Hmm," she murmured with approval, whispering to herself, "I look even better when I smile."

Nodding her head convincingly, she decided there was nothing wrong with her actions and her desires. 'I have a right to my own feelings,' she told herself. 'I have a right to enjoy Carl. We're both adults, and I am no longer married. There is nothing wrong with what I'm doing, no matter what Ephraim says. He is not an impartial judge. After all, he wants me for himself, so it's easy to see why he discourages my friendship with another man.'

The next day, she sat at her writing table and penned a response to Jon and Carl. She told them of her experiences in Washington D.C., and her elation at the passage of the Anthony amendment in the House of Representatives. She commented upon the virulence of the anti-German feelings in Prairieville as well as Waco. *"It's a shame that some pig-headed people behave the way they do,"* she commented, *"but when I consider the appearance of Carl's name, I confess I like it better with a 'C'.*

"Please thank Carl for the kind compliments you wrote about," she concluded. *"He appears to be an unusually fine man. . ."*—she had started to write, 'young man', but quickly changed her mind, *"and I am delighted that he is such a close friend of yours."* She puzzled how to send Carl a coded message of her own warm feelings for him. Several times she started to write, and stopped. Finally she wrote very simply, "You may tell him that I like him very much."

The letter was delivered in New Jersey just a few hours after the quarantine was lifted, so the day was doubly blessed. Jon smiled as he read the message from home, and of course he passed the letter to Carl as well. Prudence's approval of Carl was welcomed by them both.

The last twelve members of the 128th Infantry Regiment, including Lee and Carl and Jon, boarded the troopship *Powhattan* on the morning of March 22nd and by evening the ship was on the high seas.

The *Powhattan* was actually a German merchant ship, known as the before the war. It was one of the ships trapped away from home in 1914 when the British asserted their control of the seas and established a blockade against the Kaiser. It sought sanctuary in a neutral port of the United States, where it was eventually seized by Uncle Sam and converted to military use against its own country.

The *Powhattan* sailed in a convoy of just four ships, and everyone was extremely conscious of the threat of German submarines. During the day, the ships bunched together in a pack, guarded by the U.S. battleship *Arizona*. Toward evening, they would steer apart, out of sight of each other.

For the first time in his life Jon felt he had friends of the finest kind. Growing up on the farm had afforded little time to spare with others his age. Of course he loved his family, and had always felt close to each of the members including Uncle Eeph. He had never felt lonely nor deprived, to be sure, but now that he and Carl and Leo had begun opening their hearts to each other he suddenly realized the importance of sharing confidences with a comrade.

His discovery of this fundamental phenomenon of life occurred the evening Carl revealed the unhappy story of his life at home. The simple disclosure of such a secret opened a door of communication between the two young men that clamored for expansion.

The long days of idleness aboard ship allowed the three boys to become well acquainted with each other. They freely described the facts of their personal histories, and continued talking in the realm of their feelings and fears.

Eventually they caught up, chronologically, to their presence together aboard a military troopship headed for war.

"I don't have a good feeling about going to war," confessed Jon.

"That's only natural," commented Carl. "I don't think anyone could have a good feeling about killing or being killed."

"On the one hand, I feel it is something I had to do. I thought it through very carefully on the night I spent in the marsh—the night I told you about, when Eeph finally came to get me. There is no question that I had to enlist. It was my duty; it was a big way to say 'thank you' to this great country of ours. That sounds artificial even as I say it, but it still has an enormous significance to me."

"I understand that feeling, and I agree with it," said Leo.

"It was also a very graphic way to tell our neighbors that we are patriotic even though we have a German background."

"You said that to us in the cafe," Carl acknowledged, "and I know what you mean. I felt the same way, although I had other more powerful reasons for enlisting and getting out of town."

"You sure did," agreed Jon.

"Then why don't you have good feelings about what you're doing?"

"Well, I had a very strange dream last night," said Jon.

"That's no surprise," laughed Carl. "I'm not a sailor, and just being on this boat—even on a smooth sea—makes me nervous. Scratching those cooties all the time gives me the willies, too. I've had a bunch of wild dreams every night since we left New Jersey. But tell me about your dream last night. . . ."

"Well, I don't usually dream. I'm a landlubber, too, just as much as you, but I have slept pretty well on the *Powhattan*, even a couple of nights ago when we were rolling so much.

"So I don't think the ship has anything to do with my dream. And it really wasn't much of a dream; there was no action and no words."

"You're right," smiled Carl, "That doesn't sound like much of a dream."

"And yet it was. It was so powerful!"

"Well, what was it?" asked Leo.

"It's hard to describe. It was, ummm, like a vision. That's right, you'd call it a vision. It was a vision of my father. He came through a doorway, and just stood there. I don't think I recognized the doorway, and I don't know where this happened, really. But he stood there and looked at me with such a powerful sadness in his face. I don't ever remember him looking so sad in real life. Stern, yes. Unsmiling, yes. But not sad. His face was always positive, and vigorous, as I remember it."

"Do you know why he was sad?" asked Carl.

"No, I don't. He didn't speak, or move, or convey any message except for that indescribable mournfulness."

"He wasn't angry with you, nor critical, nor disapproving?"

"No, not at all. Just sad, like you might see on your neighbors' faces at a funeral. In fact, yes, maybe I did see him like that once in real life, and it was at the funeral of his father—my grandfather."

"How old were you?" asked Leo.

"Let's see—my grandpa died in 1910, so I was twelve years old. He was the last of my grandparents—my mother's parents both died when I was very young, and I don't even remember them. My other grandmother—my father's mother—died just before my grandpa—everybody said he died because he couldn't live very long without her."

"Was your father sad like that at your grandmother's funeral?"

"I don't remember seeing him sad, not real sad."

"Tell me more about the dream," insisted Carl.

"Golly, there isn't much more to tell. All I can remember is the expression of extreme grief in his face. He conveyed a sense of regret that was traumatic for us both. His eyes seemed to look right through me— his gaze was sharp and penetrating."

"What do you suppose it meant?" asked Leo.

"I don't know, unless it has something to do with the war. Maybe he was unhappy because there is so much suffering in the battles that are being fought."

"Maybe he wished he could go along and experience all the excitement with you—maybe he wished he weren't dead?" suggested Carl.

"Maybe so, but I didn't get that feeling at all. I think his unhappiness was caused by something more tangible," Jon replied.

"Is it more personal?" inquired Leo. "Something regarding you? Can he see into the future? Do you think he knows something bad that's going to happen to you in France? Is that what makes him so sad?"

"That's possible, but I don't really know. All I know is that he stood there looking at me, and he had the saddest eyes I have ever seen."

"You started this conversation by saying that you don't have a very good feeling about going into war," Carl reminded him. "Did you have that feeling before the dream? Or is it your father's expression that makes you uncomfortable?"

"I've been uneasy about it from the very beginning, I think. I didn't really want to enlist, unlike some of the other guys in the company. There are a lot of the guys who are pretty eager to start fighting. I don't feel that way, and never have. I think it is something that has to be done."

"Like an unpleasant duty," suggested Carl.

"Yes, exactly."

The voyage required fourteen days, giving the three comrades plenty of chance to talk. Their friendship deepened to a rich friendship among equals. Jon, planning for the future, decided he would like to have Carl settle in Prairieville after the war. There was nothing to draw him back to Michigan. Therefore, one afternoon as the boys were standing at the rail of the ship, looking out at the endless expanse of gray water, Jon said, "I'm going to be sending a letter to my mom as soon as we make shore. Why don't you write a little note for Sarah? I'm sure she'd love hearing from you."

Carl readily agreed with the suggestion. "Sure. I'd like to do that. And I did think your sister was mighty nice!"

The two boys smiled at each other, and resumed their informal watch of the waves.

The journey was tiresome and everyone was relieved when land was finally sighted. Word was quickly passed that they had arrived at the harbor of Bordeaux in southern France. The German submarines had missed them, and the *Powhattan* had delivered them safe to Europe.

They were eager to set their feet on solid ground again, but the ship anchored at noon in the entrance to the harbor. "The tide is out," they were told. "We have to wait until evening to go ashore."

The boys stood at their favorite spot at the ship's rail, staring at the coast of France, wondering what their future would hold.

Chapter 13

Following his confidential covenant with Sarah, Ephraim sought opportunities to advance his courtship of Prudence. He was quite aware of the rapidly approaching anniversary of Zachary's death, and he hoped that the passage of a year had diminished her previous loyalties and opened the way for himself.

On a gentle evening in March, Ephraim and Prudence were standing alongside the barn watching the cattle file inside to their stalls.

"Spring is comin'," remarked Ephraim to start the conversation.

"Yes, it is," Prudence agreed amiably.

"It's a good time fer settlin' down 'n puttin' things right," he ventured.

She shrugged her shoulders uncomfortably, anticipating his words.

He pressed on. "I been thinkin' how lonely ya' must be, 'n how ya' must be longin' fer some permanent companionship."

"Oh, I've got my children," she said.

"But Jon is gone now, and Sarah oughta' get married afore long."

"They're company for me, even if they aren't home on the farm," Prudence pointed out philosophically. "They don't have to be here right under my feet."

He reflected for a moment, chewing on a straw. "It ain't right," he said at last, "it ain't right for you t' be alone. It ain't natural. The Good Lord fills the earth with pairs, not wit' singles."

"I don't mind being alone," insisted Prudence wearily, "and I think it's okay with the Good Lord, too. And now, let's get on with the milking, or we'll never get through with the chores."

The last of the cattle had disappeared into the barn and found their way to their stalls where they began munching their evening treat of ground oats. Ephraim and Prudence followed them inside.

Ephraim dreaded the approach of mid-March, the time of Zachary's death in the mill. He didn't like to remember that awful event; it evoked within him a vague, suppressed sense of uneasiness and guilt. He had been only partly successful in pushing that bloody remembrance from his mind. As the anniversary approached, Ephraim was uncertain whether he should commemorate the occasion in some way or simply ignore it.

He thought of asking Sarah's opinion one cloudy morning as she was cleaning his house, but he stopped suddenly when he realized she too might be sensitive about the subject. A deep-buried memory surfaced in his mind—the recollection of the night shortly after the funeral when Sarah had dissolved in tears of agonized grief, surprising him. Although she had revealed the profound depth of her feeling, it was an expression she had never repeated and therefore he had forgotten it until now.

As if she could read his mind, Sarah paused with dust-cloth in hand, and said thoughtfully, "It's been almost a year since Dad died."

"Yeah, I been thinkin' the same thing," Eeph replied.

"Things haven't changed as much as I feared they would," she reflected. "A year ago, I thought . . . well, I don't know what I thought, except that the world as I knew it would be torn apart. I had visions of being very lonely, and moving away from the farm, and maybe even going hungry. I didn't know what to expect."

"Changes don't come easy t' nobody," observed Eeph. "Everybody is scared o' the unknown—and let's be honest, the future is always somethin' ya' can't count on."

"You're right, Uncle Eeph, anything can happen at any time. Only God knows when we're going to get sick, or get hurt, or die."

"He's a merciful God, though," added Ephraim. "He looks after us purty good."

"He's dependable," Sarah agreed. "You can count on the sun coming up every morning, and setting again in the evening. The seasons succeed each other in a regular rhythm. We plant in the spring as winter retreats, and when you put the seeds into the ground you know the corn and the oats are going to grow through the summer. In the fall the air turns nippy and it's time to pull in the harvest which you know is going to be there. And of course you'd better hunker down by Thanksgiving because winter arrives again without fail."

"It's purty predictable," Ephraim observed.

"You don't have to worry about it," she agreed.

"Take no thought for tomorrow," Ephraim quoted. "The Lord will provide."

"Yes, so long as you follow His rules," she added.

176

"Of course."

"And when you die, it's really just going back to Him," she said. "Dad went back. I know Dad's in heaven with Him."

"Yah. Yer dad was a godly man. There's no doubt about it. He's in heaven."

"That's what life is all about, isn't it," she mused. "I've thought about that during the past year. There's millions and millions of people in this world, and we don't have to be the best one, nor the richest one, nor the most powerful one. All of that is vanity, says the Preacher. A striving after the wind. We just live though our own seasons, following His laws, and then we go back to Him."

"I reckon yer right," said Eeph.

"It's like being a flower," Sarah continued. "I never saw an unhappy flower. It just blooms wherever the seed happens to fall, and doesn't even think about whether the next flower might look prettier, or attract more butterflies, or keep its petals longer. And when it wilts and dies, it does-n't complain. It just goes back quietly to the earth where it came from. It has served its purpose—it has been beautiful in its season, and hopeful-ly it has left some seeds behind it to sweeten the next generation of ten-ants on the earth."

"That's a good message, t' just be yerself an' be satisfied," comment-ed Ephraim.

"That's all God expects from us, I'm sure," said Sarah confidently.

"I know ya' been at peace with Zachary's death," said Ephraim. "Now I think I understand why."

"Yes, that's why. Oh, I missed him at first. He had always just been there, the head of the family. You know what I mean. So I missed him. And I worried about what might happen. But nothing bad happened."

"Nothin' bad happened," echoed Ephraim.

"Of course, *you* were here," she said, touching his arm and looking up into his eyes. "How could I feel bad when you are here? I loved my father, to be sure, but I feel closer to you than I did to him. You've always been like a father to me."

"I'm glad of that," he said. "An' you know I feel the same way about you."

"Thank you," she breathed, adding softly, "You know I love you."

"Yes, I know that." He took her hand and squeezed it.

Then he remembered his question. "What about yer mom?" he asked. "How should we handle this first anniversary? Should we talk about Zachary with her, or should we say nothin'?"

"I'm not sure," replied Sarah. "It seems to me Mom hasn't really been overcome by grief during the past year. Instead, it's like she was set free by Dad's death. When you think about the changes in our lives since he died, you have to recognize that most of the changes happened to her, not to the rest of us. She has made friends—she has become a club woman—she has taken to riding a motorcycle—she has traveled, to Texas and to Washington—almost everything in her life has changed."

"Yeah, I know," grumbled Eeph, thinking of Carl.

"It's true she wore dark clothes for a while," said Sarah. "I think she was simply following the custom, though, rather than being in mourning, until she bought that new dress in Waco. And after that she started wearing her normal clothes again."

"She never really acted like she was in mournin'," agreed Ephraim.

"So I don't know what's the right thing to do," Sarah concluded. "I suppose we should just wait and see what Mom says and does."

"Yeah, I think mebbe that's best," Ephraim agreed.

The anniversary day arrived. Without mentioning Zachary, Prudence invited Ephraim for dinner in the evening—something she did not often do.

Ephraim wanted, as always, to present himself well to Prudence—a desire which carried even more urgency since she had met Carl. He returned to his home after the chores were finished so he could wash and put on his Sunday clothes. When he arrived for dinner, he was surprised to find Prudence wearing the flowery frock she had bought in Waco after meeting Carl. He had not seen her wear it since their return from Texas.

The table in the dining room was covered with white linen for the first time since Zachary's death. Prudence's fine bone china—bordered with a pattern of wild roses and rimmed with gold—was set at each place, flanked by the sterling silver which had been her mother's. Delicate crystal goblets completed the scene. Ephraim wondered at the festive setting, but still he was not sure whether Prudence intended to impart an unusual significance to the occasion.

Sarah served the meal, allowing Prudence and Ephraim to dine without interruption. The fried chicken with mashed potatoes, milk gravy, and creamed corn kept the appearance of the table cheerful and sunny. Thin slices of home-made bread smeared with raspberry jam added a touch of bright color. Prudence was in a lively spirit, almost frivolous, as she chattered lightheartedly about a variety of subjects.

Ephraim listened to her with growing apprehension. He had never seen her in quite such a mood before. In his nervousness, he became clumsy. Midway through the meal he dropped his fork on the table, and in trying to catch it he upset his goblet and spilled the milk across the linen.

"I'm sorry," he said sheepishly, mopping the tablecloth with his handkerchief.

"It's all right," laughed Prudence. "Sarah, get a wet dishrag to clean it up so the linen won't be stained."

When they resumed eating, their feelings were even more divergent than before. Although the room was cool, Ephraim began perspiring profusely and was forced to wipe his forehead with his damp handkerchief. Prudence continued her lighthearted twittering.

Finally, when Sarah served the lemon meringue pie, Prudence asked gaily, "Do you know what day it is today, Eeph?"

He was flustered, but he stammered out a slow answer: "Y-y-yes."

"It's the day Zachary died," she went on. "It's been a year today. Do you remember?"

"Y-yes, I 'member," he muttered in confusion.

"The year has gone by rather quickly," she observed. "At least, it seems that way to me."

"Yeah," he assented.

"And yet, a year is a long time. Even at my age, a year is a long time. A lot of things have happened in that year."

"Yeah," Ephraim said again, speaking only because the inflection in her voice called for an acknowledgement.

"A year is long enough for mourning, isn't it?" she asked.

"Yes," he said slowly, puzzled, still not sure where the conversation would lead.

"Well, I'm ready to let go of Zachary," she declared. "It's been a year, and it's time to forget. I've got my own life to lead."

"Yes," said Ephraim again, his pulse quickening at the possibility that in letting go of Zachary, she might be responsive at last to his own courtship.

"Oh, I don't mean I will forget Zachary," she hastily added. "I would never forget him, of course. He was my husband for twenty-five years, a good husband, although . . . ." her sentence dangled unfinished as her eyes glanced out the window into an unseen distance.

"Twenty-five years is a long, long time," she resumed. "And, of course, he was the father of my children." She scrutinized Ephraim's face carefully, and saw no hint of contradiction. Instead, she identified an expression of eager expectation—an expression which puzzled her. Not knowing what to make of it, she suppressed her curiosity because she didn't want a distraction from her train of thought.

"What I mean is," she continued in a rush, "what I mean is, I want to start over in life. I feel almost like I've been re-born. I'm standing on the threshold of spring—outside as well as inside. I feel young, and the world is full of promise. I want to take part in life. For twenty-five years I have been tied to this farm, and tied to my family. I'm tired of it all. I want something more."

She stopped, suddenly aware of her daughter staring at her with a touch of pain and reproach in her face. "Oh, Sarah, I don't mean anything against you! I love you. You know I love you. It has been a great joy to raise you from babyhood onward. But you're grown up now, you know that; you don't need me anymore, and so I can be free, can I not? Do you understand?"

Sarah nodded. "Yes, mother, I understand." Her voice was compassionate, but she concealed her true feelings. "Yes, I am grown up. You have done a good job of taking care of me as a baby and a child. But you are free now. I recognize that, and I understand it."

"You forgive me?" Prudence asked quickly.

"Yes, I forgive you. But there's nothing to forgive. There's a time in life for everything, and the time for you to mother me is past. I want you to be free, just as I want to be free myself. There's nothing wrong with that."

"Thank you, Sarah," she said. Then she turned triumphantly to Ephraim. "You see? It's all right. There's a time for everything, as she says, and right now in my life it's a time to be free. My year of mourning is over. I don't feel like a widow any longer." It was as though she felt Ephraim were trying to restrain her, and a trace of chiding appeared in the tone of her voice.

"You probably thought this dinner was to honor my dead husband." Ephraim and Sarah looked at her quizzically. "Well, it's not. It's to honor me—myself. I'm celebrating this night, and I'm celebrating myself. I'm young. I'm free. It's spring. New life is starting over again, and I want to be part of it. I want to start over!"

She paused, turning her attention to the half-eaten slice of pie on her plate, and there was silence around the table. Ephraim and Sarah glanced at each other, not knowing what to say. The two of them had agreed that Prudence should get married again, to Ephraim of course, but this was certainly not the time to suggest a marriage. Not with all the commitments and responsibilities it entailed. How could they promote such a union in the face of her strong declaration of independence?

In the days that followed, they could not detect any change in Prudence. She believed she had been restrained during the previous year, but Ephraim and Sarah knew better. They recognized she had become free the moment her husband died.

She was, indeed, acting like a young heifer or a spring chicken, as Jon and Ephraim had described her, and there was no taming her. Nevertheless, Sarah tried.

"You should be nice to Ephraim," she said to her mother one evening. "He really likes you, and he has looked after our whole family all these years."

"I *am* nice to Eeph," replied Prudence with a touch of irritation in her voice. "When haven't I been?"

"Well, I mean something more than just being nice," Sarah explained. "I think Ephraim is courting you."

"Yes, I think so too," smiled Prudence. "He started courting me before I was married, and he never really gave up, not even when I was married to Zachary."

"Well, don't you like him in return? Not even a little bit?"

"Of course I like Ephraim."

"Why don't you give him a little encouragement, then?"

"He doesn't need any encouragement," laughed Prudence. "He has incredible optimism."

"No, I mean why don't you respond to his courtship? I think you two would make a very fine couple together."

Prudence became serious. She wrinkled her forehead. "I don't think I want to be married to him," she said slowly. "He and Zachary are too much alike. I don't think I want to marry another farmer, especially one as old as Eeph."

"Oh, Mom, he's not very much older than you are yourself."

"He's fifty," Prudence replied. "Almost fifty-one. That's a lot older than me. I'm only forty-five."

"But you're almost forty-six. There's five years' difference. That's still not very much for a husband and wife."

"Maybe I don't want another husband."

Sarah paused for a moment. "Maybe you don't want a husband, but maybe I'd like a father again."

"Oh, Sarah! You're too old to need a father. If I married Eeph, you wouldn't want him as a father very long. In a couple of years you'll be married yourself, and when that happens, you can just walk away. You'd be gone, as you should be, but I'd be married to Ephraim for the rest of my life. And I don't think I want that."

Sarah glanced at her mother, her wrinkled brow showing her vexation. "You don't plan to get married again, ever?" she asked.

Prudence caught her breath, flushing slightly. "I wouldn't say that for sure, Sarah. If the right man came along, and we were in love with each other, I might consider it."

"Well, I think Ephraim is the right man," said Sarah boldly. "I think he is in love with you, and I think you are in love with him even if you don't recognize it yourself."

Prudence laughed pleasantly. "Look at who is playing the role of match-maker," she exclaimed. "I've heard of mothers choosing mates for their daughters, but I've never heard of a daughter choosing a husband for her mother! At least, not until now."

"I'm sorry, Mom," Sarah laughed. "I didn't intend to be pushy. I just wanted to give you my opinion, that's all."

"Your opinion is always welcome," Prudence replied, "but I like being independent. I think I'll stay that way for a while. Men can be a foolish distraction in life. I don't want any distractions right now, for there are many important things I want to do. I'm going to ignore men, at least for now."

When Jon's next letter arrived, however, it was quickly evident that there was at least one man in the world whom she would not ignore. She had been eagerly awaiting the news from the three boys in France, and she had watched for the mailman each morning. When she saw him stopping at the foot of her driveway, it didn't matter that a steady drizzle was falling. She dashed out the door, pulling a shawl around her shoulders as she went, and hurried through the rain to receive his paper treasure.

It was indeed a letter from Jon. When Prudence returned to the house she opened the damp envelope and removed the thin pages. A smaller scrap of note paper fell from the envelope and fluttered to the floor.

She leaned down and retrieved the note. It was written in an unfamiliar handwriting, and it was addressed to Sarah. Prudence's eye dropped to the bottom of the script, and the bold, confident signature of Carl leaped out at her.

Immediately her heart exploded with disbelief, confusion, and jealousy. She sank into a chair and rested her forehead against her hand.

This combination of emotions was new to Prudence. All her life, among her limited circle of acquaintances, she had been universally admired by all men. At public meetings, she had become quite aware of her own attractiveness. The men she encountered were not sophisticated, and their clumsy expressions of admiration were completely transparent. Although she never gave them much encouragement, she enjoyed their awkward compliments and in her heart she reveled at the knowledge that they liked her.

Of course, the chief nourishment for her vanity came from the longstanding competition between Zachary and Ephraim.

After vanquishing his rival, Zachary had not felt threatened by Ephraim's presence. He trusted in the stability of his marriage and the faithful integrity of his spouse. From that fortress of security he was able to accept outside attention to his wife with equanimity. He was secretly pleased that another man found his wife desirable. It enhanced his own sense of satisfaction and pleasure. Prudence had rejected Ephraim and chosen him, and the knowledge of that choice girded him with a sense of mastery and confidence.

For his part, Ephraim understood and respected his lack of official position in the relationship. He never overcame his love for Prudence;

indeed, he never wanted to overcome it. His passion for her never cooled, but he was content to admire her from next door without intruding into the marital scene. He promised Prudence not to speak openly of his love for her, and he kept that promise.

Nevertheless, throughout the twenty-five years of her marriage, Prudence was constantly aware that she was the primary object of two men's deep and abiding affections. It bolstered her self-confidence and supported a sense of inner serenity in her personal life.

Consequently, it was a new and terrifying feeling which surged through her body at the sight of Carl's note to Sarah. In the past, accustomed to being the desideratum of all men, she had never experienced the emotion of jealousy. Now it struck her with full force, like a summer thunderstorm following a long season of tranquility.

She raised the note again to reading level, fearful of the private message she might find.

There was no wrestling with her conscience, although the note was not addressed to her. It was included in her own envelope and was not sealed separately. In her eagerness to learn its contents, the thought that it might be confidential did not occur to her.

"Dear Sarah," Prudence read, suddenly aware that her hand was shaking with excitement. *"Forgive my boldness, but your brother suggested that I write a few words to you."*

'Why would he suggest such a thing?' Prudence thought to herself. 'What possible motivation could there be? Couldn't he sense the warm friendship I felt for Carl? Why wouldn't he have Carl write to me, instead? Why Sarah?'

"So I just thought I'd tell you how much I enjoyed talking with you at our Christmas Dinner in the mess hall at Camp MacArthur."

'At the Christmas Dinner?' Prudence asked herself. 'Christmas Dinner? Did they talk together then? I guess they did. All I remember is how I wanted to sit near Carl, but somehow I ended up where I couldn't even see him. Oh yes, I remember now—Sarah was right across from him.'

Thinking hard, Prudence recalled Sarah's animated face during the dinner. At the time, it meant nothing to her—she was too occupied with her feelings of frustration at not being near Carl herself. But in retrospect she was struck by the excitement in Sarah's face—excitement she hadn't seen there since Sarah was very young.

"I think you are a very pretty girl, and you are so smart! You had a worthwhile comment about every subject we discussed."

'He's talking about Sarah?' Prudence asked herself incredulously. 'Pretty? Smart? Well, in a way, I guess she is. After all, she's my daughter. But I always think of her as rather quiet. Plain and simple. Just a pleasant little child.'

"*We don't see many girls over here,*" Carl wrote, "*so your memory has no competition. I shall go into battle remembering your face and your lovely red dress.*"

'Red dress? What red dress?' thought Prudence. 'Oh, yes, I remember—why, that was just an old dress Sarah took along because she didn't care if it got rumpled in traveling. And he thought it was lovely?' She smiled in spite of herself. 'That's funny!'

"*Well, that's all for now. The weather has been very cool, but things will warm up when we start fighting. Write me a note if you want to.*"

It was signed simply, "*Sincerely, Carl*".

The note was brief and it didn't really say very much, Prudence concluded. She read it again from the beginning. 'He was just being polite,' she decided. 'Jon asked him to write something, so he did. That's all there is to it.'

After a while she remembered the main letter from Jon, and picked it up from the table. It described the voyage across the Atlantic in the *Powhattan* and told of their watch for German submarines. It mentioned the cooties which infested them from the very first day aboard ship.

"*We were mighty glad to set our feet on solid land again,*" Jon wrote. "*But we got some bad news as soon as we were ashore. All the guys from our regiment, the 128th, have been sent into other units as replacements. That means our buddies are gone. We had been promised that Prairieville's company would be kept together as a unit, but it didn't work out that way. The whole division was designated as a replacement organization for the First Division, and our regiment was hit the hardest. We've been told that all the captains and privates alike were transferred.*

"*By the time we arrived, they were no longer using the 32nd Division as a replacement source. The twelve of us who were delayed by that quarantine in New Jersey are the only original soldiers remaining in the 128th Regiment. Even Captain Martin is gone. Other newcomers have been transferred in to join us, so each infantry company is back up to a strength of about 150 men.*

"*Of course, now we have to get acquainted and start over again in forming a team that can work together.*"

'How discouraging,' Prudence thought.

"*From the sound of things, it won't be long before we'll be at the front lines fighting the Germans. The whole world knows of the great German offensive which was launched while I was at sea. Field Marshal Von Hindenburg promised his people that he would be in Paris by April. Well, April has arrived and the Huns are still quite a few miles away from that prize. But we all know they have not given up, and if they are to be stopped it will be the Americans who stop them. I'm sure the 32nd*

Division will be in the thick of the battle.

"But don't worry, Mom. Whatever happens will be God's plan, for He looks after His own."

Prudence's eyes welled with tears at this point. She was a Christian and she wanted to believe the brave words of her son. Yet her heart was heavy with foreboding, and she longed for the unquestioning confidence her husband had always shown. She was at war with herself, torn between faith and despair. It was quite a few minutes before she was able to continue reading.

"I wanted to see France, but to tell you the truth right now I'd rather be back in Prairieville helping you plant the oats." She smiled.

"Give my love to all, and keep up your good cheer." The letter was signed with his familiar signature.

"P.S. I'm enclosing a note from Carl to Sarah—please see that she gets it."

This epistle too she read a second time. Its contents were as unsettling as the note from Carl, although the emotions they aroused were quite different.

She would have to show the letters to Sarah and Ephraim as usual, but she was not prepared to do so at once. The mailman had delivered the envelope into her own hand, and no one else knew it had arrived. She secreted it among other papers in her writing-desk, and went about her day's work with a vigor stirred by the violent agitation within.

The warm spring drizzle continued through most of the day, matching her melancholy mood. In the evening, after the dishes were dried and restored to their places in the kitchen cabinet, she pulled a shawl over her shoulders and quietly left the house.

She walked without hurry, but with resolute purpose, away from the buildings in a westward direction toward the river. There was no crackling of twigs, no rustle of leaves, no sound at all as she moved. She was a ghost-like apparition drifting effortlessly along. Within ten paces, she was enveloped in the swirling gray mists which blotted out all features of the landscape. The air was heavy with moisture rising from the cold damp earth as well as drifting down from the soggy skies above.

Even though she could not see more than a few yards ahead, she found her way without hesitation. She knew every tree, every clump of shrubbery, every mound and every hollow of the earth.

Eventually she reached the very edge of the river, at a high spot perhaps ten feet above the water level. Here she smoothed a place in the short grass and spread a cloth she had brought with her. Like a hen on her nest she settled herself comfortably, her feet tucked beneath her skirt.

She peered out across the river into the depths of the marsh. She could see nothing, not even the opposite riverbank only ten yards away.

Nevertheless, she felt comforted because the marsh was there. It was unseen, but its effect was felt into the depths of her soul. All her adult life had been spent at the edge of this marsh, and it had become a sheltering presence for her. She knew she would find a balm for her troubled emotions.

She dissolved slowly into the mists, her gray clothes merging into her surroundings. Perfectly camouflaged, she watched a pair of early green-winged teal paddling briskly in the frigid water close to the brown reeds before her. A muskrat headed across the river, leaving behind it a gentle vee-shaped wake which rapidly dissipated.

In her mind she reviewed Carl's note to Sarah. She had pulled it from its hiding place a half-dozen times during the day and studied it until she knew it word for word.

Of course, the parts that bothered her the most were the compliments: *"I enjoyed talking with you at our Christmas dinner. . ."* and *"I think you are a very pretty girl, and you are so smart!"*

And then there was the thought that he would remember Sarah's face and her *"lovely red dress"* when he went into battle.

Each of those lines was etched indelibly into her memory, and she kept repeating them to herself, exacerbating her sense of injury with every repetition.

If only that note had been addressed to her instead of to her daughter. What a difference it would have made!

'Did he like Sarah better than he liked me?' she asked herself as she stared into the mist. 'Does he think I am too old? Should I forget about him for the sake of my daughter?' These thoughts and others like them tortured her mind.

Finally the thought of Jon and the likelihood of his going into battle soon, and she felt guilty that her worries were centered on Carl.

'I'm worried about Jon, too,' she thought, 'but there's nothing I can do about him and his safety.'

For a long time she had tried to block from her mind the fear she harbored for Jon's life and limb. From the very beginning, she felt that he would not return unharmed from the war. His death would be a divine retribution for her Great Sin. The guilt was hers, and hers alone. She had read and re-read the twelfth chapter of Second Samuel, and repeatedly quoted from memory the condemnation of Nathan the prophet: *"The child that is born unto thee shall surely die!"*

The vision she saw from her window the day Jon enlisted—was it Zachary, or was it Nathan?—filled her with terror, a terror it was impossible to suppress despite her most diligent efforts. She was completely helpless, unable to protect her son from the consequences of her own sin.

His fate was in the hands of God, and she tried to forget her fears and replace them with a blind faith.

She wondered sometimes whether she was drawn to Carl as a subconscious device to spread her emotional risk—surely one of the boys would survive the war!

Such thoughts made her feel all the more guilty, and now she fell forward onto her knees in the soggy brown marsh grass. "Forgive me, oh God!" she cried aloud, her head cradled in her hands.

As she allowed her mind to remember Carl, she suddenly felt a blinding realization that her yearning for him might be another outbreak of her sinful spirit. It was clear, only too clear, from his note to Sarah that his affections were directed, quite naturally, in the direction of her young daughter.

Her assumptions that he had responded to her own warm feelings were simply delusions of her sinful mind.

Was that the sacrifice being demanded of her? That she should surrender her love for Carl? If so, she would bring her rebellious sentiments under control. She would stifle her craving for him. She would deny herself the pleasure of remembering his vigorous hug. No longer would she imagine herself locked passionately in his embrace. She would punish herself by forswearing her innermost desires.

She raised her eyes to the colorless sky, feeling the tiny raindrops splash into her face. They sprinkled a purification for her soul like the holiest of water; they gently and insistently washed away her sense of contamination.

"Oh Father, dear Father," she cried aloud, "In demanding the surrender of my fondest dreams of Carl, You ask only what is right. I give him up to You. Protect my son, my only son, and bring him home to me happy and whole again, and I will never think of Carl again!"

Motionless as a granite statue, she remained at her watery altar for an hour or more. Her knees began to ache, and her clothes were soaked through to the skin. Even though the weather was unusually warm, she began to shiver.

Finally she rose stiffly and retraced her steps to the farmhouse. She had struck a bargain with God and felt absolution from her iniquity. Her fears were relieved. The nurturing comfort of the marsh had worked wonders in her life.

Nevertheless, she couldn't immediately bring herself to show Jon's letter, with its note from Carl, to Sarah. Her intention was to disclose it later, but as the days went by she realized how embarrassing it might be. How could she explain the delay? Eventually she pushed the matter from her mind, and the letter remained hidden in her desk.

Chapter 14

At the end of May the German armies were concentrated in the center of the western front. The decisive attack toward Paris was soon launched. At first they succeeded in overwhelming the defenders, and it appeared that nothing could stop them short of their goal.

"We are fighting with our backs to the wall!" declared Field Marshal Haig, and the military strategists for the Allies were making new plans for continuing the war after the fall of the French capital.

Encouraged by their success, the best German battalions struck southwest and reached the banks of the Marne River at Chateau-Thierry, just thirty miles from Paris. Here in mid-July the exhausted French soldiers were relieved by fresh American troops. The orders given by General Foch to this new, untested army from the New World were to delay the enemy as long as possible while falling back to newly prepared defenses in the rear.

Instead, contrary to the expectations of both the French and the Germans, the Americans launched a full-scale counter attack. In desperate fighting the invaders were stopped and driven out of the town. The Germans were forced to retreat and it was quickly evident they were over-extended. "The history of the world was played out in three days," said German Chancellor Count von Hertling.

After the turnaround the Allies kept a steady pressure against the Kaiser's troops to prevent a stabilization of the enemy's defenses. Jon and Leo and Carl would play their small part in applying that pressure.

While these decisive events were occurring on the Marne, a climax of another sort was approaching on the banks of the Pishtaka River south of Prairieville.

There was plenty of work for the farmers near the great Vernal

Marsh. The oats had all been planted and the last of the corn was being sowed. The first crop of alfalfa was almost ready to be cut. In addition to the usual daily chores of feeding, milking, and cleaning, there were fences to mend and tools to repair.

On a warm morning in early June, a solitary, lanky figure strolled along River Road. On his back was a small knapsack. A close observation would disclose that he was a young man, in his early twenties perhaps, although he appeared to be much older. His face was long and thin, with deep-set vertical wrinkles set in his cheeks, and corresponding horizontal wrinkles in his forehead. Prominent cheekbones emphasized the dark hollows of his eyes. He was dressed in well-worn working clothes; his faded plaid shirt, ragged at the elbows, had once been green and white.

Reaching the entrance to the Bruno Hilley farm, the youth paused to read a crude hand-lettered cardboard sign which had been tacked to the wooden gate-post. He mouthed the words slowly one at a time: 'WON'T JOIN THE LOYALTY LEAGUE'.

His expressionless face was highlighted by a ray of sun which slanted down at him through the burgeoning leaves of the big oaks which lined the old driveway. He leisurely wiped his bony cheeks one at a time with a blue bandanna, while his deep-set eyes lolled listlessly in their oversize sockets.

After long thought, the youth glanced quickly around him in all directions, and then reached out with his long fleshless fingers. He grasped the yellow placard and wrenched it from the post. Folding it carefully, he tore it into tiny pieces which he dropped into the muddy ditch alongside the road. Then he shambled up the graveled drive toward the house, the pack on his shoulders giving him the appearance of a tall, chicken-legged hunchback.

Bruno was seated on a wooden bench, busily repairing a leather harness inside the doorway of his tidy barn, when the stranger approached. He glanced up, his tiny pig-like eyes glistening from the recesses of his square, fleshy face, and peered at the tall skeletal figure before him.

"Howdy," said the young newcomer in a high-pitched, reedy voice.

Bruno said nothing, but simply stared at the intruder.

The youth glanced quickly and nervously around the shadowy interior. "Mighty neat-lookin' barn," he observed.

Bruno remained motionless.

The youth cleared his throat. "My name is Fritz Kraus. I come lookin' fer work," he said.

Bruno stirred. His lips moved tersely. "I don't need no help," he replied.

"Sure ya' do," the visitor contradicted him pleasantly. "There's always work t' be done on a farm, 'specially in the summer. Even on a farm as nice as this one."

He paused, and strolled a few steps down the central runway. "I've worked in lots o' barns," he commented, "but I've never seen one kept as well as yours."

Still holding his leather harness in his hands, Bruno rose and followed the gangling youth with his eyes as he wandered around poking and peering into dark corners.

"I got lots of experience," said Kraus. "You won't hafta' teach me nothin'. Just tell me what ya' want done, and I'll do it."

Bruno remained silent but his face softened.

"You really got a showplace here," said the youth, ambling back to face the porcine farmer. "I'd sure like t' help ya' keep it up."

"Can't afford help," said Bruno, clipping his words.

"I don't need much money," countered the scrawny youth, stepping closer to Bruno and looking down at his stocky form. "Fifty cents a day would be fine, along with room and board."

"I said I can't afford help," Bruno repeated.

The thin lips of the young man stretched into a smile expressing unexpected warmth. "I like your farm. I want to help you keep it up. An' I don't care much about the money." He wrinkled his forehead and pursed his lips. "How 'bout twenty-five cents?" he wheedled.

"I can pay you nothing," said the German with an air of finality.

Kraus smiled at him with a friendly smile. "I accept," he said grandly, with just a touch of condescension. "I like your farm so much that I will work fer nothin' at first, until you can see what I am really worth. Then maybe I can get a raise." He stuck out his spindly arm, indicating his desire to shake hands.

Bruno hesitated momentarily; then he laughed a short, hard laugh. There was something likeable about this scarecrow youth, and he seemed so pathetic and lonely.

He set his harness aside and extended his thick hand. "I am Bruno," he said. "Bruno Hilley. I live here with my sister Elizabeth. And you are Fritz. Fritz, er, ah-h. . . ."

"Kraus," the youth reminded him.

"Fritz Kraus," repeated Bruno. "Well, Fritz, when do you want to start?"

"Right now," came the quick response. "I'm ready right now." He slipped the straps of the knapsack off his shoulders and swung the light pack down to the ground. "I've got my things right here," he explained. "I'm ready t' go t' work at once."

"Good!" exclaimed Bruno. "I've got a garden that needs hoeing before the weeds get too big."

"I like workin' in gardens."

"But first, you should meet my sister. C'mon inside, and you can see your room."

Elizabeth was not pleased. As soon as Kraus was in the garden, she turned angrily to her brother. "We shouldn't let him stay," she told him. "He is so skinny; he will not be able to work. He will be worthless."

"Now, 'Lizabeth, it will be all right," he said reassuringly. "It will cost us very little t' feed him. He looks like he don't eat very much. And he is willing t' work fer nothin'."

"We've been able to get along fine without him up to now," she observed. "There isn't enough work to keep him busy."

Bruno laughed. "Of course there is work for him to do. I'll find plenty of worthwhile jobs for him."

"What about poor little Ernst Wyman? He is counting on doing odd jobs for us this summer. He's coming tomorrow, in fact, to work in the garden."

"Ernst can work here too, 'Lizabeth. I'll find things for him to do. He don't want t' work very much, anyway; he's only a boy." Bruno patted his sister on the shoulder. "Now stop complaining about every little imaginary problem."

"You have a soft spot in your heart for young boys, don't you," she said crossly. "You've given so many gifts to little Ernst that one would think he belonged to you."

"Don't be jealous of him," Bruno admonished.

"Well, you've done too much for him."

"He's a nice boy," said Bruno.

"And don't go giving things to Fritz like that," she said meanly.

"You don't need t' tell me what t' do and what not t' do," her brother responded with similar feeling.

"You should have gotten married," Elizabeth went on, "and then you could have a son of your own."

"No, Elizabeth, you understand better than anyone that I would never want t' get married."

"Yes, I know," she said sardonically. "I know only too well."

"Besides, if I had married, who would look after you?" he asked rhetorically. "You'd be all alone."

"Humph! We'd both be better off," she said bitterly.

"Now, 'Lizabeth," he remonstrated.

She glanced through the window and watched the scraggly form of their new hired hand as he bent vigorously to his task in the garden thirty paces away.

"The truth is," she said at last, "I don't like the looks of your new boy. There is something frightening about his eyes. Something. . . well, almost sinister. I don't want him around here."

"Oh, 'Lizabeth!" exclaimed Bruno. "You don't even know the lad. Don't jump t' any foolish conclusions just by his appearance."

"That's just the point," she said. "I don't know him, and neither do you. Where did he come from? He's not very old; where's his family? Why is he out here wandering around with nothing to his name?"

Bruno didn't have the answers to his sister's questions. It was true that they knew nothing about this stranger. He had wormed his way into a position through his own witty determination.

"Ah, perhaps you are right," he conceded with a sigh. "But we made him no promises. We can get rid of him at any time. Let's keep him fer a day or two and then decide what t' do."

Kraus proved to be a hard-working young man despite his fragile appearance. He helped with the chores quite willingly, and quickly learned all the daily tasks which occupy much of a farmer's time. He showed equal enthusiasm for field work, outlasting his boss without grumbling.

The garden became his favorite workplace, where he spent every spare moment pulling weeds almost as soon as they popped their heads through the ground.

Even Elizabeth began to like him. "Bruno, guess what?" she said one day. "Fritz talks to the plants. I heard him talking to the plants in the garden today. He was encouraging them to grow tall and strong."

"He's an unusual young man," replied her brother. "And he works harder and longer than I do."

"Yes, and he has become such good friends with young Ernst. Together, they are growing the best garden I've ever seen."

Soon Bruno began taking Kraus with him when he worked on Prudence's farm, and he proved to be diligent and industrious there as well.

With the Great War reaching its climax in France, it was only natural that Germany would be discussed around the dinner table at night. Kraus was the first to open the subject.

"I found a picture of the Kaiser in the dresser drawer of my room," he said innocently one evening. "Do you mind if I put it up? I won't have t' pound a nail in the wall, for there is already one there exactly where I want t' hang the picture."

Bruno and Elizabeth exchanged cautious glances.

"Maybe it's better t' leave it in the drawer," Bruno said.

"It must have been on the wall before," persisted Kraus. "There's a very clear outline on the wallpaper which shows something was hanging on that nail, and it exactly matches that very fine picture of the Kaiser. Isn't that right?"

"It was hangin' there a long time ago," muttered Bruno. "But let's leave it alone fer now."

"All right, whatever you say," Kraus shrugged.

The next night, the subject of Germany was revived.

"Are you members of the Loyalty League?" Kraus inquired, knowing of course that they were not.

Bruno and Elizabeth remained silent; they had learned to say nothing about their views of the war.

"I wouldn't sign the pledge myself," Kraus continued, "just as I wouldn't enlist. They put a lot of pressure on me, but I don't believe in fightin' against the Kaiser, and I wouldn't give in."

"I assume from yer name that you have a German heritage," commented Bruno.

"Yes, my father was born in Stuttgart," said Kraus. "But that has little t' do with my feelings about the war. After all, I am an American now."

"Yes, we are all Americans," said Elizabeth.

"But we are on the wrong side in this war," continued Kraus.

"We support our boys overseas with all our hearts," said Bruno. "Prudence's son Jon is fighting over in France, and a finer boy you would never find anywhere."

"What a shame he has to be there, though," observed Kraus. "President Wilson should never have gotten us into this war. He should have listened to Senator LaFollette. We should have stayed neutral at the very least."

"You are right," grunted Bruno. "We should have stayed out."

"Sh-h-h," warned Elizabeth, glaring at her brother. "It's better not to say things like that."

"Don't worry," said Kraus. "This is a free country, and everyone is entitled t' his own opinion on everything. Besides, you can see I agree with you."

"Germany has been treated so unfairly by England and France through many, many years," volunteered Bruno, ignoring his sister's advice. "I won't feel sorry at all when Paris falls."

"The sooner the better," added Elizabeth.

"Then maybe the Kaiser can get some decent international agreements," said Bruno, "if that traitor Wilson will keep his nose out of it."

Several days later, when Elizabeth was cleaning Kraus' room, she noticed a small notebook atop his knapsack alongside the bed. She could not restrain her curiosity. After glancing around and assuring herself that the men were not in the house, she opened the cover of the notebook.

It was apparently a rough and incomplete diary, she discovered, scratched in pencil. The first entry was a brief account of how Kraus had wangled his job from Bruno by agreeing to work for nothing.

The second entry hinted at some secret purpose in Kraus' heart. *"Aha!"* it started, *"Success already! There is a picture of the Kaiser face-down in the top drawer of my dresser. I can tell by the marks on the wall that it was hanging above the bed not too long ago. What a find! . . . ."*

The next pages were filled with a mundane recounting of the various chores and farm tasks which occupied most of Kraus' days. Elizabeth skimmed through them but there was nothing of interest.

Then came a reference to their recent discussion at the dinner table. *"The time was ripe tonight,"* it read. *"I brought up the key subject, and both B and E were eager to incriminate themselves. B said we should have stayed out of the war. He said he hopes the Germans capture Paris. E said 'the sooner the better.' B even called Wilson a traitor."*

Elizabeth flushed as she read the entry. What did Kraus mean when he wrote that they had 'incriminated' themselves? Was it merely a harmless scribbling for his own entertainment, or did he intend to put it to some nefarious use?

She left the notebook where she found it, but she had virtually memorized the troubling passages. She took her brother aside in the barn and told him of her discovery.

"What does it mean?" she asked him. "What do you suppose he plans to do with it?"

"I don't know," said Bruno, "but we should not ignore it. I think we should ask him point blank why he wrote down our words."

Accordingly, after the evening dinner was through, Bruno turned to address the young man. "Fritz, today my sister happened t' glance at a notebook while she was cleaning yer room." He watched Kraus' face carefully and saw a pink tinge flood through the gray complexion.

"What are you writing in yer notebook?" asked Bruno.

"It's none of yer business," Kraus answered defiantly. "My notebook is private, and yer sister ain't got no business nosing through my private things!"

"I didn't mean to disturb your private things," Elizabeth insisted. "It was lying out there in the open and it didn't appear you meant it to be anything secret and confidential."

"Well, it certainly is confidential," asserted Kraus, "and you ain't got no business readin' it."

"Stop avoiding the question," said Bruno, his anger rising. "Why did you write what you did? Why did you write down what we said the other night?"

Kraus was silent, his countenance betraying his guilt.

Bruno stood up and glowered down at the thin figure below him. "Answer me!" he demanded.

Kraus look frightened, his face now turning pale.

Bruno flexed his arm in front of the youth, threatening him with clenched fist. "Answer me!" he shouted.

Young Kraus made no motion to defend himself. Instead, he looked up coolly into the eyes of the furious farmer. "All right," he said, "if you want t' know the whole truth, I'll tell ya'."

Bruno stepped back and lowered his arms. "I'm listenin'," he said.

"The truth of the matter is that I am a government agent. I am an agent of the U.S. Secret Service."

"What?" exclaimed Bruno in loud disbelief. Elizabeth gasped, and stifled further outcry with the back of her hand.

A stunned silence ensued. Nobody moved. The ticking of the mantel clock seemed to increase in volume until it filled the room.

"You are lying," declared Bruno.

"No, I am not lying," retorted Kraus. "Some of yer neighbors reported their suspicion that you are both traitors, and I was assigned the job of finding out the truth about you."

"You took advantage of our kindness," scolded Elizabeth, "of our hospitality. That's not right. That's not fair."

"In war, everything is fair," replied Kraus.

"You are lying," repeated Bruno, his voice rising. "You are no more a Secret Service agent than me."

"All right," shrugged Kraus. "I am lying, if you say so. You will find out soon enough." He fixed his spectral eyes upon the farmer. "Look at me," he directed. "Look at me, and tell me if I am lying."

Bruno did not look at him. Instead, he pushed his chair back from the table and rose to his feet.

Fritz, too, began to rise, but Bruno stopped him with a fierce pointing of his stubby finger. "You stay right where ya' are!" he commanded in a sharp staccato voice.

Bruno stepped into the hallway and returned quickly with his shotgun. He cocked it as he entered the dining room, and brandished it in front of Kraus. The gangly youth was draped loosely over his chair, one elbow hooked over the back. He looked up at the threatening farmer with insolence and admonition.

"Don't be foolish, Mr. Hilley," he said wearily, as one would address a naughty child. "You're in enough trouble already. Don't make it any worse by doin' something you'll regret later."

"I kin get rid o' you here an' now and nobody will ever know," said Bruno through clenched teeth. His eyes were darting around the room quickly from corner to corner, as though looking wildly for other enemies.

"Don't add murder to your conscience," Kraus responded in patronizing tones.

"I kin shoot rats all day long an' it don't bother my conscience one whit," replied Hilley, leveling the barrel at his adversary. He noticed with surprise that he could not hold the gun barrel steady, no matter how hard he tried.

Elizabeth stirred. "Wait!" she cried. "Don't shoot. It will just get us in deeper trouble. They're out to get us already, and we mustn't give them anything tangible to hold against us."

"They'll never know, 'Lizabeth," replied her brother. "We'll bury this vermin so deep in the cornfield that no part of him will ever see the light o' day again." He was perspiring now even though the evening was cool; the front of his blue work shirt showed dark streaks of moisture.

"Ya' won't save yerself by killin' me," said Kraus in steady tones. "Ernst knows all about ya', too. He's got everything I got. And he knows where to go and what to do if I disappear. I gave him all the instructions just in case something should happen t' me, God forbid."

"I kin get rid o' him, too," snarled Hilley, but his voice was shaking.

"His parents are in on it," Kraus said smugly. "Are you gonna' bump them off too? How many people do you think can disappear around here without everyone getting suspicious?" He laughed briefly with a tight, mirthless sound.

"They're gonna' get me anyway," Bruno replied nervously. "I might as well have the satisfaction of takin' ya' with me." He sounded absolutely determined, but the barrel of his shotgun wavered momentarily and finally lowered, eventually coming to rest pointed at the floor.

Kraus leaned forward, ready to seize the advantage. "I got a deal for ya', Mr. Hilley," he said. "I got a deal that will get ya' out of trouble an' keep yer dirty little secrets."

He looked up at the dejected farmer, arching his brows.

Bruno's eyes were cast down at the tip of his gun, inches from the floor, and he didn't lift them. Nevertheless, he was interested. "What's the deal?" he asked.

"It's simple enough," replied Kraus, his eyes still on Bruno. "I'm broke. I could use some money. You want secrecy, and I want money. Let's make an easy little swap. You pay me a small sum of money, and I forget about everything I discovered while I was here."

"Everything?" asked Elizabeth.

"Everything," he answered decisively.

"How much money?" she asked.

"Not much," he responded. "Just one hundred dollars. Fifty fer Ernst, and fifty fer me."

"One hundred dollars!" exclaimed Bruno with great anger. "That's a small fortune!"

"Fer me, yes, but not fer you," Kraus said. "I know what ya' got in yer bank book."

"What bank book?" demanded Bruno.

"Don't play so innocent," said Kraus. "I know all about you and yer sister. I know everything you are hiding. And I know about the bank book you keep in that secret compartment in the back of the sock drawer of yer dressing cabinet."

"You dirty little sneak!" exclaimed Bruno, raising his gun again. "I oughta' blow your brains out!"

"Go ahead, if you want the world to know all your secrets," taunted Kraus.

"You know too much for yer own good," said Bruno under his breath.

"Maybe so," said Kraus. "Maybe not. But I know ya' got a strongbox in the basement, mortared right into the wall behind the potato rack."

He grinned up at the farmer in triumph, as Bruno seemed scarcely able to control himself. The shotgun barrel was jerking as skittishly as the eyes of its owner.

"I bet ya' got enough money in that strongbox t' pay me right now," Kraus continued. "Why don't ya' jus' go down and get a hundred bucks for me and Ernst, and then I promise you'll never see me again. Your secrets—all of 'em—will be safe forever."

"I'll never pay you a single penny as a bribe!" declared Bruno.

"Don't look at it as a bribe, then," said Kraus. "I worked long and hard fer ya'. Just think of it as wages. After all, you never paid me nothin' at all for my labor."

"You agreed to work for nothin'," Bruno reminded him.

"Yes, so I did. But you could easily decide t' pay me anyway, out of your good conscience, an' I could hardly refuse."

"Never!" shouted Bruno, waving his gun to indicate the conversation was over. "Get up, get yer things, and get out of this house before I lose all my patience with you."

"Yer not gonna' fire me, are ya', Mr. Hilley?" asked Kraus. "I really like it here on yer farm."

"Are you kidding? You expect t' keep working here after everything you said and done? Hah! Get out! I never want to see ya' again!"

"Don't be so hasty, Mr. Hilley," protested Kraus, but he began pulling his bones together to rise.

"Get movin'," ordered the farmer, and Kraus stood up and shuffled up the stairs to his room. The knapsack was quickly packed and Bruno escorted the lanky youth to the door, his sister trailing behind.

"Now get off this farm and don't you ever come back," Bruno warned. "I'll shoot you on sight!"

"I'm goin'," Kraus said, "but I'll be back. And when I come back, yer gonna be sorry!"

Bruno and Elizabeth stood on the porch of their farmhouse and watched the tall youth as he trudged down the driveway in the long twilight of the mid-summer evening. They saw him turn north on River Road, toward town. They stood silently, their eyes fixed upon the tiny speck of his silhouette in the distance. There was nothing to say.

Neither of them could sleep that night. They stayed awake together, huddled in their chairs in the living room, listening for any strange sound which might come to their ears. When the early dawn began to fill their room with a gray light, they finally relaxed enough to sleep fitfully for a few hours.

They were together outside the house at mid-morning when their watchful eyes spotted a youthful figure walking up the driveway. It was the young boy, Ernst Wyman.

"I told Fritz I'd come and help him in the garden this morning," he said as he walked past them into the toolshed.

When he emerged with a hoe in hand, he asked, "Where is he?"

"Ernst, a terrible thing happened last night," said Bruno.

"What was that?" asked the lad. "Fritz ain't hurt, is he?"

"No, he ain't hurt. But he don't work here no more."

"Why not?"

"Because he said he was a secret agent spying on us," Elizabeth informed him.

The boy looked puzzled, and for a moment Bruno hoped he was completely innocent.

Ernst whistled through his teeth. "He wasn't supposed to tell you so soon!" he blurted out.

"What did he say t' you?" asked Bruno. "How much do you know?"

"He told me everything," replied Ernst disarmingly. "We're best friends."

"Tell me exactly what he told you," demanded Bruno.

"He told me he was working fer the government," replied the boy. "They hired him t' prove that you are German spies." He made the accusation openly and without hesitation, as though he were relating a childish story that had no actual meaning.

"German spies, eh?" repeated Bruno. "And did he get his proof?"

"Yes, of course. He said you wanted the Germans t' win the war. You wanted our side t' lose. You wanted Paris t' be captured by the Huns. You called President Wilson a traitor. And you even keep a secret picture of the Kaiser in your house."

"Ernst, do you believe everything he told you?"

"Of course I do. Fritz is my friend. He wouldn't tell me anything that wasn't so."

"Do you think my sister and me are German spies?"

198

"I don't like to think that, Mr. Hilley, but Fritz wouldn't lie t' me," said Ernst.

"Did he say anything else about us?" urged Bruno.

The boy hesitated, and looked back and forth between the brother and sister several times. "Yes, he said some other things."

"What things?"

The boy looked very uneasy. "I . . . I . . . I can't remember anymore," he said.

Bruno looked down at the small boyish figure. "Ernst, we have been friends fer a long time. We have given ya' many gifts, and we have been very good t' you. Tell me, do you *really* think we are German spies?"

Ernst stepped back a pace or two. His eyes filled with tears. "Well, ya' are, ain't ya'?" he said.

"No, Ernst," Bruno said gently. "We are not German spies. We're loyal Americans, just like you."

The boy backed away farther. His facial expression was rippling with conflicting emotions, and the tears began spilling down his tanned cheeks.

"Liar!" he called out in his shrill, childish voice. "Liar! Fritz said you would lie about it. I thought you would tell the truth, but I was wrong!"

Bruno looked at him sadly and shook his head. "If that's the way ya' feel about us," he said, "then you'd better leave. You'd better leave and never come back."

Ernst took two more steps backward, and glanced behind him. Then he dropped the hoe on the ground and began running down the driveway toward the road. He did not look back.

Bruno turned to his sister. "It's hopeless," he declared. "They're out t' get us, and it's absolutely hopeless. Nobody is going t' believe us. They'll all be like little Ernst."

"Maybe we should pay them the money and be done with it," suggested Elizabeth.

Bruno sighed. "You're probably right. When Fritz first asked fer money, I was dead-set against it. But maybe that's the only way out."

"They won't leave us alone. I know they won't," said Elizabeth. "When they come back, let's pay them what they're asking and get rid of them."

Their opportunity came when Kraus phoned them a few days later.

"I called to see whether you had changed yer mind," he said. "I felt we should give you one last chance."

"Come t' the farm and let's talk about it," Bruno told him.

Shortly before noon, Kraus arrived along with young Ernst. Elizabeth met them at the door and invited them into the living room.

"I'm glad you decided t' be reasonable," Kraus said. "It's better fer everyone that way."

"Well, yer not bein' very reasonable yerself," grumbled Bruno.

"Let's not say nasty things t' each other," said Kraus. "Just give us the money and we'll be gone."

"We're not rich," said Bruno. "We can't give you what ya' asked. But we're prepared t' give ya' fifty dollars."

"Oh, come now, Mr. Hilley, you didn't make us walk all the way to yer farm just t' insult us, did you?"

"We're not insultin' you," Bruno said grudgingly. "But we need t' keep the money we've saved. We've got taxes t' pay on the farm, and we're gonna' hafta' buy some hay this year, and we've been tryin' t' get enough t'gether to buy an automobile."

Kraus laughed, and Ernst joined in. "Yer gettin' mighty fancy, wantin' an automobile an' all," he said. "But you'd better put us first, or you won't have any need for luxuries like that. Give us fifty dollars apiece, or quit wasting our time."

"We can't afford to pay you that much," said Elizabeth. "You boys have no idea how much money it takes to keep up a farm and harvest the crops."

"Miss Hilley, you won't even have a farm, unless ya' take care of us first. We'll have you behind bars so fast that yer crops will rot in the fields."

"You are so cruel!" she exclaimed.

"We don't have the money you think we have," said Bruno. "But we'll raise our offer. We'll give you a total of sixty dollars fer you t' split. We can't go no higher."

"Mr. Hilley, you forget that I know exactly how much money ya' got. Yer bank book don't lie. So just give us fifty dollars apiece, that's a total of a hundred dollars, and we'll be on our way. This is yer last chance." He rose from his chair and took a step toward the door.

"All right, all right," said Bruno wearily. "We'll give ya' what yer demandin'." He pulled an envelope from his pocket. "I've got fifty dollars here. I'll have to go downstairs and get the rest."

"Yes, we know ya' got piles of money in yer strongbox," Kraus commented.

"We want a written receipt fer the money," Bruno said.

"You can trust us," said Kraus.

"No, I can't trust ya'," said Bruno. "I want a written receipt, so you can't say ya' didn't get the money."

Elizabeth went into the kitchen, and returned with a pad of paper and a pencil. Bruno handed it to Kraus. "Write the receipt while I go downstairs and get the rest of the money."

Kraus handed the pad to Ernst in turn. "Here, kid, write a receipt for them," he directed.

"How do I write it?" asked Ernst.

"Just say, *'Received one hundred dollars from Bruno Hilley'* and put the date on it," Kraus told him.

"Put the reason on it, too," said Bruno. "We're payin' ya' so we will be safe from yer threats."

When Bruno returned with the money, Kraus handed him the receipt. Ernst had written it out as directed, along with the terse explanation: *'For Protection against Exposure.'*

"I guess that'll be okay," mumbled Bruno as he counted out fifty dollars for each of them. They pocketed the bills, and rose quickly to leave.

"Now get out of here, and never come back!" Bruno told them. "I don't ever want to see either one of you again."

Kraus' pencil-thin lips broke into one of his rare smiles, but it was twisted into a sneer. "Oh, we'll be back next month," he said, "and you'd better have another hundred dollars ready fer us."

"You goddam crooks!" shouted Bruno. He started for the doorway. Kraus realized he was headed for the shotgun, and he leaped in front of Bruno. The two of them raced for the gun. Kraus reached the gun-rack first, but Bruno was stronger and knocked him to the floor. Then he grabbed the gun from the rack and pointed it down at the fallen youth. "Get into the living room again," he ordered. "We got some talkin' to do!"

While the two men were racing for the gun-rack, Elizabeth had quietly headed for the telephone in the kitchen. She soon had Prudence on the line.

"Send Ephraim over here right now," she pleaded. "They are after us," she said. "Bruno and Fritz are fighting over the shotgun, and we're all going to die!"

Ephraim and Robert were working in the fields, and Prudence was home alone. The desperate words from Elizabeth gave wings to her feet as she rushed along River Road to her neighbor's driveway.

She was only twenty feet from the house when she heard the loud explosion of a shotgun blast from inside. She stopped abruptly just as the kitchen door flew open and the small figure of Ernst Wyman dashed out, followed almost immediately by the stocky form of Bruno Hilley.

The farmer paused for a second or two on the porch as he completed the re-loading of his gun. Then he leaped down the steps to give chase.

Prudence stepped in front of him. "Bruno!" she shrieked. "What's going on?" She grabbed at his shotgun as he rushed toward her. "Give me that gun!" she commanded, but he was beyond control. He pushed her aside roughly and began sprinting after the fleeing youngster.

Unable to intervene, Prudence cautiously entered the house. Elizabeth was in the kitchen, looking dazed. "Thank you for coming," she said, "but it's too late." She thrust an envelope forward into Prudence's hands. "Here. I want to make sure everyone knows the truth."

"What is the truth?" cried Prudence. "What's happening?"

"They're after us," Elizabeth said quietly. "It's the end."

Not making any sense of those words, Prudence brushed past her and glanced into the living room. The body of Fritz Kraus was slumped in a rocking chair. Fresh blood was spattered everywhere.

Prudence turned quickly back to the kitchen. Elizabeth had disappeared. She heard another explosion at some distance from the house. She peered from the door and saw Bruno striding rapidly back toward her, his smoking gun still in his hands.

"Bruno!" she wailed as he approached. "Why are you killing those boys? What are you doing?"

His eyes were wild with hate and fear, and the savage expression of his face would remain with her for years afterward. "You couldn't stop this," he said stolidly. "There was no way t' prevent it. They were after us. It had t' happen."

He started up the stairway, and she began to follow him. He turned, loading another shell into the firing chamber of the gun. "Stay back," he warned. "It's too late. We're all dead." He went onward up the stairs, and moments later she heard a third deafening report from the gun.

Prudence grabbed the telephone in the kitchen and called the sheriff. Then she listened at the foot of the stairs for several minutes. All was quiet. Cautiously she climbed from step to step until she reached the top. She glanced into a bedroom and saw Bruno's body sprawled from a chair. He was dead, the tip of the gun's barrel imbedded in his chest. His hand still clutched the broken yardstick which he had used to trip the trigger.

Walking carefully into the next room, Prudence found Elizabeth lying on the bed. She, too, was dead, with an open bottle of arsenic on the table nearby.

While she waited on the porch for the sheriff, Prudence opened the envelope which Elizabeth had given her. She unfolded the sheet of tablet paper with trembling hands.

"*Goodby to everyone in this world,*" she read from the hasty handwriting. "*They are after us, and I know there is no escape. They are only toying with us, leading us along. They don't mean to let us alone, ever. But don't take it hard. Bruno would be in jail for the rest of his life anyway. It's better this way. Ephraim, you pick the pallbearers for us. Goodby, everyone.*"

Chapter 15

"*General Pershing himself came to inspect our Division,*" Jon wrote in a letter dated in mid-July. "*He looked us over very carefully, every single unit. General Haan, our Division Commander, told Pershing that we are ready to fight. I myself heard General Haan say that we are weary of training exercises. 'Fed up with it, eh?' Pershing commented with a smile. 'Yes, sir,' replied General Haan. 'Our boys have been well trained, and they will give a good account of themselves when they get into battle.'*

"All of that is certainly the truth," commented Jon. "*We thought we would be thrown against the Germans as fast as we could march to the front, but instead we have been cooling our heels here in Alsace, week after week. It's all a big waste of time. I wanted to tell that to General Pershing, but when he inspected our ranks and passed by in front of me I couldn't get the nerve to open my mouth.*

"But I did hear him say that he likes our spirit. 'This Division has a lot of snap,' is the way he put it.

"*We've come together pretty good with all new men in our regiment, but we still miss our company leaders. I wish Dan Martin and Red Welch were still with this group. At least I've still got my two best friends, Carl and Lee, with me.*

"Afterward, General Haan told us we would probably be heading for the front line pretty soon. It can't be any too soon to suit us."

Despite her emotional resolution to never think of Carl again, Prudence examined the letter for news about him and she felt a keen sting of disappointment at its absence.

Jon and his comrades didn't have to wait very long for action. "They need us now!" declared their lieutenant on July 19th, after a hurried meeting of the regimental officers. "There's no time to waste."

Without delay they were loaded into the familiar 'Hommes 40' French railway cars, so named because forty soldiers (or eight horses) could be crowded aboard each car.

They rolled and rattled through Paris, where they were lustily cheered by the civilians who realized their city and their whole country were being rescued by the American doughboys. "Vive L'Americain!" they shouted, crowding around the railway cars. The soldiers responded with genuine enthusiasm.

The question remained: would the new troops of the 32nd Division be shunted aside for more training, or would they go directly into battle? If they were to fight, would it be at Chateau-Thierry where the American 1st Division had turned the tide, or would they go farther north to the British front?

Shortly after leaving Paris, the troop train halted near Compiegne, the place which would later become famous as the site of the armistice ceremonies. The soldiers were quartered in several small towns west of the forest. None of them knew their immediate destination, which added to their pervasive sense of apprehension. Overwhelmingly, the boys hoped they would soon be in battle.

Despite their hasty journey, they now remained inactive for several days. The hours dragged by, filled with anticipation and dread.

"I'd rather be fighting than waiting," said Lee, and everyone agreed with him.

When their orders finally arrived, they learned they would fight on the American front at Chateau-Thierry after all. Once again, everyone was in a hurry. "On the double!" their leaders bellowed constantly.

This time the boys were squeezed into trucks, with scarcely enough time to stuff the last personal items into their packs. Soon they were bouncing along the rough country roads. Everyone was in a mood of high excitement, and they filled the air with the boisterous strains of army ballads:

> Good-bye, Maw! Good-bye, Paw!
> Good-bye, Mule, with yer old hee-haw!
> I'll git you a Turk an' a Kaiser too—
> An' that's about all one feller can do!

Before long the wide-eyed soldiers realized they were passing through an area which had recently been re-captured from the Germans. The ground was pockmarked from the explosion of artillery shells; the trees and bushes were shattered. A few blackened hulks of burned-out vehicles littered the landscape, looking like giant carcasses. Scattered around them were the untidy remnants of war—belts of machine gun bullets, helmets, small arms, scraps of military clothing, and twisted pieces of metal. The occasional whiff of a dead body assailed the nostrils of the innocent soldiers.

"Wow!" exclaimed Carl. "This must have been quite a battle!"

"And how," agreed Jon, surveying the field. "Look at that truck, Lee—the doors are bulged out—I bet a shell exploded inside."

"Sure. Look at that!" exclaimed Leo. "It must have come in through the windshield—a direct hit."

"I wish we could get off and walk around a bit," said Carl. "I'd like to pick up some souvenirs."

His wish came true just moments later as a roadblock developed and the whole convoy of trucks lurched to a stop. The three boys jumped from the back of the truck and ran out into the field, surrounded by dozens of their comrades.

Carl picked up a German helmet and bounced it lightly in his hands. "I can't believe this," he marveled. "I feel like I'm in a dream."

"I wonder what happened to the Hun who wore that thing," said Jon. "Did he throw it away while he was retreating? Or was he killed in the battle?"

"Germans soldiers are well disciplined," commented Carl. "He wouldn't throw his helmet away. If he did, he'd likely lose his head later. If that guy were alive he'd still have the helmet. I think he's dead."

"From the smell in the air," replied Jon, "there must have been a lot of dead ones."

"Yeah, and it looks like they were buried right here where they fell," observed Leo.

"It's hard to tell—some of this fresh dirt is from shell blasts," speculated Jon.

"That's true," agreed Carl, "but there are a bunch of shallow graves scratched out too. Look over there—see that dead hand sticking up? Looks like the guy was trying to scratch his way out of the grave!"

They looked where Carl indicated, and not more than ten yards away they saw a set of stiff grayish fingers protruding from the ground. "Ugh! You're right."

Filled with fascination and dread, the three boys walked over and stared at the rigid hand. They were silent for a few moments. At last, Jon spoke. "War is awful, isn't it."

"It sure is," agreed Carl.

They were occupied with their own thoughts until Jon noticed a pistol lying on the ground nearby. He picked it up gingerly, turning it over in his hands while he examined it.

"Is it German?" asked Carl.

"I don't know," Jon answered. "I would assume so, but it could be French or British. I don't think it's American." He opened the breech. "It's not loaded," he observed. "I think I've got my first souvenir." He stuck it in the pocket of his pants.

"I think I'll go back and get that helmet," said Carl. "It'll make a good souvenir, too."

The helmet was still where he had thrown it down. Even though there were dozens of doughboys milling around on the battlefield, there were plenty of souvenirs for them all.

It was a sobered group of young soldiers who climbed back into their trucks, many of them displaying their strange souvenirs. There was no singing as they resumed their journey.

The truck convoy stopped many times during the afternoon, blocked by a jumble of heavy traffic which seemed to converge upon their route. They played the familiar military game called 'Hurry up and Wait.' The hours stumbled past, and the boys grew increasingly hungry as the supper hour came and went.

The sun was below the horizon when the trucks finally reached their destination. The boys jumped down with their packs, amidst a great confusion of men and matriel.

"Where's the mess kitchen?" Carl asked innocently.

Someone snickered. "About twenty miles behind us, I'd say. Those horses ain't so dumb."

"The lieutenant says we're on our own," another man announced. "That's what our reserve rations are for."

"Grab what you want," said a non-com. "We've got a pretty good supply of canned goods."

Jon and his friends each took a couple of cans; the selection seemed to be limited to beans and hash.

As the boys followed their company away from the road, they heard the intermittent rumbling of staccato thunder ahead of them to the northeast. Looking in that direction they saw red blotches filling the sky. They realized with a sudden panic it was the relentless stabbing of heavy artillery.

Their company assembled together in an open field some distance from the road and marched about half an hour before reaching their assigned overnight area. When they finally put down their overweight packs, the men were dog- tired and very hungry.

"You have your choice of seats for dinner," said the lieutenant wryly, sweeping his arm out into the darkness. "And while you're at it, you can reserve your sleeping area, too. We won't stand on formality tonight, boys, you can sleep wherever you like—just so long as you're within shouting distance. Use your pup-tents if you have them."

Jon and his two friends didn't have any tents, nor did they know any of their buddies with such a luxury. For the first time since landing in France, they would be sleeping without a roof over their heads. They wanted a bit of privacy, which was hard to find amidst so many men. They wandered as far as they dared from their company's leaders, and finally chose a spot with a patch of grass. In the darkness, they organized their belongings as best they could.

When they were settled, they realized they had lost most of their appetite. Jon opened a can of beans with his knife and forced himself to eat some of them cold, right from the can. He also ate a chocolate bar. Everything was washed down with swigs of water. In the darkness he couldn't see what his friends were eating, nor did he care.

Then he stretched out on the ground, staring straight up into the black sky.

Tired as they were, sleep did not come easily. They lay quietly for a while, their eyes wide open.

"Tomorrow could be the big day," Carl said at last.

"I wouldn't be surprised," agreed Jon.

"Well, we've trained long enough to know what we're supposed to do," commented Leo.

"Yes, that's true. Now the only thing left is to do it."

They were silent for a while. Then Carl said, "At least we're not stuck in the trenches. Somehow I feel safer when we're on the move, even though we're more exposed to enemy fire."

"I don't like the trenches, either," agreed Jon. "Even the ones we had in training gave me claustrophobia."

After another pause, Jon said, "I wonder if we'll make it through the battle okay."

"The odds are in our favor, I'd say," speculated Leo, "now that we've got the Huns on the run."

"I don't know," said Jon. "Even with good odds, some of our group is sure to be killed or wounded."

"That's true, but there's not much chance of our whole company being wiped out, or even most of it," commented Carl. "It's not a situation like General Custer against the Sioux Indians."

"I'm sure of that," agreed Jon. "The great majority of our boys will make it through. The question is, which ones—the unlucky ones—will catch a German bullet?"

"I'm going to make it, I think," said Carl. "I'm going to tell my grandkids about it someday."

"Well, I'm not that confident," Jon admitted. "I don't have a very good feeling about my chances of survival."

"You've told me that before, and I think it's because of the dream where you saw your father staring at you," said Carl.

"That might have something to do with it," conceded Jon, "but I told you I had these feelings even before then."

"Yes, I remember," said Carl."

They had run out of words, and once again they became quiet. The frequent thump, thump of the heavy guns, firing in the distance at targets the boys could only imagine, reverberated through the still night air. The darkness seemed to magnify the sound. They lay motionless, staring up into the black sky, until Jon could stand it no longer.

"I'm scared," he said in a small voice.

"I am, too," responded Leo promptly.

"I want to see Prairieville again," said Jon wistfully.

"Me too," echoed Leo.

"And I want to go there with you," added Carl.

"I want to show you through the Vernal Marsh," said Jon. "You can't imagine what a wonderful place it is! It's so quiet, out away from all the noise of other people. There's lots of birds, and frogs, and turtles."

"Beautiful!" exclaimed Carl.

"It's nice when the sun is shining, especially in the spring," Jon elaborated. "But I think it's even better when it's raining, or at least when it's foggy."

"Do you have a favorite spot in the marsh? Tell me about it," urged Carl. "I want to picture it in my imagination."

"Yes, I do have such a spot. It's a little patch of ground, covered with grass, and it's higher than the surrounding marshlands. If you stand up, you can see a long way in all directions. But if you lie down, you are screened on all sides by the shrubs and reeds, and you are safe from the world. If you want, you can peer through the reeds and see out pretty well. It's a great spot for a lookout; nobody can creep up on you without you seeing them."

"Delightful!" commented Carl. "I can see why you like it so much."

"I've never been in the marsh," said Leo. "I guess I'm a city boy; I've lived all my life in town. But the way you describe it, I can't wait to get back and have a look for myself."

"After a while, the marsh kinda' gets into your blood," observed Jon. "Uncle Eeph says it seems to straighten out your whole outlook on life."

"What do you mean?" asked Carl.

"Well, it's been there so long, and it changes so very little. It makes you realize how tiny and insignificant you are by comparison."

"And that's good?" asked Leo.

"Yes, that's good, Lee. It's good to understand that even your biggest worries are meaningless in the long scheme of things. Somehow, it puts everything in the right proportions—you recognize that the things in life which you think are so very important don't really mean anything at all. It's the big principles that really count. No matter what happens in your own life, the marsh goes on forever without changing. Uncle Eeph told me all this more than once."

"I think I'm beginning to understand," said Carl.

"It's impossible to take yourself too seriously when you're in the marsh," explained Jon. "I think Uncle Eeph is right. It's true that your problems of the moment seem very small indeed, when compared to yourself and your life. But that's only the beginning. You yourself are very small when compared with the ageless marsh itself. It's a good tonic just to sit out there and meditate."

"What a wonderful way to look at it," breathed Carl.

"It's the same feeling I get when I read the Book of Ecclesiastes in the Old Testament," confided Jon.

> "Vanity of vanities, saith the Preacher,
> Vanity of vanities; all is vanity.
> What profit hath a man of all his labour
> Which he taketh under the sun?
> One generation passeth away,
> And another generation cometh,
> But the earth abideth forever.

"A couple of times when I was a kid I took my Bible out there and studied Ecclesiastes while I soaked up the atmosphere of the place," Jon said. "People come and go. Babies are born and old men die. No matter what a person does on earth, whether it's trivial or monumental, he still dies and gets forgotten while the earth just keeps on spinning. I don't suppose the Vernal Marsh has changed in a thousand years, but all kinds of people have come and gone during that time. It makes me realize how futile everything is, and how puny I am myself."

"What you say is true," agreed Carl, "but still everyone is important in the eyes of God."

"Oh sure, I'll grant you that," said Jon. "Man himself is important, but what he does is not. That's the liberating message. We don't have to knock ourselves out to accomplish some great goal, because that goal—whatever it is—has no lasting significance. Build whatever you want to build, whether it's a skyscraper, a great ship, or even an empire. It doesn't matter. It'll fall apart eventually and disappear."

"You're talking about material goals, right?" asked Carl.

"Yes, of course. Matters of the soul are different, for the soul itself is eternal."

"Even personal relationships are different, don't you agree?" suggested Leo. "It's important to treat other people right and to build deep friendships."

"Yes, it's crucially important, Lee. I think all that contributes to the development of the soul."

"And that's what you learned from the marsh?"

"Yes, I guess so," replied Jon.

"I wish we were there now," said Carl. "I wish the three of us were sleeping out in the Vernal Marsh tonight, listening to the croaking of the frogs and the quacking of the ducks instead of the rustle of a huge army all around us."

"And how!" agreed Lee. "I wish those distant flares in the sky were simply the lightning flashes of a far-off thunderstorm."

"So do I," said Jon.

"If you close your eyes," suggested Leo, "the tumult of those guns sounds just like thunder."

"Yes," said Carl dreamily, "it's easy to imagine we're camping out in the marsh and there's nothing more threatening than a thunderstorm around us."

"I'm going to take you there someday," promised Jon, "if we live through this war. Lee and I are going back to Prairieville, and we're going to take you with us."

"I'd like that," said Carl.

In the darkness, Jon felt brave enough to add, "And you're going to marry my sister Sarah."

"I am?" Carl laughed.

"Yes," said Jon decisively. "I want you with me as my friend forever, and what better way to keep you there than to have you marry my sister?"

Carl laughed again. "Sounds good to me," he said. "But I'm afraid she has no interest in me. I never got a reply to the note I sent her."

"Don't hold that against her," begged Jon. "She's probably embarrassed to answer you. She's never had a boyfriend. But I think she liked you when she met you in Texas. She's really very nice, even if she is my kid sister."

"I'd like to get to know her better," agreed Carl. "I'll go with you, all right. Certainly there's no reason to go back to Michigan."

The boys were quiet again for a while. Then, wistfully, Jon said, "Carl, I want you to go back to Prairieville even if I'm not around any more."

"Don't talk like that," admonished Leo. "It's bad luck."

"No," said Jon. "I don't mind saying it. I don't feel real good about the fighting ahead. And if I don't make it through alive, Carl, I want you to promise me you'll go back to Prairieville, at least for a little while. I want you to tell my mom and my sister how much I love them."

"That's fine," said Carl, "but don't say such things. You're being too morbid."

"Promise me," persisted Jon.

"Fine, fine, I promise," said Carl. "Now let's get off the subject. Let's

210

talk about something cheerful."

Nobody could think of anything cheerful to say, however, so the three friends were silent as they listened to the myriad noises around them—the noises from hundreds, even thousands, of boys like themselves who were lying apprehensively in the dark wondering what the morrow would bring.

The next morning the soldiers were allowed to wander around the area, so long as they didn't stray too far from their leaders. They had a few hours to look over the area which had been the tip of the famous salient of the German forces—their farthest advance toward Paris, reaching the banks of the Marne River.

Now, thanks to the Americans, the tip of the salient had been recovered by the Allies, and with General Pershing's men in the vanguard, the task ahead was very clear. The Germans must be pushed back steadily, without giving them an opportunity to re-group. The dullest private in the ranks understood the strategy, and suffered no illusions about how hard the task would be.

Late in the afternoon, the expected orders arrived. The entire division was to march forward to replace two battle-weary divisions in the line. The troop movement would take place that night under cover of darkness.

Accordingly, the men lined up on the hot dusty road as the sun was setting. Their packs were on their backs and their rifles were slung over their shoulders. There were no bands playing, no flags flying. The men were admonished to be as quiet as possible, and their mood was somber and determined as they started off.

Although they were marching along a major road between Paris and Metz, the conditions were extremely rugged. Thousands of marching feet kicked up a storm of dust which swirled in the hot night air. The men choked and coughed as they kept their cadence.

The heat of the night was oppressive. Although they were supposed to march in full uniform, most of the sweating men soon stuffed their olive drab shirts into their packs, wearing only the lightweight blouses above their khaki pants.

The division struggled along like a giant frazzled caterpillar, with frequent starts and stops for each segment of men. Their packs, already well over the recommended weight limits, seemed to grow heavier with each passing mile. Before long the men were sorting through their personal belongings whenever they stopped, and throwing out everything that wasn't absolutely essential.

"Carrying this stupid German helmet doesn't seem like such a good idea any more," said Carl. He pitched it blindly into an adjoining field, where it landed with a satisfying thud. "I'll have plenty of chances to get real souvenirs from our own battles."

"I think you're right," said Jon, as he pulled the German pistol from his pack and heaved it out into the darkness.

Others were following their example, throwing away extra clothes as well as miscellaneous pieces of military equipment. "By morning," joked Leo, "there's going to be so much junk alongside this road that it'll look like Napoleon's army passed through here on the way back from Moscow!"

The long night was filled with confusion and frustration as thousands of soldiers struggled forward under a moonless sky. The fatigue of the men added to their misery, and many of the doughboys dropped to the ground and caught a quick catnap whenever they were blocked by the unit in front. The pounding of the heavy guns constantly reminded them of their proximity to the battle, and gave them ample proof that they were headed toward the front line.

As dawn was breaking they arrived at their immediate destination in the rear of the two American divisions they were to replace. There they bivouacked, feasting again on canned beans before stretching out full length on the ground for a well-deserved rest. It had been twenty-four hours since they had slept.

The day passed in a blur for Jon and his friends. They woke some time after noon, but they were so drowsy they simply sat around and waited for time to pass. Like many of his comrades, Jon dashed off a short letter to his mother. The men were quiet; they didn't feel like talking now, or even thinking. When night came, they were satisfied to flop down again where they had lain the night before.

The next day was different. During the night, their orders had arrived. Their brigade, the 64th, was to replace the American 3rd Division during the coming night. They were busy throughout the day, bustling here and there with feverish excitement, even though there was little for them to do.

The arrival of their horse-drawn mess kitchens boosted their morale, They enjoyed hot meals again, and nobody complained about the 'greasy water'—known by the U.S. Army as stew.

As the twilight deepened into darkness on the night of July 29th, Jon and his friends started forward again. Their packs were firmly in place on their backs, but this time they carried their rifles in front of them, ready to shoot if necessary.

Their own scouts, who had reconnoitered the area during daylight, guided them toward their new front-line positions along the Ourcq River. There was no road to follow, and the darkness of the night was broken only by the firing of the artillery. Jon could see scarcely ten paces ahead through the damp gloominess of his surroundings. He was jumpy. He felt frightened and alone. He knew there were thousands of American soldiers around him, but only a few of them could be seen as they drifted in and out of his vision.

Suddenly he was threatened by a straggled group of strange-looking soldiers emerging from the darkness in front of him—coming straight at him, rifles poised for action. His heart jumped into his throat. He quickly raised his own weapon, finger on the trigger, before he realized they were Americans. They looked haggard. Their uniforms were dirty and torn. These were the men they were replacing. These were the men who had stopped the Germans at Chateau-Thierry and had pushed them back to their present position. They deserved a rest.

He lowered his rifle and said "Hi!" in low tones as the men passed him. No one returned his greeting.

Soon there were dozens, even hundreds of these bedraggled men with dazed eyes who stumbled past him toward the rear lines.

Jon had been steadily approaching the line of heavy artillery which he had been hearing for the past several days. Now, suddenly, he came upon the gun batteries in action. Their crews were firing as fast as they could load the shells. By their flashes of light Jon saw a bit of the broken countryside. On a dusty road to his left he saw several military ambulances moving slowly in the gloom, their dark crosses plainly outlined against their white backgrounds. A shiver ran through his body, even though the night was hot and his face was covered with rivers of perspiration.

"Gas! Gas! It's a gas attack!"

Jon heard the shouted warning as though he were in a dream-like trance. In his panic, he stopped in his tracks and could not move.

"C'mon, kid, get your gas mask on!"

Jon grabbed his mask and soon had it in place over his sweaty face. He imagined the smell of mustard gas, remembering his experiences in training. He began to choke, and he could taste the bitterness of bile backing up in his throat.

He couldn't breathe. Was his mask working?

'I'm going to die,' he thought, 'I'm going to die right here where I am, and I haven't even seen a German soldier!'

"False alarm!" somebody called. "No gas. It's a false alarm."

Jon left his mask in place for a few more steps, still gagging, just in case there actually was poison gas in the air. Finally he could stand it no longer. He ripped the mask off his face and returned it to his belt. Gingerly he took a breath of the damp night air. It was non-toxic.

When the gradual return of daylight finally put an end to the terror and confusion of the night, the fresh troops of the 64th Brigade were settling into their front-line positions. Jon and his two friends found themselves with elements of the 127th Regiment, separated from their own company, but they stayed where they were because they didn't want to wander around during daylight.

Across the field before them they could see the enemy line, anchored by a strong German force in a clump of woods—the Grimpettes, they were told. This stronghold had stopped the American advance. It had to be overcome.

Accordingly, just a few hours after moving into the line, General Haan ordered his troops to drive the enemy from the woods. Jon and his two comrades had no choice but to advance with their new unit.

They waited with growing apprehension as a fierce barrage of American artillery splintered the woods, and then they dashed forward across an open field toward the German lines.

At first he felt exhilarated as he ran. There was a measure of safety in the massive numbers of men around him.

Then a shell exploded in front of him so close that the concussion lifted him off the ground with his legs still churning. He was back down in an instant, but as he swept ahead he saw several bloody bodies crumpled on the ground. Other shells were bursting around him on all sides. He felt terribly exposed in the open field with an invisible enemy pouring steel down upon him.

The first line of doughboys was approaching the woods, and they were met by the rattle of machine gun fire from concealed positions.

Jon reached the woods and considered it a haven even though he knew it was filled with German soldiers. The sharp crackle of rifle fire, punctuated with the louder whomp from grenades, sounded like a thousand Fourth of July celebrations compressed together.

Running with a line of other soldiers as they swept through the underbrush, he almost fell into a deep pit hidden behind a row of bushes. He stopped, out of breath. It was a short trench, not more than twenty yards long, and at one end he saw his first German soldiers. There were two of them, huddled over a machine gun. Quickly he raised his rifle and fired in panic, sending his bullet into the underbrush well behind the Germans. They did not move, and he realized they were already dead. One of them was bare-headed, his helmet upturned beside him. His arm was thrown out at a grotesque angle, and his shoulder was saturated in blood.

But were they really dead? The helmeted soldier appeared to be watching him through half-closed eyes. Was he playing possum, waiting for his chance?

A lull settled around him, and Jon found himself alone, momentarily between the waves of advancing infantrymen. His heart was pounding. He was sure now that the man was alive. Jon could see no visible wounds. He fancied he could see his chest moving almost imperceptibly as he breathed.

Jon raised his rifle again and pointed it at the soldier. "Hands up!" he called out in a voice he did not recognize. "Surrender!"

There was no response.

"Hands up!" he repeated in wavering tones. "Or I'll shoot!"

Still there was no reaction. Jon felt foolish. He couldn't stand there forever, delayed by a single stubborn German, while the rest of his unit was rushing ahead already out of sight.

He fired. The force of his bullet knocked the man over, and Jon saw that he was horribly mangled—there was virtually nothing left of his torso below the waist except a bloody mass of entrails.

A sudden nausea racked Jon's body. He doubled over, threw down his rifle, and vomited into the weeds.

When he recovered, he rose unsteadily to his feet and took a deep breath. He reached down for his rifle, and hurried off after his comrades without looking back.

The battle in the Grimpettes Woods would never become famous like Verdun or Chateau-Thierry, but for Jon and his friends it was the very essence of war in all its horror. When the three of them found each other afterward, each had been seared with his own experiences, which they preferred to keep private.

The next day Jon and Carl were held back from the fighting because they had been chosen to be 'mess runners' for their company. Since the rolling mess kitchens were kept far enough behind the lines to be reasonably protected, it was the custom for five mess runners from each front-line fighting unit to deliver food from the kitchens. For safety, they traveled only at night. Enormous buckets filled with coffee or stew were suspended from yokes around their shoulders. Round loaves of bread were strong on wires and looped around their necks.

The German soldiers were still smarting from their defeat at Chateau-Thierry, and they recognized the vital necessity to defend their lines and stop the Allies. Consequently, they fought with wild desperation. Their artillery kept up a ceaseless barrage, even at night, so there was no place for the men of the 32nd Division to escape the noise of battle or the risk of being blown apart by exploding shells.

As Jon and Carl and three other mess runners from their unit headed through the crowded rear lines late that night, they had only a vague idea of where their mess kitchen was located. They wandered across open fields and through dense woods, often back-tracking, asking directions from anyone who looked knowledgeable. Many times they took temporary shelter as they heard the whistle of an artillery shell overhead. They located their kitchen an hour or two before dawn and tried to get some sleep.

They remained with their kitchen through the next day, and when the darkness gave them some protection they set out with their supplies of food to find their own company again on the front. They hoped their unit hadn't traveled too far and that they could find it quickly to get their food to their buddies.

They were about halfway back when they heard the whining approach of an artillery shell. The noise became so intense that the two boys hastily set their buckets down and dove for cover.

"Look out!" shouted Carl just as the nearby explosion sent up a shower of debris. He felt a sharp stab of pain in his left leg just as he lost consciousness.

When he opened his eyes again, several men were clustered around him. He felt an intense throbbing pain while someone was wrapping a bandage very tight around his leg just above his ankle.

"Where's Jon?" he called out, raising his head.

Nobody answered.

"What happened to Jon?" he asked again. "Tell me, guys, where's Jon?"

An older man leaned over his face. "Do you mean the other mess runner with you?"

"Yeah. That's Jon. Is he okay?"

The man hesitated. "No, son, he's not okay. He's dead. That shell landed right next to him. He got blown to bits. There's nothing left of him but a memory."

"No!" cried Carl. "It can't be! We're gonna' go back to the marsh together. I'm gonna' marry his sister!"

"I'm sorry, son," said the older man, turning away. "I'm sorry."

"It can't be!" screamed Carl. "It can't be!" Then he sank back again into unconsciousness.

On the night Jon was killed, Prudence was restless. Her motherly intuition warned her of impending tragedy, but she was acutely aware of her own helplessness. She had tried to keep Jon at home, and failed. There was nothing more she could do.

When supper was over and the dishes washed and put away, she wandered outside and made her way to the riverbank. There she stood watching a brilliant crimson sunset radiating through a gash in the gray clouds of the western sky. She remained there, an unsmiling statue at the edge of the river, until daylight had faded into the dingy dusk of night. Then she retraced her steps slowly to the ancient stone farmhouse.

She walked past the lamp glowing on the kitchen table and idled her way into the living room where she sank down onto the sofa. She wanted to be alone.

Her reverie took her back to Jon's birth, and the joy she felt at having a son. This child was Zachary's, and she fervently believed it would be the bond which would completely restore the happy days of their early marriage and firmly unite her husband to her in joy and compassion.

She remembered Jon as an eager, inquisitive young tot who would melt her heart by throwing his stubby arms around her neck and blubbering "I love you Mommy" as he planted a wet kiss on her lips. Then he was the boy of ten who helped on the farm, insisting he could do the work of a man. And how could she forget the stubbornness of his early teenage years, when she almost gave up on him in despair? But now he was a soldier—he was a boy playing a man's deadly game.

Suddenly, sitting in the murky shadows of her living room, she felt a familiar coolness growing upon her. It was the feeling which had presaged the appearance of the ghost-like silhouette of her dead husband more than a year earlier. It had happened on Registry Day, when Jon signed up for the draft.

Instinctively she looked toward the window where she had seen Zachary's likeness, but there was nothing visible in the blackness of the night. She searched the other windows of the room without success, but the sensation of a close presence grew stronger.

A slight motion in the doorway of the room attracted her eyes. There, outlined in shadowy form by the flickering lamp in the kitchen, she saw a familiar masculine shape.

The palms of her hands felt cold with sudden perspiration, but there was no fear in her heart. She stared at the apparition with patient understanding.

"Zachary," she called gently. "Zachary, what is it? Why are you here?"

The figure remained motionless.

A feeling of comfort and consolation drifted over Prudence, although the sensation of coldness remained. The apprehension which had tormented her throughout the day seemed to drain slowly away.

"Zachary, I'm glad you're here," she said. "I wish you could speak to me, but I can feel your compassion and I appreciate it."

She strained to see the expression of his face, but it was completely hidden in the shadow of the dim light coming from the kitchen.

"I'm scared," she said softly. "I'm scared for Jon. You know that. I am afraid he will be killed. I have been afraid of that ever since he said he wanted to enlist.

"Actually, you know I've lived in fear for his life ever since he was born. You know about my fear that God will take away my firstborn son as a punishment.

217

"Are you here as a messenger of that punishment? It would be only fitting, wouldn't it, since I sinned against you as well as against God.

"And yet, I feel that you are here to console me, not to punish me. Am I right, Zachary?"

She leaned forward, earnestly seeking his response, and started to rise from the sofa. The shadow quickly slipped sideways, gliding out of the doorway toward the kitchen. Prudence leaped to her feet and dashed forward, but when she reached the spot where he had been, there was nobody there.

She rushed into the kitchen, toward the flickering lamp, but she found the kitchen empty. The ghost had vanished.

Chapter 16

The military car drove slowly along River Road and turned into the driveway of the Hartmann farm. Prudence, drawn to her living room window by the sound of tires crunching on the gravel, peered from the window without surprise.

She met the young man at the door. He was wearing a uniform like the ones she had seen at Camp MacArthur at Christmas, except that it was perfectly neat and spotless.

Later she could not remember anything the young soldier said, except the bitter words "your son Jonathan was killed in action." There was only the recollection of staring downward at the sharp crease in the soldier's trousers and the reflected glare of sunlight from his spit-shined shoes. She felt lightheaded and dizzy, but she knew she would not faint.

When he was gone, she returned to the living room and sat down noiselessly on the sofa. She cried silently, her tears spilling heedlessly in rivulets down her face and onto the front of her dress. So, Jonathan was dead. Zachary's only child. The dreaded event had actually happened. Almost simultaneously, she could remember him as a baby, a child, an adolescent. His cuteness, his energy, his deviltry, his warm devotion, his independence, his rebellion, his love.

And what of Carl? The two boys were fighting together as soldiers. Jon had been killed; was Carl also dead? How would she find out?

After a while, she heard the kitchen door open. The reassuring form of Ephraim entered the living room and sat down beside her.

"Is it bad news?" he asked.

"Yes," she said listlessly, not bothering to dry her tears. "Jonathan is dead."

"I feared as much when I seen the soldier come." He slipped his arm around her shoulder. "The Lord giveth, and the Lord taketh away," he recited.

"I was afraid, but I didn't really believe he would be killed," she said. "I thought God would be more merciful."

"Of course. By all the odds, Jon shoulda' made it through the war and come home t' us."

"I knew it would happen," she said in contradiction to herself. "It had to happen. But still I can't believe it. I didn't prepare myself for his death."

"No one is ever prepared fer someone dyin'" Ephraim commented. "Even when ya' know someone is very old or very sick, and you know they're gonna' die, ya' can't get ready for it. That's jus' the way people are."

They sat a long time without speaking. He pulled her close to him, quieting her sobs, comforting her with his presence the way only long-time friends can do.

"He was a good boy," she reflected.

"Yes, he was."

"Other than the ordinary little childish squabbles, he never gave us any trouble."

"No, he didn't."

"It isn't fair," Prudence protested. "He was so young."

"Yer right," he agreed. "But life itself ain't fair."

"I suppose he and Zac are together again," she observed.

"Yep. I bet they are," said Ephraim. "They both led good lives. They gotta' be across the Jordan, in the Promised Land."

"I wish I were with them," she said. "I'm tired of the troubles and the worries and the misfortunes of the world. I'm tired of suffering."

"Now, Prudy," Ephraim said softly, "don't say such things. Don't question God's will. His world is still a purty good place fer us t' be. We got lots of years in front of us yet, I reckon."

"Was it God's will for Jon to die so young?" she asked. "What was his life all about, anyway? Was he put down here on earth just to carry out God's judgment against me?"

"No, Prudy, I don't believe that fer a minute. Jon's life had a real purpose. I don't know what it was. Nobody can know fer sure what God's purpose is. But Jon brought a lot of happiness and joy to a lot o' people. He was always doin' good things fer others."

"But his life was so short!"

"In the eyes o' God, it was a full life. It don't matter how many years he was here."

"If Jon's purpose on earth was to be a punishment to me," Prudence continued her philosophical thought, "then what was my purpose? Why did God put me here?"

"I don't know, of course."

"And why did he fix it so I would be led into such a sin? He could just as well have fixed it so I wouldn't have sinned."

"I can't answer that," Ephraim replied. "But I don't think God ever fixes to lead someone into sin. We all have free choice in whatever we do, to sin or not to sin."

"He led me into my sin," insisted Prudence. "And you were led right along with me."

"I didn't have to do it," he observed. "I could have said no."

"Not really," she countered. "No man who was really a man would have said no, given those circumstances."

"Well, I'm not sure that we sinned. I know you have felt that way a long time, but I'm not sure about it. We didn't hurt nobody. I don't think it was a sin."

"Oh Eeph!" she scolded. "Don't make such fuzzy-headed excuses. What we did was a clear-cut violation of the Seventh Commandment, and you know it."

"No, I don't know it," Ephraim said defensively. "Not fer sure. The Sixth Commandment says 'thou shalt not kill,' but it's no sin to shoot yer enemy in war. If the Lord makes some exceptions for one commandment, mebbe he makes some exceptions for the others too, for good reasons like ours."

"Oh, Eeph!" she said again, and then was silent. They said nothing more, but they leaned against each other helplessly for a long time.

More than a week later, Jon's last letter, written on the eve of battle, arrived in Prairieville.

"What a strange feeling, to get a letter from the dead," exclaimed Prudence. She was almost afraid to read it; she took it with her into the living room and held it in her hands for a long time before she slit the envelope and extracted the single sheet covered with Jon's distinctive handwriting. A pang of guilt coursed through her body as she remembered Carl's note to Sarah from a previous envelope—a note which was still hidden in her desk. She had honorably intended to give it to her daughter, but somehow she had never done so. Now she nervously searched the new envelope for a similar missive, but there was nothing.

Jon briefly described his rapid trip through Paris and the deployment of his unit near the front. The short letter then closed with the following thoughtful comment:

"It is almost certain that we will be in the front lines by tomorrow or the next day. We can hear the constant thunder of the artillery at very close range.

"Fortunately, Carl and Lee are together with me. Just having my

buddies at my side gives me more confidence.

"*Our chances of making it through the fighting in one piece are very good. The losses among our troops are very few, they say. Nevertheless, we know that a few of us will be hit. If I am one of the unlucky ones, you can be proud that I did not flinch from my duty. And remember that I love you and Sarah and Ephraim with all my heart.*"

That was it. Those were the last words she would ever have from her son. She would treasure them for the rest of her life.

Prudence gathered Sarah and Ephraim and read the letter aloud to them. All of them wept, and embraced, and finally Sarah gave voice to a prayer on behalf of them all. "We praise Thee for Thy graciousness in letting us enjoy the life of our brother Jonathan for a few years," she said. "We thank Thee for his faithfulness, and for his kind heart, and for his honest conscience. His time on earth is now over, and he has returned to Thee. Thou hast called him home. Help us to let go. Help us to give him back freely. Help us to put ourselves in harmony with Thy divine will."

"What a beautiful prayer," said Ephraim. "You always been close t' God. Thank you fer helpin' t' set our thinkin' straight."

Near the end of August another letter arrived from France. Even before she read the name of the sender, she recognized the bold, handsome script of Carl. She had seen it before on the note to Sarah—the hidden note.

This time, however, the message was addressed to herself. Eagerly she tore the flap and began reading even as she walked up the driveway from the road.

Carl described the battle in the Grimpettes Woods, and the events of the following night when he and Jon had been hit by the exploding artillery shell.

"*I'm lying in a big army tent somewhere behind our front lines,*" he wrote. "*My left leg was shattered above the ankle, but the doctors were able to set the bones and they think I will mend okay. That leg will never be the same again, but I pray that it won't become infected and have to be amputated.*

"*Another piece of shrapnel hit me in the head and nearly scalped me like an Indian,*" he revealed. "*Once again, however, if it doesn't get infected, I shall be all right. Thank goodness my head was too hard to break!*"

Prudence sat down on the grass outside the house and went on to the next page. "*Lee packed up Jon's personal things and sent them along with me. There isn't much of anything, but I'll keep them and make a special trip to Prairieville to deliver to you as soon as I can. I can hardly wait to see the farm and the Vernal Marsh that Jon has told me so much about. I hope to be there by fall; it must be really beautiful then.*

"*Remember me to Sarah and Ephraim.*"

He signed the letter, *"Love, Carl."*

During the next few weeks, Ephraim took the first steps toward fulfilling his avowed intention of becoming a candidate for the State Assembly. He was driven by his desperate desire to endear himself to his beloved Prudence.

Ephraim was perhaps much better at recognizing his problems—even philosophizing about them—than he was at solving them. He was not generally a man of spontaneous action. Throughout his life, he had tiptoed around the edges of his desires and his fears. He tended to temporize, even when the need for urgent action became obvious. Events were usually things that happened to him; they were not things he initiated.

When a man is deeply in love, however, he will do almost anything to win his woman. Love is one of the greatest motivators in the world.

Now, faced with what might be the last big opportunity of his emotional life, Ephraim was determined to make a supreme effort to become the man he thought Prudence would love—a man who shared her goals and worked with her to attain them.

Typically, he had mulled over this decision for months—ever since January, when Prudence had celebrated the passage of the Anthony Amendment in Congress. His careful consideration of the question, though, was largely irrelevant. He was rushing ahead at the impulse of his heart, and rational matters were of little importance.

When he discussed his plans with Prudence, she discouraged him with a laugh just as she had done in January.

He was not deterred by her attitude. He enlisted Sarah's aid, and she became his informal campaign manager.

Ephraim had never participated in civic matters before, except for voting in the general elections. Wisconsin voters displayed an easy willingness to vote outside the two major political parties. The LaFollettes achieved statewide victories with their Progressive Party, while Congressman Victor Berger as well as Mayor Daniel Hoan of Milwaukee were Socialists. Ephraim was one of many who shunned a party label. Therefore, he decided to run as an independent candidate against the incumbent, Republican John Buckley.

That meant he must collect the signatures of many of his fellow voters to get on the ballot. Sarah learned the requirements, and she directed his efforts as he and Robert took turns driving through the district on the Harley-Davidson motorcycle asking people to sign his nomination papers.

Those weeks of frantic activity passed quickly for Ephraim, while Prudence suffered a severe emotional depression. In one sense, it was a relief to know for sure the fate of her son. Sometimes it is better to know the grim certainty than to suffer a cruel suspense. But in another sense, the knowledge that Jon was dead deprived her of all hope and left nothing in her heart but an aching emptiness. For most of her married life she had lived in dread of the punishment she felt was inevitable. Nevertheless, so long as Jon was alive there was always the possibility that she might be forgiven and the sentence might be stayed. Now that possibility was gone, and she was bereft of all reason to live.

She went about her daily chores through force of habit, without allowing herself to think. There was solace and reassurance in performing the routine tasks which required her attention—the housekeeping, the milking, the harvesting of her garden.

Gradually a speck of light appeared in her darkness; it was the anticipation of the promised visit from Carl. With plenty of time available, the lonesome soldier wrote to Prudence from his hospital bed every few days. Each letter gave her a step upward from her dungeon of despair.

It was of great significance, she felt, that every letter was addressed to her alone, and not once did he mention Sarah in any of them except for a casual greeting. With an easy conscience, Prudence passed all of Carl's letters to Sarah and Ephraim.

The first letters were written from France and arrived a few days apart. Along with the third one, however, came its successor written two weeks later in New Jersey. Carl was back in America!

"What a relief to leave Europe!" he wrote. *"And what a surprise, as well. The Army was just as secretive about my return voyage as they were when we shipped over a few months ago; I knew nothing about it until they sent me hobbling down the gangplank with my crutches.*

"Of course, my leg is still in a heavy plaster cast—from my toes almost to my hip. It's extremely awkward, but I don't really mind because the doctors say it will mend well enough that I will be able to walk again when the cast is removed after a few months.

"They are keeping me here for a day or two, but then I will be free to come to Prairieville. I want to see you in person and deliver Jon's last little belongings to you. Let me know if it is convenient for me to come in the next few days."

Prudence tucked this letter into the pocket of her dress, and as soon as the noon dinner was over she left the house and headed once more for the riverbank. This time there was no rain or mist to obscure her passage. She returned to the knoll and sank into the tall clumps of grass.

There she re-read the letter, alternately scanning its words and gazing out across the panorama before her.

The marsh was decorated in its lavish autumn colors. Softened hues of goldenrod and sumac accented the gray-green background. Hazy sunshine bathed the landscape in a gentle light. There was no breeze; the air itself was hushed as though it were suspended midway between the scenes of summer and winter. The muted quacking of wild ducks unseen in the distance emphasized the underlying tranquility. The pungent aroma of the marsh, emphasized by a recent rain, filled Prudence with its familiar scent.

So! Carl was coming to Prairieville to see her! Just the thought of it made her heart beat faster. She remembered again their first meeting in Texas, when they had exchanged glances. There was no doubt he felt the same strong attraction as herself; she knew it instantly as they met. She had never really doubted it since, not even when his note had arrived for Sarah. That worrisome note had been prompted by Jon, no doubt, Carl had clearly explained in his first sentence. It showed how considerate he was of the feelings of others.

The fact that he had ignored Sarah afterward showed very clearly that he was not interested in her. No, he was not being drawn to Prairieville by Sarah, but by Prudence herself. He wouldn't be coming to Prairieville if it weren't for his keen interest in knowing her better. It was too soon to call it love, of course, but she had certainly caught his attention.

The last time she had sat on this ground in meditation, she had wondered whether her feelings for Carl were generated by an inner desire to protect herself against total loss in case Jon were killed. She had attempted to bargain with God—if Jon were kept safe, she vowed never even to think of Carl again. It was an impossible vow, of course. But now Jon was gone; the bargain was broken. There was no reason any longer to attempt an unnatural forbearance.

Besides, perhaps God had provided Carl to assuage her loss. No one could ever take the place of her son, but Carl would make life worth living again. It was the appearance of the rainbow after the flood; it was like the birth of Solomon to David and Bathsheba after the death of their firstborn. God was infinitely merciful; He did not stay angry forever.

Undoubtedly, Ephraim would be bitterly disappointed. She remembered his unhappy face and his resentful words on the train back from Texas. But she didn't belong to Ephraim; she had never made him any promises nor given him any false hopes. He had no right to expect anything from her. He had followed her all his adult life, but that was his choice, not hers. She had her own choices to make.

And Carl was coming to see her! There was no reason, absolutely no reason at all, why she shouldn't allow him to bring joy into her heart.

Thinking of him now gave her mixed sensations of contentment and expectation. She turned her face upward into the cool radiance of the declining sun and smiled broadly with unrestrained joy.

Like a schoolgirl, she skipped a rapturous dance along the lane as she returned to the farmyard. She wanted the whole world to know of her wild ecstasy.

Yes, Prudence wanted everyone to know, but yet she didn't rush to tell Ephraim or Sarah. She intended to read Carl's letter to them, but somehow the right opportunity did not present itself. It was much the same as her earlier intention to give Carl's special note to Sarah—somehow the deed was never done, although there was no conscious decision against it.

She replied to Carl's overture, inviting him to come at once, but she contrived to meet the postman at the roadside to hand him the letter instead of leaving it in the mailbox with the red flag upraised.

"You look so happy, Mom," Sarah commented a few evenings later. "I haven't seen you smile so much, I don't think ever before."

"Oh, really?" replied Prudence, surprised that her feelings were so evident to others.

"I don't see how you can recover so quickly from Jon's death," continued Sarah reproachfully. "I certainly can't. I think about him all the time, and feel like crying."

"Well, what's done is done," said her mother. "While Jon was still alive, I feared for him and tried to keep him home and prayed for his safety. But now that he is dead, there is nothing I can do any more to save him or bring him back to life. He will not return to me in this world, so I might as well turn my face forward and go on without him."

"You're right, of course," reflected Sarah. "You sound just like King David after the death of his first son with Bathsheba. It's the right thing to do, and I'm glad you can do it. I can't."

To herself, Prudence thought 'Sarah would certainly be surprised if she knew how apt her comparison really is. She has stumbled upon more of the truth than she knows.'

"It will take a lot of time for all of us to learn to go on without Jon," said Prudence aloud. "It isn't easy."

Prudence thought again about the story of King David; it gave her comfort. 'He and Bathsheba recovered and had another son right away,' she remembered. 'That's impossible for me; Jon is dead and so is his father, and I am past the age for child-bearing. It's just got to be true that Carl is being sent to cheer me up. He is my Solomon,' she surmised.

The next few days dragged slowly past, and Prudence began to think Carl wasn't coming after all. But then a new letter arrived.

"*I'll be arriving on the* Chicago and North Western *railroad on the tenth,*" he wrote. "*If it's convenient, please meet me at the station in mid-afternoon. But don't put yourself out. I know you live on the River Road a few miles south of town, and I can find my own way out if necessary.*"

"If it's convenient," Prudence repeated aloud with a gentle laugh.

"I've been waiting for this day. I'd drive all the way to Milwaukee to meet you!"

Now it was necessary to inform Sarah and Ephraim. Carl's impending visit could not be concealed, whether or not she was prepared to announce it.

That evening, when the chores were finished, Ephraim and Robert stopped by the door to the old stone farmhouse along with Sarah. "Guess what!" Prudence blurted out. "Carl is coming to Prairieville."

"He is?" said Ephraim. "When?"

"Next Thursday," Prudence replied, and she pulled the letter from the pocket of her dress and read it aloud.

"Ah-h-h," breathed Sarah softly to herself. "Now we know. . . ."

"It'll be good to see Jon's friend," remarked Ephraim casually. "It'll be good to hear his war stories." In his heart, though, Ephraim was distressed. He quickly said "good-night" and walked up the road to his house.

The young man was clearly a formidable rival for the attentions of Prudence. He was young and undeniably handsome. In addition, he seemed better educated, or at least he was more recently educated. And he had the advantage of having traveled abroad, even if just as a soldier.

Ephraim ate a cold supper, scarcely speaking to Robert across the table. He was in a grumpy mood, and he escaped from the kitchen and retreated upstairs to his solitary bedroom as soon as he could. There he unlocked his tin box of memories and sifted through its meager contents—the ticket stub from the harness race; the old penny; the fountain pen; the letters; the dried marigold.

His attitude was gloomy. The approaching presence of Carl did not challenge him; it merely depressed him. By every reasonable standard, Prudence should become his own. Yet he knew in his heart that she had responded to Carl at Christmas with an enthusiastic vigor which she had never shown to him at any time, not even when he was courting her before her marriage to Zachary.

In addition, he feared Carl would replace him in Sarah's affections as well. Just a few months ago, Ephraim had suggested to Sarah that she should become better friends with Carl, in an attempt to draw Carl away from Prudence. Outwardly he would still support that plan, but inwardly he felt threatened by it. He didn't want Carl to take his place in the heart of Prudence, nor in the heart of Sarah either.

Ephraim was profoundly depressed by the prospect of Carl's early appearance. He felt overwhelmed by approaching events. His one heroic action—becoming a legislator in order to help Prudence with her suffrage efforts—suddenly seemed too little and too late. He had obtained the required signatures, and his name would be on the November ballot.

But the chances of his winning the election were very slim, he realized, and his loss would simply confirm Prudence's low opinion of him. Yet he could not think of any other promising course of action. In fact, it was hard to think at all. It was easier to withdraw within himself and accept whatever befell him.

Sarah, too, was apprehensive about Carl's coming. She was attracted to him, but she had little reason to think he returned her feelings. To the contrary, his letters centered around her mother and seemed to ignore her. It seemed unlikely that he even remembered her from their brief meeting at Camp MacArthur nearly a year before.

His presence would simply be an embarrassment, especially if he showed too much interest in her mother. He was so much younger than Prudence and it would be unseemly for him to be interested in her. And what would the neighbors think of her if Carl courted her mother instead of herself? Just the thought of that possibility made her blush with humiliation.

When Thursday arrived, Prudence dressed herself once again in the flowery frock she had bought in Waco, admiring herself in the mirror before descending the stairs from her room.

She allowed Ephraim to hitch Kaiser to the buggy, but she insisted upon driving into town without him.

"I want to go along," begged Sarah.

"No," replied her mother in a tone that was harshly abrupt. "I will go alone."

With an hour to spare, she was at the ornate train station which had been built years before to accommodate the wealthy visitors to Prairieville's healthful mineral springs. Unable to relax, she paced up and down the platform remembering the crowds of fancy people she had seen here when she was a child. Her eyes constantly searched the tracks to the east, alert to any clue that might herald the approaching train.

She thought of Jon as she had bid him goodby at this very spot just a year before. He had stood so tall and straight, like the magnificent man he had become, and he had marched along this platform willingly, from his ingrained sense of duty, knowing he might never return.

At last her ears discerned the distant huffing of the approaching locomotive, and she rushed to the end of the platform in eager anticipation. It arrived; it passed her; its cars coasted to a stop and a number of passengers began alighting. She ran alongside the coaches and paused in the midst of the small milling crowd.

Suddenly she saw him descending. Wrestling with his crutches, Carl was the last one out. He was wearing his khaki uniform with a brimless cap. He looked much older than she remembered. His face was pale, and to Prudence it appeared wan, but there was a sharp sparkle in his eye as he glanced apprehensively around the station platform.

When he saw her, a broad smile spread quickly across his face. He stopped on the bottom step of the coach and waited for her to reach him.

"Carl!" she exclaimed.

"Mrs. Hartmann," he responded with a certain shyness.

She sprang up on the step of the coach and threw herself upon him, crying and laughing and hugging him with great intensity. Her deepest emotions, pent up for so long, burst from her without restraint.

Carl's hands were encumbered with his crutches and his duffel bag, and he was unable to thwart her demonstration despite his obvious surprise and embarrassment.

"Oh Carl, Carl!" she exclaimed again and again. "I was so afraid I would never see you again. But here you are, my poor wounded boy. Wounded, but alive. Alive, and here where I can look after you like my own son." Her tears wetted his face as she impulsively pressed her cheek to his with a renewed hug.

His own eyes moistened. "I'm sorry about Jon," he said, his voice choked. "One minute he was alongside me, and then he was gone."

Prudence burst into a new spasm of weeping. "My son, my son!" she cried. "To think that I shall never see him again."

"Not on this earth, to be sure," Carl replied. "But we shall meet him again in Heaven, Mrs. Hartmann."

"Yes, yes, oh yes," she replied, seizing him by the shoulders and leaning back to look at him. "But please call me Prudence," she insisted. "Don't let's be formal. I feel like we are old friends." She hugged him again, craving a kiss but restraining herself because she felt him turn his face away.

"All right . . . Prudence," he said tentatively.

"Where is your luggage?" she asked.

"I don't have much—everything is here in my duffel bag. When you are a soldier, you have to travel light."

Prudence seized the bag with one hand and took his elbow with the other. "Let me help you down."

When he was firmly on the platform, he dismissed her aid. "I can get around pretty well with these crutches," he explained.

She led him to her buggy, where Kaiser was waiting with impatience. She helped him up into the seat, stored his crutches carefully in the back, and climbed in alongside him.

At last she was alone with the young man who had become the center of her thoughts and dreams. After Kaiser was headed south on Grand Avenue toward home, she turned to look at him.

For many months she had doted upon him in her imagination; now she examined him cautiously, measuring him against her fantasy and being slightly jarred at finding little discrepancies. In reality, his jaw was more angular; his eyebrows were thicker; his whole body was thinner; his voice was harsher. Perhaps the most noticeable difference, however, was the way his head jerked occasionally when he spoke. All things considered, he was less attractive to her than she had remembered.

They drove along through the tartness of the October air. Now that her paragon was present in the flesh, Prudence felt disappointed. Meeting Carl again did not measure up to her expectation. She had anticipated something different, something more, but she could not define the shortcoming.

"I've worried so much about you," she said. "I've been so very concerned about your leg. Does it still give you a lot of pain?"

"Yes, Ma'am, it does. The doctors say the pain will gradually go away, but it might take several months or more. I don't mind; I can stand it."

"But it didn't get any infection, did it?"

"No, thank God. Oh, the wounds were sore enough, and they festered a bit at first. But it was nothing like the gas gangrene that so many of the guys got. I was real lucky."

"What about your head?" she inquired. "Where were you hurt?"

He pointed to the right side of his head, well up into the hair. "Whatever it was, it got me right there. It cut my scalp open, but it didn't crack my skull. They put a lot of stitches in it to sew it up, and it's all pretty much back to normal. You can feel the scar, but fortunately it's all up in the hair where you can't see it."

"May I touch it?" she asked, already reaching upward toward him.

He removed his cap and leaned over. "Yes, Ma'am. It's healed up real good."

She pressed the reins between her knees to hold them, and used both her hands to position his head carefully while she examined it. The feel of his bushy dark brown hair was like magic to her. She could see the ugly jagged line of the torn scalp, but she was relieved to verify his optimistic report—it was healing very nicely.

"It looks good," she said.

"Yes, Ma'am; it feels good."

"Please don't be so formal," she told him with mock reproach. "Don't call me 'Ma'am.' Just call me Prudence."

He laughed, and the merry tone of his laughter pleased her ears. "Okay, Prudence," he said. She continued to stroke his head afterward as though he were a pet; the touch of his hair and his forehead made her tingle with excitement.

"This is River Road," she informed him as they approached the farm. "It's known informally as 'Lovers' Lane.'"

Carl did not comment.

Prudence was so engrossed with Carl that she did not see Ephraim awaiting them at the gate to her driveway until she heard the loud "Hallo!" boom out at them. With a guilty start, she released Carl's head and reached for the reins.

Frowning, Ephraim thought, 'She didn't waste no time,' as he walked alongside the buggy to the house. 'But they do make a handsome couple t'gether. You'd never know she was twice his age. She is so beautiful!' He helped Carl down, and then volunteered to take care of Kaiser.

Carl was able to go up and down stairs with his crutches, so Prudence settled him in the upstairs bedroom which had been Jon's.

"You'll probably want to rest up a bit after your journey," she said. "We'll eat supper about seven o'clock, after the chores are done. We'll call you in plenty of time."

She invited Ephraim and Robert to eat with them.

Carl attacked the meal like a starving man. "This is the first good food I've had since my mother died," he said. "Everything tastes so good! Thank you for including me at your table." He looked around the room as though he had never seen a house before. "This is like being in heaven."

The solid food of the farm table—beef ribs, mashed potatoes, and squash—began to satisfy his appetite, and Carl began relating the events that had happened to Jon and Lee and himself. Expanding upon the account he had written in his letter, he told again of their march to the front lines, and their baptism into fire.

"It's impossible to describe the battlefield," he told them. "You would think that you would be scared to death when you begin an attack. But you really don't think about anything at all. Everybody is charging ahead, and you don't want to be left behind. You just get caught up in the whole thing, and move right along, scarcely aware of what is happening around you.

"I was about as lucky as you can get," he said. "I was in the front lines only a couple of days, and I fought only one battle. I didn't kill anyone, at least not that I know about. I ran forward with the rest of my unit when they told us to go, and there was a lot of noise and confusion, and when I got to the Grimpettes Woods where the Germans were supposed to be, I didn't see any. They had already been flushed out by the leading group of our soldiers, and had retreated to their next line of defense.

"The next night I was wounded, and with this broken leg there was no thought of fixing me up and returning me to the front. Fortunately I was behind our lines when I was hit, so I got immediate medical attention and they didn't have to amputate."

"We are so glad," murmured Prudence.

"We've heard a lot about trench warfare," said Ephraim. "Did you fight in trenches?"

"No, we didn't, at least not the long formal zigzag trenches like they used in the earlier part of the war. Of course, we dug in whenever we stopped, because we wanted some protection from the artillery barrage which seemed to go on both night and day. But our little holes weren't very deep, and our boys were moving forward a couple of miles every day so then we had to start over.

"From what we heard the trenches were terrible, especially in cold rainy weather. The floor of the trench was flooded with dirty water, turning the bottom into a slimy ooze. The walls would cave in, even though they were shored up with sandbags or stones or tree limbs. Can you imagine living in a mess like that day after day, and night after night? How could you sleep, when there was no place to lie down out of the mud? How could you even stay alive? It sounds awful!"

"You poor thing!" exclaimed Prudence. "Even though you weren't in those trenches, your conditions were bad enough. We are so grateful your life has been spared, and you have come home."

"Thank you, Prudence," he said.

His familiar use of her first name chafed Ephraim. 'What a young upstart,' he thought to himself. He looked at Sarah across the table, and their eyes expressed mutual disgust.

"This feels like home to me already," Carl added warmly. "You know, of course, that I don't really have a home."

"Yes, Jon told us a little about your background," replied Prudence.

"My mother died a year ago in the spring, and I joined the National Guard. My father and I don't get along very well. He wasn't very kind to us. He has no idea where I am, and I don't care. I don't ever want to see him again."

"You poor thing," Prudence repeated with extreme sympathy, slipping her arm around his shoulders and giving him a squeeze.

Ephraim and Sarah exchanged doleful glances again.

"What are ya' plannin' t' do after yer recovery," inquired Ephraim.

"Oh, I don't know," replied Carl. "I'll get a job somewhere, and start a new life I suppose."

When they had finished eating, Carl produced a little packet he had been carrying. "As soldiers on the march, we didn't carry very much with us unless we had to," he apologized, opening the packet and presenting a few papers. "All Jon had of a personal nature were a couple of your own recent letters from home and the tiny New Testament which he said came from you, Sarah. He read from it every day. And, of course, there was the lovely picture of his mother." He handed over the little photograph from O'Brien's she had mailed to Jon after Christmas.

232

Prudence accepted the items with tears in her eyes. She wished he would keep her picture, but it seemed awkward to give it back.

She insisted upon getting Carl to bed. "It's been a long day," she told him. "You need your rest so your bones will knit together again."

He went up the steep stairs one at a time, with Prudence right behind him in case he should lose his balance. She fussed over him as though he were her own son, scarcely allowing him the privacy of his own bath. Afterward, she tucked him into Jon's bed and leaned over to give him a goodnight kiss on the forehead.

Then she retreated into her own bedroom, shut the door, and wept.

Robert headed for the barn to take a last look at the cattle, and Sarah decided to walk with Ephraim part way to his home.

"Wasn't that revoltin'!" exclaimed Ephraim. "He plays on her heart-strings like a fiddle. It was like there was nobody else in that room; the two of them was jus' talkin' t' themselves wit' the rest of us jus' lookin' on."

"Uncle Eeph, what's going on between those two? Mom acted so strange about Carl when she met him last Christmas. She seemed so excited, almost giddy."

"Yah, we've talked about it before. She's kinda' nutty about him."

"He was Jonathan's buddy," commented Sarah. "He could be her son. I keep telling myself she is feeling a motherly instinct for him, and that's all. But she acts like it might be something more."

"I have the same worries," said Ephraim. "I'm afraid she could make a fool outta' herself."

"Uncle Eeph, I've said this before, but more than ever I want you to marry my mother," reminded Sarah.

"Well, I'm quite willin'," replied Ephraim, "but she don't seem t' have much interest in me."

"She ought to. I'd like to have you for a father."

Ephraim changed the subject. "How about yerself? If Carl takes a fancy fer ya', are ya' still interested in him?"

"Yes, I think so. Of course, I don't really know him yet. But I like him, if only he'd like me."

"Well, let's stick to our little pact," suggested Ephraim. "Let's get you n' Carl goin' together, an' mebbe we can swing Prudence back in my direction."

"I think I would like that very much," Sarah said.

They gave each other a vigorous, heart-felt hug before they parted.

Chapter 17

Prudence intended to help Carl get dressed the next morning, but she didn't want to disturb his rest so she went downstairs to start preparing breakfast.

Carl did not linger in bed, however. He made his way downstairs and surprised Prudence by being ready to eat with the family.

She rushed to his side and took his arm to guide him to a chair.

"You could have slept longer," she told him.

"No, I really couldn't," he said. "I've been awake since dawn, and I was itching to get up and around."

She helped him sit down, making room for his bulky leg alongside the kitchen table.

"Here, Sarah, take his crutches—you can lean them against the wall."

"Thank you," he murmured.

"It must be difficult to dress yourself," Prudence sympathized.

"Oh, I'm a little slower at it because of the leg," he agreed. "But it's a great feeling just to be able to take off my clothes at night and climb into a real bed. I don't mind the extra effort of dressing and undressing; it sure beats sleeping on the ground in a sweaty uniform."

"Oh, you poor thing," Prudence exclaimed, patting his shoulder comfortingly.

He shrugged off her hand, laughing. "It wasn't all that bad," he said. In fact, I'd have to admit we enjoyed the experience—most of the time."

Prudence set a steaming cup before him. "Here," she said, "you can get started. Do you like coffee?"

"Yes, I do, Mrs. Hartmann."

She winced and gave him a look of mock disapproval.

234

"I mean, 'Prudence,'" he corrected himself.

"That's better," she smiled. "Now, what would you like for breakfast? I can fry eggs and bacon, or cook some oatmeal, or dish up some corn flakes. Would you like some toast?"

"I'll be glad to eat whatever you normally serve," Carl said. "Please, don't put yourself out for me."

"It's no trouble," she assured him. "It's the least I can do for a war hero."

He laughed. "I'm no hero," he protested. "I was worse than useless over there. Never even saw a German soldier."

"Well, I was planning on scrambling some eggs," she said.

"That would be fine," he said. "I have a hankering for scrambled eggs this morning, and I was about to tell you so."

"Her scrambled eggs are delicious," Sarah testified, eager to join the conversation.

"Sarah, I saw Robert and Ephraim heading up the road to their house," said Prudence. "Aren't they going to stop by for breakfast?"

"Not today, Mom," Sarah replied. "They said they didn't want to trouble you."

"It's no trouble for me," Prudence commented. "As long as I'm cooking breakfast for the family, two more mouths don't make much difference." She turned to Carl. "Sometimes they have breakfast with us, and sometimes they don't," she explained. "I think that's the only good meal they get all day, when they come here." She shrugged indifferently. "Men are so helpless by themselves!"

Carl laughed. "You're right, Prudence," he said. "Every man needs a good woman. Even Ephraim." He had seen the look of loneliness in Ephraim's eyes and the flash of affection whenever the old farmer glanced at Prudence.

"Yes, even Ephraim," repeated Sarah.

Prudence smiled warmly at Carl. "Yes, but it's got to be the right man, and the right woman," she said.

"Of course," he replied.

Prudence set a sauce dish before him. "Here's some canned prunes," she said. "You can eat them while I get the eggs ready."

Carl wrinkled his nose. "I don't care much for prunes," he said.

Prudence smiled patronizingly. "They're good for you," she said, "and you're going to eat them whether you like it or not."

He laughed. "Yes, Mother," he said.

"I'm not your mother," she said quickly. "I'm your friend."

"You are right, Prudence. You are indeed my friend." He picked up his spoon.

She put a restraining hand on his arm. "Let's say our morning prayer first," she said.

He rested his hand on the table, still clutching the spoon, and closed his eyes.

"Our Father in heaven," recited Prudence, "bless this food to our use, and bless us to Thy service." She paused, and then added, "And kindly put Your hand of healing upon this wonderful man, and restore him to perfect health in Your good time, amen."

"Amen," repeated Sarah.

After breakfast Carl wondered aloud whether he could see the marsh that Jon had described to him in such attractive terms. Prudence was pleased to oblige him, and she guided him on a walk to the river and back. The distance was not great, but it took the crippled young man most of the morning to complete the trip.

"I'm beginning to understand Jon's fascination with the marsh," he remarked. "It's hard to describe, but I can feel it deep in my heart."

Carl settled easily into his new role as the beloved son recuperating from his heroic injuries. He helped Prudence to surmount her grief for Jon. She was eager to pamper him, and he was hungry for personal attention.

He showed his appreciation by offering to help the family with their farm work.

"There ain't nothin' ya' can do," Ephraim told him rather abruptly, when Carl showed up in the barn the next morning during the milking.

"I can't walk without crutches," Carl conceded, "but surely there must be something I could do that would be helpful."

"I can't think of nothin'," replied Ephraim.

"Maybe he could curry the calves," suggested Sarah.

"I'd be glad to do anything at all," Carl said.

"They git along jus' fine without curryin'," grumbled Ephraim.

"But they do get dirty in their pen," Sarah said. "They look so much nicer when they're clean, and I'm sure they feel better, too."

"Yer welcome t' do it if ya' want," shrugged Ephraim.

"Yes, I'd like to do it," replied Carl. "I want to make myself useful as much as I can."

"Go ahead n' show 'im how," said Ephraim. "I don't s'pose he's ever seen a currycomb, much less used one."

Carl laughed. "You're right about that, of course. But I want to learn, and I catch on fast." He turned to Sarah. "Please teach me how to curry a calf."

Sarah was grateful for the opportunity for a little time alone with Carl. "Come along," she said, "The calves are down at the end of the barn."

She led him slowly down the central aisle to a small pen with three calves inside.

"This one is Arlene," she said, pointing to the biggest one. "The next one is Carolyn, and the one lying down in the corner is Snowflake."

"Do you name all your calves?" asked Carl.

"Oh, yes, as soon as they are born. Every cow in the barn has her own name. Each one knows her own name, but most of the time they are so stubborn they won't respond to it."

"Don't you have any young bulls?" he asked.

"No, we don't keep any bull calves," she said. She laughed disarmingly. "The males are useless. They don't produce any milk and of course they don't have any baby calves of their own."

"I don't know much about farming," grinned Carl, "but I read somewhere that a cow can't have a calf without getting a bull involved somewhere."

"Of course," Sarah said without embarrassment. "We keep one grown-up bull. That's all we need."

"I guess that's right," Carl agreed. "So what happens to the bull calves if nobody wants them?"

She laughed again, teasingly. "What do you think they make baloney out of? Most males are full of baloney, you know!"

"Is this your commentary on men, as well as bulls?" he asked with a smile.

"Oh, no," she said quickly. "In the world of people, men are very useful. We need men to do most of our work. They're a lot stronger than us women."

"Men are important, then, because of the work they can do," he repeated. "Is that all?"

Sarah flushed. Normally she was quite shy around men, but she suddenly realized she had been babbling like a child. She could talk freely about farm animals, and she had been led along farther than she had intended.

Hiding her confusion, she plucked a small circular hand tool from its nail on a post and displayed it to Carl. "This is a currycomb," she said. "Its purpose is to scrape all the dirt and straw and other crud off the hide of the calf. It also helps to make all the hair to lie down in the same direction, so the calf looks prettier." She demonstrated by stroking Arlene's flank.

"That's simple enough," Carl commented. "Let me try it."

He put one crutch aside, and stood unsteadily on one leg alongside her. He took the comb from her hand and began working vigorously with it.

"You're doing it just right," she said.

He worked in silence for a few moments. Then he said, "Your mother is certainly a marvelous person. I just love her."

"Yes," replied Sarah.

"It is so nice of her to take me in like this. I have no home to go to, and she has made me feel so welcome that it's just like I'm part of the family."

"You're a boy almost the same age as my brother Jon," observed Sarah. "Your being here helps my mother get over the loss of her son. You can be her little boy for a while."

Arlene suddenly shifted her stance, bumping Carl, and he wobbled precariously for a moment. Sarah quickly seized him, one arm around his waist, to steady him.

The touch of his body was magic to her. She continued to hold onto him long after the danger of falling was past, until he said, "I'm okay; you can let go of me now."

"Oh, yes," she acknowledged, flushing crimson for the second time. She could not speak again, but watched him silently as he worked.

Later in the morning, Ephraim and Sarah found an opportunity to talk privately while they strolled together beneath the colorful maples bordering River Road.

"I'm outclassed," Ephraim confessed to Sarah. "Carl is young, handsome, and better educated than me. He's been overseas. But I don't feel hopeless about my chances. I've known Prudence a lot longer. An' I know she's got good common sense deep in her heart."

"She's a wonderful woman and she's been a good mother," Sarah responded, "but she's been acting so strange lately. Ever since Dad died. Maybe even a little before that. I'm confused by her, and I don't really know what she is likely to do."

"Well, I think she'll do the right thing in the end," said Ephraim. "She's treatin' Carl like a son, an' that's okay with me. We gotta' remind 'em once in a while about the difference in their ages."

"I think you should treat Carl nicer, though," suggested Sarah. "You were not very civil to him when he came to the barn this morning."

"I know, I know," Ephraim replied. "I'm sorry. I know it don't do no good t' be mad at him. I'll try t' be better."

They walked a few minutes without talking. The morning air tweaked their noses with its frostiness. Overhead, the sky was crisp and cloudless, the solid China blue contrasting vividly with the reds and yellows of the leaves.

"I've got t' be worthy o' her, though," added Ephraim. "That's why it's so important fer me t' beat John Buckley n' go t' the Assembly."

"I think you've got a good chance," said Sarah.

"I'm running as an Independent," he reminded her. "I don't have the support of any political party."

"I know," she said, "but the citizens who like the major parties are going to split their votes between the two big-name candidates. John Buckley has the Republicans behind him, and George Dwinnel has the Democrats. It helps us that Dwinnel is such a strong challenger, because that cuts down on Buckley's votes. There won't be many Democrats who vote for Buckley. And that gives us a great chance to win. We can win votes from Republicans and Democrats alike."

"I see what you mean," Ephraim said.

"Like I told you before, I figure we can win if we get twelve hundred votes," Sarah said. "There will be about three thousand ballots cast, maybe a little more. We don't have to get a majority to win. With three candidates, all we have to do is get more votes than either one of our opponents. So if we get twelve hundred, and they split the rest and get maybe a thousand votes apiece, we win."

"We ought to be able to do it," Ephraim commented.

"What helps us the most is that Buckley and Dwinnel apparently are not in favor of woman suffrage," Sarah said. "From what I hear, they spend their time talking about other things."

"That gives me an open field," Ephraim observed. "If I can jus' talk t' enough people and let them know that I support votes fer women, then I win."

Sarah laughed. "Yes, that's our best chance. But remember, not everyone is in favor of votes for women."

"That's hard t' believe."

"Yes, but it's true," she assured him. "You and I have been listening to my mother's opinions for so long that we are completely convinced. But it's a new idea to lots of our friends and neighbors, and they aren't sure they want it."

"Well, I'm gonna' tell everybody how I feel, anyway. There oughta' be a lot of people who agree with me. Mebbe enough to win, huh?"

"Maybe so. You've got a couple of natural advantages. Out here in the country, many of the voters know you—and that should help you. And in Prairieville itself, there is a lot of support for woman suffrage."

"I never looked at it that way, but yer absolutely right," Ephraim commented, pursing his lips and rolling his eyes.

"When you are talking with the farm people, you should emphasize the fact that you are one of them—that you've been farming here for thirty years."

"That's right," Ephraim agreed.

"And when you talk with the city folk, you should talk about your support for woman suffrage."

"Whew!" It was more of an exhalation than a word, and his breath formed a misty plume as he blew it from his mouth. "Yes, I see what ya' mean," Ephraim said. His face clouded, and he was silent as they continued to crunch the early fallen leaves beneath their feet.

"I hadn't even thought about goin' in t' Prairieville," he confessed finally. "I don't know none o' those city slickers. I think they would laugh me right outta' town."

"Uncle Eeph, there aren't enough farmers out here to win the election, even if every one of them voted for you," Sarah explained. "You need some of the votes in the city, too."

"I s'pose yer right."

"You don't have to win all of them," she said. "But you've got to win some of them to add to the ones you get out here in the country."

"But how can I get at 'em?" he asked. "I can't jus' go knockin' on their doors like I do out here."

Sarah wrinkled her forehead thoughtfully. "I know what we'll do," she said at last. "We'll have Mom introduce you to some of her friends from the Woman's Club. They are mostly on the side of suffrage. And they can tell their friends."

"Okay," Ephraim agreed doubtfully. "We can try it."

"If we want to win, we don't have any choice," she observed.

Sarah suggested the idea to her mother later in the day. "Mom, Ephraim needs to meet some of the people from Prairieville to try to pick up enough votes for his election. How about introducing him to your friends from the Woman's Club?"

Prudence was momentarily taken aback. "Oh, I don't think that's necessary," she said hesitantly. In her mind's eye she saw her elegant and refined friends from the city meeting Ephraim—Ephraim the farmer, looking like a bumpkin, smelling like the manure pile, and unable to speak a single sentence in accordance with the rules of good grammar.

"He's got to get some votes from the city," Sarah explained, "and those votes are most likely to come from suffragists. That's why we thought of your friends."

"Oh, no," protested Prudence. "I don't think that would work at all."

"Why wouldn't it work?" inquired Sarah.

"Oh, I think my friends already have their minds made up. They've probably already decided how they will cast their votes."

"Oh, do you think so? Do you think they would vote for Buckley or Dwinnel if they knew about Ephraim and his commitment to their cause? You can be darned sure that Buckley and Dwinnel won't work very hard for woman suffrage. But Ephraim will. That ought to change the minds of some of your friends, at least."

"Well, perhaps," Prudence conceded.

"How about Theodora Youmans herself?" persisted Sarah. "Surely she would vote for a man who will advance her cause."

"I suppose so," said Prudence.

"Well, of course," said Sarah. "Now, how's the best way of going about this? Is there a meeting of the women before the election?"

"No, I don't think so," replied Prudence.

"Well, how about having Theodora invite some of the friendly women over for an afternoon tea where they could meet Ephraim and talk with him?"

"I don't know," temporized Prudence. "Let me think about it."

"Oh, Mom!" exclaimed Sarah, "You're not being very enthusiastic. Don't you want to help Ephraim win the election? He's doing it all for you, you know."

"I didn't ask him to do this," Prudence said defensively, "and I hate to encourage him very much because there is no chance at all that he can win, and I don't want him to get his hopes up too high."

"Well, that's a dumb reason not to help him," observed Sarah. "I think he can win. But let's say you're right about him losing. Don't you think he'd feel worse about losing if he hadn't given it his best efforts?"

"I suppose so," acknowledged Prudence.

"Well, I would certainly think so. Now, will you do it? To help Ephraim? And our cause? Even if he loses, it's a good thing to have him reminding everybody about the importance of woman suffrage."

Prudence thought once more about her friends meeting Ephraim, and this time the setting was Theodora's fancy parlor. An involuntary shiver made her shoulders twitch.

"Well, how about it?" Sarah pressed. "What's holding you back? Are you ashamed to have your lady friends meet Ephraim?"

Prudence hesitated. "Well. . . ."

"Oh, Mother! Remember, you're a farmer too. That didn't keep you from being friends with the women in those clubs." It occurred to Sarah as a surprise that perhaps one's social class made a difference, even in America. She herself had always been proud of her farm heritage, but suddenly she realized that her mother might be embarrassed by it. Perhaps that was one of the sources of her discontent which had been so noticeable in the past several years. And perhaps that was a barrier between her mother and Ephraim. Perhaps her mother could no longer be comfortable with the social status of a farmer.

"That was different," Prudence weakly protested. "I met those women as an equal, almost—I understand their point of view; I speak good English; I'm just like them in many ways."

Sarah thought for a moment. "It's true that Uncle Eeph doesn't always use good grammar," she said hesitantly.

"Yes, he'd probably feel awkward and embarrass himself," Prudence suggested.

"Well, I still think we should do it," Sarah said more firmly. "I'll try to help him a bit with his English. To win this election, we've got to swing a pile of votes from Prairieville, and add them to our farmer friends. The numbers are very convincing. It's got to be done."

"Will Eeph be willing to do it?" asked Prudence.

"Yes, he will," replied Sarah. "We've already talked about it. He's not exactly thrilled by the idea, but he realizes it's the only way to win and so he'll do it."

"Maybe we should invite some of the women out here to the farm," suggested Prudence, beginning to yield. "That way, they will meet Eeph in his own territory."

"I think that's a good idea," said Sarah thoughtfully. "How many of your friends would come?"

"Oh, I'd guess maybe a half-dozen or so," speculated Prudence. "Not very many more than that, surely. Everybody's afraid to go out in public because of the influenza epidemic."

"Let's do it," Sarah said decisively. "Let's invite them out here. We should hold the meeting in our house, I would think, rather than Uncle Eeph's; it would take too much work to make his place presentable."

"You're beginning to talk me into it," Prudence admitted, "but let me see what Theodora thinks about it."

When she telephoned her friend she found a very receptive audience. "Your plan certainly has my full support," Theodora told her, "even though Mrs. Dwinnel is a member of the Woman's Club. If Ephraim is an ardent supporter of suffrage, we all ought to meet him and hear what he has to say. We need every voice we can enlist on behalf of our cause."

Convinced at last, Prudence began calling the clubwomen and inviting them to an afternoon reception at her farm.

She was pleasantly surprised at the positive responses she received. During the next several days, many of her friends promised to come, and they seemed pleased to be asked.

Carl was enthusiastic about Ephraim's campaign as soon as he learned about it. "We've got to treat women better in this society," he declared. "We've got to give them more respect. I saw what happened to my mother, the way she was brutalized by my father. She had no place to turn; there was nobody who could help her. It was like she was a slave to my father. He could do anything he wanted with her, and there was nobody she could appeal to."

"That is awful," sympathized Prudence. She had learned the story from Jon, but it seemed more terrible now that she heard it directly from Carl's lips.

"Giving women the right to vote isn't going to rescue all the wives who are threatened by their husbands," Carl said, "but it is certainly one step toward the goal of giving them more power."

"That's absolutely right," agreed Prudence, "and that's why I'm fighting the suffrage battle."

"Uncle Eeph must be a brave and forward-looking man to stake his campaign on that issue," observed Carl. "There aren't very many men who would be willing to speak up so forthrightly for such a cause."

"Yes, Ephraim is a good man," said Prudence faintly.

"A very good man," Sarah added firmly.

"I like him," Carl continued. "I've been out in the barn with him enough during the past several days to recognize that he is a very knowledgeable farmer. But more than that, he seems like quite a Christian gentleman."

"Yes, that he is," Prudence agreed quietly.

"He's all of that," Sarah agreed expansively. "We've known him for years, and you will never meet a finer gentlemen or a more devout soul."

"Jon told me a little about him," Carl explained. "Jon said he wasn't really a part of the family, despite the fact that you all call him 'uncle.'"

"That's right," confirmed Prudence. "He's a good-hearted neighbor who stepped in to help us after Zachary died."

"He's never been married?" inquired Carl.

"No, he's been a bachelor all his life," replied Prudence.

"I thought that's what Jon told me," said Carl. He grinned mischievously. "He seems to think very highly of you. I think one of the reasons he's running for office, in addition to his own personal convictions, is because he respects you so much, and wants to help you in your suffrage efforts."

Carl searched her face inquisitively, but she glanced away and said nothing. Sarah caught Carl's eye and sagely nodded her head at him.

With a disarming smile, Carl asked bluntly, "Is he courting you?"

"Heavens no!" exclaimed Prudence quickly. "Don't be ridiculous. He's just a good neighbor."

"I think he still likes you a lot, Mom," Sarah said eagerly. "You see, Carl, he courted my mother years ago, before she married my father."

"Maybe you should give him a little encouragement," pressed Carl.

Prudence narrowed her eyes, and pinched her lips together uncharacteristically. A touch of color surfaced in her cheeks. "I have no interest in him," she declared vigorously. "Please, let's not even talk about it."

When the day of the reception arrived, all was in readiness. Ephraim looked a bit stiff in his Sunday suit, which Sarah had taken into Prairieville for cleaning and pressing. It was a size too small, and the white cuffs of his shirtsleeves seemed to extend halfway to his thumb. Every hair was slicked down. His face was ruddy from the sun and from being scrubbed absolutely clean.

It was a warm day for mid-October, with the temperature in the sixties. Robert had scrubbed and re-painted the family's half-dozen wooden outdoor chairs, and they were scattered around on the lawn. Their pure whiteness marked a vivid contrast to the still-vibrant emerald green grass. Even though there had been several nights with a hard frost, there were a few hardy chrysanthemums still showing their colors. The sky was cloudy, but the outline of the sun could be seen throughout much of the day as it tried valiantly to break through the overcast.

Plates filled with sugar cookies, baked by Prudence and several neighbors, crowded the kitchen table. The coffee was ready in the dining room, along with freshly squeezed apple cider.

Ephraim had been carefully coached by Sarah, who had learned as much as she could about the race. She told him that the incumbent, John Buckley, was a young man in his mid-twenties. He graduated from the law school of the University of Wisconsin in 1915, and was elected to the state assembly the next year. In his first term he championed the university and its law school, supporting everything from street improvements near Camp Randall to state-sponsored scholarships for university students.

Sarah suggested that Buckley's Democrat opponent, George Dwinnel, seemed to be promoting himself as an older and more experienced man.

Neither candidate, apparently, was making an issue of the suffrage amendment.

The cars began arriving early for the three-o'clock event. Theodora came first, bringing three other women with her. Bertha Palmer followed soon afterward with another group. Before long, at least twenty-five women were milling through the house and overflowing onto the lawn, munching daintily on cookies and gossiping lightly.

"I'm amazed that so many women are coming, considering the threat of influenza," remarked Theodora.

The pleasant weather was fortuitous because it became obvious as more and more women arrived that the crowd would surpass the highest expectations. It would have been impossible to accommodate everyone inside.

Without a doubt, there had never been a more elegant party at John Hilley's seventy-year-old house. The graceful women with their fastidious coiffures and their long flowing dresses represented the highest ranks of Prairieville society.

"Mom, you've got to take Ephraim around and introduce him to every woman here," Sarah directed. "Later, he can give his little speech." She watched with satisfaction as Prudence took Ephraim by the arm and marched him toward a cluster of her friends. Then she turned to Carl and the two of them set off separately.

Ephraim was welcomed warmly by the women. "We've been hearing about this man who is brave enough to run against two powerful politicians," said Martha Walton. "Do you really think you have a chance to unseat John Buckley?"

"Yes, Ma'am, I really think so," replied Ephraim.

"On what grounds?" she wanted to know.

"Because I think the citizens are in favor of votes for women, and I am openly supporting the idea," he said, enunciating his words slowly and carefully the way Sarah had instructed him.

"Good for you," beamed Mary Lockney.

Prudence and Ephraim wandered from group to group, trying not to miss anyone in the crowd, repeating the same message again and again.

Ephraim was well received, but he was very nearly upstaged by Carl. Led by Sarah, the young soldier also circulated among the guests. The women were eager to hear of his experiences at war, and plied him with countless questions.

"What did you think of France?"

"Do all the doughboys really have cooties?"

"Were the French girls as bold as the stories we hear about them?"

"Did you see any other Prairieville boys besides Jon?"

"How many Germans did you kill?"

"How much longer will the war go on?"

"Tell us how you were injured!"

Among themselves, the women gossiped freely, speculating upon Carl's presence in the Hartmann household.

"Is he Sarah's boyfriend?"

"No, it's just that he was a close friend of Jon."

"He's very handsome."

"Yes, they make a perfectly matched couple together."

"Why is he staying here?

"I hear he's an orphan."

"He's taking the place of Jonathan, sort of."

"I'd certainly be proud of a son like that."

"Yes, Prudence seems very proud of him."

"Speaking of Prudence, what's her relationship to Ephraim?"

"Oh, they're just friends, I'm sure."

"He's been a very good neighbor to her, especially since Zac died."

"They make a perfectly matched couple too!"

After an hour or so, Sarah directed Ephraim to the solid little wooden box which would serve as his speaking platform. The chattering of the crowd subsided as he gazed out over his new friends. He smiled broadly and began speaking slowly and carefully.

"I suppose it seems strange for a farmer from the Vernal Marsh to decide all of a sudden to run for a political office," he began.

"Well, believe me, it seems strange to me, too. Before this year, I would never have considered makin' such a race.

"But then my neighbor, here," he gestured toward Prudence, "this woman I trust and respect, began talkin' about how important it is to have all the womenfolk votin' in the elections.

"Now, I'd never thought about that before. Like many men, I just figured the women belonged at home and had no business votin'.

"My friend Prudence opened my eyes on this subject and convinced me that we need to have women talkin' politics and takin' part in the elections. They will add some common sense and compassion which has been missin' from our considerations."

Many of the guests were smiling and nodding their heads approvingly.

"It seems to me," Ephraim went on, "that the men in our state legislature have not supported votes for women. They have fought against the idea and given ground only grudgingly. As of right now, you women can vote only in school elections, and it took fifteen years of fightin' after the law was passed just to enforce its provisions.

"The House of Representatives has already approved the Anthony Amendment. When the United States Senate finally agrees, it will be up to the states to ratify it.

"When that day comes, I want to be in the State Assembly so I can lead the fight for ratification. I want Wisconsin to overcome its past. I want Wisconsin to make amends for its backwardness. I want Wisconsin to be one of the first states to ratify the Anthony Amendment!"

At this, many of the women broke into spontaneous applause, which spread until almost everyone participated. Looking around the crowd, Prudence could see only five or six women who stood motionless in stern disapproval of Ephraim's declaration.

Afterward, as the women gradually drifted back to their cars, they paused to shake Ephraim's hand and wish him well. Several of them even made small cash contributions to help him with his campaign expenses.

Theodora was one of the last to leave. She paused long enough to comment privately to Prudence, "We were all greatly impressed by your friend Ephraim. He appears to be quite knowledgeable, and he comes across as a sincere and trustworthy gentleman."

Prudence blinked back her amazement. "Thank you most kindly," she murmured.

Ephraim's efforts were energized by the encouragement the women had given him. In the following days, he rode Robert's motorcycle out of the yard almost every morning, even in the rain, as he went from farm to farm through the southern half of the county.

Talking to each voter one at a time was long, slow work. There were a few men who knew the issues, but usually he had to start from the beginning and explain the history of the suffrage movement and its rationale. He was seldom sure of the response to his message, even after he finished. The men who listened to him usually kept their own counsel, making no commitments. They sent him on his way with a smile and a handshake, but few promises.

At first he went alone. But after the first week of steady calls, Carl lightly scolded Prudence for her lack of support.

"The very least you can do," he told her, "is to accompany Ephraim on his neighborhood campaign visits. After all, he's running for office because he wants to help you win your suffrage campaign."

After that, Prudence went along whenever the weather was suitable. Ephraim was delighted.

"You're a pleasant companion," he told her, "and you make it a lot easier to open doors and get the conversation goin'".

On those trips Prudence was impressed by Ephraim's loyalty and dedication to her. Campaigning, even in the best circumstances, was not easy for him. Yet he did it cheerfully and tirelessly, without complaints. It was all for her, she knew. He was, after all, a man of deep quality.

One afternoon late in the campaign Ephraim parked the motorcycle alongside the road not far from the farm.

"The world is so beautiful today," he said. "Let's take a little walk together before we go home."

He opened a gate for Prudence, and they meandered down a grassy lane into a pasture alongside a tiny creek. The autumn sun, already low in the sky in mid-afternoon, was warm on their faces. A light breeze ruffled their hair. Occasionally a lonely leaf fluttered down from the nearly bare branches of a tree. Overhead a vee of wild geese scurried past, their urgent honks lingering in the quiet air.

They came upon a small grove of hickory trees. The ground was covered with the green unopened nuts. They gathered a few, stripping away the husks and pocketing the solid little brown shells.

"I like autumn," Ephraim said. "I like the soft colors, the harvest, and the feelin' of bein' almost through with yer work."

"It is a beautiful time of year," Prudence agreed.

"We're kinda' in the autumn of our lives, too," he said. "I know it bothers some people when they get older, an' I guess it bothers me a little, too. But mostly I feel a sense of contentment. Like I'm lookin' forward to a well-earned rest."

Impulsively, she took his hand in hers. "You have done well, Eeph," she said. "You certainly deserve a little rest, especially after your hard work campaigning. But we're still young, and there's lots of work ahead of us."

"Yeah, I s'pose so," he grunted.

"Eeph," she said, "I do appreciate all the work you have put into this campaign. I am really grateful to you."

She looked up at him, and he looked down at her. He bent his head and kissed her, wrapping his arms around her and pulling her so close to him that she could feel the hickory nuts in his jacket pockets as they pressed against her ribs.

After that, it didn't matter so much that he lost the election. John Buckley returned to his seat in the state assembly, defeating George Dwinnel by a few hundred votes. Ephraim ran third, and stayed on the farm where he was happy just being close to Prudence.

He had made the effort; he had demonstrated his devotion to her; she was grateful. That was all he had really wanted from the election. His heart once again was full of hope.

Chapter 18

As the Allied armies pursued the Germans eastward, the American forces under General Pershing increased rapidly. Nearly two million doughboys would fight in France, tipping the scales heavily against the Kaiser's troops. There was no time for anyone to stop and dig the trenches which had stalemated the opposing forces during the earlier years of the war.

With ultimate disaster looming ever closer, the German people abandoned their support of the war and their own government. Sailors mutinied and refused to sail their ships; revolutionaries raised the red flag of triumph over many key cities; the government collapsed and the Kaiser himself abdicated his throne and fled to Holland.

The Armistice, which was tantamount to a complete surrender of the German forces, was announced on November 11th. It was received with relief and joy throughout much of the world.

"Everything for which America fought has been accomplished," declared President Wilson, not being able to foresee the future.

In Prairieville, news of the Armistice spread quickly even to the most remote farms of the county.

"Whoopee!" yelled Robert. "The war is over!"

"It didn't end soon enough to save Jonathan," Prudence reminded him soberly.

"No, but without Jon and his comrades-in-arms, it wouldn't have ended at all," commented Ephraim.

"We paid an awful price, in many different ways," said Carl, "but given the problem we faced, it was absolutely necessary."

With the war ended, everyday life quickly focused upon things closer to home: the Spanish influenza epidemic; the Republican control of both the U.S. Senate and the House of Representatives; the battle for ratification of the Prohibition Amendment.

For Prudence, these national issues were of little interest. Even the constant efforts of her sisters-in-arms to secure Senate passage of the Anthony Amendment failed to excite her.

Her attention was fully occupied by matters on her own farm—mostly matters of the heart.

There was Ephraim, of course—dear, attentive Ephraim—who tried to anticipate her needs. One of Robert's children had come down with influenza, so Robert had gone home to help the family. Although Prudence had jealously asserted her control over the farm immediately after Zachary's death, Ephraim had gradually assumed its management. Without Jon and Robert, he now performed most of the work. Prudence accepted his devotion, as usual, without thought or comment.

But it was Carl who was foremost on her mind. With his leg encased in plaster, he found it difficult just to get dressed each morning. Prudence was eager to help him, but he steadfastly maintained the privacy of his person. Against her wishes he insisted upon getting up early and he would not allow her in his bedroom until he was decently clothed. Then he would go out to the barn with Sarah in the pre-dawn darkness for the morning chores. Although he wasn't much help, he felt a strange comfort just being there in the cozy warmth of the barn. He savored the sound of bovine noises as the cows grunted into wakefulness and began swallowing their breakfast of ground grain. He delighted in watching the barnyard cats beg for the first squirt of milk aimed at their faces by Ephraim. Sometimes he curried the calves, as Sarah had taught him to do, but usually he just leaned on his crutches and enjoyed the ambience. He even learned to love the aroma of manure.

"If you must get up so early," Prudence protested, "wouldn't you rather stay in the kitchen with me and help get breakfast on the table?"

"Of course I like being in the kitchen," Carl replied, "but I like the cow barn too, and I feel guilty if I'm not there during the milking."

"I'm sure you're not really needed in the barn," Prudence persisted. "Isn't that right, Sarah?"

"We like him there," Sarah said defensively. "He can't do a lot of work while he's on crutches, of course, but we need his cheerfulness and his sense of humor."

"But I'm all alone in the kitchen," complained Prudence. She turned back to Carl. "I like being with you. I need your companionship more than they do. Won't you stay inside and give me some of your cheer?"

"I like being with you, too," Carl responded, "but I really feel I should be in the barn during chore time."

"Oh, I think you are being ungrateful!" exclaimed Prudence. "I think you like Sarah more than you like me!"

"Please, don't say such a thing," Carl pleaded. "Don't be like that. I like you both, of course."

Prudence was contrite at once, afraid he would think her unpleasant. "I'm sorry," she apologized to him, forcing a smile. "I don't know what made me say that. Forget it."

"That's all right," Carl reassured her. "I don't want to displease you. I'll keep you company from now on while you make breakfast. I promise."

The next morning Carl remained behind in the kitchen with Prudence when Sarah went out to join Ephraim for the morning milking. Prudence tried very hard to interest him in herself and her work, but he was obviously restless and discontented.

After a few mornings of uneasiness, Prudence released him from his promise. "Go ahead to the barn if you want to," she told him. It was an unhappy decision for her, but she concluded she had more to lose by keeping him with her against his will than by letting him be with Sarah during the milking.

Thanksgiving Day approached. It was a significant holiday for the Hartmann family. Zac ordained it beginning with the year they were married. He said he was the most fortunate man in the world, just to have Prudence for a wife, and so their first Thanksgiving together in 1892 was virtually a wedding feast. Afterward, Prudence considered that day the most joyful holiday of her life. A few months later, the pressure from Zachary's mother about childbearing rubbed the luster from her marriage. Although they celebrated the holiday seriously every year thereafter, it was never quite the same again.

Prudence ignored the occasion completely the year Zachary died. She was a widow and Jonathan was away in the army. There was little reason to celebrate.

Now things were changed again. Now Prudence determined to make it a feast day honoring Carl.

She threw herself wholeheartedly into the preparations with an enthusiasm as high as her first Thanksgiving with Zachary. Her dining room was thoroughly cleaned and dusted; the windows were washed inside and out. An entire evening was devoted to polishing her heirloom sterling silver, unused since the dinner in March when she declared an end to her season of mourning.

Nothing in her wardrobe satisfied her, not even the flowery dress she had purchased in Waco. 'I've worn it twice for him already,' she thought. 'Besides, it's too thin for our cold November weather.' Instead she bought a new wool suit, going all the way to Milwaukee on the electric interurban train to find the right one. It was goldenrod in color and it had a jaunty style.

Sarah didn't like it. "The skirt is too short," she complained.

"I want a change from the long drab dresses we've been wearing during the war," Prudence explained.

"It's something a young girl might wear," Sarah continued.

"I'm not so very old," said Prudence. "I'm not exactly tottering on the edge of my grave. And my legs are still quite beautiful, don't you think? Zac always said I had the prettiest legs in the county." She lifted the hem of her skirt slightly and struck a provocative pose with one foot raised off the floor.

Sarah shrugged, rolling her eyes, and turned away while Prudence adjusted a gold necklace over the lacy throat of her new white blouse.

Even the right turkey was hard to find; Prudence visited three neighboring farms before she was satisfied. She brought it home alive in a gunny sack in the back of the wagon. Like an executioner, Ephraim chopped off its head just as the Thanksgiving Day sun was peeking over the eastern horizon.

It was a sumptuous banquet for just the four of them. Prudence took her customary chair at one end of the table, placing Carl at the other end. Ephraim and Sarah sat on opposite sides facing each other through the tall tangerine-colored candles of the centerpiece.

Prudence herself delivered the invocation, carefully written and memorized beforehand. "Our heavenly Father, we come to thank Thee for Thy bountiful blessings. We have so much to be grateful for—the abundance of food on this table; the end of the terrible war in Europe; Thy protection from the deadly influenza in our midst. Most especially we are grateful that Thou hast protected the precious life of Carl and that Thou art healing his wounds. We thank Thee for bringing him to this home where he can love and be loved. We ask that we may become a rich blessing to each other. In Thy name, Amen."

Prudence deserved the praise she received for the banquet for she had prepared almost all of it herself. The roasted turkey was tender and moist, lightly browned on the outside, accented by a tangy cranberry sauce. The sweet potatoes were served in halves mixed with chopped apples and smothered with melted brown sugar. The green peas, which had been canned in Mason jars after ripening on the vine, were unusually sweet. Homemade whole-wheat bread added its savory aroma to the delightful smells permeating the entire house.

"I'll bet you never had such a feast in Michigan, Carl," declared Prudence, openly seeking a compliment.

"No, of course not," the boy replied. "Nor in France, either. All the food is absolutely delicious. Everything has changed quite dramatically in my life," he said thoughtfully. "Changed for the better, of course. I was so fortunate to meet Jon and to be accepted into his family here."

"We are fortunate too," Prudence responded. "It's very comforting to have a man in the house again. You look very nice there at the head of the table, Carl." She nodded her head approvingly. "That's where Zachary always sat."

Ephraim squirmed and started to say something but stopped suddenly with his mouth already open.

"I miss Jon the most," said Sarah quickly, her eyes moistening at her own words.

"Of course I miss Jon too," Prudence added. "Carl, I guess you'll have to be a substitute for both Zachary and Jon."

"That's an enormous assignment," replied the youth, "and I'm not worthy of being a substitute for either one. "I hope you'll let me just be myself."

"Yes, surely," Prudence said softly.

"I'm just a little boy, a homeless little boy with a broken leg who is lucky to be among friends while he gets well again."

Prudence made a sympathetic face.

"But I know I'm a great burden to you, and when I am able to get around better I'll be on my way again."

"I see," commented Sarah. "You're like an injured bird who has dropped in from the sky while your wing gets mended."

"You're not a burden," objected Prudence, "you're a blessing. We want you to think of this as your home. We want you to settle down here in Prairieville. I'd like to have you right there in that chair at every holiday dinner in all the years to come."

"That would be very nice," said Carl, "but it's probably best for me to move along when I am able to go."

"You said you like the Vernal Marsh," prompted Prudence.

"Yes, it's a great place to live," he agreed.

"Then don't even think about leaving," Prudence told him.

"Now Prudy, let the young man make his own decisions," said Ephraim.

"Well, of course he'll make his own decisions," she replied. "But I want him to know he is loved and he's welcome to stay here even after he's well."

"It's too soon to decide," said Carl diplomatically, and he turned the conversation to a less controversial subject.

Afterward, more than ever before, Ephraim was apprehensive about Carl and Prudence living in the same house together. "Keep yer eye on 'em," he warned Sarah privately. "They're both a little daffy, I think. You gotta' be the chaperon, I guess."

"I'll do my best," Sarah promised.

Ephraim felt an unusual loneliness that night as he lay restless in his empty house, reflecting upon the words spoken around the Thanksgiving Day table. The personal disaster he feared seemed much closer to reality.

When Prudence, as was her custom, entered Carl's bedroom to tuck him in, he took her hand and gazed up at her from his pillow with gentle eyes. "Thank you for such a wonderful holiday," he said. "It was so nice to celebrate an occasion like this with your whole family, and not have it end with a drunken fight."

"Yes, it was one of the best holidays I can remember," Prudence agreed.

"At home," Carl added, "we never got through such a meal without my father exploding into a violent outburst over something, over nothing."

"You poor thing," Prudence said softly, squeezing his hand.

"I do like living here in the Vernal Marsh," he confided. It's like being in paradise. Especially since I have an excuse not to work." He thumped his knuckles through the bedclothes against his plaster cast.

"There's no place on earth I'd rather be," Prudence said. "I am so grateful to God for all our blessings. Every day ought to be Thanksgiving Day for us."

"It's like a Garden of Eden," Carl agreed. "Jon used to talk about the marsh and about growing up here on the farm. He really loved it and he made me envious of his childhood."

Prudence needed little invitation to embellish the joys of her native soil. Dropping his hand, she responded at some length.

Sarah, in her own bedroom a few steps away, wondered suspiciously why her mother was so long in Carl's room. Remembering Ephraim's earnest adjuration, she padded silently along the wood floor and stopped at Carl's door. It was slightly ajar; she could hear low voices but she could not see the speakers.

"Farm work is not easy work," Prudence concluded, "and I don't like the absolute necessity for milking the cows twice a day, but the advantages of living here make it all worthwhile."

There was silence for a moment; then Carl said softly, "Thank you for taking me in and letting me live here for a little while. Thank you for looking after me."

"I hope you'll stay a long while," she corrected him.

"Perhaps I will," he said. "You are a wonderful mother, and I love you for it."

Encouraged by their tender conversation but frustrated by the implication of his last words, Prudence dared to say, "I hope you love me for more than being a mother."

He furrowed his forehead. "What?" he asked.

"I want you to love me for more than being a mother," she repeated with a touch of irritation. "I want you to love me for being myself."

"What?" he asked again with a look of confusion.

"I want you to love me for being a woman," she said boldly, seizing his hand again with both of hers and kneading it with passion. "I don't see why I shouldn't be honest with you. I don't have to be ashamed of how I feel. I want you to love me as a woman."

He looked up at her with enormous soft eyes, as though he were seeing her for the very first time. He started to speak, but his throat was choked and no words came out.

She leaned down closer to him. "Can you do that?" she asked plaintively. "Can you love me?"

He did not speak, but slowly he reached upward with both hands and clasped them together behind her neck. He half raised himself from his pillow, tugging her head down to meet him. His wondering eyes gazed into her agitated face just inches away, and then he impulsively pulled her closer and kissed her full on the lips.

Outside the door, Sarah could not see what was happening during the extended silence. But she could guess, and her heart began beating furiously. She waited a few moments, and then retreated into her own room, where she stood shaking in a hot sweat until she saw her mother emerge from Carl's room and cross over to her own bedroom.

None of the three in that farm household, each in their own beds, slept much during the night.

Carl had been oblivious to Prudence's true feelings from the very beginning. His words and deeds, from which she had inferred so much, had been innocently spoken and done. But now that she had revealed herself to him, he thought back over their history together and recalled everything in the light of a new meaning.

He had admired her from the start. He envied Jon for his wonderful mother. She impressed him as a thoughtful, sensitive woman with great capabilities in her public service as well as her private life. And he considered her very attractive, although her position as Jon's mother had blocked him from any consideration of a romantic attractiveness.

Certainly he had grown to love her during the two months of his convalescence at the farm. It was the love of a boy for his mother, or the love of a patient for his nurse, he thought. But now it was something more than that. The kiss which still burned his lips was proof of the difference.

Although he was twenty-six years old, he had never really known a girlfriend. It wasn't for lack of interest on his part; it was because he considered his position in life inadequate to attract the right kind of girl and provide for her.

There had been, in fact, a particular girl who had filled his heart with longing. He dared to take her to the movies once or twice before withdrawing from her life, and he even kissed her once, tentatively, as they stood on her doorstep afterward. But that kiss was nothing like the intensively passionate kiss he had now experienced. The eagerness of Prudence's lips upon his own conveyed an unreserved yearning suddenly revealed to his awakening eyes.

From that moment on she was no longer a mother or a nurse to him. She was, as she wanted to be, a woman.

Prudence spent the night alternating between feelings of rapture and shame. For many months she had contented herself with hopes and guesses, jumping blindly to wild inferences to feed her hungry imagination. Repeatedly she had been disappointed at Carl's response. At last she had found the courage to reveal her true sentiments to him, and he had not rejected her. She was delighted, but yet she was astonished and dismayed at her own boldness.

After he thought about their new relationship, how would he react? Would he still love her and respect her? Or would he consider her a brazen hussy?

Such fears tormented her, but it was no worse than the torment of uncertainty she had endured beforehand. Carl had not repaid her hints and suggestions in like currency. It was necessary for her to be more aggressive. After all, he was not an experienced man of the world. She was forced to be his teacher, as well as his nurse. The question remained: would he allow himself to be taught?

In the next room, Sarah's mind was a hopeless jumble of suspicions and fears. She had hidden her own romantic feelings from Carl as well as her mother. Until now she had not really accepted the thought that her mother could be romantically interested in Carl. After the events of the day, however, there could be no doubt. Could Carl actually feel the same way? Maybe she should just forget her own feelings about him. She was not a fighter by nature; how could she possibly compete for Carl's affections against her mother?

She waited impatiently for morning, for an occasion to talk privately with her mother in the kitchen while the two men were outside.

"Mom, I heard what you said to Carl last night in his bedroom," she began.

"What did I say?" asked Prudence, unruffled.

"It was absolutely shameless," Sarah continued.

"What do you mean?" asked Prudence. "I said nothing to be ashamed of."

"Oh, Mother!" exclaimed Sarah. "You asked Carl . . . you asked him to love you . . . to love you . . . like a woman."

Prudence smiled weakly. "Well, I love *him*," she declared slowly, with emphasis. "I wanted to find out whether he could love me in return."

"Mother! That's awful."

"What's awful?"

"He's Jon's age."

"Not quite," Prudence corrected her. "He's twenty-six."

"That's still young enough to be your son."

"Yes, technically you are right. But he is not my son. At twenty-six, he is a fully grown man."

"Mother, you can't be serious about loving a man—a mere boy—who is twenty years younger than you."

"Why not?"

"It just isn't done. What do you think the neighbors will say?"

"Well, they ought to be happy about it. Happy that I've got a man for a partner again."

"Oh, Mom, that isn't what they will say. You know that's not what they will say. They'll say you're robbing the cradle. They'll say you're taking advantage of a young boy, a virtual orphan, who has no one to protect him. No kidding, Mom, they'll say you're making a victim out of him."

"Well, then, who cares what they say?" asked Prudence defiantly. "Let them say anything they want. I have no obligation to them, and their words can't hurt me."

"Maybe not your neighbors, but what about Ephraim? I think you have an obligation to *him*. If you fall in love with any man, it ought to be Ephraim. He has been faithful to you through all these years, and I know he loves you. Don't you have any sympathy at all for his feelings?"

Prudence paused momentarily and sucked in her breath. Then she declared, with studied carelessness, "Ephraim has been very kind to me, and in my own way, I love him, too. But I have never asked him to follow me around and look after me. Contrary to what you say, I have no obligation to him. He has done what he has done because he wanted to do it, and I must do what I want to do, too."

"You will hurt him terribly, you know," said Sarah.

"No, if he is hurt he will have hurt himself. I'm not going to sacrifice my life for him. I have a chance at personal happiness, and I'm going to seize it while I still can. I'm sorry if Ephraim gets hurt, but that's something I can't help."

"Oh, Mom, think about it a little."

"Sarah, I have thought about it a lot, believe me. I know it's not customary for a widow my age to fall in love with a younger man. But I can't help my feelings. I can't put him out of my mind. I've been in love with him ever since I first met him down in Texas."

Sarah grimaced. "I think it's positively sinful," she commented. "It's almost like incest, to have a romance with your son's best friend. Especially when your son is dead."

"It's not incest, you know it's not, Sarah. And sinful? No it's not sinful, either. You know your Bible, and so do I. There is nothing in the Bible anywhere that says it is a sin to love a younger man. My husband is dead, and Carl has never been married. There is no sin in our being in love with each other, or even getting married if we choose. I challenge you to tell me where in the Scriptures it says that I am wrong."

Sarah thought a moment, and then conceded the point. "I guess you're right about that; there's nothing in the Bible against what you're doing. But I still think it's wrong. It just isn't customary."

"I'll grant you that it isn't customary. But there's nothing wrong with going against customs. It isn't customary for a woman to take part in politics, either, but I'm doing it. I really don't care if I follow the customs or not, so long as I believe in what I'm doing."

"You'll just make a fool out of yourself," said Sarah.

"Maybe so. I suppose I made a fool out of myself by riding Robert's motorcycle, too, but I don't care."

"Well, maybe your family cares. Try to imagine how embarrassed I'll be if you start running around with a boy scarcely older than me."

"Well, I wouldn't like you to be embarrassed, Sarah. I love you with all my heart and I wouldn't want to cause you any unhappiness. But you've got to think about my happiness, too. Maybe it's worth a little embarrassment on your part to allow me to find new happiness with a man, maybe even a husband."

"But what about *my* happiness?" demanded Sarah. "Don't you think I'd like to have a husband, too?"

"Yes, of course, but you'll have to find someone other than Carl. He isn't in love with you, Sarah. He's in love with me."

"Well, maybe he *would* have fallen in love with me," complained Sarah bitterly, "if you hadn't monopolized his attention and literally thrown yourself at him."

"Sarah, what are you saying? You've had the same chance with him that I have had. Perhaps even more. You've been with him in the barn while I've been stuck in the kitchen. And you are more his age, which gives you an advantage. But in spite of that, he's in love with me, not you. I think you're just jealous of me, and I think you're being very mean-spirited."

"Oh, Mom!" exclaimed Sarah, throwing one arm across her eyes and beginning to cry.

Prudence stepped alongside quickly, her motherly instincts returning momentarily, and put her arm compassionately around her daughter's shoulders. "I understand your feelings, Sarah," she said. "We are caught up in a situation that is not going to be easy for us. But let's remember that we are mother and daughter. Let's not get angry with each other."

The two women clung to each other silently for a few moments, and then Sarah broke away and ran up the stairs to her room, where she remained, weeping, for a long time. She had learned that a daughter cannot change the mind of a headstrong mother, any more than a parent can change the mind of a headstrong child.

Later in the day, Sarah huddled with Ephraim in the barn loft. She was distraught, with reddened eyes, and as she recounted the conversation with her mother she had to pause frequently to compose herself. He listened quietly, nodding occasionally.

"I ain't surprised," he commented when she had finished. "The handwritin' on the wall has been purty plain."

"What are we going to do?" Sarah wailed.

"What *can* we do? Nothin'. Nothin' but let 'er go. She's got the bit in 'er teeth an' she ain't stoppin' fer nothin' or nobody."

"But she's making a bad mistake," insisted Sarah.

"Yep. She sure is. You know that, and I know that, but she won't see it until it's too late."

"I feel awful," Sarah said. "And you must feel worse. How can you possibly stand the thought of it, when you've waited so long for your chance? It would be torture just to see them together day after day."

Ephraim chewed on a haystem for a while, his thoughts slowly forming in his mind. Finally he said, "Well, I couldn't stay here no longer, of course. I'd have t' give it all up. I'd have t' say good-bye t' Prudence and to the marsh and I'd have t' go somewhere else."

"But where could you go?"

"I got an uncle up near Fond du Lac who's been wantin' t' give up his farm. He's gettin' old n' wants t' retire. I kin sell my place here. Albert Jones has been wantin' me t' sell it to 'im for a long time anyways. Mebbe I'll jus' let 'im have it. Then I could buy my uncle's place and move up there."

"Oh, Uncle Eeph!" exclaimed Sarah, putting her arms around him and burrowing her head into his shoulder. "I couldn't stand it if you went away. You have been the only true friend I have ever known." She began crying again, her tears quickly dampening his plaid wool shirt.

"Now, now, Sarah, don't take on so," he said soothingly.

"But you're the only one who has ever loved me," she sobbed, "and now you're leaving me. When you are gone, I'll never have another friend who will talk to me. You are everything to me. Nobody else will ever love me, I know it. Nobody."

"Oh, come, come, that's not true. The right young man will come along any day, and sweep you off yer feet, and you'll be married with a passel of kids and never think of me again."

"There is no right young man," Sarah declared. "No one will ever love me. I must be completely unlovable. I thought maybe Carl might love me. He had every opportunity. He even lives in the same house with me. He sees me first thing in the morning and we work together during the day and he sees me last thing at night. And what happens? He falls in love with my mother!" She burst into a spasm of tears, her whole body shaking.

"Not so fast now, Sarah. From what you told me, we don't know fer sure that Carl has fallen in love with yer mom. We know *she*'s makin' a fool of herself, but we don't know that *he*'s gonna' be crazy too."

Such words were little comfort to the stricken girl, but it was the only comfort to be found. She lingered for a few moments in his strong embrace, and then she wiped her eyes with her sleeve and left the barn.

It wasn't long before their fears were confirmed, however. Now that Carl knew the true feelings of the woman who was caring for him, he responded like a flower awakening to the sun.

They began opening flirting with each other, ignoring the presence of Sarah and Ephraim. Their faces glowed whenever they were together, which was most of their waking hours. They laughed like schoolchildren at the weakest opportunities.

Carl changed his mind about the morning chores, and stayed in the kitchen with Prudence until breakfast.

He even allowed Prudence to help him put on his clothes each morning. And when she entered his room to help him prepare for bed in the evening, she carried a wash cloth, a bath towel, and a basin filled with warm water. Sometimes Sarah listened at the door, which stayed closed longer and longer as the evenings went by. She could hear soft murmurings and an occasional giggle from within and she imagined all kinds of shameful activities occurring.

On Christmas Eve, as the four of them prepared to leave for church, Prudence presented Carl with a hand-knit yellow woolen muffler. Sarah was disturbed to recognize it as a duplicate of the one her mother had given to Zachary two years earlier. "Here's a little something to keep you warm," Prudence remarked as she positioned it snugly around Carl's throat.

Sarah was even more disturbed during the candlelit worship service in the Reedsville Town Hall when she noticed Carl take Prudence's hand and hold it tenderly through most of the hour.

"What a sacrilege!" Sarah complained to Ephraim later. "Right there in the same room where she married my father and attended church with him Sunday after Sunday. How could she do it?"

"I can't understand it either, Sarah," Ephraim commented sadly. "It's not the Prudence I've known all these years. She just ain't the same woman no more."

Chapter 19

Prudence stood alone in her bedroom, leaning down slightly to see herself in the big mirror over her dresser. She ran her fingers over her face, pulling the skin tight and smoothing the wrinkles.

'I must be smiling too much,' she said softly to herself. 'Smiling causes lines like crows' feet around the corners of my eyes. I've got to look pleasant, but without a lot of smiling.' She set her face grimly, trying out several different expressions as she examined herself in the glass.

'Am I really forty-seven years old?' she asked. 'I don't feel that old. I feel like I am twenty. Maybe in my mid-twenties. But certainly no older than that.'

With her fingers she pushed her cheeks upward. 'My skin doesn't seem as firm and tight as it used to,' she observed. 'If I didn't know better, I would think my face is sagging a bit. But it's only because I'm leaning over.' She straightened up, and tilted her head back. 'See? Now it feels normal again. And when I smile, it's just like it used to be. Maybe I should smile more, not less. Should I smile and show my crows' feet, or should I not smile and let my jowls sag?' She chortled hopelessly at the dilemma.

Giving up on that question, she leaned down to peer into the mirror again. 'My face looks so pale,' she fretted. 'But surely that has nothing to do with my age. It's simply a matter of not getting enough sunshine. It's February in Wisconsin; the days are short and it's been cloudy for weeks; I don't get outside much anyway. That's why there's no color in my complexion. Maybe I should buy some rouge to use on my cheeks, just during the winter. They probably sell it at Hoeveler's Drugs, or maybe at McCoy's store. I suppose Theodora could tell me where to get some.'

She shivered, suddenly aware of the wintry chill invading her room.

She clutched her woolen sweater closer around her, and glanced out through the frost-encrusted window at her side. The snow-covered landscape was bleak and barren. The oak trees with their scattering of dead leaves still clinging to their outstretched limbs appeared old and gaunt against the cheerless gray sky. "So depressing," she murmured. It was like the world had reached the end of its life span and was dying. Summer was long since gone; could she even remember what it was like? She rubbed her hands together; would they ever be warm again?

Carl was limping across the snow-covered lawn, coming toward the house. The doctor had sawed the cast off his leg soon after Christmas, and he was learning how to walk again as he gradually regained his strength and confidence. The winter wind whipped the tails of his new yellow scarf, the one Prudence had knit for him at Christmas, and she smiled wanly as she watched the frosty plume from his breath trail upward behind him and disappear into nothingness.

Her eyes returned to the mirror. She seized a handful of her own hair and ran the strands slowly through her fingers. She was sharply aware of the gray ones proliferating among the brown. "Oh, no," she sighed. "One calamity after another."

She heard the door close downstairs, and the rustle of Carl's coat and scarf as he hung them in the closet. 'What does he really think about me?' she asked the aging figure in the glass. 'Does he worry, like I do, about the margin of years between us? Twenty years. I was married before he was born. I am almost twice his age. Does he think about that? Does he notice the wrinkles in my face? Does he see the grayness of my hair? Does he care?' She would never ask him those questions; she would never call his attention to those facts which filled her with such dread. 'He always treats me so tenderly. I know he has fallen in love with me, but I wonder—are there some quiet moments in his reverie when he thinks of me as just a foolish old woman?'

His uneven footsteps sounded on the stairs, and he entered her bedroom without knocking. He came up behind her and slipped his hands around her waist, glancing at her face in the mirror.

"Isn't it a wonderful winter day out?" he asked rhetorically. "Everything seems so bright and crisp. It makes you feel so young and alive! You can almost feel the buds on the trees building their energy to break loose in the spring."

She turned in his arms and forced a weak smile as he kissed her with an easy air.

"What were you doing, admiring yourself again?" he teased.

She didn't reply, but nestled her face against his shoulder.

"Don't worry, Prude," he said, "you are young and good-looking. You will never change."

"Thank you, Carl," she said, adding to herself 'You are concerned about my age, that's why you called me *young*—you are simply trying to give me false assurances.'

He pulled her head away from his chest and was surprised to see a tear in each eye. "Is something wrong?" he inquired earnestly.

"No, dear, nothing is wrong," she said, laying her head against him again.

He squeezed her gently. "I love you, Prude," he said.

"I love you too," she replied.

"You are happy, aren't you?" he asked.

"Yes, I am very happy," she assured him without enthusiasm.

"You frightened me," he said honestly. "I thought for a moment you were crying."

She couldn't tell him the real truth. "I am sad once in a while when I think of Jon," she said to divert him.

"Yes, of course. It must be horrible to lose a son like that." He hugged her again. "But let me be your consolation, as best I can. Let me try to fill a little of the empty spot he has left in your heart. You can love me all you want; I've never enjoyed much of it so far in life."

"Yes, yes," she agreed. "We are both hungry for love. We can feed each other."

After her bold approach to him at Thanksgiving, Carl lavished upon Prudence the devotion she craved, the devotion and approval she had seldom received from Zachary. In her turn, she poured out a full measure of motherly affection. Their attraction for each other seemed to deepen with each passing day.

Ephraim and Sarah observed this escalation of feeling, but they were mere spectators at the scene. Each of them tried again and again to turn Prudence away from her new romance, but nothing would deter her.

Ephraim became so dispirited that he began avoiding Prudence's farm. He no longer opened each day by milking the Hartmann cows, but seemed content to let Prudence and Sarah fend for themselves. Carl's injury was repairing itself quite well, and as spring approached he began assuming an increasing share of their work.

From time to time it was necessary to take a wagon load of corn to be ground at the Reedsville mill. This chore was usually performed by Robert, but he was still with his family in Janesville. Although his son appeared to be recovering from the attack of influenza, he had not yet returned to the farm.

Consequently, as the supply of ground grain dwindled, Carl decided to make the trip to the mill. It was a cold blustery day in March when he and Sarah loaded the wagon box with the bags of dull golden nuggets.

Carl was proud of the wagon, for he had refurbished it himself soon after getting the cast off his leg. He painted the box a crisp apple-green, while the tongue and the wheels were bright Chinese red. It was his first solid contribution to the farm; the first payment on the enormous intangible debt he owed to Prudence.

Prudence helped him hitch Kaiser into his harness, and praised him for his work. "This old wagon sure looks smart again," she said. "Thanks for fixing it up."

"It was fun," he replied. "It's so much more pleasant working with a wagon that looks nice."

They connected the last snap on the harness. Carl squeezed her hand, and turned to mount the wagon.

Her heart was abruptly filled with apprehension. "Do be careful in the mill," she begged. "It can be a very dangerous job."

"I know, Prude," he said. "My best friend in Michigan lived on a farm when I was a kid, and we helped his dad grind corn more than once. I'm no stranger to a mill."

"Please; don't even try it if Mortimer Reed isn't there."

"He'll be there, I'm sure," Carl replied. "He said he'd be back from Prairieville by noon."

"It was two years ago this very month that Zachary was killed there," Prudence reminded him.

"Yes, Prude, I know. I'll be careful."

"I asked Ephraim to do this for us," she said. "He should have done it, but he begged off for no reason at all."

"That's all right. It's my place to go. I don't mind."

"Your leg isn't strong enough yet. It can't stand a lot of strain. I even told him that, and he still said no."

"My leg is doing fine," he said.

"You still favor it when you walk," she observed.

"Yes, of course. I know I still have a limp. But it's getting better every day."

"I'm upset with Ephraim," Prudence continued. "He doesn't seem like himself lately. He's never turned me down for any favor I asked, no matter how trivial. But this time he was irritated when I asked him, and he didn't even bother to think about it. He just said no."

"He was probably in a bad mood," suggested Carl.

"That's not like him. He's never been in a bad mood before," Prudence said. "He doesn't come over to help with the morning chores very often of late, and even then he never stays for breakfast any more."

"He's getting older," suggested Carl, "so he probably tires easier. He's got farm work of his own to do, too."

Carl climbed up to his seat at the front of the wagon, and gathered the reins into one hand. Prudence tugged at his sleeve, and he leaned down to kiss her.

"Keep that scarf tucked around your neck," she told him. "I don't want you coming down with a cold."

"Yes, Mother," he laughed, and she winced.

He flicked the reins, and Kaiser began pulling the wagon down the driveway. It rolled away on its brightly painted red wheels, and Prudence shuddered briefly as she thought again of the day, just like this day, when Zachary had started on his way to the mill with a similar load. She had watched him leave, just as she was watching Carl now. The wagon turned south on River Road, holding her eyes like a magnet until it disappeared from her sight. It was all the same as before, except the wagon was freshly painted and the man on the front board, whom she loved, was younger. She stood as though rooted to the ground, staring at the empty road as it ran to the river and through the marsh.

After a long time, her reverie was interrupted by the motion of a second wagon. She recognized the dark gray horse as it emerged from Ephraim's driveway and turned south following Carl's path.

A vague feeling of alarm shuddered through her heart as she remembered that Zachary had not returned alive. Ephraim was the one who found him mangled in the mill, she recalled. She took a sudden step forward as though to pursue the wagon, but then she laughed inwardly at her apprehensions and turned with a shrug to enter her house.

Carl's face was thoughtful, as Zachary's had been, as he rambled along on the lonely country road through the marsh. With the return of the sun to its more northerly orbit, spring was loosening winter's grip on the landscape. A few patches of snow remained in well-sheltered declivities, but life had returned amidst the long dry grasses. Tiny green sprouts were asserting themselves, and Carl's sharp eye caught the motion of a muskrat several times as his wagon crunched along the graveled road.

'Prudence has been through a long cold winter of her own,' Carl thought, 'but I think she is arriving at a new spring in her own life. Her face is so lively when it smiles. And what a smile! When she smiles, it makes you feel so good. It wakes you up inside, and you are glad to be alive. Everything in the whole world is lovely when she smiles.

'She's got to be the most beautiful woman I've ever met, anywhere, no matter what her age.

'She doesn't seem nearly so old as I know she is. She's got to be in her late forties, because she is Sarah's mother and Sarah is almost my own age. But she sure doesn't seem like she's that old. If I didn't know better, I'd think she was only a few years older than me.

'But who cares how old she is? Not me. What's important to me is that she makes me feel good. She makes me feel like I belong. She makes me feel wanted, and loved.'

When Carl arrived at the mill, Mortimer was not in sight. "Might as well get started," Carl mumbled to himself. He entered the mill and glanced around. 'Looks just like the one at home,' he thought.

He hoisted a bag of corn to his shoulder and carried it inside, returning several times for more. Then he moved the levers to set the mill in motion. A deep rumbling of the gears began slowly, the pitch gradually rising as the speed increased. He filled the hopper with corn and watched as the millstones began their work.

Nearly a half-hour later, the second wagon arrived at the mill, and Ephraim jumped down to tether his horse alongside Kaiser.

He strode to the wooden door and pushed it open slowly and noiselessly, covered by the sound of the grinding millstones.

In the depths of the mill, half-hidden in the shadowy interior, Carl's head and shoulders were framed starkly against the glare of the nine-pane window in the far wall. He stood before the millstones with his back to the door, silently contemplating their work.

Ephraim stopped just inside the door, closing it carefully behind him. His mind returned vividly to that day two years before when he had come upon a similar scene. Everything was exactly the same—the noise of the grinding millstones, the dim light, the silhouette of a man's upper torso against the far window—only this time it was Carl, not Zachary, who was the central figure.

Ephraim's heart began pounding as he remembered the flood of emotions which had engulfed him that day. Here was Zachary—the rival who had usurped his own position and stepped into place alongside his beloved Prudence. He had learned to hate that man with an intensity that hardened through a full quarter-century of envy and resentment. It was a hatred which had festered and grown the more malignant because it was suppressed.

He had stood at the doorway several long moments, feeding upon his own jealousy, keenly aware of the pounding of his own pulse in his ears. Zachary was standing close to the mill wheel, endangered by its powerful momentum. It would be so easy, thought Ephraim, to step up behind his adversary and catch him unawares.

The tasseled ends of Zachary's bright yellow scarf were dangling so close to the open gears that a sudden unexpected push from behind would undoubtedly snag them and eliminate his enemy forever.

Ephraim brushed his hand across his forehead to wipe away the old memories. He crept forward a few paces and paused again. It had taken only a few months for his loathing and hatred for this younger man Carl to equal and surpass the corrosive feelings he had nurtured earlier against Zachary. The years of his life were running out; he did not have another quarter-century to wait for Prudence. The long-suffering patience which had bolstered him through the years was gone. He had borne out God's time, and the fruit was there almost within his grasp when suddenly Carl had intervened and snatched away the prize.

The grinding of the millstones seemed to be rising to a crescendo just like before, making it impossible to think. He remembered pausing at this same spot before; he remembered watching the ends of the scarf swinging hypnotically ever closer to the voracious spinning gears; he remembered his feeling like a panther about to spring.

But now he remembered how the horror of what he was about to do had swept across his mind and he had stopped, paralyzed by the sudden recognition of the unthinkable evil which he had been planning. 'Oh God! How could I!'

He had stood transfixed; he remembered the sweat emerging on his forehead and cascading down his face. And then, unbelievably, he had seen the ends of Zachary's scarf snatched by the gears and suddenly his old friend had been jerked down against the machinery.

He had been unable to move at first; his body was like a granite statue. He finally sprang forward not to take a life but to save it, but even as he reached Zachary he knew his efforts were futile. He had tried to tear his friend loose from the deadly embrace of the machine but his own strength was no match for the remorseless water power generated by the surging mill stream.

Realizing his helplessness, he abandoned the unequal contest and grabbed the long wooden handle to stop the action. It was too late. He gave a fleeting agonized glance at the mangled and lifeless body of Zachary; the horror of what he saw drove him from the mill.

Now, as he leaped toward Carl's unsuspecting form, the terrible vision of the past was throbbing in his mind. His body was moving in slow motion, he felt, even as he watched the fateful swinging of Carl's yellow scarf close to the deadly gears.

Then his body collided with Carl and knocked him away from the millstone. The astonished young man lay sprawled on the floor with Ephraim on top.

"Why did you do that?" asked Carl, more in amazement than in anger.

"Didn't ya' see?" asked Ephraim. "Yer scarf was about t' be caught by the gears!"

Carl laughed. "You are dreaming, man," he said. "I'm not even wearing my scarf. It's over there with my coat. I wouldn't wear such clothes around the machinery; it isn't safe."

It was true. Carl was clad in overalls and a green plaid shirt. His scarf was lying out of harm's way on a nearby bench.

Ephraim crawled off the young man. "I'm sorry," he said in confused embarrassment. "I thought . . . I thought I could see . . . ."

"It's awfully dark in here," said Carl, "with only that one bare light bulb. I can understand how you made the mistake." He rose to his feet and brushed the flour-dust from his pants.

Ephraim remained sitting on the floor. "An' here I thought I was gonna be such a hero this time," he said.

"That's okay," said Carl.

"Y' see, last time, last time wit' Zachary, I was too late." Suddenly he was sobbing. He couldn't help it; the collapse of his enormous emotions rendered him helpless. He sat there on the wooden planks of the floor and bent over, burying his head downward against his knees, his whole body shaking uncontrollably.

Carl pulled the levers to shut down the millstones. He sat down next to the older man and put an arm around his trembling shoulders. "It's okay, Eeph," he repeated again and again. "It's okay."

The dreadful sobs subsided along with the momentum of the millstones, and Ephraim felt an urgent need to tell his story.

He raised his head and began speaking, haltingly at first, of how he had met Prudence so many years ago, and how she had been 'his girl' until Zachary appeared. He told how his love for Prudence never diminished; how he bought the farm next door to remain close to her; how he favored her children; how he watched over her interests and helped her and her family at every opportunity.

When he came to the day Zachary died, he told sobbingly how he had chanced to enter the mill at the fateful moment, and how he tried in vain to save the husband of the woman he loved.

Finally, he recounted his latter-day hopes to win Prudence and how those hopes had been thwarted by Carl himself. "I was just beginnin' t' make some progress when you came along and ruined everything."

His young listener remained quiet and sympathetic until the older man had finished.

"That's quite a story," he said when Ephraim finally was through. "Now I understand why you came hurtling at me from behind."

"Y' see, I've been in love with Prudence even before she laid eyes on Zachary," Ephraim explained.

"I believe that," said Carl. "She is a very attractive woman."

"There's one thing more I gotta' confess," said Ephraim. "When I walked into that mill an' saw Zachary standin' there, I thought . . . I thought about the possibility o' pushin' 'im into the machinery t' get ridda' him."

"Really? You thought about . . . murder?"

Ephraim winced at the word. He had never allowed himself to think that his intentions constituted such a monstrous crime. He put his hands over his face. "I guess that's what it really was," he said with a tone of incredulity. "It was horribly evil for me even t' think about doin' it, but I did."

Carl sat there, huddled alongside Ephraim in the flour-dust on the floor, and pondered the story he had heard. There was silence except for the rushing of the water through the sluice below.

"You must hate me as much as you did Zachary," said Carl at last. "Did you think about murdering me, too?"

"No, no, of course not, never!" Ephraim insisted. "That wicked thought against Zachary was only a fleeting one, from the devil himself, an' I put it outta' my mind. I would never do such a thing, and I would never even let myself think about it now."

Carl grinned. "That's a relief," he said.

"I could never harm ya'," Ephraim continued. "Yer perfectly safe around me."

"Thank you," replied Carl.

"But the decent thing for ya' t' do, now that yer all healed up, would be t' pack up n' move on. Go back to yer family in Michigan where ya' belong."

"I have no family to go back to," Carl replied.

"Well then, go anywhere ya' want. But get outta' here."

"But I like it here. I'm not planning to leave," said Carl.

"Go," said Ephraim sternly. "There's no good reason fer ya' t' stay now. There's no future fer ya' on a mucky farm in Prairieville. Yer still young. Ya' oughta' go somewhere an' make somethin' outta' yerself."

"I don't have any big hopes for myself," replied Carl. "My beginnings aren't very promising. I don't have much in the way of education or skills. My expectations are not very high. I can't think of nothing better than to settle down here and stay on this farm the rest of my life."

"Yer not bein' fair t' yerself," Ephraim said.

"Maybe not. But it's my decision. It's my life."

"Prudence herself ain't bein' fair wit' ya'," Ephraim added.

"Don't say anything bad about Prudence," warned Carl. "She is a wonderful woman and would not be unfair to anyone."

Ephraim thought about that for a moment, and then went on. "Yer not bein' fair t' Prudence, neither," he said.

"In what way?" inquired Carl.

"It ain't fair t' her t' lead her on like yer been doin'. Lemme tell ya' the honest truth. She's old enough to be yer mother. Lemme be blunt wit' ya'. It's unnatural fer the two o' ya' t' be romancin' together the way ya' been.

"Sarah's more yer own age," Ephraim suggested, "an' she loves ya' as much as 'er mother does. Take my advice. Fergit about Prudence, an' start thinkin' about 'er daughter. She's just as purty, and she's a heck of a lot younger."

Carl said nothing although his heart had suddenly started pounding. This new revelation about Sarah was a complete surprise to him. Sarah loved him? She had not responded to his note from France, and certainly she had given him no signs of attention since he arrived at the marsh. Yet Ephraim said it like a foregone fact. Sarah loved him!

He sat motionless on his haunches and stared out the far window.

"Yer not gonna stay wit' an old woman very long, anyway," Ephraim continued. "Yer gonna wreck her life an' when ya' leave her she ain't gonna have nothin' left. Not even her self-respect. Yer makin' a fool outta her, and there ain't no fool like an old fool."

Ephraim paused and glanced at the younger man. Carl did not meet his eyes. Instead, he said slowly, "You are wrong, Uncle Eeph. You are in love with Prudence, but I am in love with her too. Surely I don't have to tell you, of all people, how wonderful she is. She is the one person I have ever known who has brought joy and comfort into my life. I would never leave her. I will stay at her side and love her and protect her as long as she will have me."

"Look, kid, yer gonna make a laughingstock outta her. Everybody around here knows what's goin' on."

"If everybody knows, then it's too late to do anything about it, isn't it?" countered Carl.

Ephraim could think of no new arguments, and threw himself on the mercy of the younger man. "If for no other reason, Carl, take pity on me. Think how you would feel if ya' loved her fer thirty years an' then lost 'er to a new young man. Please, I beg ya', pack up and move on so she and I can build a new life together."

"I don't think that's what she wants," said Carl carefully.

"Not while *yer* around," replied Ephraim. "She's flattered t' get the attentions of a young buck like you. It's only natural. It makes her feel like she's back in her springtime again."

"Our love goes a lot deeper than what you think," protested Carl. "And it doesn't matter that she's few years older than me. She's still a very young woman."

"Look at it this way, kid. Fifteen years from now, when yer barely forty, she'll be in 'er sixties. Think of it. Sixty-two, in fact. She'll be sixty-two years old. Believe me, that's *old*!"

Carl laughed. "That's a long way off," he shrugged.

"It's not so long as ya' think," Ephraim replied.

There was a pause in the conversation, as both men thought about what had been said. It was Carl who resumed the discussion. "I don't think you are being fair with me," he said. "Even if I left town, I don't think it would make any difference between you and Prudence."

"Why not?"

"You two have known each other for many years, and I wasn't around to get in your way. You knew her before Zachary, even. And after Zachary died, I wasn't in your way then."

"She was in mournin'," said Ephraim.

"Maybe so," said Carl, "but I was just pointing out that you have had plenty of chances with Prudence. Before her marriage, and afterward. If she favored your courtship, she would have let you know."

"She don't know her own mind," Ephraim grumbled.

Carl threw off his caution, and proceeded boldly. "I think she knows her own mind," he said. "She's in love with me. She's not in love with you. It's as simple as that."

The blunt words struck Ephraim like a club, and he groaned at their impact like a wounded animal. Carl pitied him then, and softened his approach. With a wisdom beyond his years, a wisdom perhaps imparted to him from the presence of the eternal marshlands which he too had grown to love, he continued with a tender, expressive voice.

"Ephraim, you have your vision of a perfect love with Prudence. It's a dream you have had ever since you met her. It's a longing for happiness with her in a world where there is no pain nor sorrow.

"Every man in the world has that same desire," Carl continued in a pensive tone, "and every woman too, I suppose. In the midst of our daily conflict and suffering, we all stubbornly yearn for peace and comfort.

"And we men think that if we can just find the right woman, if we can win the love of the right woman, then our agonizing hearts will be satisfied and nothing else will matter. We think we can snuggle together and ignore the struggles of the outside world and all will be well with us. We will live happily ever after.

"You're inspired by that vision, as all men are. And you think Prudence is the right woman for you, and if you can win her love, you will have entered your paradise."

"Yer right," commented Ephraim. "I have clung to that dream for thirty years. It's all that has kept me goin'."

"But your dream is just an idle fancy, nothing more," Carl insisted gently. "It's a mirage that disappears whenever you approach. It's not based on reality, because Prudence's feelings for you will never match your exalted expectations."

Ephraim squirmed dejectedly in the flour-dust on the floor, his shoulders sagging, afraid to examine Carl's thoughts too closely.

"But what is only a fantasy for you," Carl continued, "is a reality for me. It has become evident that Prudence and I were destined for each other. Our love really does bring us complete satisfaction."

"She's old enough t' be yer mother," Ephraim insisted.

"It's a very imperfect world," acknowledged Carl, "and in this case the timing got all muddled up."

"Humph!" exclaimed Ephraim.

"But other than that," said Carl earnestly, "everything fits together like the right pieces to a puzzle. Our love for each other is deep and pure."

"It was that way for Prudy n' me in the beginnin', too," complained Ephraim darkly.

"But it's going to stay that way for us," said Carl. "It's different this time."

"Mebbe," muttered Ephraim.

"Uncle Eeph, you understand what I'm talking about; you understand the dream. You understand what Prudence means to me, because you've been down the same road."

"Yeah," assented Ephraim.

"Uncle Eeph, I know that you are a man with a good heart. You are a devout Christian. I want to ask a favor of you, a very big favor."

Ephraim said nothing.

"Uncle Eeph, I want you to recognize that your hopes for a future with Prudence will never come true. Can you do that? Can you accept the real truth, no matter how unpleasant?"

Ephraim's shoulders seemed to sag even lower.

"I want you to lay aside your fantasy about Prudence. Can you do that? And I want you to give Prudence and me your blessing. I want you to bless our love. It will be the noblest thing you ever did in your whole life."

Ephraim moaned again, letting his head droop between his knees. His shoulders resumed their shaking. When his words finally came, they were so muffled that Carl could scarcely understand them. "No, no, no," he said. "Yer askin' the impossible. I can't do it. No way. I been countin' on winnin' Prudence someday, and I still believe I will do it. Yer wrong about what she wants, and yer wrong about what she'll do."

He raised his head and fixed Carl with a rigid, steely gaze. "Even if yer right," Ephraim said, "I couldn't do it. I can't give up my dream. I can't live without it!" Suddenly he was sobbing as he had done before, with deep spasms rending his body. "I won't give 'er up!" he declared. "I won't, I won't, I won't."

"Then we'll just have to wait and see what happens, I guess," said Carl pleasantly.

"Yeah," said Ephraim. "Like two billy goats fightin' it out on a mountain ledge."

"Prudence herself will be the judge," observed Carl.

Their conversation was finally ended by the arrival of Mortimer, who set them back at their task of grinding corn.

While their work had been delayed, Prudence's apprehensions had been quietly gnawing within her. She busied herself with cleaning the kitchen, but her heart was not in the assignment and she made little progress.

'It's not possible for Ephraim to do him any harm,' she told herself again and again. 'He's an honest God-fearing man and he wouldn't do anything to hurt Carl.'

Nevertheless, her eyes kept glancing out the window, scanning the River Road coming from the marsh.

'I love Carl even more than I thought,' she mused, 'if I can be so distraught over such a groundless fear.'

When at last she saw the two familiar horse-drawn vehicles arriving from the south, she relaxed with the air of one who has completed a day's hard physical work.

Ephraim turned his horse into his own driveway, while Carl came on alone.

Prudence rushed out in the cold March wind to welcome Carl and to give him a long, solid hug.

"I'm so glad you're back safe," she breathed. "I love you so much I can hardly stand to have you out of my sight."

Carl smiled. "I feel the same way about you," he said. "You are the answer to my lifelong prayers."

Chapter 20

Although President Wilson personally appeared before the U.S. Senate to plead the cause of woman suffrage, the senators rejected the Anthony Amendment in October 1918 and again the following February.

It was a doomed last-ditch stand and everybody knew it, for the November elections had dramatically changed the political landscape. The time for woman suffrage had arrived. Republicans had seized control of both houses of Congress, but of greater importance was the fact that the sentiment for suffrage had increased substantially on both sides of the aisle. The new legislators who took their seats in March were expected to approve the Amendment upon presentation.

Wilson was in Paris during the early part of the year 1919, where he tried to get the Allies to accept his plan of Fourteen Points for peace. He returned to America with only partial success, and promptly called a special session of Congress to convene in May.

The Anthony Amendment—Joint Resolution 1—was first on the agenda, and Theodora went to Washington to watch the House of Representatives pass it again. This time, she wrote later, "there was no excitement, no jubilee on our side. We knew the outcome beforehand. The fight had been so long and the victory had come so gradually that it was difficult to grasp. We filed out smiling quietly at each other and that was all."

The new U.S. Senate passed the Amendment on June 4th. The 'Suffs' had finally triumphed in Washington.

Theodora was already back in Wisconsin, ready for the ratification battle.

"Our national leader, Carrie Chapman Catt, judged Wisconsin to be hopeless in the suffrage battle," Theodora pointed out. "Now we have a chance to redeem ourselves at the end, if we can ratify the Amendment quickly."

Ephraim was anxious to help, even if he wasn't a state legislator. "I ain't got much chance t' prove myself t' Prudence," he told Sarah. "This is about the only place where I can do somethin'."

"But what can you do to help the ratification?" asked Sarah. Always close to the man she called "Uncle Eeph," she had become even closer to him as a direct consequence of the ripening romance between Prudence and Carl. In the past, Sarah had gone to Ephraim's house twice a week to sweep the floors and dust the furniture and wash the stack of dirty dishes. Now she went almost every day, soon after breakfast.

"I wish t' heaven I had that seat in the assembly," Ephraim replied. "But at least I can work on Buckley t' support the Amendment. He don't seem t' be very enthusiastic about it, but mebbe I can talk him into votin' fer it."

"You'd better hurry," said Sarah. "Congress has already approved the Amendment, and it's before the states for consideration."

"Yer right," agreed Ephraim. "I better get right t' work on it. I'll walk to yer house with you this morning so I can call Mr. Buckley on the telephone. I want to talk t' Prudence anyhow; I ain't seen 'er fer a long time."

Assemblyman Buckley was willing to listen, and agreed to an appointment for discussion.

After hanging up the telephone, Ephraim turned to Prudence. "Prudy," he said, "I'm goin' to meet with Buckley Monday mornin' at ten. I'd like you t' be there an' help me wit' my arguments. Will ya' come wit' me?"

"Oh, I'd like to," replied Prudence politely, "but I think I'll stay here on the farm. There's lots of work to do."

"Please, Prudy, I need you. I need somebody to support me. Please come along."

"I don't think so," answered Prudence coolly. "But thanks for inviting me, anyway."

"I'll go with you, Uncle Eeph," said Sarah.

"You don't need to go," admonished her mother.

"But I want to go," protested Sarah. "It'll be fun."

Accordingly, early on Monday morning Ephraim and Sarah rode into Prairieville in the buggy behind Kaiser. Ephraim rehearsed his introductory remarks several times, and then the conversation turned, as always, to Prudence.

"Why wouldn't she come with me today?" Ephraim asked.

"I don't know," answered Sarah. "She sure surprised me when she turned you down."

"Of course, we both know she's all rattleheaded about Carl,"

Ephraim admitted. "When a female gets that look in 'er eye, it comes down to a foot-race between Mister Bull and Father Time. Nothin' else will set 'er straight again. Ain't no sense wastin' yer breath with arguments. That's why I stopped comin' over. I figgered I'd jus' stand back and wait it out."

"I'm afraid you're right," said Sarah.

"But I didn't think she'd lose interest in woman suffrage," he said sadly. "She was so set on makin' women important an' gettin' 'em out of the kitchen. Now that the battle for women's votes is almost won, I can't believe she's turnin' her back on it."

"It certainly seems strange, that's for sure," said Sarah. "But she's so wrapped up with Carl right now that I guess she doesn't care about anything else at all."

Buckley had agreed to meet them at the Elk's Club on the corner of Wisconsin Avenue and Clinton Street. After leaving Kaiser at Thiel's Livery, Ephraim and Sarah arrived at the Club early and waited on a sofa in an anteroom. Sarah leaned her head against Ephraim's shoulder and they rested comfortably while they watched for their legislator. No words were necessary; they were two old friends who simply enjoyed being together.

The ruddy-raced assemblyman eased into the room, displaying a genial exterior overlaying his well-organized personality. He was young, only twenty-seven, but he was already into his third year in the state legislature.

The two men exchanged greetings, and Ephraim introduced Sarah.

"I haven't seen you since the election," said Buckley, moving a chair so he could face his constituents. "You ran a good race. As an independent candidate, you did very well."

"Thank you, Mr. Buckley."

"Oh, please call me John," said the young politician. "I'd like the freedom to call you by your first name, too."

"That's all right, John. Call me Ephraim; I'd like that."

"Thanks, Ephraim. Now, what topic did you want to talk about with me?"

"The Anthony Amendment, John. Our ratification of votes fer women."

"Oh, yes," said Buckley reflectively, as though he were recalling it from a very distant place in his mind.

"The measure has passed both houses of Congress," Ephraim reminded him, "and it should be brought before the state legislature very soon."

"Yes, yes, I understand it is coming up tomorrow," Buckley said.

"Well, I'm assumin' you'll vote fer it," said Ephraim.

Buckley did not reply in words, but he sat quietly and nodded his head up and down almost imperceptibly. Perhaps he meant he would vote for the ratification. Or perhaps he simply indicated he understood Ephraim's request.

"And I'm hopin' you'll encourage the other legislators t' vote fer ratification, too."

"Hmmm, I see," responded Buckley. "If you were in my place, what would you say to convince them?"

Ephraim remembered his coaching from Sarah. "Tell them the Anthony Amendment is a sure thing t' be ratified, even if Wisconsin holds out. Those women suffragists have been very active all over the whole danged country, and they have more than enough states lined up t' ratify. They vow t' change the constitution in plenty of time so they can vote in the next presidential election. What's more, they are right. They've got the votes. There ain't no way t' stop 'em."

Buckley rubbed his hand on his jaw in a gesture of meditation.

"Then tell 'em," continued Ephraim, "we can't afford t' be known as a backward state which stubbornly held out against giving votes t' women. It's bad enough t' be considered unpatriotic and anti-American. We're known across the country as a bunch of backward bums wit' beer bellies and no brains. Here's a chance t' make some good news fer a change. Here's a chance t' make people all over the country sit up straight and say, 'Wow, maybe I was wrong about Wisconsin!'"

"I'm afraid you're right," conceded Buckley, "about the Amendment being ratified. But I don't think it will happen in a year or two. It's going to take a long time."

Ephraim pulled a wrinkled sheet of tablet paper from his pocket and unfolded it. "John, here's a list o' the states where we know there are enough votes t' ratify. It's only a matter o' months until all o' these states convene their legislatures and ratify the Amendment. We're talkin' months, John, not years. There are only five states missin' from this list, and one o' them is Wisconsin. Even though the Wisconsin legislature gave women the right to vote in presidential elections a couple o' months ago, the national leaders don't really believe our hearts are in it. We're still looked upon as a backward state."

Buckley looked uncomfortable.

"But we can change all that by becomin' the first state t' ratify the Amendment. Our legislature is already in session. We don't have t' wait for it t' convene. We have the chance to print good headlines across the nation. We gotta' do it. We don't dare muff that chance."

"You are very convincing," said Buckley. "And you certainly have done your homework."

"Then you'll go t' Madison and support a quick ratification t'morrow?"

"Well, I've got to think it over. I'm sure you know I voted for the bill last February to let women vote in presidential elections. But I have heard from many eloquent friends who think I voted wrong, and in any event the Anthony Amendment is a lot broader in scope. Even if ratification is a foregone conclusion, perhaps it's not the right thing for us to do, and maybe it's not the right time."

Sarah had remained quiet throughout the discussion, but now she couldn't restrain herself. "How can you say it's not right?" she asked, her voice rising. "Women are just as smart as men, and many of them are better informed. Besides, they bring a better sense of compassion to the political arena than men do. The country will be a better place when women can vote on everything."

"Now, now, Miss, let's not get drawn into an argument about the wonderful qualities of women. I surrender at once. I'll be the first man to confess that women are delightful creatures and in many ways they are superior to men."

"Don't be condescending," Sarah scolded lightly. "If women are so wonderful, then why shouldn't they have the right to vote?" she demanded with a disarming smile.

"Perhaps they should, Miss, perhaps they should," Buckley replied smoothly, smiling back at her. "I'll give it my full consideration before I vote upon it."

Ephraim could see that there was no reason to belabor his position. "Thank you fer listening t' us, John," he said, extending his hand. "Do think it over, and I trust yer gonna come t' the right conclusion. I'm gonna be in Madison tomorrow, by the way, t' watch the vote, and if you think of any more questions I'll try t' answer them."

"I'm glad you are so interested," replied John. "I'll get you into the gallery so you can watch the proceedings in the assembly, if you like."

"Thank you, John. Yes, I would appreciate that very much. Sarah and I will both be there."

As they rode home, Ephraim and Sarah compared their reactions to the assemblyman's words.

"I think he'll vote yes fer ratification," Ephraim said. "He seems like a purty smart man. When the actual moment arrives, I think he'll go along with it."

"I don't think so," said Sarah. "He's got some powerful friends who are pressuring him to vote no. Even if he wants to vote in our favor, it might be a political necessity to go against ratification."

"Well, maybe so. We'll find out when the vote is taken."

The two rode along without speaking for several miles. The countryside around them was radiant in the fullness of early June. In the fields along the road, young corn sprouts with their pointed leaves were reaching up toward the warm sun. The aroma of freshly cut alfalfa from the first cutting wafted gently across the topless buggy. A young calf bawled loudly for its mother.

Sarah leaned against Ephraim's shoulder as she had done while they were waiting for the assemblyman.

"I'm so worried about what's going to happen," she said..

"Why, what's gonna happen?" he asked with pretended innocence.

"You know what I'm talking about," she said. "What's going to happen with my mother and Carl."

"Well, we don't know what's gonna happen, do we?" he responded

"No, but it doesn't look very favorable, that's for sure," she observed.

"I'm gonna give it one last shot," he said. "I'm gonna go t' Madison an' try t' help get the Amendment ratified. I hope yer mom will come along an' help, but I don't know if she will."

"If she wouldn't go to Prairieville with us today," observed Sarah, "then there isn't much chance she'll go to Madison tomorrow."

"Probably not," Ephraim agreed. "It ain't a very good sign fer my chances, is it. Well, I'm gonna do it anyway. I'm gonna help get that Amendment ratified, an' then I'm gonna go t' Prudence an' lay it at 'er feet like a trophy an' maybe then she'll love me."

Sarah couldn't help laughing, in a gentle way. "Oh, Uncle Eeph,!" she exclaimed. "You are so sweet. How could anyone harden their heart against you?"

They were quite right; Prudence had no interest in going to Madison. "Theodora is going to be there," said Prudence, "and she tells me she's got the votes. I don't see anything that I can do. Besides, there's work to do on the farm, and somebody's got to do it. Carl can't do it all by himself, although his leg is getting stronger every day."

Ephraim wrinkled his face. "Would you rather I stayed here on the farm to help ya' with the work?" he asked. "I'm only tryin' t' please you. I'll do whatever ya' want."

"You can go to Madison if you want," said Prudence grandly. "I suppose one day won't make that much difference."

"I'd really like ya' t' come with me," Ephraim pleaded. "We're right up against the goal line, an' it would be such a great victory fer us t' celebrate t'gether. One day on the farm won't make that much difference fer you, neither. Please come along."

"No, I won't go with you," she replied with a touch of exasperation, shaking her head sharply to dismiss him.

"Well, *I'm* going," declared Sarah. "It's going to be a great historic occasion, and I want to be a part of it. Someday I'll tell my grandchildren about it."

Prudence frowned. She started to speak, but thought better of it and clamped her mouth shut.

The State Capitol building in Madison is an imposing stone structure whose huge dome can be seen for miles; it is perhaps the most beautiful state capitol in America. It is situated on the isthmus between Lakes Mendota and Monona.

Both Ephraim and Sarah were strangers to the building. They arrived by cab from the *Northwestern* railway station, and entered the building with some degree of trepidation. Scurrying around them were hundreds of people, but there were no familiar faces. Their inquiries for Assemblyman Buckley met with no success; nobody seemed to know him and nobody seemed to care. When they finally arrived at his office after following imperfect directions, the door was locked.

Feeling slightly bewildered and entirely useless, the untutored couple managed to get seats in a back corner of the crowded gallery overlooking the assembly chamber.

Ephraim looked as uncomfortable as he felt. Wearing a business suit was a violation of his nature, and made him self-conscious to the point of awkwardness. He seemed to bulge out of it as though he were larger than life-size. His rough, outdoor complexion and his shaggy black hair were a ludicrous contrast to the fine-woven texture of the wool. The unnaturalness of it all made him hot and sweaty.

"Ain't much we can do, I guess," ventured Ephraim.

"It'll be interesting just to watch and see what happens," Sarah replied brightly.

"I'm kinda' glad Prudence ain't with me t' see how helpless I am," he confessed.

"Now don't go feeling that way," she told him. "After all, this is the first time we've ever been here. We can't expect to walk right in and know everything right off."

"I guess yer right," he agreed.

They glanced cautiously around them. An air of expectancy permeated the atmosphere. The gallery was crowded and noisy, with many women in attendance. A large authoritative woman sitting in front of Ephraim attracted their attention. She wore a somber gray dress, and her severe black hair was knotted in a tight bun at the back of her head. She was very agitated, waving her arms and busily pointing out over the assembly hall, talking rapidly to the meek-looking woman sitting next to her.

Following her gestures, they gazed down over the floor of the assembly and saw many empty desks.

"Why aren't there very many assemblymen down there?" asked Sarah.

"I don't know," replied Ephraim. "Maybe they're just late in coming in."

The black-haired woman turned around quickly and addressed the subject without introduction. "The ones that aren't here aren't coming at all," she said with disdain. "Some of them say they have work to do at home, especially on the farm. But there's a lot of cowards among them. They are not in favor of votes for women, but they haven't got the guts to come and vote against us."

"Oh, I see," said Ephraim.

"Some of them were hoping there wouldn't be a quorum, but we've counted noses and we know we got enough," she added.

"Ahh," responded Ephraim.

"Assemblyman Thomas Nolan, chairman of the assembly judiciary committee, is going to present the resolution. We don't expect much opposition from the members who are here on the floor," she declared.

"That's good to know," said Ephraim, nodding his head. "Thank you very much."

The woman turned back to her friend and continued her monologue without missing a beat.

The gallery was talkative until Assemblyman Nolan took the floor. Then a sudden hush swept the noise away, and everyone turned their eyes expectantly upon him.

Nolan was a handsome, square-faced man from Janesville. A staunch Republican, he had been the chairman of his party in Rock County for many years. He was newly elected to the assembly, having won a landslide vote in his first attempt at public office. Although he was in his sixties, he was part of the wave of progressive new ideas which had swept the nation in November, ensuring the passage of the Anthony Amendment.

"Mister Chairman," he began, speaking in rich sonorous tones, "this is a truly historic occasion, as we are about to consider the ratification of an amendment to the Constitution of the United States—an amendment which will right an immense wrong.

"Half of our citizens are denied the right to vote in our elections. The time has come for us to set things straight. We shall give women the franchise because it is right—and because we need their wisdom and judgment in our public decisions."

There was a quiet murmur of approval from the gallery.

Nolan then read Joint Resolution 108A which included a brief recital of the passage of the Anthony Amendment: *The right of citizens of the United States to vote shall not be denied or abridged by the United States or by any state on account of sex.*

"Resolved by the assembly, the senate concurring, *That the said proposed amendment to the constitution of the United States of America be and the same is hereby ratified by the legislature of the state of Wisconsin. . . .*

"Mister Chairman, I hereby propose this resolution."

The gallery applauded.

"The notification from Congress has only recently been received in Madison," Nolan continued, "so the resolution is not listed on the calendar of the assembly. Therefore, I ask unanimous consent for suspension of the rules so the resolution can be engrossed immediately."

A slender, straight-nosed assemblyman with a dapper moustache leaped to his feet as Nolan relinquished the floor. He was John P. Donnelly, a veteran Democrat from the third and fourth wards of Milwaukee. Although he was a young man, not yet thirty-five years of age, he would champion the old order. "I object," he declared, "to the suspension of the rules. I see no reason to give this measure any special treatment. It can be considered in due time. It will wait for us." It was clear that he sought to delay what he knew he could not defeat.

A chorus of feminine groans emanated from the gallery. "We want to be first!" someone shouted. A very pointed frown from the uplifted face of the chair quickly restored order.

Since the consent was not unanimous, Assemblyman Axel Johnson moved a suspension of the rules, and a call of the roll was required. This would be a test vote, but the knowledgeable observers in the gallery already knew there was overwhelming support for the resolution among the assemblymen who were present on the floor.

A preponderance of 'ayes' answered the roll, and the official count was forty-eight to eight in favor of suspending the rules. The gallery applauded with enthusiasm.

The roll call confirmed the extent of the missing members, as forty-three assemblymen—including John Buckley—failed to respond.

"The rules have been suspended," announced the chair.

Assemblyman Donnelly had not yet given up. Adjusting his small, wire-rimmed eyeglasses, he looked down his long nose and said in a brisk, businesslike tone, "There are many of our members who are not here. Perhaps they do not know that we are changing the rules to consider this important amendment to the U.S. Constitution. They deserve the right to be heard, and they deserve the right to vote on this measure. It is only fair to give them enough time so they can participate. Therefore, I ask unanimous consent to place this resolution at the foot of the calendar."

"I object," called out Assemblyman Nolan.

"A point of order, Mister Chairman," interjected Assemblyman Donnelly. "This resolution is not on the calendar, and therefore it can not and ought not be considered at this time. We need to give timely notice to all of our members."

The women in the gallery expressed their disapproval again with a loud groan in unison which sounded as though it had been co-ordinated by a conductor. "I can't believe this!" exclaimed the authoritative woman in front of Ephraim. Someone else shouted, "Give up, Mister!"

The chairman pounded his gavel twice with great deliberation. "Spectators will remain quiet," he announced, scowling upward again. "You are here at our invitation, and you are expected to remain courteous and refrain from disrupting the proceedings."

The commotion quickly subsided.

"Your point of order is not well taken, Mister Donnelly," the chair continued, "because the rules have been suspended."

"I appeal the ruling of the chair," called out Assemblyman Donnelly. "I demand a call of the house."

A loud murmur of disbelief swept through the gallery. The woman in front of Ephraim muttered "Ridiculous!" to her companion, and then yelled loudly "Quit stalling!" Several others took up the call.

Donnelly could not get a sufficient number of seconds for his appeal, so his effort to force another roll call failed.

"The resolution is ordered engrossed," declared the chair. "It will now be read again."

After the reading, Assemblyman Axel Johnson took the floor. "I ask unanimous consent for a suspension of the rules so we can have immediate consideration of this measure."

"I object," Assemblyman Donnelly called out. "We are not being fair to the members of this assembly who are not present."

"Lacking unanimous consent," said Assemblyman Johnson, "I move the suspension of the rules."

Another roll call was required, which was easily carried by a vote of fifty to seven.

An amendment to the resolution, which would delay its final approval by making it different from the version being passed by the senate, was then offered by Assemblyman Donnelly. It was overwhelmingly rejected.

The opponents of the measure had run out of time and maneuver. The resolution was read for the third and final time.

The chairman declared, "The question now is, 'Shall the joint resolution be adopted?'"

A roll call vote was required, and only two defiant votes were recorded against the measure. Even Assemblyman Donnelly voted "Aye;" with the battle lost he wanted to be on the winning side.

"The resolution has been adopted," announced the chairman.

The visitors in the gallery applauded and cheered. The woman in front of Ephraim stood up and shouted, "It's about time!"

Afterward, amidst the milling crowds in the hallway, Ephraim spotted Theodora. He and Sarah worked their way to her side.

Theodora introduced them to Ada James, one of the most dedicated suffragists in Wisconsin.

"Ada's father David and his brother introduced the original suffrage bill in the state legislature years ago," Theodora explained. "Ada herself has worked tirelessly for a long time to win votes for women."

"Yes, I've heard Prudence speak of her many times," Ephraim said. He turned to Ada. "I've got the greatest respect fer people like you who made our victory possible today. I congratulate you on our success!"

Ada smiled politely and nodded her head.

"She's hard of hearing," Theodora explained.

Ephraim spoke louder. "I congratulate you!" he said again.

"Thank you," replied Ada, smiling. "I'm pleased to meet you." She studied his face for a moment, and then gazed at Sarah. "Is this your daughter?" she asked.

Ephraim was flustered and could not speak, but Sarah shook her head and said with a slight smile, "No, Ephraim is just a neighbor. He is a good friend of my mother, Prudence Hartmann."

"It's just that you look so much alike," said Ada.

"You know Prudence Hartmann," Theodora spoke loudly into Ada's ear. "She's a Suff from Prairieville. This is her daughter, Sarah."

"Oh yes, I see," said Ada, nodding her head.

"I've known Ephraim since I was just a little child," explained Sarah. "He has a farm right next to ours. He ran for the assembly last fall, but he didn't make it. He has been a strong advocate of woman suffrage, and we came here together to celebrate our victory."

"It's a complete victory now," said Theodora. "The state senate has just approved the resolution, too. Their action was quick and easy, with no obstructions. There was only one vote against it—Senator Herman Bilgrien, that old farmer from Dodge County, just couldn't be convinced that us poor misguided women should be allowed the franchise. Every other senator voted in favor."

"How about Senator Mulberger from Prairieville?" asked Ephraim.

"He was conveniently absent," replied Theodora, "just like last February when we won the vote in presidential elections."

"This time, Prairieville's representatives didn't help us none, then, in either house," observed Ephraim.

"Well, at least they didn't try to fight it," Theodora pointed out philosophically.

Ephraim laughed. "That's true enough," he conceded.

"Now there's still work to do. We want to be listed as the first state to ratify the Anthony Amendment," said Theodora. "But we've just heard from our friends in Illinois, who sent a telegram saying that their legislature completed their ratification earlier today."

"Oh, how disappointing!" exclaimed Sarah.

"Yes, but we haven't given up yet," declared Theodora. "We think Illinois will send their ratification certificate by certified mail. We can beat that. Ada was just telling me that she's got her father standing by with his bags packed. He's going to personally deliver our certificate to Washington. You have to change trains a couple of times to get to Washington," Theodora said knowingly, "and David James can change trains faster than the mailbags can."

"Good for him," Ephraim said.

"The Secretary of State is drawing the document right now," Theodora said, "and Governor Philipp is standing by. It won't take long to get it signed and sealed. Then Mr. James can be on his way."

"Uncle Eeph, why don't you go with him?" asked Sarah with sudden inspiration.

"That's an excellent idea," said Theodora. "Mr. James is not so young any more, and he is apprehensive about making the trip. He would really appreciate a traveling companion."

Ephraim hesitated. He looked at Sarah, and Ada, and Theodora in turn. His mind was churning. "I'd kinda' like t' do that," he said tentatively, "but I don't have no money with me fer the trip."

Theodora opened her purse and withdrew several bills. "Here," she said, thrusting them at him. "Take these. You can repay me when you get back to Prairieville."

"Well, thanks," he said, still uncertain of himself. He looked at Sarah dubiously.

"Go, Uncle Eeph; of course you should go," she said at once. "What a great experience you'll have."

"I can't jus' leave you here," he said. "How you goin' t' get home?"

Sarah laughed. "We'll be on the same train, I'm sure. It goes right through Prairieville. I'll get off there and you can go right on with Mr. James. Just think about how proud Prudence will be of you."

Ephraim's eyes suddenly sparkled. He was convinced. "I'll go," he said decisively. "I'll go."

"It's the *Chicago and Northwestern* train," said Theodora. I think it leaves a little after four o'clock."

"We'll be on it," promised Ephraim.

With a couple of hours to spare, Ephraim and Sarah decided to enjoy a late lunch together. Afterward, they strolled down to the lake front and looked out across the peaceful water of Lake Mendota.

There was a gentle breeze blowing inland, carrying with it the scent of freshwater lakes. They watched the small ripples which ruffled the surface of the water as they rolled up against the beach and splashed harmlessly against the pebbles. A pair of sea gulls circled effortlessly off-shore, surveying their tranquil world.

"It's been a great an' noble effort," Ephraim said reflectively, "and it sure feels wonderful t' win a victory at last."

"Yes, it certainly does," Sarah agreed. "But somehow, I wonder how much difference it's really going to make."

"What do you mean?" asked Ephraim. "It'll make a lot o' difference, of course. Women will be able t' vote now, just like men."

"Sure, we can vote, but will it really make that much difference?" she asked again. "I think it will be a long time before men take women's ideas seriously. It's going to be a long time before we gain any kind of equality with men."

"In that sense," said Ephraim, "I'm sure yer right. But this fight was simply to give women the right t' vote, nothin' more. Men and women are different from each other. They ain't equal, and everybody knows it. That's just the way God made 'em. Women are s'posed t' be the home-bodies. God made 'em t' have babies and t' take care of the home an' t' be a helpmeet to their husbands, as the Bible says."

"I guess you're right, Uncle Eeph," said Sarah.

"Now that doesn't mean yer anything less than men are," Ephraim continued. "Yer just as important as men, mebbe more so. Yer ideas is just as good, an' that's why ya' oughtta' vote."

"I guess you're right," Sarah said again. "But there are times when I think women should be able to run businesses and fly aeroplanes and fight wars just like men."

"I guess that'd be okay," conceded Ephraim, "if they can do it with-out neglecting their primary duties of motherhood and homemaker. Those are the things that come naturally, as duties from God."

"It is kind of natural for women to be homemakers," admitted Sarah. "I really enjoy keeping house for you." She looked up at him shyly. "Sometimes I pretend that it's my own house, and you're my very own husband, and then I get such a wonderful feeling of contentment and sat-isfaction."

Ephraim slipped his arm around her shoulders, and looked into her eyes. "I know what ya' mean," he said gently. "I'd sure like t' have the right woman in my house."

"But for now, we'd better get on over to the train station," Sarah reminded him. "We don't want to be left behind."

When they arrived at the depot they were met by a distraught Theodora. "I'm so sorry," she said, "I was wrong about the time the train was to leave. It's already gone, and you have missed it!"

Ephraim and Sarah looked at each other, and shrugged. "Well, we ain't gonna catch up to it," Ephraim said. "I guess Mr. David James will just have t' do it all by himself." He reached into his billfold and retrieved the bills Theodora had given him.

"Here's yer money back," he sighed. "I won't be needin' it. We already got the tickets t' get home with tonight."

"I'm so sorry that you missed going to Washington with Mr. James," Theodora repeated.

"Oh, that's all right," said Sarah. "It was only a last-minute thought anyway; it doesn't matter."

"That's the way it's been wit' me and Prudence all the way through," commented Ephraim with a touch of bitterness. "I've always missed the train so far as she's concerned."

"What do you mean?" asked Theodora.

"Well," began Sarah, giving Ephraim a mischievous glance sideways, "Ephraim tried to get my mother to marry him when they were young, but she married my father instead."

Theodora looked quizzically at Ephraim, who reddened noticeably.

"Then when my father died a couple of years ago, Ephraim got a second chance. But my mother still isn't interested; she's caught the eye of a younger man."

Ephraim put a restraining hand on Sarah's elbow. "I don't think you ought to be saying this," he chided.

"Oh, why not?" Sarah brushed him off. "It's no secret that my mother and Carl are crazy about each other."

Theodora looked sharply at Sarah. "Carl?" she asked. "You don't mean Jon's young friend from the army, do you? The injured one?"

"Yes, that's the one," replied Sarah, her lip beginning to tremble now at her own boldness. "My mother and Carl think they are in love with each other."

Theodora looked skeptical. "But Prudence is so much older than Carl!" she exclaimed.

"I know," said Sarah. "There's twenty years difference. But that doesn't seem to bother either one of them."

"Well, I married a widower myself," said Theodora, "and he is older than I am. But not twenty years!"

"I don't think it's right," pouted Sarah. "Carl is my own age, and my mother should leave him alone."

"I take it that you like Carl yourself," suggested Theodora.

"You're very perceptive," Sarah smiled.

"I think very highly of your mother," said Theodora, preparing to leave. "I've got to get back to the Capitol, so I can't stand and talk any longer. But don't despair. I know your mother rather well, and I'll bet she'll come to her senses in good time."

"I certainly hope so," replied Sarah.

"Don't count on it," cautioned Ephraim. "When it comes to romance, she ain't never been very prudent."

Chapter 21

Prudence answered the phone on the third ring. It was Theodora.

"David beat the Illinois mail to Washington," she told Prudence. "He turned in our documents at one o'clock on Friday, and Wisconsin has the honor of being the first state to be listed in ratification of the Amendment."

"Well, that's very wonderful indeed," replied Prudence.

"Yes, it's wonderful, and ironic at the same time, that we should claim that award when we have been about as backward as any state could be in giving women the right to vote."

"It's due in great measure to your efforts, Theodora," said Prudence, "and you'll be remembered by grateful women whenever they go to the polls to vote."

"I did what I could," said Theodora, "but it was really women like Olympia Brown and Ada James who got the job done."

"You are too modest," remarked Prudence. "Every woman in Wisconsin knows the truth. You were their leader."

"Well, thank you," acknowledged Theodora. "But you can take some of the credit yourself, you know. There were many women who played their part, whether it was large or small. I'll always remember you buzzing around the state on that Harley-Davidson motorcycle. That was a real scene to behold."

"It was a lot of fun," confessed Prudence. "I enjoyed driving that motorcycle, and I'm sorry Robert stayed in Janesville this summer. I miss him and his motorcycle."

"At least you had the motorcycle when you needed it."

"Yes, and I had Robert too. Now that he is gone, thank goodness Carl is strong enough to pitch in with the farm work. There's an awful lot of work to be done, and Sarah and I can't do it all."

"Doesn't your friend Ephraim help you this summer?" asked Theodora.

"No, he hasn't been around much this year. I guess he's got farm work of his own to do."

"Carl has replaced him?" inquired Theodora.

"In a way, yes, that's true," admitted Prudence.

Theodora pressed on in her usual bold manner. "Sarah says you are in love with Carl."

Prudence hesitated momentarily. "Well, yes, I suppose that's true, too. Carl and I like each other a great deal."

"He's very young, isn't he?"

"Not really. He's twenty-six. And he is very mature. I think being in the war has made him old beyond his years."

"Twenty-six still seems very young to me, Prudence. I don't know your age exactly, but he's got to be about twenty years younger than you are."

"Yes, you're right. He's twenty years younger than me. But twenty years isn't all that much. After all, we're not living in the Victorian age any more."

"Well, you can do what you like," said Theodora abruptly. "But I think he is too young for you. You should leave him to your daughter. She likes him, too. She told me as much. And you're not giving her a fair chance."

"I don't think you are in a position to judge," protested Prudence, her voice quavering. "We all have our own lives to lead. Sarah's not a baby any more. She is a grown woman in her own right, and she can take care of herself."

"Forgive me," said Theodora. "I'm always too quick to speak my mind. I don't really mean to sit in judgment."

"No, no, that's all right," said Prudence. "I'm glad we're good enough friends that we can be honest with each other."

Prudence hung up the phone and resumed washing the breakfast dishes but she found it very hard to quiet her thoughts. She could tell herself a thousand times that her love for Carl was legitimate and acceptable, but she knew in her heart it wouldn't stand up to scrutiny from her respectable friends. She felt like her secret immorality had been suddenly uncovered and now she stood naked and ashamed for the whole world to see. The criticism from her esteemed friend drove daggers deep into her heart.

She was still ruminating an hour later when she heard an automobile in her driveway. Peering out through the curtains of her window, she saw a young man emerge and stand alongside the unfamiliar vehicle. He glanced at the barn and then turned slowly to gaze across the open fields toward the river.

He was tall and slender, with medium brown hair, and he seemed in no hurry to move. For a long time he stood meditating before he finally turned toward the house. Only then did Prudence recognize Jon's comrade, Leo Herbst.

She met him at the door with a hesitant smile.

"Hello Mrs. Hartmann," he said brightly. "It's a pleasure to see you again."

"Yes, yes. Do come in."

When they were seated in the living room, she said, "You have changed a great deal since I saw you at Camp MacArthur."

"Of course, Mrs. Hartmann, it's been a year and a half."

"Yes, I guess it has. But still, you seem so much older."

"War does that to a guy," Leo replied soberly.

"I'm glad you are back home safe," she said with a sad smile. "Jon didn't make it."

"Yes, I know. We were in the same unit, you remember."

"Of course."

"I was injured slightly," Leo volunteered, "but it didn't amount to much."

"I'm glad it was not serious," Prudence said.

"Me too," Leo agreed.

"How good it is to have the war over," Prudence said. "It's such a foolish waste of lives."

"How true," he agreed. "It was a terrible thing to lose Jon. I got to know him pretty well during our year together, and I think he was one of the grandest guys in the world."

"Yes, he was certainly very precious to me," Prudence agreed.

"Jon was a good soldier. He never faltered. We were all scared as we could be, especially on that first day of battle, but he never showed it. He followed his orders and he did his best. He was only in the first fight, in the Grimpettes Woods, but he fought bravely."

"Yes, that's what Carl has said," Prudence commented.

"Oh, have you seen Carl?" Leo asked in surprise. "I lost track of him after he was injured. I wrote a letter to his home in Michigan but they couldn't find him and the post office returned it to me after a while."

"Carl came here to recuperate," Prudence told him.

"Humph. Of course. I should have thought of that. Jon loved the Vernal Marsh so much, and this farm in particular, that he made us all love it too, even though we had never seen it. Of course Carl would come back to have a look.

"In fact, that's why I'm here. Jon made me love the marsh, and I felt guilty that I have lived in Prairieville all my life and never even seen it. I had to come out and meet you and ask you to take me to Jon's special hidden places."

"We'll be glad to show you around," she said. "I know what! I'll pack a picnic lunch. Sarah and I can take a couple of hours from our farm work and enjoy a little outing. Even Carl can come along; his leg is pretty well healed up now and he gets around as good as ever."

"Oh, is Carl still here?" Leo was surprised again.

"Yes, he stayed on to help us," Prudence said innocently. "There's a lot to do."

Leo's eyes brightened. "Ah yes, I remember. Jon always told Carl to come back here after the war and marry his sister." He nodded knowingly.

Prudence's blush went unnoticed as she quickly said, "I don't think that's going to happen."

Leo laughed. "You never know. I remember your daughter being a very pretty girl. Her name is . . . ."

"Sarah."

"Oh yes. Sarah. She really was a pretty girl. And Carl is about as nice a guy as you'd ever want to meet."

"Yes, Carl is wonderful," Prudence agreed with enthusiasm.

"Then why don't they get together?"

Prudence shrugged.

"Oh, I get it," Leo said. "There's somebody else."

Prudence felt a pang of guilt. "What do you mean?"

"I mean Sarah must have a different boyfriend."

"No, that's not it."

"Then what?"

"It's just one of those things," Prudence said. "They weren't meant for each other."

Leo didn't understand, but he did not pursue the subject.

At noon, the foursome strolled out into the marsh, with Carl carrying a brown wicker picnic basket. The day was warm, with a southerly breeze which indicated the approach of rain. The sun was shining, but overcast skies to the west were moving slowly toward Prairieville.

Carl and Leo talked with animation as they told each other their experiences after being separated at the front. Carl described his odyssey from one makeshift military hospital to another, and his voyage back to the States.

"As soon as I could get loose," he explained, "I headed for Prairieville. I was in love with this marsh long before I ever saw it, just from all the wonderful things Jon told us. This was my goal, the happy destination of my life. I couldn't wait to get here."

"And we were just as anxious for him to come," added Prudence cheerfully. "It was almost like having Jon return home."

"I was injured too," said Leo, "but not very seriously. It was just a flesh wound in the arm." He pulled up his right sleeve to disclose the scar. "It was late in the war and it healed quick. They actually gave me a choice between going on into Germany with the occupation troops of the 32nd Division or staying in a military hospital.

"I thought I'd get home faster if I stayed in the hospital system. I figured the boys would be held in Germany a long time, but I was wrong. As it turned out, the rest of the troops beat me home."

"Did you just get home now?" asked Carl.

"I got home in April. I intended to get out here right away and look for Prudence, but you know how it goes. Anyway, I guess June is the best month to see the marsh, huh?"

"Any time of the year is good," Sarah said. "Even in the winter. My favorite time is in the fall, in September and October, but June isn't bad at all."

"I'll be busy in September," Leo said with a twinkle in his eye. "That's when Clara and I are getting married."

"Congratulations!" everyone exclaimed.

"Oh, look!" exclaimed Leo, to change the subject. "What's that animal?"

"That's just a muskrat," explained Sarah. "There's lots of them around here. They like the marsh, and they spend a lot of time at the edge of the river." They watched as the small furry animal crawled rapidly through the grass and reeds about fifty yards away.

"It looks like a beaver," said Leo.

"Yes, and it loves the water like a beaver, too," said Sarah. "But a beaver has a broad flat tail, while a muskrat has a thin, hard tail."

"Like a rat," said Carl.

"Sure," said Prudence. "That's why they call it a musk-rat."

"I want to see it closer," exclaimed Leo. "Is it dangerous?"

The two women laughed. "No," said Sarah, "It's not dangerous. You can chase it if you want. It'll just scurry to the river and escape underwater."

Leo took after the little animal, with Carl at his heels. "I'm going, too," declared Sarah, and she followed them, dashing along with her yellow skirt dancing in the sunlight as she went.

Prudence was left on the trail holding the picnic basket. She was not inclined to run through the marsh.

The muskrat quickly realized the three young people were on its trail. It stopped abruptly and gazed in their direction for a second or two, as though sniffing the air. Then it disappeared into a patch of heavy marsh grass. Its progress was evident for a few yards by the motion of the foliage, but then there was nothing.

"Where is it?" asked Leo. "Where did it go?"

"I thought it would head straight for the river," said Sarah, "but instead I think it's hiding somewhere here in the bogs."

They walked on toward the point where they had last seen the grass tips moving. The animal remained motionless until Carl got within a few feet, and then it suddenly bolted, surprising everyone. Before they could react, it was safely out in front of them, moving swiftly parallel to the river.

The three started after it again. From time to time they caught a glimpse of the furry gray back as it flashed along with astonishing speed. Even the boys could scarcely keep up as they ran through the marsh, sometimes fighting their way through waist-high reeds, sometimes sinking inches into the black mud, sometimes backing off and working their way around pools of stagnant water. Sarah was close behind, paying no attention to the dark splotches accumulating on her bright dress.

Several times it appeared the muskrat had successfully evaded them, but eventually they flushed it again. Finally, as Sarah had predicted, it headed for the river which had never been more than a few yards to its right. There was a subdued splash, and when the three young people gathered at the edge of the water all they could see was the concentric ring of ripples spreading out across the surface and gradually disappearing.

"That was a merry chase indeed," commented Leo. "What a pleasant introduction to the marsh!"

They turned back to look for Prudence. She was standing on the trail where they had left her, a small solitary figure against the far horizon.

"I guess it wasn't very polite to leave her behind," observed Carl ruefully, and the thought slightly dampened their exuberance.

Prudence showed no displeasure, though, as they returned to her side. The group of four resumed their stroll.

"Was this Jon's trail?" asked Leo.

"It's really a deer path," explained Prudence, "But it was a favorite trail of Jon. He came out here a lot when he wanted to be by himself. He had a particular hummock, a patch of higher ground in the midst of the marsh, which he loved. It's up ahead not too far; I thought we might eat our lunch there."

"You'll like the spot," said Sarah.

Prudence related how Ephraim had found Jon in his little hideaway on more than one occasion, including the fateful night he decided to enlist in the army.

By the time she finished they arrived at the familiar spot of seclusion, a generous space of shorter grass on dry ground surrounded by shrubs and reeds. Prudence opened her basket and produced a red-checkered cloth which she spread on the grass. Soon a tempting array of sandwiches, lettuce, radishes and milk was laid before them.

"I can see why Jon loved this spot so much," said Leo. "It feels like a sacred place, God's little haven. We are privileged to visit this modern Eden."

"Jon certainly drew inspiration from being here," affirmed Prudence.

"He was a remarkable person," said Carl. "He was concerned for others. He was sensitive, caring, and smart. What more could you ask in a human being?"

"You are being very kind," replied Prudence, "yet I think you are right. I felt the very same way about him. He was almost too good to be a real person."

"He was my brother," said Sarah, "so he had his share of faults." She laughed. "But we don't remember them any more."

"It is strange," mused Leo, "how much a person can be influenced by a particular place. I think when a person lives close to the earth, close to nature, he learns strong moral values almost like he absorbs them."

"I certainly agree with that," said Prudence. "Having lived here so long, I can almost feel the presence of this marsh. It's a deep, eternal, brooding presence which makes me philosophical and reflective. In a sense, it purifies me. It forces me to consider the basic principles of life. It makes me do what is right."

"It certainly sustained Jon," Carl testified. "He had an inner confidence which strengthened his spirit."

"He felt his job as a soldier was absolutely crucial," added Leo. "He was doing his part to 'make the world safe for democracy,' as President Wilson put it."

"Now that the war is over," said Prudence, "is Jon's faith going to be rewarded? Is Wilson going to be able to win a lasting peace?"

"I don't think so," said Leo. "His lack of success in Paris showed that the other world leaders have extremely strong selfish interests. None of them really have the long range goal of peace and freedom for the world."

"Yes," agreed Carl, "and Wilson won't have the strength to push it through. He can't work with the senators because he is too proud and arrogant."

"His health worries me, too," said Sarah. "I've seen pictures of him in the paper, and I think he is headed for a physical collapse."

"We don't need another president to die in office," said Leo.

"Carl, where were you when you learned McKinley was shot?" asked Prudence. "Everyone seems to remember exactly what they were doing when they heard the shocking news. I was washing the dishes when

Ephraim came into the house and told me," she said.

Carl smiled weakly. "I was only a little boy when that happened," he shrugged. I can vaguely remember my parents talking about it, but of course I didn't have the slightest idea what a president was, so it didn't mean anything to me."

"Oh yes, of course," murmured Prudence. "I forgot."

When the sandwiches were gone and the chocolate cake was devoured, the remains of the outdoor feast were stowed again in the basket. The sky had become completely overcast, the breeze had disappeared, and the scent of rain was in the air.

"We'd better get moving," Prudence said, "or we might get caught in a shower."

Reluctantly the picnickers prepared to return to the farm. First, however, Leo grabbed the low branch of a solitary tree growing at the edge of the high ground. "How far down the river can you see from here?" he asked as he swung himself higher into the branches.

"Not very far, I think," said Prudence. "All you're going to see is more of the marsh.

Leo was near the top of the tree, up so high that the main trunk was smaller than his wrist. It swayed with his weight. "Hey, I can see a railroad off to the south, on the other side of the marsh."

"Yes, that's the *Soo Line*," said Prudence. "It runs through Prairieville down to Chicago."

"I want to see too," said Carl, swinging up into the branches.

"Let me come down first," said Leo. "This tree isn't strong enough for both of us at the top." He scrambled down, passing Carl on the way.

When Leo was back on the ground, Sarah insisted on going up. "It's my turn, Carl," she said. He gallantly cut short his sightseeing at the top and made his way down past her, allowing her to climb all the way up.

"Hey, Mom, come on up," she called out. "You'd love it up here!"

"Thanks for the invitation," smiled Prudence, "but I think I'll stay right here on the ground."

"Oh, come on, Mother. It's easy. It's just like climbing a ladder."

"No thank you," Prudence demurred.

"Don't badger her," said Leo without malice. "She's too old to be climbing trees."

When Sarah was satisfied, she started down again. Carl was sitting on the lowest limb, and it suddenly snapped with his weight, dropping him seat first onto the ground five feet below.

Prudence rushed over. "Are you hurt?" she asked, leaning down to put an arm around him.

He laughed reassuringly. "I'm okay," he said. "Just surprised, that's all. It was a soft landing." He rose quickly to his feet with her assistance.

"Hey," called Sarah, looking down. "How am I going to get down? The bottom step is missing!"

Leo laughed. "I guess you're stuck there for the rest of your life," he suggested.

"Not at all," said Carl, reaching up toward her. "Just slide down and hang from that last branch you're on, and then drop so I can catch you."

She squeaked and squealed, but in the end there was no other choice. When she was hanging by her hands, Carl could reach her legs just above the ankles. After a moment's hesitation, she let go and fell into his grasp.

He caught her deftly and for a moment her arms were around his shoulders and their faces were only inches apart. Their eyes met, and Carl remembered the words Ephraim had said to him in the mill about Sarah: *'She loves ya' as much as 'er mother does, an' she's just as purty.'*

Ephraim was right. There could be no doubt about Sarah's feelings, not the way she looked at him with such warmth and wistfulness.

As soon as he put her down, Prudence was alongside him. "Now that everyone is safely back to earth," she said sweetly, "it's time to head back." She gave him the basket to carry, and she took his hand in her own for the first few steps, until the trail narrowed.

They started homeward, hurrying to beat the approaching showers. By the time they reached the farmyard, light sprinkles of rain were tickling their faces.

Later, at chore time, Prudence told Sarah to stay in the house and entertain Leo while she and Carl went to the barn.

Sarah and Leo sat together on the sofa in the living room. "I always loved my brother," she said, "but I didn't realize how much until he left for the Army and got killed. Now I really miss him."

"Jon was a friendly, cheerful comrade," said Leo. "Everybody liked him."

"He was a couple of years younger than me," said Sarah, "but it always seemed like we were the same age. He looked after me."

"He was good at looking after people," agreed Leo. "He took his responsibilities seriously."

"Yes, that's why he volunteered for service in Prairieville's Company," said Sarah. "He couldn't live with himself at home while other young men were headed off to fight for their country."

"He was a real deep thinker," said Leo. "He talked to Carl and me with a great depth of feeling a night or two before we entered battle. It was like he had a premonition about dying."

"I wonder," said Sarah.

"I know he wrote a letter home during the last day or two. What did he say? Did he give any indications?"

"My mother read the letter to Ephraim and me," said Sarah, "but I don't remember anything very specific in it. Let me see if I can find it."

Sarah stepped across the room to her mother's writing-desk and opened a drawer or two, riffling through various papers. After a moment she discovered a letter from Jon, written in March—it was the one Prudence had hidden and never shown to anyone.

Sarah began scanning Jon's letter. It began with a description of the voyage and his early days in France.

"I don't remember reading this before," she remarked innocently. "It's very strange. He tells about scratching cooties almost as soon as they got aboard ship, and taking turns watching for submarines—surely I would not have forgotten such things."

She returned to the letter with renewed interest, finally reaching the postscript: *"I'm enclosing a note from Carl to Sarah—please see that she gets it."* She gasped involuntarily, and her heart began pounding with an unfamiliar excitement.

The next page was Carl's note, brief and to the point. She was glad she wasn't reading the letter aloud. Many of his phrases startled her and sank deep into her heart. *"Forgive my boldness . . . I enjoyed talking with you at our Christmas Dinner in the mess hall . . . I think you are a very pretty girl, and you are so smart! . . . I shall go into battle remembering your face and your lovely red dress . . . write me a note if you want to . . . ."*

Sarah instantly remembered Carl's brief glance as he had caught and held her a few hours earlier in the marsh, and the tenderness of his brief possession returned to her mind. She felt her face flaming as she glanced up from the letter and met Leo's inquisitive expression. She couldn't speak.

"What does he say?" Leo asked.

"He says . . . he says . . . he says the trip over to France was exciting, with fears of German U-boats attacking at any moment." She couldn't possibly tell Leo about the note from Carl.

"No premonitions of death, or anything?"

She remembered suddenly why she had looked for his letter. "Oh, no, nothing like that," she said. "But I think there was another letter afterward."

She set the first letter aside and began rummaging anew through her mother's desk. Her mind was whirling and it was hard to concentrate on the search.

Eventually she found the letter she sought, written by Jon just before the battle. She read it aloud. *"Our chances of making it through the fighting in one piece are very good. The losses among our troops are very few, they say. Nevertheless, we know that some of us will be hit. If I am one of the unlucky ones, you can be proud that I did not flinch from my duty. And remember that I love you and Sarah and Ephraim with all my heart."*

"Well, there's nothing very dire about those words," remarked Leo. "I suppose he didn't want to frighten his family, so he didn't mention his deep inner fears. He was a lot more open with Carl and me. He told us on several occasions that he didn't expect to live through the war."

Sarah was scarcely aware of Leo's words. Her heart was aflutter, and her mind was racing in circles with new thoughts she had never dared to think before. Carl liked her! Carl thought she was *'a very pretty girl, and so smart!"* Well, she liked him, too. Their feelings were mutual.

Then why didn't Carl declare himself to her when he arrived at the farm? She knew the answer even before she phrased the question in her mind. She had never responded to his note—the note she had not received. Of course, he thought she didn't like him. Having been rebuffed by her lack of response, he wouldn't risk another overture. She had failed to write back to him. Maybe he hoped she would at least encourage him a little when they came face to face, but she had failed him again. No wonder he kept quiet!

But while she was seemingly ignoring the invitation he had extended in his note, her mother was actively pursuing him. The result, she could clearly understand, was inevitable.

She was terribly frustrated at the revelation, and terribly angry at her mother for keeping Carl's letter from her. It was difficult to suppress her feelings, but she didn't want to discuss them with Leo so she forced a friendly smile to her face and turned the conversation in a new direction.

She was relieved when he said he must return home. The showers had diminished for the moment, and together they walked through the damp air to the barn where he bid his goodbys.

Afterward, Sarah found an opportunity to talk privately with her mother in the kitchen. "I wanted to read Jon's last letter to Lee," she said, "and I found an earlier one in your desk. It's a letter I don't think you showed to the rest of us."

"Oh?" Prudence stiffened.

"Yes. Jon wrote about his voyage over to France."

"I remember," said Prudence.

"But there was a page addressed to me—from Carl," Sarah said tersely. "You never gave it to me!"

"No? Didn't I?" Prudence said blandly.

"You know you didn't!" exclaimed Sarah.

Prudence cocked her head to one side, as though trying to remember. The familiar vertical wrinkles appeared at the center of her forehead. "I thought you read all Jon's letters," she said tentatively. "I remember talking with you about his voyage."

"But you didn't let me read his letter—I know you didn't," insisted Sarah. "And you didn't say a word about Carl's note to me, even though Jon told you to be sure to give it to me."

"Well, I thought I did," Prudence said defensively. "I certainly intended to."

"But you didn't. I never saw the letter Carl wrote to me."

Prudence shrugged. "I'm sure it's of no consequence. And besides, Carl is here now, and the two of you can talk any time you want."

"That's not the point, Mother," Sarah declared. "In that letter, Carl said he liked me. He asked me to write back. And I never wrote back because I never got his letter. I never got a chance to tell him I like him, too. Things could have been so different!"

"Well, you can tell him now."

"But don't you see, Mom? All this time he thought I didn't like him, because I didn't answer his letter. And I thought he didn't like me, because he ignored me most of the time. I thought he wasn't interested in me at all."

"Well, I really don't think he is," said Prudence.

"But he could have been," Sarah protested.

"We've had this discussion before," Prudence reminded her. "Carl is in love with me. That's the whole truth of the matter, and I don't think there is anything you could have said or done which would have changed the course of events."

"Oh, Mother! How can you pay so little heed to your daughter's hopes and dreams? There was a time when you cared for me and went far out of your way to do good things for me. I think you would have sacrificed your very life for me."

"Yes, I would have," answered Prudence. "That's what mothers are for."

"But you have changed. You don't look after me any more."

"Of course not," replied Prudence, "because you have changed. You are not a little child any longer. You are an adult. You don't need me to look after you now that you have grown up."

Sarah frowned.

"Do you remember the summer you found your first duck's nest in the marsh?" Prudence continued. "You went there every day and you came back and told me about it. At first it was just the eggs, but soon the tiny, fluffy ducklings emerged. You watched them grow bigger and bigger until they overflowed the nest. Then you saw them paddling about on the open water in their mother's wake."

"I remember," Sarah murmured, her eyes softening a bit.

"The point is this: their mother looked after them when they were little—she kept the eggs warm; she guarded the nest; she brought food for their tiny bills; she protected them while they learned to swim and forage for themselves. But when summer was over, the ducklings were grown up and they took their place in the flock. When they left the marsh to fly south for the winter, you could hardly tell them from their parents."

"I know what you're going to say," said Sarah. "Ducklings need their mothers only when they are young. But I am not a duck. Human beings are different. I think human beings need someone to look after them, even when they are adults. I think mothers should do good things for their children, even when the children are grown up. And it was not a good thing when you hid Carl's letter and wouldn't let me see it. It was mean and selfish and very unbecoming a mother. It may have ruined my life."

Prudence blanched, stammering, "Y-y-you're the one who is being selfish. I'm a widow. I've lost my husband, as well as my son. And here's a young man who can make up for both of them in my life. It's my last chance for happiness, perhaps. And you would deny me that chance!"

"Oh, Mother!" Sarah wailed in frustration. "How you can twist things around!"

Sarah retreated to bed that night and could not sleep. Her mind would not rest no matter how hard she tried to find a comfortable thought. Knowing that Carl had once liked her, and had asked her to reply to his letter, filled her with desolation because his invitation had gone unanswered.

The situation which followed, with her mother stepping in to win Carl's favor, disgusted her. And it could have been avoided, if she had simply known of his liking for her. Her mother betrayed her, and what feelings of wretched frustration she felt!

The rain intensified with nightfall, and the gloomy darkness outside matched her miserable mood. After an hour or two of brooding she rose from her bed and stumbled to the window of her room. There she knelt, staring out across the black void of the marsh. She looked up into the utter obscurity of the sky, and began to pray timidly for guidance.

Gradually, as though in answer to her prayer, the conviction grew that she should tell Carl the truth about her recent discovery. She should reveal that her mother had withheld his letter. She should tell him that she would surely have replied with eagerness if she had only known. By the time she finally crept back to her bed, her course of action was fully determined in her mind. She would seek him out, tell him everything, and hope for the assurance of his love.

There were heavy mists over the river valley when Sarah walked to the barn with Carl shortly after dawn the next day, but the yellow-white sun was brilliant as it rose in strength over the wooded hills to the east. The weather would be perfect when the morning miasma melted away.

Even though she was eager to tell her story, Sarah hesitated. Together she and Carl measured the morning ration of ground grain for each cow, and together they prepared the milking equipment.

Finally, she found the right opportunity. "What a surprise to have Lee drop in on us yesterday," she began.

"Yes, it was good to see him again," Carl agreed.

She could feel the pounding of her heart. "When Lee and I were alone in the house," she said, "he asked about Jon's last letter home."

"Oh?"

"When I looked for the letter, I found an earlier one—one that Mom had never shown to me."

"Yes?"

"It contained a page from you, addressed to me."

"Ah, yes, I remember," Carl said cautiously.

"Carl, it was a beautiful letter." She touched his arm gently, trying to establish deeper communication.

"Thanks," he mumbled.

"You said some very nice things about me. You said . . . you said . . . I was very pretty, and smart too."

He nodded.

She plunged ahead boldly. "If I had only read that letter, I would have written right back to you."

"Oh? Why?" He stalled, not knowing what to say.

Her boldness suddenly vanished. The shy, sensitive girl who avoided confrontations reasserted itself, and she retreated into silence, her eyes downcast.

Carl waited patiently for a moment, and then gently lifted her chin with one hand. "Why?" he repeated, forcing her to look at him. Ephraim had told him that Sarah liked him, but he wanted to hear it from her own lips.

"You really want to know?" she inquired softly.

"Yes, I really want to know," he insisted, taking her hand.

"You won't be angry with me?" she asked.

"No, I promise I won't be angry. Please tell me what you would have written to me if you had read my letter."

"I . . . I would have written something nice back to you," she said.

"And what would you have said?"

"I would have said thank you for your kind compliments."

"Is that all?"

"I . . . I would have said that you were a very nice young man, and I liked you very much." There! She had said it. She freed her hand from him and stepped back to look at his face.

Carl was quiet. He looked down the central runway of the barn, out through the big doorway, out where the white morning sun was lighting the landscape.

Then he looked back at her tender face. "I wish I had known this when I first came here," he said softly.

"I know," she agreed. "I wish I had read your letter before you came here, too."

"It's too late now, of course," Carl said. "I'm in love with your mother, and she is very much in love with me. If I were to leave her—it would break her heart . . . I just couldn't do that."

"But you could break my heart instead," Sarah suggested in a voice so low he scarcely knew she was speaking.

"It's too late," Carl repeated, stepping close to her again and seizing both her hands in his own. He looked straight and deep into her eyes, and his voice was husky. "It's too late. I've made commitments and I can't break them."

"Commitments to my mother?" she inquired.

"Yes, of course. We are engaged to be married at Thanksgiving, as soon as the harvest is in."

Chapter 22

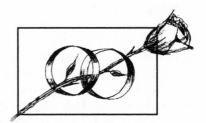

Sarah was stunned at the news from Carl's lips. She turned away so he would not see the tears which sprang quickly into her eyes.

Her heart turned to wood in self-defense; her emotions were caught and held in a breathless suspension while she refused to think.

Somehow she blundered through the morning chores, going through the motions mechanically, her body moving according to long-established habit. She avoided Carl as much as possible, and never looked directly at him.

When the last work was finished, Sarah fled from the barn into the dazzling white sunshine. Half blinded by its glare, she stumbled out the familiar driveway. Forgetting her waiting breakfast, she dashed up the River Road to seek solace from the man who had comforted her through all the big and little trials of her life.

"Uncle Eeph!" she cried, bursting into his house without knocking. "Uncle Eeph!" He was there, as she knew he would be, and she collapsed into his arms, her whole body racked with emotional convulsions. She now cast aside all restraint and the tears rushed out in such a torrent that she was not able to talk.

"Now, now, m' girl, settle down," said Ephraim, patting her shoulders with comfort and assurance. "Now, now, just take it easy." He held her in a sheltering embrace until her shudders finally subsided.

"Now, then, what's makin' m' little girl cry like a spring flood?" he said gently. "Jus' tell Uncle Eeph all about it, and you'll feel better." He led her to the sofa and they sat down together. He put his arm around her shoulders.

Sarah swallowed hard once or twice, and then she blurted out, "Carl says he's going to marry my mother at Thanksgiving!"

Ephraim stifled his own sudden panic. "Well, now, m' girl, when did he tell ya' that?"

"Just this morning. During the milking."

"How'd he come t' tell you such a thing?" inquired Ephraim.

"Well, yesterday I found an old letter written by Jon. It was in Mom's desk and she had never given it to me. It was sent from Europe a couple of months before he was killed."

"What'd it say?"

"Jon's part was a description of his voyage to France, and it was very interesting, with things I had never heard—stories about watching for submarines and scratching his cootie bites and things like that. But the important part was an extra page written by Carl to me. Carl said he . . . well, he said some pretty nice things about me, and he asked me to write back to him. But I never got the letter, so I never wrote back. Everything could have been so different if I had only written back. I would have told him how much I liked him and how wonderful he was and then when he came here to the marsh he would have come to see me instead of my mother and this whole nightmare would never have happened and I know it's too late now and oh, Eeph, what am I going to do?"

"Yer mother hid the letter?" Ephraim asked incredulously.

"It wasn't exactly hidden, but it was in a drawer of her desk where I seldom go. It was under some other papers, not really tucked away at all but tossed in carelessly. She says she intended to give it to me, but she never did."

"You can tell from the letter that he likes you?" asked Ephraim.

"I think so. At least, he did when he wrote the letter. I'm not so sure about how he feels now that he's actually here."

"Carl knows ya' found the letter?"

"Yes, I told him this morning. That's how come he said he had promised to marry my mother."

"Are you sure about that? Did he come right out n' say fer sure they're gonna' get married?"

"Yes, Uncle Eeph, there is no doubt about what he said. They are engaged, he said, and they are planning to get married as soon as the harvest is safely in this fall."

Ephraim pulled her close, his face contorted with agony, his mouth working silently with an imaginary cud of chewing tobacco. They sat huddled together saying nothing, two unhappy creatures thinking their own gloomy thoughts.

Finally he said, "That settles it fer sure. I'm gonna' get outta' here."

"No, Uncle Eeph," Sarah protested. "Don't leave. Don't leave the marsh." She turned toward him and seized his shoulder with her hand, looking straight into his eyes. "Don't leave *me*!"

306

"I don't really wanna' go, Sarah," he replied with deep emotion. "But I can't stay here. It says in the Bible that every man is to die once. But if I stayed here, I would die every single day jus' seein' them two t'gether. I couldn't stand it."

"What are you going to do, Uncle Eeph?" she cried in desperation. "Where are you going to go?"

"Like I told ya' before, Albert Jones wants t' buy my farm. He's been after me fer years. He's offerin' me a price now that's purty reasonable. I'm gonna' take it."

"Then what? Are you really going to leave the marsh?"

"You know what I'm gonna' do. I ain't kept no secrets from you. My uncle in Fond du Lac is gonna' retire from farmin' and sell his place. He's been beggin' me to buy him out. It'd be like tradin' my farm fer his. I figger I'd be far enough away up there. I'll start a new life and forget about Prudence and everythin' down here."

"That means you'll forget about me!" Sarah wailed.

"No, no, I could never ferget about *you*, Sarah," he said. "You and me understand each other. We're very much alike. I love ya' like ya' was m' own daughter. No, I could never ferget about you."

Sarah squeezed his shoulder tighter and pressed herself against him. After a few moments, she said, "Uncle Eeph, why can't you stay here and keep on looking after us? You were our friend when Dad was still alive and married to my mom. Why can't you stay here even if Mom is married to someone else like Carl?"

"Because I love yer mom too much fer that," Ephraim replied. "I love her with all m' heart, and I jus' couldn't stand to see her married to another man."

"But up until Dad died, you and Mom were friends even though you were in love with her. Can't you go back to the way it used to be?"

Ephraim hesitated, and then in a low voice he said very slowly, "Sarah, ya' know I been in love wit' yer mom since before she married yer dad. We talked about it that night underneath the Northern Lights."

Sarah's forehead puckered up with that familiar set of wrinkles that touched Ephraim's heart. "Yes, I know," she said tentatively, "and you told me that you have been in love with her through all the years since."

Ephraim stood and walked slowly up the stairs. Puzzled, Sarah rose and followed him as he entered his bedroom.

He went straight to the chest of drawers beyond his bed, and took in his hands the little tin box which he had bought at Perkins Hardware. Sarah knew it well, for she had dusted it many times through the years. It had always been shiny like he had just polished it. He inserted a miniature brass key into its lock as he sat on the edge of his bed.

He motioned her to sit alongside him with the box between them.

Sarah had never paid much attention to the box; she assumed it contained his private papers of no interest to anyone else. Suddenly she was curious, and she peered inside as soon as he raised the lid. There were some papers, yes, but with them was a small handful of old relics.

"Here is the ticket from a harness race in Prairieville," he said, handing her a cardboard stub. She saw a number imprinted on it, along with a rubber-stamped date in July 1889. "That was where I first met yer mother. It was her seventeenth birthday and she was the purtiest girl in the world."

He pointed to the pencil portrait of Prudence in its plain wooden frame. "See? That's what she looked like when I met her. A gypsy drew that picture of her right there that very same day."

He pressed a copper penny into Sarah's palm. "I bought her a strawberry soda pop t' sip on while the artist was workin'. Here's the change I got back."

Sarah looked at the ancient objects with an air of wonderment. "You saved these!" she breathed.

"Yep," he nodded proudly. "I loved yer mom from that day 'til now, with no letdown. I love her with all my heart! These things oughtta' prove it. I wouldn'ta kept 'em otherwise."

There was more. The fountain pen with which he had written his love letters. The ornate printed invitation to the wedding of Zachary and Prudence. Newspaper clippings of the wedding, and the births of Sarah and Jon. A cloth button from an old summer frock which Ephraim himself had given to her. A delicate lock of hair tied neatly by a white thread. Finally, a dried marigold.

"What does the flower represent?" asked Sarah. "Why did you keep it?"

"Oh, it's just a remembrance," replied Ephraim. "It was from a very sentimental occasion. I kept it 'cause it reminds me o' what things coulda' been like between us."

Sarah sifted through everything reverently. At last she looked up at him with glistening eyes. "All these years," she murmured, "you have been so much in love with my mother. You never really got over it!"

"Yep."

"It must have been torture for you," she said, "living so close and seeing Mom every day with my father."

"No, it warn't torture. Jus' bein' with 'er, an' bein' able t' watch over 'er, brought me joy," he said wistfully. "Without Prudy, my life would have been unbearable with all its meanness and drudgery. There wouldn'ta been no purpose to it a'tall. An' I knew in my heart, I don't know why, that someday I'd have another chance t' make 'er my own. I didn't really mean fer Zac t' get hisself killed; I really never thought about what would happen t' him; he would just disappear, I guess. But somehow I always felt, deep inside, that m' last years on this nasty ole' earth would be happy ones with Prudence at m' side."

"Now I understand so much," Sarah said thoughtfully. "I never really thought about it, not even after what you told me a couple of years ago. How could I have been so blind! Of course you were head over heels in love with my mother. Your devotion to her showed itself in a thousand ways, now that I think back upon it. Over and over and over again, in the things that you said, and the things that you did."

Ephraim blushed.

"I took you so much for granted," Sarah continued, "because you were part of my life from the very beginning. You were just there, like my solid stone house and the sky overhead and the marsh all around. I should have known better, because none of my friends had an 'Uncle Eeph' to watch over them. But I didn't really understand—not until now."

She reached across the box and took his hand. "My heart aches for you," she said. "After twenty-five years, you finally get the chance to fulfill your dream—and then Carl comes along and cheats you out of it!"

"That's the long and short of it, honey," Ephraim said. "An' it looks like my luck has finally run out. I've come to the end o' the string. There's nothin' left t' hope for anymore."

"So it's off to Fond du Lac," Sarah said dismally.

"Yep. I'm off t' Fond du Lac."

They were silent for a few moments, before Sarah said impulsively, "I'm coming with you!"

Ephraim laughed. "No," he said, shaking his head. "You can't. You've got t' stay here."

"No, I don't have to stay here. What for? There's nothing to keep me here. You are the most important thing in my life—you mean more to me than my house, or this farm, or even the Vernal Marsh itself. If you were here, then I'd be happy here too. But if you go to Fond du Lac, then I'll be happy in Fond du Lac. I want to be near you, wherever you are. You're the only person in the whole world whom I love."

"There's yer mom."

"Not any more. She's not my mother any more. I don't know her at all. Ever since she fell in love with Carl, she's been a stranger to me. I don't want to stay here with her any more than you do. I'd be as out of place as a thistle in my flower garden."

They fell into a morose silence. Outside, a cow bellowed from a nearby pasture. The chirp of a robin added a more delicate touch. A car puttered by on River Road. The morning was slipping past, and they weren't getting any work done, and they didn't care.

Their mood was interrupted by the sound of rapid footsteps approaching with firm tread on the gravel drive. The steps—definitely the steps of a determined woman—marched across the wooden floor of the porch, and a rapid staccato of three knocks sounded through the house.

Ephraim rose and went down the short hallway to the door with Sarah following close behind.

It was Prudence. "I came to see where you were, Sarah," she said. "You didn't come in for breakfast, and Carl wasn't sure where you'd gone."

"I'm right here, Mom," replied Sarah politely.

"Is everything all right?" inquired Prudence. "Usually you eat breakfast before you come to keep house."

Sarah's glance hardened into a glare. "How can you stand there like that and ask sweet questions about me?" she asked. "No, everything's not all right, and you know it!"

"What's wrong, honey?" repeated Prudence. "Let's talk about it."

"What's wrong!" shouted Sarah. "Carl says you're getting married to him at Thanksgiving, that's what wrong."

"I'm sorry he said that," Prudence said quietly.

"It's true, though, isn't it? Isn't it, Mom? You're planning on getting married to him?"

"Yes, it's true, but we weren't going to announce it just yet. I'm sorry he told you, because I wanted to tell you myself in my own way."

"I'm *glad* he told me," Sarah said defiantly. "It's the same news, no matter how it's told. And the sooner the better, since you've made up your mind."

Prudence was silent.

"Well, you *have* made up your mind, haven't you?"

"Yes," Prudence sighed. "I've made up my mind."

"Do you have any idea what this is doing to our dear Uncle Eeph?" Sarah charged.

Ephraim laid a restraining hand on Sarah's shoulder. "Don't, Sarah, don't," he said.

With a display of her newly found boldness, Sarah shook off his hand and plunged on. "Here's a man who has been in love with you for more than twenty-five years," she said with a gesture of her hand toward him. "He is a God-fearing man who is honest and dependable. He has shown incredible devotion to you, and he has spent his life watching over all of us."

"He is a good man," Prudence interjected weakly.

Sarah left the room abruptly, dashed up the stairs, and returned swiftly with the little tin box. She displayed the items to her mother one at a time, fingering them with thoughtful respect as she recounted their significance.

Prudence endured the iteration without comment.

"See?" demanded Sarah. "See how much he has loved you, through all these years?"

"Yes, I see," murmured her mother.

"How can you not love him in return?"

"Yes, I love him, Sarah," responded Prudence. "But then there is Carl."

"You love Carl more?"

"Yes."

"Well, all right. Ephraim's too good for you anyway," Sarah went on scornfully. "You don't deserve him. You are too selfish and short-sighted. But at least give him your sympathy: he still loves you, and he still wants you, in spite of what you are."

Prudence lowered her gaze.

"Come to your senses, Mother," implored Sarah. "You love him too, more than Carl, I know you do. Wake up before it's too late!"

Prudence glanced from one agitated face to the other. After a moment's hesitation, she said quietly, "Ephraim is a wonderful man, and I respect him for all of his many virtues."

"You do more than just respect him, Mother," Sarah insisted. "You love him deeply. I know you do."

"Yes, you're right. I love him. But fate has brought Carl into my life, and I love him too. Carl and I have committed ourselves to each other, and we have decided to get married."

"You're driving Uncle Eeph away," Sarah pointed out. "If you go ahead with your plans, he's going to leave the marsh. He's going to buy another farm somewhere and move away!"

Prudence gazed at the solemn man who stood before her. She detected a slight trembling in his solid frame. "I suppose that would be for the best," she said coolly. "Of course, it's got to be his own decision, but I suppose it would be for the best."

"No, Mother, no!" Sarah shrieked. "Don't say that!"

Prudence turned to go. "Come home and eat your breakfast," she said abruptly, "it's on the stove to keep warm."

Sarah followed her mother out onto the porch. "I'm not hungry," she said. "I'm not coming to breakfast."

Prudence continued down the steps onto the gravel. "Mother," said Sarah in a controlled voice, "I'm going with Ephraim."

Prudence stopped and turned. "You're *what*?" she asked.

"Ephraim is buying a farm up at Fond du Lac," Sarah said, "and I'm going with him."

"Sarah, don't," protested Ephraim again.

"Shush, Uncle Eeph," said Sarah. "Mother, Ephraim and I have discovered that we are in love with each other."

Ephraim stared at Sarah in disbelief, and started to speak, but Sarah silenced him with a glance.

"We are going to get married and have our own farm," Sarah said.

Prudence was stunned. "Y-you can't do that!" she declared.

"Of course we can," Sarah insisted.

"You can't do that," repeated Prudence. "You're just making this up."

"And why can't we?" challenged Sarah.

"Ephraim is too old for you!" stated Prudence. "It's a mismatch, if there ever was one."

A smile appeared on Ephraim's face, and Sarah laughed out loud. "We're about the same ages as you and Carl," she reminded her mother. "If it's okay for you, then it must be okay for us, too."

Prudence looked hard at Ephraim. "Say something, Ephraim," she demanded.

Ephraim shrugged. "I got nothin' to say," he replied.

Prudence turned back to her daughter. "Get that crazy notion out of your head," she said, and she spun around and resumed walking toward the road.

When she was gone, Sarah looked at Ephraim with a sparkle in her eye. "Hello, future husband," she said.

"You shouldn'ta done that," scolded Ephraim.

"Why not? She hasn't listened to anything else we've said."

"But we aren't in love with each other—not in a romantic sense. And where did you get that crazy idea about getting married?"

"It just popped into my head," Sarah laughed. "I thought it might get her attention."

"I think it did," Ephraim said.

Sarah took him by the arm and together they walked back inside the house. She went up to his bedroom again and returned with his big Bible. "This is the right time to ask for a little help from the Lord," she said. They sat on the sofa and she opened the Good Book, leafing through a few pages until she found what she wanted in Psalm 57. She read aloud, her mellifluous voice soothing them both.

> Be merciful unto me, O God, be merciful unto me,
> For my soul trusteth in thee:
> Yea, in the shadow of thy wings will I make my refuge,
> Until these calamities be overpast.
> I will cry unto God most high;
> Unto God that performeth all things for me.

They have prepared a net for my steps;
My soul is bowed down:
They have digged a pit before me,
Into the midst whereof they are fallen themselves.
Be thou exalted, O God, above the heavens:
Let thy glory be above all the earth.

She finished the psalm and began to pray: "Dear God in Heaven, please hear our fervent prayer: speak to my mother's heart and help her to see clearly the path to follow.

"If it be thy will, O God, turn her heart away from Carl and let it rest in your servant Ephraim who loves her so dearly.

"Nevertheless, not our will, but thine, be done. Amen."

Ephraim echoed, "Amen."

While the two forlorn souls were sending their petitions toward heaven, Prudence wandered back toward her home in confusion. How could Ephraim possibly be thinking of marrying Sarah, his own daughter! Was it a ruse? It must be a diabolical trick they were trying to play upon her.

Well, their trick wouldn't work, she told herself grimly. Ephraim surely must know that a marriage to Sarah would be both illegal and immoral. He wouldn't go through with it, of course.

Carl was in the front yard as Prudence approached the heavy stone homestead. "Is she at Uncle Eeph's?" he asked with concern.

"Yes, she's there," answered Prudence. "She's not coming to breakfast."

"Why not?"

"She is upset because we are planning to get married. The news was quite a shock to her."

"Yes, I know," Carl acknowledged.

"She's lost her reason. She says Ephraim is moving to Fond du Lac, and she is going with him—as his wife!"

Carl laughed incredulously. "That's mighty sudden," he commented.

"I don't think she means it," Prudence said. "But she's just gone crazy, that's all. I wish you hadn't told her just yet about our plans to get married."

"Why not? It's only a few months away, and she has a right to know. After all, she is your daughter."

"She's such a sensitive girl," replied Prudence, "and she wasn't expecting us to get married so soon. I was planning to break the news more gradually to her, to let her adjust to the thought. You shouldn't have told her so suddenly."

Carl was stung by her reproof. His face reddened. "It would be a shock to her no matter how gradually she found out," he said. "And besides, I don't think it is right to keep secrets from her. Is it true that you didn't give her the letter I wrote to her from France?"

It was Prudence's turn to redden. "I . . . I meant to give the letter to her," she stammered. "I really think she saw it, even though she doesn't admit it."

"Oh, Prudence! If she had read the letter when it arrived, I'm sure she would have answered it."

They did not discuss the matter any further, but for the first time a chill developed between them.

As she thought back over the episode with Sarah, Prudence concluded that the whole thing was a sudden contrivance of her daughter. Ephraim had looked as confounded by Sarah's words as Prudence herself, she thought. Sarah had simply tried to play a bad joke on her.

However, during the next few days Ephraim resumed his visits to the barn at chore time in conjunction with Sarah. They began to look like a couple in love. Prudence, peering from her kitchen window, watched Sarah walk to the end of the driveway and wait for Ephraim to approach along River Road. They greeted each other, exchanged hugs, and held hands as they strolled to the barn. The sight infuriated Prudence, and it didn't help when she recognized little signs of jealousy in Carl's eyes as he observed the warmth of affection displayed by the other couple.

Worse was to come. Ephraim and Sarah began following Carl and Prudence as they walked from place to place around the farm, mimicking them. If Carl and Prudence held hands, then Ephraim and Sarah would hold hands. If Carl put his arm around Prudence, Ephraim's arm would soon follow suit with Sarah. If Prudence paused to give Carl a little kiss of affection, she could be sure that Sarah would quickly kiss the grizzled cheek of Ephraim.

Remonstrating with Ephraim and Sarah was useless. Whenever Prudence complained about their behavior, Sarah would reply "We're merely following your own example!"

The game of copycat was bad enough on the farm where there were no outside observers, but to Prudence's chagrin Ephraim resumed going to church with them in the town hall on the very next Sunday. The two couples, sitting side by side during the service, were a ludicrous sight. If Prudence patted Carl's knee, Sarah would pat Ephraim's. If Carl dared to hold Prudence's hand, Ephraim would quickly seize Sarah's. Prudence heard the titters from other parishioners, and with embarrassment she refrained from any further show of affection, small or large.

That afternoon, Ephraim arrived with his horse and buggy.

"I'm moving out," Sarah announced.

"You're doing *what?*" Prudence exploded. "Where are you going?"

"I'm moving into Uncle Eeph's house," Sarah explained.

"Why are you doing that?" Prudence demanded.

"We like being together," Sarah replied blandly. "And besides, we thought you'd like to have a little more privacy with Carl."

"No, don't go," Prudence protested. "I don't want you to move out. There's plenty of room for you here at home. I won't let you go."

"I'm going anyway, Mom," Sarah answered. "I'll just be in your way here when you get married; I would rather move out now and get it over with."

In spite of Prudence's objections, Ephraim helped Sarah carry most of her clothes and personal belongings out to the buggy.

Prudence watched in disbelief as the buggy rolled down River Road and turned in at Ephraim's driveway. Where would Sarah sleep? The house was so small!

Afterward, Prudence put supper on the table for herself and Carl, but she had no appetite. The two of them went through the motions grimly, with scarcely a word said between them.

While she was clearing the table and washing the dishes, her mind was not on her work. She was clumsy and accidently dropped an heirloom creamer. It shattered into tiny fragments.

"Oh Carl! Look what I've done. That was a gift from Zachary's grandmother."

Carl was little consolation to her.

Finally she could stand it no longer. The thought of Sarah sleeping in the same house alone with Ephraim horrified her.

As the dusk settled over the Vernal Marsh, she pulled a shawl around her shoulders and started down the driveway with Carl at her heels.

When Prudence marched through her neighbor's doorway, she found Ephraim and Sarah sitting close together on the sofa with the Bible spread upon their knees.

"It's time for us to tell Sarah the whole truth," Prudence declared without preliminary conversation. "This game has gone too far!"

Ephraim looked up in surprise. "What is there to tell?"

"Are you hiding something else, like Carl's letter?" asked Sarah.

"More than that," said Prudence. She stepped over to her daughter and grasped her by both hands. "Sarah, Ephraim is more than just a neighbor. He is your father. Your real father."

Sarah looked quizzically at Ephraim, whose face was impassive. Her glance then met Carl's, and she recognized his genuine astonishment. She looked back at Ephraim. "Is this true?" she asked incredulously. "Is this really true?"

Ephraim nodded his head slowly, almost imperceptibly. "Yes, it is true, my daughter," he confirmed.

"How can it be?" Sarah demanded. "How did I live all these years thinking my father was Zachary?"

In subdued tones, Prudence related the story of how she had persuaded Ephraim to father her first child. "I was desperate to save my marriage," she said, her voice finally faltering. "Don't judge me too harshly. What I did was wrong, I know. Believe me, I have had years to meditate upon my sin. And I am sure that God took Jonathan, my only son, as punishment, just as Bathsheba and David lost their firstborn son."

There was a hushed stillness as she finished her confession. Ephraim's eyes were downcast, but Carl and Sarah stared at her in shock. Prudence's composure melted and she began sobbing with loud, enormous convulsions.

Ephraim rose from the sofa and put his arm around her shoulders. "Now, now, Prudy, don't take on so. You did what ya' thought was right, an' I agreed wit' ya'. Jon's death was nothin' more than an accident o' war. Don't hold yerself responsible fer it. Our God is a merciful God, an' he don't go around punishin' ya' twenty years later."

Prudence put her arms around Ephraim and laid her head on his shoulder. The quaking of her shoulders gradually subsided.

Sarah stood up and faced Ephraim. "Dear Uncle Eeph," she said. "My father! Now I understand why I have felt so close to you all my life. You know I have always loved you even more than him—the man I thought was my father—Zachary. Many times I have wished that you actually were my father."

"My heart ached t' tell ya'," said Ephraim.

"It seems impossible to believe. Can it really be true?"

"Yes, Sarah, it is really true."

"You are my one and only real father!"

"I am."

Ephraim swiped the corner of his eye with his knuckle, and then he hugged his daughter.

In a quiet voice, Prudence admonished him with a gentle smile. "Now, Eeph, you've got to quit this crazy romance with Sarah. You're not allowed to be in love with her."

"On the contrary, Prudy," said Ephraim with a smile, "although I don't love 'er in a romantic way, now I can openly love 'er like a father, an' that's probably the deepest and best love any man can give."

Carl had observed the scene with keen interest and amazement. Now he stepped forward. Prudence reached out her hand to him, and he took it in his own. Then he seized Ephraim's hand as well. "I think this sets us all free to do what we know is right," he declared. "There's only one proper solution to this complicated tangle. I want both of you as my in-laws." He put Prudence's hand together with Ephraim's.

"Ephraim," he said boldly, "I want you for my father-in-law."

He looked at the woman who had nursed him back to health, the woman who wanted him, the woman who was on the verge of giving up her family for him. "Prude," he said, "I love you dearly, and I want you for my mother-in-law."

"He's right," agreed Ephraim heartily. "It's the only proper outcome o' this whole danged mess." He gazed down into Prudence's eyes. "Surely you agree, don't you, Prudy?"

There was a moment's hesitation, and there was absolute silence in the room. "Looks like I don't have much choice," Prudence said, glancing around at the faces of the people she loved. "But to be truthful, I . . . I agree. I agree completely. In my heart I knew from the beginning that this was the inevitable outcome. I don't know why I fought it so long. Vanity, perhaps. A rebellion against my growing older.

"But now I realize I couldn't live with myself if I tried to live with Carl. What you say is right, Carl, and I'm ready to accept it.

"I am comfortable with who I am . . . even . . . even with my age.

"And Carl," she continued in a choked voice, "I am ready to let you go—to go to the woman you deserve."

Carl's face broke into a broad smile as he and Prudence exchanged deep glances. Then he withdrew his hand from her and turned to the younger girl. "Sarah," he said tenderly, "will you marry me?"

She burst into tears, but he knew from they way she hugged him that her answer was 'yes.'

When that fateful summer was ending, and the days grew shorter and cooler on the reeds and rushes of the Vernal Marsh, two well-matched couples prepared for their weddings. The farmland's harvest was safely in for the season, and a sense of orderliness and contentment settled over the river valley.

Mother and daughter recited wedding vows with their respective husbands in the familiar Town Hall where Zachary had claimed his beloved Prudence many years before. Theodora was the Matron of Honor for Prudence, and Leo served as Best Man for both couples.

Afterward, their friends and neighbors spoke freely of their benevolent feelings.

"Sarah was so beautiful, she looked just like her mother."

"Carl is a lucky man. He's got no family of his own, so this one is all the more important to him."

"He's walking into a perfect situation. He'll inherit one of the best farms in the county."

"Yeah, two farms really. Together, Ephraim and Prudence have some of the best farm land in the county, thanks to the Vernal Marsh."

"In one way or another, the marshlands have been good to us all."

"Prudence herself never looked better. What a radiant smile!"

"I hope I look that good when I'm her age. You'd think she was Sarah's sister instead of her mother."

"But did you see Ephraim? That look of love on his face was what you hope to see when you get to heaven."

"Yeah, he's certainly moon-struck if ever a man was. They say he has loved her since she was seventeen."

"That's a long time. I always wondered why he never got married. I thought maybe there was something wrong with him."

"There is nothing wrong with Ephraim. In fact, I think he's almost like a saint. His life demonstrates just about the greatest love anybody can find here on earth. His love was long suffering, just like it says in the Bible. He was completely unselfish, and he bore everything patiently with quiet hope and endurance. What more could you ask?"

"Saint Ephraim? Well, why not? He even looks like a character right out of the Old Testament!"

"I knew," said Theodora, "ever since I saw these two couples together during Ephraim's campaign last fall, that all would be well."

"Yes, they certainly make two perfect couples!"

Theodora Youmans, president
Wisconsin Woman Suffrage Association

Leo Herbst, U.S. Army, 1917

Waukesha's Infantry Company
with wooden rifles on Main Street, 1917.

Leo Herbst with Mary Sue Harter in 1993.